He grabbed her by the arm . . .

"You came here and started this, and by Christ I'm going to bloody well finish it! I'm warning you, Evelyn. If I catch you so much as within a yard of that bloody Yank, what the Krauts did that day to scare hell out of you will seem like something out of kindergarten—do you hear me?"

"Let go of me!"

"I'll let you go when I'm good and ready!"

"You're hurting my arm!"

He forced his lips on her, brutally. But as she felt her mouth crash onto his she bit his lip with such force that he gave a shout of pain and let her go. "You bloody little bitch . . ."

DANGEROUS DECEPTIONS

"Slickly paced . . . satisfying!"

—*Booklist*

"An exciting conclusion . . . If you enjoy stories of suspense . . . DANGEROUS DECEPTIONS is the book for you!"

—*Pittsburgh Press*

DANGEROUS DECEPTIONS

ARABELLA SEYMOUR

BERKLEY BOOKS, NEW YORK

This Berkley book contains the complete
text of the original hardcover edition.
It has been completely reset in a typeface
designed for easy reading and was printed
from new film.

DANGEROUS DECEPTIONS

A Berkley Book, published by arrangement with
G. P. Putnam's Sons

PRINTING HISTORY
G. P. Putnam's edition / January 1987
Berkley edition / March 1988

ISBN: 0-425-10882-1

A BERKLEY BOOK® TM 757,375
Berkley Books are published by The Berkley Publishing Group,
200 Madison Avenue, New York, NY 10016.
The name "BERKLEY" and the "B" logo
are trademarks belonging to Berkley Publishing Corporation.

PRINTED IN THE UNITED STATES OF AMERICA

10   9   8   7   6   5   4   3   2   1

Especially for Frank.

CONTENTS

PART ONE

LONDON

1

Far below, from one of the downstairs apartments, faint strains of a Cole Porter tune drifted upward, mingling with the distant sounds of late-night traffic from the street outside. It was still snowing. As she lay there, trying in vain to sleep, Evelyn could see the white, glistening flakes fall gently against her window, then disappear into the darkness on their way to the ground below.

Her eyes were still sore and swollen from crying. Her head still ached. Slowly, she turned toward the clock on her bedside table and tried to make out the time. Ten minutes past one. Another six hours to get through, somehow. Another six hours before she could get up and get dressed. Seven and a half before she could leave her apartment and walk to her job at Pellini's art gallery in Bruton Street, twenty minutes away, the only place she knew where she might find some kind of relief from the anguish that had tortured her for months, a temporary panacea for the misery of being in love with a man she wanted more than she'd ever wanted anything . . . but couldn't have. Another woman's husband.

She turned over and stared up at the ceiling. She thought about him and wanted him, as she always did before she slept. She grasped a mascara-stained pillow from the other side of the bed and hugged it to herself, pressing her lips against the linen, pretending it was his body that she held instead. But it was no use. The Cole Porter tune from the party downstairs became louder, and as the lyrics went round and round in her head she could feel more tears coming, stinging at the backs of her eyes, and that lump in her throat, big as a man's fist. *Night and day, you are the one.*

There was no photograph of him on her bedside table. Nor among the dozens of pictures that adorned the piano top or the walls of her sitting room, nor in the stack of albums that she kept piled up on the chest of drawers on the other side of her bed. Married men with socialite wives and important careers rarely, if ever, made the mistake of giving pictures of themselves to young women whom they would never dare to be seen with in public. Jack Neville was no exception.

But it made no difference to her. She could see every feature of his face as clearly as if he were here beside her, and she was putting down every detail onto a blank canvas. *Only you beneath the moon and under the sun.*

She threw back the covers and got up.

Without turning on the light, she felt her way to the studio room next door, opened one of the big, iron-bound chests that held most of her materials, then rummaged inside it until she found a sketchbook and a piece of charcoal. There was a small work lamp on a stool near the window. Switching it on, she sat cross-legged on the floor, the sketchbook on her lap, while she flicked through its pages, searching for a blank sheet.

Faces and scenes that she'd drawn, from six years back, leaped at her from the assortment on the crowded pages; some still vivid in her mind, some long since forgotten until now.

A dozen or more portrait sketches of her mother. Full-faced, profiles. One of her sitting in the embrasure of an imaginary window; others of her in long, elegant expensive evening gowns she'd never in reality owned, leaning against a piano in the nightclub where she'd sung, in a background of faces and instruments. The noise and the sound of the music came back to her as she looked at the picture, remembering that small, claustrophobic place, filled with humanity and clouds of cigarette smoke and the wail of saxophones. She remembered herself from then, a shy, gawky fourteen-year-old who'd blush to the roots of her hair if one of the musicians winked at her, peeping out from a crack in the door to listen when her mother took the floor, or, in the early hours, bleary-eyed from lack of sleep, curled up on the couch in her mother's dressing room with a coat thrown over her and a cushion on her head to blot out the din from the music and people outside.

She imagined herself back there, half asleep, wishing that she were tucked up safe and warm in her own bed, when one of the men from the band would come in and pick her up, wrapped in a blanket, and carry her to a taxi outside the club, and all the way home she'd lie there on the back seat, her head resting on her mother's lap, dimly aware of the passing cars and the lights along Piccadilly that would flash on and off as they passed.

Slowly, almost reluctantly, she turned the page over and hesitated as she looked at another face, the only face in the book that she'd drawn from a photograph and not from life.

She was beautiful, Blanche Tregeale, her father's sister. Not in the same stark, startling way her mother had been. Her mother could have gotten up in the morning after singing at the club until 2:00 A.M., pulled on a crumpled dressing gown, not bothered with lipstick or a hairbrush, and still have taken any man's breath away . . . as she had Gilbert Tregeale's. But Evelyn could never imagine her aunt being seen in a crumpled dressing gown with no lipstick and untidy hair; everything about her was perfection. She looked up from the page with her beautiful, soulful eyes, as she did in the photograph that she'd sent in one of her earliest letters: perfectly groomed, perfectly dressed, without a hair out of place, even down to her eyebrows. The likeness to Gilbert Tregeale was so great that they might have been twins.

Evelyn thought of her own father, the father she could never recall clearly, the father who had come from an old, proud Jersey family whose ancestry went back to the time of the Normans. The family had never forgiven him for marrying not only someone outside the island but someone they considered too scandalous even to recognize. The car crash had happened when she was three, too long ago for him to have seemed a real person to her. All she had now were the photographs, and the things her mother had told her to go with them, like illustrations with a book.

She turned over the remaining pages in the sketchbook one by one, until she found a blank sheet near the end. For a moment she stared at it, suddenly back in the present. Then, with quick, deft, almost frantic movements of the hand, she transferred the face that haunted her onto the whiteness of the paper.

When it was finished she lay back against the chest and stared at it for a long while.

It was three months since they'd met, in the corridor at Pellini's; he was on his way into Guy Pellini's private office to discuss the shipment of a painting; Evelyn had been on her way back to one of the workrooms where she was engaged in repairing the damaged canvas of a Fragonard that was destined for the castle of a Scottish baronet. As usual the corridor had been crowded with other people going to and fro, and neither of them had spoken a single word. But the way he'd looked at her as they passed had sent her heart racing and her pulse leaping. He was the most good-looking man she'd seen in her entire life. When she had gotten back to the workroom and sat down again in front of the canvas, her hands had been shaking so much that she'd laid down her brush for several minutes to compose herself.

Half an hour later, the door behind her had opened, and when she'd turned round to see who it was he had been standing there, smiling, with the same look in his eyes other men had, when they saw her. She remembered the way he'd closed the door noiselessly behind him and leaned against it, casually, everything about him proclaiming to her how used to charming women he was.

"So you're Evelyn Tregeale, the girl Pellini rates so highly," he'd said, taking out a silver cigarette case and flicking it open. She had shaken her head when he'd held it out to her. "He reckons you're so clever with a brush that even the cream of the experts would have trouble drawing a line between the original painting and the bits you've repaired."

She'd half smiled, shyly.

"Anyone with a modicum of talent can go over something that's already there. Or make a copy that superficially resembles the original. But to paint the real thing from scratch in a style that no other artist has ever created is something different altogether."

Slowly, his eyes still on her face, he'd lit his cigarette and replaced the lighter in his pocket. A column of smoke began to wend its way toward the ceiling.

"You're too modest. Anyone who knows anything about painting can see at a glance that your talent is way out of the ordinary." He'd come farther into the room and stood beside her looking at her work on the damaged canvas. "And I've been in this business long enough to know that you're in a class all by yourself." With difficulty, she'd raised her eyes to a level with his. "I saw your watercolor of Mrs. Leo d'Erlanger in Pellini's office. That isn't just talent, Evelyn; that's sheer genius." He'd put out his cigarette and moved closer to her; so close that his arm was touching her shoulder. Then he'd reached out, taken the brush from her fingers and stroked her hand, almost imperceptibly, with his own. "You don't mind if I call you Evelyn . . . do you?" Unable to speak, she'd made no answer. "I should be intrigued to see any other paintings you've done, in your own style." And again, that smile. "I really must call in on you sometime . . ."

That was how it had started.

He was already married, of course. No man as attractive or as successful as he was could have been a bachelor . . . unless he was also a homosexual; and that Jack Neville certainly was not. Nor could he be divorced. Divorce was a severe social stigma that not even royalty could survive; only two and a half years ago King Edward VIII had been compelled to give up his throne as a punishment for marriage to an American divorcée. That Wallis Simpson was charming, witty, had immaculate clothes sense and would, no doubt, have made a fascinating and excellent queen was beside the point: to be divorced or to marry a divorced person spelled certain social death, and Jack Neville cared too much about who he was and what he wanted to risk that. Common sense should have warned her. Only when it was too late, when she had already fallen in love with him, did he tell her the truth.

"Of course, I'd leave her if I could. Neither of us ever pretended it was a love match." A shrug of the shoulders, the charming smile that went straight through her, like a warm breeze on a chilly day. "But her father was president of Delacroix Art Syndicate, I wanted to get where I intended to go by the quickest possible route, and she was attractive, his only daughter, and moved in all the right circles . . . I saw the advantages. I approached the whole thing like a good investment; and it worked out, for both of us." She should have realized then that she was making a grave mistake; that she was in for nothing but heartache and misery if she didn't stop seeing him . . . she'd watched it happen to too many of her friends. But he'd already become like a drug that she couldn't do without. And there was no cure.

She'd remembered retorting, almost angrily, "But if you don't love her how can you go on sleeping with her?" And he'd answered, with the same smile and same nonchalant shrug, "A man can go with a woman he doesn't care for as easily as . . . that . . ." He'd dotted the ash from his cigarette into the nearest ashtray. Another smile. "But it's different with you and me . . ."

Slowly, Evelyn closed her sketchbook and put it down, then turned off the lamp and went to the window. Where the curtains were not quite pulled all the way across, she pressed her face against the pane and stared out into the night.

Despite the thick fall of snow the London streets were far from deserted. Every now and then, taxis or sedans crammed with late-night revelers chugged past, slower than usual because of the slippery state of the roads, on their way from one of the theaters nearby to late-night supper or early breakfast at Ciro's or the Embassy Club. Evelyn could not see their faces clearly from where she stood, two floors up; but she glimpsed flashes of sleek white fur and sequined evening gowns, and in her misery imagined their high, raucous laughter, as they made endless jokes, or repeated the latest society and theater gossip. She thought of Jack Neville's wife, so like the gilded, useless occupants of those expensive, chauffeur-driven sedans, the spoiled little rich girl who had to have everything, including the best-looking husband she could get; and who made sure that her doting daddy's wallet was thick enough to buy her what she wanted . . . Jack Neville. If Evelyn hadn't loved him so passionately she knew she would have despised him for letting himself be bought like this season's exclusive Chanel.

A tear welled up in the corner of her eye, then spilled over. She pulled the curtains tightly together, angrily, and went back to bed.

Minutes later, she sat bolt upright, her heart racing. Beyond the sitting room in the tiny hallway she could hear the unmistakable sound of a key turning in the lock; and only one person besides herself had a key to her front door.

Rubbing her eyes, half incredulous, she got up and went into the next room, pulling on her peach-colored satin wrap as she went. Then she screwed up her eyes as they met the sudden, harsh glare of lights.

He stood there, in immaculate evening dress, top hat and overcoat dusted with snow, smiling at her in that charming, casual way he had, as if they'd seen each other only a few hours before, instead of weeks.

Staring at him, she shielded her eyes from the dazzle of the sitting room lights.

"What are you doing here, Jack? For God's sake, where have you been for the last three weeks? I've been half out of my mind . . ."

He tossed his hat onto the sofa and came across to where she stood.

"Well, there's a welcome. And I thought you'd be pleased to see me. What's wrong? Did I wake you up?"

"Jack, it's nearly two in the morning!"

Mixed with her delight at seeing him there was anger rising in her. Three weeks and not a word and then in he came, as casually as if nothing had happened. He took her by the shoulders and held her at arm's length.

"You're the only girl I know who can get straight out of bed in the middle of the night and still look like a million dollars." Gently, he stroked a loose strand of hair back from her face. "Well, what d'you say, beautiful? Shall we have a drink together . . . and then I'll really show you how much I've missed you." He glanced toward the bed through the half-open door.

"If you'd missed me that much, you'd have telephoned." Her voice shook.

"How could I? The old man's got a new merger on the horizon and I've had him on my back day and night . . . in the office and out of it . . ."

"You could have called me from a public box!"

"Only if I'd been by myself." He reached out and touched her cheek. "Every day for the last three weeks he's been like a shadow. Calling for me in the morning in his car so that we can go over final details before I leave for Brussels; then insisting on coming home with me every evening and staying for drinks. He's my boss and Laura's father . . . so what could I do?"

Evelyn's face had gone white at the mention of leave and Brussels in the same sentence.

"So he's sending you away? Again?"

"Only for a fortnight. When we get back—"

"Is your wife going with you?"

He hesitated momentarily. "Yes, but . . . Look, Evelyn. I don't want to take her with me . . . that was her father's idea. He thought we could go via Paris and she could do some shopping on the way. If he hadn't suggested it and she hadn't agreed, I was going to ask you to come with me. I swear it. We could have had two weeks together and nobody the wiser."

"They seem to have your life pretty well sewn up between the two of them, don't they?" Two weeks alone with him, traveling through France and Belgium, two places she'd never been to in the whole of her life. No one to recognize them, no one to care what or who they were. But it wasn't to be. Robert De Braose's spoiled daughter wanted to go shopping in Paris, and Evelyn Tregeale had to stay behind and work for her living. The irony and the injustice of it all brought fresh tears to her eyes. Irony, because she was in love with him and his wife wasn't, but it was his wife who was going with him and not her. And injustice because someone like Laura Neville could go shopping in Paris any time she chose to, but chose to go now, the only chance they'd ever had to be together for more than a few snatched hours. The unfairness of it all overwhelmed her and, despite her determination not to, Evelyn began to cry.

"Evelyn, please . . . don't . . ."

Angrily, she tried to push him away.

"I'm surprised you're even here tonight. And at two o'clock in the morning! Did they let you off the leash for the evening, or did you think of some brilliant lie to throw them while you sneaked in here?"

"You think I'm not sick at the way things have turned out? You think I'd rather take Laura with me than you? Well, I don't even have to answer that. You know what I want. You know who I'd rather spend my time with. But when we started seeing each other I told you I was married and I told you things would be difficult. You said you understood. You told me it didn't matter to you. Now every time I don't ring you or I can't call, you rave at me the minute I step inside the door. Evelyn, please. Don't make things any harder than they have to be. After the Brussels merger things are bound to slow down and I'll have Laura's father off my back. We'll have more time together . . . I promise you." He took her by the shoulders and gave her that smile, the smile that turned her limbs to water and made her heart jump and hammer. All he had to do was to turn on that smile and she'd forgive him anything.

He was right, of course. Everything he'd said was true. She'd known about his wife. She'd known about his father-in-law. She'd known she couldn't have him whenever she wanted him, and she'd thought she could handle that; but things never quite work out the way you expect them to. Despite all the things she'd sworn she'd never do—sit waiting by the telephone, refuse other invitations to go out in case he called—she'd succumbed to all of them, and more. But there was no point in feeling sorry for herself; she'd gone into this with her eyes wide open, believing she could cope with anything that came along. Now, in spite of promising herself that she'd never make the fatal mistake of making scenes, she was being dragged down by her longing to be with him into a treacherous quicksand of resentment and jealousy, because he was going away with his wife and she was being left behind.

But there was nothing she could do about it. She had no rights, no status, no claims. She was the odd angle out of a triangle. He was married to another woman and, as she'd already found out, she was only going to be allowed to play second fiddle, waiting perpetually in the wings for a cue that was never to come.

There was no way she could complain about what had happened; men who embark on extramarital affairs rarely, if ever, want a woman who parodies their wife, but the complete opposite. Never arguing, never questioning, never demanding . . . otherwise, the thrill is gone. Only wives have the prerogative of nagging to get what they want.

With difficulty, she gathered her anger and harnessed it.

"I'm sorry." She rubbed her aching eyes. She ran her hands through her disheveled hair. "I'm tired out . . . I haven't been sleeping well. And there's been a lot of pressure at work. More clients, more sales, bigger workloads. Instead of delegating some of the less valuable canvases, Pellini wants me to do them all. I can only do so much in a day."

At once he was all sympathy.

"My poor darling! He works you too hard! But then you ought to take it as a compliment. He knows that nobody else is in your class."

She managed a weak smile.

"Jack, you know how much I've longed to see you . . . but I have to be up at seven and it's nearly three. If I don't get a few hours sleep, I shan't be awake at all."

He reached out and took her by the hand.

"Come straight home tomorrow and have an early night . . . I'll be here at six-thirty on Thursday, and make sure you're ready and waiting. Dressed in your best. There's a cozy little country club I've discovered, thirty miles from here, just the place for a perfect evening together where there's not a chance of either of us being recognized. Well, what d'you say?"

"Jack!" Her eyes lit up, her spirits soared; not once since they'd met had he ever suggested that they go out anywhere together. "Do you really mean it?"

"Of course."

"But are you sure . . . certain there's no chance of anyone seeing you with me?" A minute flame of fear flickered, in the back of her mind, for the consequences should anything go wrong. A whisper to his wife. His father-in-law. Never see him again. Never kiss him, never touch him. Endless days and nights alone, filled with emptiness. Unthinkable. Unbearable.

"As much as I want to go, I'd rather stay in than run any risks."

He smiled.

"I've already thought them all out, and planned for the worst . . . all I have to do is to tell my wife that I'm having a business dinner with someone who I'm giving a commission to for several paintings . . . she'll think nothing of it."

Evelyn frowned.

"But that isn't true. If she checked she'd find that out."

"It is true. Ever since I first saw that watercolor in Pellini's office, and asked him who'd painted it. You've got an extraordinary talent, Evelyn. Why not get one foot on the first rung of the ladder to being an independent artist, and give us the perfect excuse we need to be together and not worry who's watching us two steps behind."

"You've talked about me to your wife?" She looked incredulous.

"I've let slip once or twice that Pellini has a very talented artist working for him at the gallery. Why? I had an idea, just on the spur of the moment, sparked off by something she said.

You know what? Her father wants her portrait painted for our anniversary. Who better to give the commission to than you?"

"I couldn't."

He stared at her.

"What d'you mean . . . you couldn't? Why the hell not?"

"I couldn't paint your wife. I just couldn't go through with it. Not in your house, the house you share with her. I wouldn't be able to paint properly because I'd be on edge from the minute I walked in. And if I saw you I know I'd betray myself. As soon as I looked at you she'd see the expression in my eyes and she'd guess the truth.

He took out a cigarette and lit it.

"Garbage, as the Yanks say. We've been in the same room together with Guy Pellini, his chief buyer, and Christ knows who else, and no one's yet had the slightest inkling. Nor will they. You feel that way because you've got a guilty conscience . . . don't ask me why. I certainly haven't. What I do and what you do in our own private time isn't anyone's affair but our own." He drew heavily on his cigarette. "For an intelligent girl you certainly talk a lot of hooey."

"Jack, I can't do it. I'll do anything you ask me and I'll paint anything or anyone else you want, but I can't paint your wife."

"You can and you will. And in any case, I shan't be at home while you're working so there's no chance of her seeing how you look at me or how you don't. Satisfied?"

"But what about my job? I'm not allowed to take private commissions in working hours, you know that."

"It'll all be arranged, no problem. I'll tell Laura's father that you should have the commission and he'll tell Pellini. Pellini'd bend over backward to please him. He couldn't afford not to . . . the syndicate put too much his way. And think of what it'll do for you. The old man'll be over the moon with the finished portrait and he'll trumpet your praises to all the people who matter. In no time you might even find that you get so many private commissions you can leave Pellini and work for yourself. So . . ." He stubbed out his cigarette. "What do you say now, Miss Evelyn Tregeale?"

"You know to live by my own work is all I ever wanted."

"Then why are you looking like you've lost a fiver and found sixpence?"

"I'm afraid."

"Afraid? Of what?"

"A feeling I've got. I don't know how to describe it. All I know is that it's there, and it scares me."

He took her by the hand and laughed, in that suave, casual way he had that both melted and exasperated her.

"Like all gifted people, you let your imagination run away with you." He tightened his grip on her hand in a way she knew well. "Now stop talking and show me how much you've missed me."

2

Guy Pellini walked slowly along the length of the gallery, pausing in front of every painting to study it with his expert and critical eye. Two paces behind, Evelyn followed him without speaking, watching his face carefully as he studied her work of the last few months. As always it stayed completely expressionless; but because she'd worked for him for so long and knew him so well, Evelyn knew by the way his eyes shone that what he was looking at pleased him more than he would ever say.

"Yes," he said, slowly, at last, "yes. They're all as nearly perfect as they'll ever be . . . thanks to you." He turned to her. "I thought you might find problems with the Domenico Veneziano, seeing that there was so much damage to the subject's face . . . but studying the canvas now I can see that I didn't have any need to be concerned on that score. Veneziano himself couldn't have made a better repair job than you have."

The thrill Evelyn always felt whenever she was praised for a special piece of work ran through her. She smiled. "Thank you, Mr. Pellini. But it wasn't the skin tone pigment that caused me the main problem in doing the restoration work . . . it was the detail in the foreground of the painting and the colors in the saints' robes. We rarely have an early

15

Italian master needing the kind of extensive work on it that this piece did . . . and the problem was that in many of them pigments like Naples yellow and Renaissance vermilion were commonly used, and they are virtually impossible to duplicate exactly with modern colors, simply because of the original method by which the Early Italian schools manufactured their pigments . . . for want of a better word." She allowed herself to laugh. "When you can't go and find lead antimonate for Naples yellow on the volcanic slopes of Mount Vesuvius, or heat mercury and sulphur together in a flask in the exact way the Italians did, you have to come up with a cast-iron alternative. That's rarely as easy in practice as it sounds."

"You're nothing less than a perfectionist, Evelyn . . . that we both know." He turned from the painting for the first time and looked her full in the face. "And I'll be the first person to admit that if you hadn't put in all the evening work you have over the last few weeks, it would have been difficult, if not impossible, to have all these finished in time. I appreciate your sense of duty and your loyalty. But I've been noticing that you haven't seemed yourself lately. In fact, for some time now . . . and I know the reason why." Evelyn's heart missed a beat. No, no. There was no way he could possibly have guessed the truth. "All work and no play makes Jack a dull boy—or Jill a dull girl. Nobody can go on working without a break, as you have, indefinitely . . . none of us are machines, after all. So I've decided that now the pressure is off and the workload is lightening, temporarily, you've more than earned a seven-day break. With full pay, of course."

The weak half smile on her lips felt like starch. Her palms were sweating.

"I really appreciate your offer, Mr. Pellini. And please don't think I'm ungrateful. But if it's all the same to you, I'd rather keep working than take any time off right now." She ignored his look of surprise. "When I looked into the studio first thing this morning I noticed the damaged Turner that arrived yesterday in the Yorke consignment . . . and it's so long since I worked on an English landscape that I'd like to start on it as soon as possible."

Pellini smiled and shrugged his shoulders.

"That I won't argue with . . . though you're the only one in this whole building who'd choose work instead of a holiday.

Just don't push yourself too hard.'' He gave her her instructions for the rest of the day and went on to his office.

Holiday! she thought, almost bitterly. A whole week of days and nights, spent alone in her apartment. Listening to the mournful ticking of the clock, counting the hours and days and weeks till Jack Neville got back from Brussels. Thinking. Crying. Imagining him and his rich, spoiled, socialite wife, dining and shopping in Paris. And it was the imagining that tortured her most of all.

Her father would have arranged for them to travel everywhere first class. The best transport, the best hotels, the best restaurants. Evelyn could see her, filling her idle days while Jack trailed in her wake like some kind of lapdog, taking him in and out of all the famous French couturiers, ordering everything she saw and wanted, knowing that her doting daddy would foot the bill. Ensconced in a private box at the theater, decked out in fur and jewels, not because she either appreciated or enjoyed the play but because she wanted to be seen . . . Laura De Braose Neville. Not for the first time, the reluctance and distaste she'd reacted with when Jack had brought up the subject of the portrait he wanted her to paint came sharply back again.

But it was too late for her to back out now. Jack had recommended her to his father-in-law and his father-in-law had rung up Guy Pellini. And Evelyn was committed.

She turned to take one last look at the Veneziano painting. Then she went along the gallery and out into the coolness of the corridor, toward the studio, reached through the small office of Guy Pellini's secretary. As Evelyn came into the room, the secretary glanced up from her typewriter.

"Well, hello there . . . I was just about to finish off this letter and go in search of my morning coffee . . . want to join me in a cup?"

"Yes, thanks. I could do with it. I left in a hurry this morning and didn't have time for seconds."

The other girl got up from her chair.

"Overslept, did you?"

"Nearly. The girl in the downstairs flat had another party last night, and it didn't break up until gone one A.M. The noise kept me awake. By the time I managed to get to sleep it was almost time to get up again." Only a half truth. Thoughts of her lover in a Paris hotel with his wife had kept her awake, that and the music from downstairs.

They walked side by side along the corridor to the staff room.

"Maybe nobody else has to get up and go to work in the morning." As they reached the door, Pellini's secretary opened it and Evelyn walked through. The room was empty. "By the way, I heard you turned down a whole week's holiday. With full pay."

Evelyn busied herself with the coffee cups.

"News travels fast."

"Give me the chance! But then, I only type his letters. If I was another Michelangelo and Vigée-Lebrun all rolled into one, I might start to go places."

Evelyn laughed without turning around.

"So would I. Do you take sugar now or are you still doing without it?"

"Doing without it. I bought a divine dress on Friday and I need to lose another two inches before I'll look right in it."

Evelyn poured the coffee and handed it to her.

"Why didn't you just get another size up?"

"You must be kidding. The looser clothes are on me, the thinner I feel and the more I eat. If I wear them one size too small, I do just the opposite." She cradled her cup in her hands and studied her long, gleaming red nails. "Now . . . since we're alone for a moment or two, you can tell me something I've been wanting to ask you." A sly note crept into her voice. "Who is he, Evelyn?"

Alarm bells sounded. "He?"

The other girl's eyes never left her face.

"Oh, come on! Don't pretend you don't know what I'm talking about! The new man in your life. And don't tell me there isn't one, because I know better. You've been mooning around for the last two months at least . . . working harder than three people put together, offering to stay and finish things on your lunch hour, and coming to work with a white face and swollen eyelids . . . only a man has that effect on a girl! I know, from bitter experience!" She sipped her steaming coffee. "You're blushing now. There is someone, isn't there?"

Evelyn sat down and stared into her cup. What a relief it would be to tell someone, anyone; to let it all come out, to pour her feelings of misery and frustration into a sympathetic ear, releasing all the jealousy and anguish that, for the past three months, she'd kept bottled up inside. But she couldn't do that, not even in the monthly letters to Jersey that she wrote to her aunt Blanche. Certainly not now. When a secret was shared by more than two people, it ceased to be a secret at all. She liked Helene Morgan. But whether she could trust her was another matter altogether . . . and there was too much at risk for her to ever take the chance.

"OK. You win." She lay back in the chair and looked up at the ceiling. Anywhere except into Helene's piercing blue eyes. "There was someone. I met him a few months back, in the old nightclub where my mother used to work . . . of all places. In the beginning I thought he was special. Then I found out that he was married, and I decided to stop seeing him. I didn't want to . . . but I knew if I couldn't make myself be strong and break it off before it got too far, I'd be hurt." She half glanced up, hating the lies she had no choice but to tell. "I'm still hurting."

"Oh, Evelyn!" Helene was off her chair in an instant and kneeling on the floor beside hers. She took hold of her hand and squeezed it. "I didn't mean to sound flippant, just now . . . or to pry. I mean, it's none of my business, I know that. It's just that when you work with someone for more than two years, you get to know at least something about them. And I knew there was something that was on your mind. You've looked so preoccupied lately."

"I'll get over it."

"Didn't he tell you he was married straight away? Oh, what a stupid question! Of course, they never do. Only after you've fallen for them. It happened to me, once." She put her hand on Evelyn's shoulder. "I know just how you feel . . . it's not fair, is it? And however much you love them, they'll never leave their wives. They'll tell you how unhappy they are and how they don't get along. That she doesn't understand them and they're only staying with her because of their children or because she can't manage on her own . . . I've heard it all. And you're damn right. It does hurt. You feel bitter. Used, cheated. You sit there at home, trying to imagine what she's like, hating someone you don't know, who you've never met and probably never will. Do you know," Helene fidgeted with the ring on her finger. "He actually showed me a photograph of her. I can almost laugh, looking back on it now. I just sat staring at it, wondering what the hell a good-looking man like him was doing married to *that!* Talk about Plain-Jane-and-no-nonsense! I can tell you, Evelyn, it took all my self-control not to snatch it right out of his hands and tear it in pieces! My God, how I hated her! If I could only describe how I felt . . ."

"There's no need. I know exactly how you felt." She tried to smile and failed. "I feel that way right now."

Helene put an arm around her shoulders.

"Look. I know it's always easy for someone else to say it . . . but you have to try and forget him. Just put him out of your mind. Easier said than done. I know that. But it's the only way you can ever get back on even keel. You've already made a start . . . by breaking it off. And remember that it's the first step that's always the most difficult."

She fought down the need to cry. She couldn't afford tears. Weakness. The almost unbearable temptation to break down and pour out everything that was tormenting her. If only her mother were still alive, if only Blanche Tregeale lived in London and not Jersey, if only her lover was any other man but who and what he was. But she was trapped in a maze from which she could not see an escape route.

"In six months' time," Helene Morgan went on, "you'll look back on all this and laugh. Yes, you will, it's true. My sister says it's like having a baby . . . you go through it all and the pain nearly sends you out of your mind and you swear you'll never go through it again . . . but six months later you can't even remember. And you're the last one to have to worry, with your looks."

"Beauty's only skin deep," Evelyn said, dryly.

"That's deep enough! Besides, look what you've got going for you with your career. Pellini's over the moon with you on this last consignment of work and Sir Robert De Braose offers you a commission to paint his daughter! Think what kind of doors a man like that can open for you. In a year's time or even less, you could be a big name in the art world. Evelyn Tregeale, society portrait painter. And you'd make a tremendous impact just because you're a woman."

"Maybe."

"Tell you what. Let's have an evening together one day,

when you don't offer to work late. Do a sketch of me!'' She laughed, and stood up. "Then when you're famous I'll be able to show it to people and say, Evelyn Tregeale drew that portrait, when we used to work together at Guy Pellini's.''

3

She had always imagined that the house where her lover lived with Laura De Braose would be different from any other she had ever been inside, and it was. More grandiose, more luxurious, more ostentatious. It was a massive, white-painted town mansion, set apart from all the others in the quiet, private, eighteenth-century square, less than a mile from the heart of Mayfair, surrounded by a high wall of gleaming railings and approached through massive wrought-iron gates . . . as any ordinary doting father might present his daughter with a doll's house furnished right down to the very last minute detail, so Robert De Braose had presented his with this, her own life-sized mansion, what he considered a fitting setting for his rich, pampered little girl, complete with husband to go with the designer interior.

As Evelyn stepped out of the taxi that had brought her, carrying her artist's case under her arm, she felt an immediate distaste for what she had come here to do. But it was too late to turn back now.

None of the feelings that she usually experienced before a new commission were part of her now; there was none of the excitement, the exhilaration of a special challenge, the sense of pleasure, the ache to create with her pastels and paintbrushes something unique and beautiful to look upon. Instead, she felt only a strange sense of foreboding that she had fought with for days, ever since Guy Pellini had called her into his office and told her the arrangements De Braose had made.

"He's having a new easel and all the sketching paper and canvas you'll need delivered to the house; all you'll have to take with you are your own brushes and paints . . . I told him you'd prefer to use your own." And, competely unaware of the truth, he'd added, cheerfully, "If he likes the result—and how couldn't he?—you'll do for his daughter what Da Vinci did for the Mona Lisa. It'll be the making of you as an artist in your own right . . . and nobody could deserve it more. I suppose you've thought about that, Evelyn? When you please a man like De Braose the sky's the limit." And she'd amazed him by answering, with an edge to her voice he rarely heard, "Does that mean he expects me to paint her as she'd like to be, or as she really is?"

He'd raised an eyebrow.

"Show me any woman living who'd say to an artist what Cromwell said to Lely—'Paint me just as I am, warts and all'—or any artist who'd do it, if he wanted to stay in business. All women are vain and they all like to be flattered . . . some more and some less than others. If you want to be a professional portrait painter you need to be a diplomat as well—that I don't need to tell you. Think of Van Dyck's portraits of Queen Henrietta Maria and Winterhalter's of Adelina Patti and you'll see what I mean; Henrietta Maria was a little skinny woman with a sallow skin and front teeth that stuck out like a buck rabbit's; Patti was a squat, dumpy, over-weight prima donna whose neck was so short that she almost didn't have one . . . but to look at their portraits you'd think they were two of the most beautiful women who'd ever lived. And what happened to the artists? Van Dyck became principal court painter and Winterhalter the number-one painter of royalty all over Europe. That's diplomacy." He'd opened the box on his desk and picked out a cigar. "All they did was to eliminate all their subjects' bad points and emphasize their good, and if they didn't have any good points, they invented them." He lit the cigar and puffed on it, slowly. "I'm afraid that when you want to make your living from painting other people, Art and Truth don't often go hand in hand."

Evelyn set down her case at the top of the stone steps and

rang the bell. It was answered by a butler so swiftly that he might have been standing behind it, waiting for her to arrive.

"I'm Evelyn Tregeale," she said, simply.

"Mrs. Neville is expecting you, if you'll come this way." And she followed him, gazing from one side of the hall to the other, momentarily taken aback by the ostentatiousness of the decor.

The whole interior of the house could have been taken straight from the palace of Versailles. The vast hall was a picture gallery, with white velvet wall coverings and a mass of gilding, Louis XVI furniture and Meissen china vases full of hothouse flowers. Individually each piece was exquisite; but crammed together their effect was vulgar and overpowering. As Evelyn passed by a mirror at the end of the hall, she glanced into it and thought how stark and simple she looked by contrast, in a plain black cloth two-piece and wide-brimmed undecorated hat.

"Mrs. Neville has asked that you wait in here," the butler said, opening one of the white-and-gold doors and showing her inside. "All the equipment that Sir Robert De Braose ordered for you arrived yesterday." He pointed to a far corner of the room. "No doubt you'll wish to look at it yourself."

"Thank you." Left alone, Evelyn stood in the middle of the room looking around her. Above the marble fireplace was an enormous gilded mirror, flanked by two rows of antique miniatures. A Boulle clock ticked away in the center of the mantelpiece, and on either side of it stood a set of Dresden figures, each one, no doubt, worth a small fortune. It was a room straight out of the Petit Trianon, with crystal chandelier, parquet flooring polished like glass, brocade-covered furniture and walls, and a carpet that could have come directly off the famous looms of Margolin. She guessed, wryly, that De Braose knew down to the last shilling what every item not only in this room but in the entire house was likely to fetch in the salesroom; a man who knew the price of everything but the value of nothing.

Everything had been bought to impress. There were several pieces of contemporary sculpture, which she disliked, and on an Empire table in the center of the window bay, one of the most elaborate and exquisite Meissen fruit stands she had ever seen in her life. Not a single piece of it, she noticed, had ever been chipped or repaired or broken; De Braose would never buy anything that was flawed.

She walked about, slowly, stopping to look at every painting and ornament, wondering how much of it was really Jack Neville's taste, or the personal selection of his father-in-law, when, unexpectedly, the door behind her suddenly opened, and she turned round to find herself face to face with her lover's wife.

"*You're* Evelyn Tregeale?" Laura Neville said, frowning, without any greeting. She held a coffee cup in her hand and stared at Evelyn with an expression in her eyes that Evelyn recognized only too well . . . that of a woman who sees a face far more attractive than her own and doesn't like it. Her heart began to beat faster.

"Yes, I'm Evelyn Tregeale. How do you do, Mrs. Neville." She glanced toward the opposite side of the room, where all the equipment De Braose had sent over was waiting to be assembled. "If you're ready to start, I'll unpack my case and set up the easel."

Laura Neville's small, deep-set eyes surveyed her critically. "May I ask you how old you are, Miss Tregeale?"

"Twenty-one."

"My husband never mentioned you were as young as that . . . nor did my father." She closed the door behind her. "I was expecting someone much older."

"I was twenty when I painted Mrs. D'Erlanger. It was after noticing the portrait in the office at the Pellini gallery that your husband suggested I paint you."

"He spoke to *you* about it?"

Time to lie. "To Mr. Pellini. I was told several weeks ago that Sir Robert was thinking of having your portrait painted as an anniversary gift, and that when you came back from Brussels the arrangements would be made." She managed to smile, with her lips at least. "Shall we make a start?"

Laura Neville put down her coffee cup. "Certainly not until I've selected an appropriate dress. I still can't decide what color I want to be painted in. And certainly you're not painting me in here. The light is far too bright."

"But a good north light is essential for any painting—"

"I want to be painted in the music room, with the window embrasure behind me. It's the perfect setting. And directly opposite where I sit is a mirror, so I can keep checking on how I'm going to look."

Evelyn was appalled.

"But if it's on the other side of the house there won't be enough light at this time of day."

"A good artist can paint anywhere." She went over to the other side of the room and pulled a bell rope. "I'll have your things moved to the music room." A frosty smile. "Will you sketch me first, or what?"

"I'll make the preliminary sketch to begin with, then paint in the face. There won't be any need for me to finish the portrait here. The secondary details can be done in my own studio."

"You have your own studio?"

"A studio flat."

A maid came in answer to the bell and Laura Neville gave her orders for the shifting of Evelyn's things. While she waited she stood there, watching the woman she'd envied and agonized about for so long.

She saw her with an artist's eye as well as with a woman's; she was slim, dark, ordinary; made superficially attractive with the aid of skillfully applied cosmetics and expensive, classic-cut couturier clothes that were far beyond the reach of most women's pockets, certainly beyond her own. Despite what the society columns of newspapers printed about her, and ambitious hostesses with an eye to pleasing De Braose said about her, there was nothing remarkable about her physical appearance except for the cost and exclusiveness of what she wore: on the mustard-colored Chanel suit—had Jack Neville bought it for her when they were in Paris together?—Evelyn noticed a diamond and sapphire brooch, four inches in diameter, and matching earrings, each the size of a florin. Guy Pellini's sage words, inevitably, passed through her mind. "Henrietta Maria was a little skinny woman with a sallow skin and front teeth that stuck out like a buck rabbit's . . . but to look at her portrait you'd think she was one of the most beautiful women who'd ever lived." She imagined Laura Neville, hanging on the arm of the man she loved and couldn't have, floating in and out of exclusive London clubs and aristocratic house parties in a cloud of Dior satin and georgette, her mediocrity lost in the brash glitter of sequins and jewels. Suddenly, she despised herself for even being here.

"Well, if you'll excuse me," her rival said, with the frosty half smile that never quite reached her eyes, "I must go back upstairs and choose what I want to wear for the sitting." She went out, leaving Evelyn to follow the servants who had come to move her things through more yards of ornate corridor.

It was a beautiful room but totally unsuitable for a portrait painting. At this time of the day, the best light was on the opposite side of the house. What little there was here was focalized in the window embrasure where Laura Neville intended to sit, leaving Evelyn to work in shadow. As the two servants set up her easel she paced the huge room, more simply furnished, save for the huge grand piano, than the one she'd just left, and wondered what she should do. Anger and resentment and all the other feelings she had for her lover's wife made every word and every gesture hazardous. She'd come here with deep misgivings, and only because he'd asked her to, only because Pellini had arranged it. But against her better judgment. From the moment they'd come face to face she'd struggled to mask her natural antipathy beneath an air of detached professionalism and the pretense that De Braose's daughter was just another client, but the instant Evelyn had met her, she'd known she'd failed. Every time she looked at her all she could see were visions—unbearable—of her and Jack Neville together, upstairs in bed. Oh, God, how she hated her!

Agitatedly, she paced the big room, clenching and unclenching her fists, while the two servants fiddled uncertainly with the unfamiliar equipment.

A crazy longing gripped her, to take hold of the easel and smash it to pieces, to march upstairs and find Laura Neville, then tell her the truth to her face. To describe in vivid detail every time she and Jack had been together. To repeat, word for word, every sentence he'd ever said, all the beautiful, passionate things he would never say to his wife, the spoiled little rich girl he'd married for her father's influence and money, and watch those cold, hazel eyes stare back at her in rage and shocked disbelief. Wonderful thoughts. Cruel, perhaps. And cruelty had never been a part of her. But the pain of sharing another human being, the pain of long, lonely days and nights without him, of being the outsider in his life, had dredged up from the very depths of her feelings of violence and bitterness she had never known existed in her.

She turned from the window and spoke to one of the servants.

"I'm sorry, but I'm afraid this won't do." They both stared at her. "There isn't sufficient light in this room to paint Mrs. Neville, and what little sun there was an hour ago has mostly gone now, and it's two parts shadow. Can you please take these things back to the room they came from, and set the easel up in there? Here . . . I'll hold the door open for you." She picked up her case and followed them as they carried the big, cumbersome easel carefully back the way they'd come. But as they reached the hallway they both stopped, abruptly, and looked uncertainly up toward the turn of the stairs.

Evelyn looked too. It was a magnificent staircase; a wide, carved semicircle thickly carpeted in deepest red, the paneled walls decorated as far as the eye could see with paintings from the French and English schools, with gilt wall lights set in sconces next to each one. And there, in a diamond tiara and a long, floating gown of salmon chiffon, stood Laura Neville.

"Matthews? Where are you going with that thing?" Slowly, holding the trailing hemline above her high-heeled shoes, she came down the remaining stairs unsteadily. "Didn't I tell you to take it into the music room?"

Evelyn stepped into view from behind the two men.

"Yes, you did tell them, Mrs. Neville. And I've taken the liberty of asking them to take it back again." Somehow, she made her lips smile. "Unfortunately, the room doesn't have a strong enough light for me to paint in; not properly, at any rate. The first room was ideal." They stared at each other, eye to eye. "But if it's the setting or the background that you're worried about, I can simply paint in the details of the music room later . . . then it will look as if you were painted in there after all."

"I see." With an imperious gesture, she motioned the two men to carry on. "Well, you're the artist. I suppose you know what you're doing." She glanced at herself in one of the hall mirrors. "But I must say if I'd known that having my portrait done would entail all this palaver, I'd certainly have thought twice about it." She went on into the room and stood there, looking about her. "So. Can I at least sit where I want to?"

Getting out her materials Evelyn wondered, dryly, if Laura would have been so deliberately unpleasant had her artist been a man instead. She thought not.

"The light in this room is so good that it really doesn't matter at all."

She was packing away her cleaned brushes and tubes of paint when the door behind her opened, so softly that she didn't hear it. Only when a long, dark shadow fell across the floor did she glance up sharply, startled. She could scarcely believe her eyes.

"Jack!" She scrambled to her feet, her heart hammering. "For God's sake! What are you doing here?"

He smiled his unique smile.

"I live here, remember?"

"But your wife . . ." Nervously, she glanced toward the door.

"Gone out. Afternoon tea at the Ritz with some of her society friends." He came toward her and touched one side of her face with the tips of his fingers. "I made an excuse to come back early, hoping to find you still here. I knew she wouldn't be." He slipped his hands around her waist; she pushed them away again.

"Someone only has to open the door and walk in!"

"They won't. Nobody in this house would ever walk straight into any room without knocking first."

"They would if they thought there was nobody there."

"Evelyn, for Christ's sake . . . if it makes you feel better I'll lock the bloody door."

"No! Please, Jack. I have to go now. I've been shut up in this house—her house—all day long and I'll go mad if I don't get out. I feel stifled, as if I can't breathe. All I want is to go home, put a record on the gramophone, run myself a hot bath and just lie there, soaking, with my eyes closed. Then I want to go out for a good, long walk somewhere. Anywhere." There was a blank look in his eyes. No, of course, he didn't understand. No man would. "It was a mistake for me to come here. A mistake for me to have ever agreed to do the portrait . . . I told you that right at the start. I knew it then, I know it now. But against my better judgment I let you persuade me."

"For your own good. I explained all the reasons why I thought you should do it . . . what De Braose can do for your career." He caught hold of her hand and held it. "Stop thinking of him as Laura's father; think of him as a means to getting what you deserve and what you want . . . as I do.

OK. I know you despise him for what he is and what he stands for. So do probably more than half the people who have anything to do with him. But in a rough sea it pays to ride in a big ship, and the bigger the better. Think about it. De Braose has only one weakness besides his love of power and money—and that's his sweet little daughter. Paint her as you've never painted before and he'll put your name up in lights."

"And spend the rest of my life licking his boots like everybody else that he manipulates? No thanks. I'll get where I want to go without his kind of help."

"That's the long way round, Evelyn. And you may not even make it at all."

"Thanks for the vote of confidence."

He looked contrite. "You know I didn't mean that the way it sounded. I just care about you, that's all. But if you want to get on in this world, you can't afford to have outdated principles that end up being nothing more than a millstone around your neck. We're living in 1939, Evelyn, not in the Age of Chivalry."

She pulled away her hand and went on packing her things. "If you want to do something for me you can call me a taxi."

"I'll do better than that. I'll drive you home myself."

She stood up, ready to go. "You know very well you can't do that. Someone might see us. And your wife might be back any minute and wonder why you're not here."

"She isn't my keeper."

"No?" She tried to keep the note of sarcasm from her voice, but failed. "That's why you couldn't see me for a whole month, before you went to Brussels . . . because she isn't your keeper."

"Wrong. Because I couldn't get her father off my back. I've told you before. She lives her life and I live mine."

"Will you ring for a taxi for me or shall I do it myself?" She looked at him with a coldness she didn't feel. She wanted to punish him. To give vent to the feelings of resentment and jealousy she'd kept tightly bottled up inside her, ever since she'd set foot in the house, and the deeper, more confused emotions about him that had thrown her whole life into disarray ever since they'd met. If she let him drive her home she knew she'd weaken, and let him make love to her . . . then leave her to spend the rest of the evening with his wife.

"Evelyn, why are you angry with me?" She hesitated by the

door, her face half turned away from him so that she didn't have to look into his eyes. "I rushed through my work today so that I could be with you when you'd finished here. I needed to see you."

"Well, you've seen me."

"Are you trying to tell me something you think I won't want to hear?" Something in his voice alarmed her.

"What do you mean?"

"If your feelings about me have changed I'd like to know."

She stared at him in disbelief. Tears sprang up into her eyes. "For God's sake . . . have you got any idea of how much I love you?" There was a break in her voice. "No, I don't think you have, have you?"

"Evelyn . . ."

"Don't you know what being here, with *her,* all day long, has been like for me? Having to look at her, listen to her, be polite to her as if she were just another client? And all the time I was painting her all I could think of was you and her, together." Helene Morgan's words went round and round in her head. *You feel bitter. Used, cheated. You sit there at home, trying to imagine what she's like, hating someone you don't know, who you've never met and probably never will.* Well, now she knew. There was no more need to conjure up pictures in her imagination because she'd come face to face with the reality. If she'd liked Laura Neville, if she'd found her amiable, talkative, interested, it would not have hurt her so much. But she'd never met anyone that she'd taken so uncompromising a dislike to; and it had almost nothing to do with her being her lover's wife.

"I'm tired, Jack." She opened the door. "All I want is to go home. To get as far away from here as possible."

"Will you let me take you for a drive?" He saw that surprised her. "A long drive. Anywhere you like. We could stop somewhere and have dinner . . . if you'd like that."

Quietly, she closed the door.

"I don't understand. Ever since I've known you, you've said we can't go out together, in case we're seen. Now this." She gave him a long, searching look. "You've always seemed so scared of the consequences if anyone found out; your wife, De Braose, someone at Delacroix or Pellini's . . . but suddenly you're flinging caution to the wind and I want to know why."

"I do have a reason . . . yes. But I can't talk to you about it here." He came and stood so close to her that she could feel the warmth of his breath across her cheek. He took the case gently from her hand. "My car's parked out front."

"You'll have to drop me at the flat first, Jack. I'll need to change my clothes." She looked down at her working suit, with a smear of paint on one of the cuffs. But he shook his head.

"You look beautiful just the way you are."

4

"The idea first took root when I was in Brussels . . . and it's been growing bigger and faster ever since." He turned off the engine and faced her. "I've been playing the role of De Braose's apprentice ever since I got married to Laura . . . nearly seven years. Up till now I didn't mind that, even with him breathing down my neck the way he does, because I knew that in the end I'd be the one who got total control of Delacroix; after all, he's got no son and he can't live forever. Being kept on his leash for a few more years wouldn't have bothered me too much, knowing what I'd get at the end of it." He paused for a moment and stared absently from the car window to the expanse of fields and forest beyond. "But the day before we left for Brussels he dropped his bombshell on me . . . I can't even remember now how the subject came up; only that he stood there, telling me as casually as if he were discussing tomorrow's weather that when he retires as president of the syndicate, his nephew steps right into his shoes. And I stay on as the resident second fiddle!" His voice was bitter. "After the way I've worked for him, after the way I've knuckled under, running his errands, bolstering his ego, having him run my life in and out of the syndicate, knowing he was always there, somewhere, peering over my shoulder just in case I happened to step out of line. Well, I've had plenty of time to think it all out, and I know exactly what I aim to do."

"Only two hours ago you were telling me to use De Braose for my own ends exactly the way you do."

"Yes. And I meant it. For now. When you have to find your way through a jungle and you don't know east from west, you have to use a compass or a guide . . . until you've been there for so long that you could find your way with your eyes shut. That's what I've been doing. And it's what I'll have to do for a while longer. But I've made up my mind, Evelyn. My days as De Braose's underdog at Delacroix are numbered." He took hold of her hand and held it between his own. "Now I'll tell you what I couldn't back at the house.

"De Braose's people weren't the only ones I met while I was away . . . there was an American, from a New York–based art consortium that has contacts all over, as far apart as Australia and Brazil . . . and he made a special point of singling me out. They've crossed professional swords with my father-in-law on more than one occasion; and they're not the only ones who don't like the methods he uses to do business. Believe me, he's made more enemies than even he realizes. And the consortium is growing fast. They want someone to join their consortium who has a first-class working knowledge of the Delacroix syndicate, and a personal knowledge of Robert De Braose." For the first time, he smiled. "They could hardly find anyone more suitable than me."

"But you're married to his daughter. How could you go on living and working in London if you left him and went over to the other camp?"

"I wouldn't be living and working in London. I'd spend most of my time, when I wasn't traveling, in New York."

"And you think your wife would tamely leave that big, furnished shrine her father's built for her and follow you to the other side of the Atlantic so that you could join forces with his competitors?" She thought of Laura Neville, transplanted from her secure, gilded existence, daddy's little girl cast adrift from his all-enveloping world of riches and power, a fish out of water. And herself, left alone again when he'd gone . . . this time for good. "You really think she'd be willing to give all that up . . . or that her father would let her?"

"I don't care what Laura wants anymore. Or him. And in any case it doesn't really matter." Another smile. "When I go to New York I don't intend to take her with me. I want to take you."

For a few moments her whole world began to spin. She felt a wild, heady joy that was so intense it was almost unreal, and she stared at him, unable to take in the words that he'd only spoken to her in her dreams.

"But, Jack . . . if you left De Braose and then walked out on his daughter, he'd never forgive you; or forget. Men like him never do . . . they just bide their time. He'd never leave you alone or be satisfied until he had revenge."

"He won't get it. I'll be part of the American consortium and it's too powerful for even Delacroix or De Braose to manipulate. Besides, he has only himself to blame. If he'd played fair with me after everything I've done for the syndicate, instead of using me to keep the seat warm for his bloody nephew, I'd have thought twice about accepting the New York offer." Suddenly, he realized what he'd said and added, quickly, "No, that isn't true. I'd have still accepted it because it's the only way I can get where I want to go and still have you."

"Do you really mean that?"

"It's not often any man can get the best of both worlds . . . but when I join the consortium and take you with me when I go, that's just what I'll have." He leaned forward and kissed her, and she slid her arms around his neck, while fire leaped through her.

"Jack, I love you so much."

"And I love you. Laura can keep anything she wants to in the house that's mine, as long as I get my freedom."

"Supposing she won't give you a divorce?"

"She'll have no choice. And she has no reason not to. In her eyes, when I leave Delacroix and join its archrival, she'll say I've betrayed her father; even without taking you into account, she'd never forgive me for that alone. She wouldn't be able to go running to her solicitor and file for a divorce fast enough."

"But Jack, being a divorced woman . . . even if she's the innocent party . . . think of the social implications for someone in her position . . . the scandal, and the disgrace . . . look at what happened when the king wanted to marry Wallis Simpson. Just because she'd been through the divorce courts—nobody cared whether she was to blame or not—Baldwin, the government, the Church and the whole royal family ganged up on her. And in the end they all got their own petty little way. It still makes my blood boil whenever I think about it." She rested her head against his chest. "In England divorce is a dirty word and if you've had one, people fight shy of you as if you've got leprosy. And it closes doors to your wife that I'm sure she'd rather were kept open."

"America isn't England. Thank Christ. They don't have time for all that hypocrisy and stand-to-attention-even-if-it's-killing-you mentality . . . that's why they're so much more successful than we are . . . they look forward and not back to Queen Victoria and the Middle Ages. They're realists. They think modern. We could learn a tremendous amount from the way they do things, but we won't. We're all tradition and tea on the lawn and the old school tie. Take a look at what De Braose has done with me and his nephew . . . that could only happen here. In the States, it's the man with the know-how and the ability to do the job that gets it, not the one with the same surname as the chairman who wouldn't know one side of a picture from the other.

"It's the same with divorce. It's far more common and accepted in America than it's ever likely to be over here. They don't believe in being saddled with a wife you don't want to be married to anymore when you can be happy with somebody else. So you've no need to worry. If Laura won't give me a divorce here, I'll get one elsewhere."

"You make it all sound so simple."

"You make it sound so difficult." He laughed, softly, and kissed her again, more strongly. "Now let me tell you something else . . . there's something I want you to do for me and for yourself." He drew away from her slightly. "When I was talking to the American in Brussels, I told him all about you."

"I don't understand."

"Simple. I just told him how brilliant you were. Gifted. A unique talent . . . that's not too much of an exaggeration, is it? After all, it's just the truth. I didn't need to gild the lily. I told him about the work you did in repair and restoration at Pellini's, and about your own painting that I'd seen . . . and he was all ears at once. Think what working for the consortium would do for your career . . . and that's what you want, isn't it? To be an artist in your own right?"

"Yes, but . . ."

"No buts. Just listen. For the next few months, maybe even

a month or two, we'll just go on as before, as if nothing's happened, while I sort out the departure details . . . it's March now and the consortium job wouldn't begin until September. Not that we'll have to wait until then . . . we'll be gone long before. But they want to see samples of your work and I did promise to be able to show some to one of their members when he comes to London at the end of April. I know you won't let me down."

"Why didn't you tell me all this before?"

"I've hardly had a chance to. And I've had a lot of things on my mind that I needed to think out carefully before I told you. Now . . . I want you to do something for me. They'll love your own work, I know that. But to give them a real idea of how gifted you are, I want you to make an exact copy of a painting that Delacroix acquired recently for a private art collection in Milan." He smiled his melting smile. "Just take a look at this." Before she could answer he turned round and lifted a carefully wrapped package from the back seat of the car. Slowly, carefully, he untied the string that bound it and stripped away the covering of brown paper, and Evelyn gasped.

"It's Giorgione's *Sleeping Venus*! One of the famous religious paintings he died before he could finish. Titian completed it." She stared at Jack Neville and then back at the painting. "Jack . . . it's breathtaking. Magnificent. My God . . . it's one of the most beautiful works I've ever seen." Her eyes moved over the canvas, absorbing the perfection of the delicate brushstrokes, the unmistakable mark of genius. "But what is it doing here, in your car? It's worth God knows how many tens of thousands of pounds . . . a genuine old Italian master . . . surely it should be locked up in the security room at Delacroix?"

"Don't get so worked up . . . it won't come to any harm. I've borrowed it for a short while, that's all."

Evelyn could scarcely believe what he was saying.

"You mean De Braose doesn't know that you've got it?"

"Of course not. Nor does anyone else. And they won't, either . . . because I want you to keep it at your flat. How else can you paint a copy?"

"But that could take weeks, maybe months."

"Not for a clever girl like you."

"When someone at Delacroix discovers that it's missing,

and they're bound to, all hell'll break loose! Jack, we can't. We just can't. It's not right. It'll cost you your job and me mine as well. And they'll never believe that you borrowed it just so that I could paint you a copy to show to the American consortium . . . your father-in-law will want to know what's going on, and then you'll have to tell him about us. And that you're leaving his syndicate and his daughter to live with me in New York. Can you imagine what he'll do to you?"

"He won't do anything. Because he's never going to find out. Delacroix bought the painting from a seller in Luxembourg, and it's been sold to a collector in Milan . . . just as I've told you. As far as anyone at Delacroix knows, it's been boxed in a custom-made crate and is already on its way to the buyer . . . and, when you've finished painting the copy, that's just what it will be. Better late then never."

"When it doesn't arrive after a reasonable time, the buyer will contact De Braose and questions will be asked."

"You'll have finished copying it long before then," he insisted finally. "Believe me, no one will ever be the wiser."

"Jack, I don't like it. It scares me."

"Rubbish." Playfully, he tapped her nose with the tip of his finger. "Think what the end result will be, for you and for me. We'll be made. Literally. The Yanks'll go overboard about your talent, they'll never stop being grateful to me for introducing you to the consortium, and we'll be able to be together, openly. Never again like this." Those last four words, like a cup of water to a man dying of thirst. "I always thought that was what you wanted."

"Yes, it is. But supposing something went wrong? Supposing somebody burgled my flat and stole the painting?" She thought of the unthinkable, and felt cold fingers on her spine. "It could happen."

"Nobody knows the bloody picture is missing and nobody would ever think of looking in your flat for it if they did. As for it being burgled . . . can you see the average housebreaker walking along Piccadilly with a four-foot-long Giorgione tucked underneath his arm? Where would he fence it? Who'd be stupid enough to buy something that was completely unique, something that'd be instantly recognizable anywhere in the world? They wouldn't touch it with a ten-foot pole. For Christ's sake, Evelyn, use your common sense!" There was a sharp, impatient edge to his voice that hadn't been there before. "I want you to do this for me. More to the point . . . for us." He looked into her eyes with that special expression he had. "Will you paint the copy or not?"

For a brief moment she hesitated.

"Anything I can do to help you break free from De Braose, I'll do."

His frown vanished and a wide smile took its place.

"My lovely, clever girl!"

"But you've forgotten something else; I did, too. Your wife's portrait. I can't work on two paintings at the same time."

"Oh? Why not?"

"Only another artist would understand that."

"But you've already finished the face, didn't you say? How long will it take you to do the body and the background?"

"Two, three weeks perhaps. And that's if I work on it continuously."

Thoughtfully he rubbed his chin.

"The Giorgione's far more important than Laura's portrait. Shelve it. Our anniversary isn't for another two months, and by that time we might not even be together." Her heart soared. "Leave it as it is and start on this one as soon as possible. If necessary, ring up Pellini and make out you're sick . . . yes, I know you don't like being deceitful, but it can't be helped, there's just too much at stake . . . and the end justifies the means. Besides, didn't you tell me that he'd offered you a couple of weeks' break and you'd turned him down?"

"When you were in Paris. But if I ask for them now he might think something's wrong."

"Pretend you're not well, then. You'll be inside the flat, painting all day, so nobody's going to be any the wiser. And if they ring up to see how you are, just say you're stopping in bed and don't feel like seeing anyone." He did some quick calculations in his head. "You can get a lot done in two or three weeks, working nonstop."

"Guy Pellini's very busy this time of year, Jack. I hate having to let him down."

He lay his hand on her thigh and squeezed it. Then he winked at her.

"He'll have to get used to it, won't he? Before long he won't have you at all."

5

Helene Morgan glanced at her wristwatch and then at the clock on the wall opposite her desk. Two minutes to one. She finished the letter that she'd started, laid it in the tray, then put the cover on her typewriter and went out into the corridor and along it. She hesitated outside the studio door; then she opened it and went in.

"Joining me for lunch?"

"No, thanks," Evelyn answered without looking up, "I'm already way behind on this. Maybe another time."

Helene leaned against the door.

"Everyone has to eat, at some time." She walked across the floor and stood beside the massive canvas that Evelyn was painstakingly repairing. "What's the point of pushing yourself like this, working yourself into the ground when you've only just got better? By the look of you, you came back to work too soon."

"Thanks."

"I didn't mean it like that. But it's true. And I'm not the only one who's noticed. You've got shadows under your eyes, your skin looks like dough that someone forgot to cook, and all the bounce has gone out of you, like a glass of shandy that's gone flat. Didn't your doctor give you a prescription for a tonic, after that virus you had?"

"I didn't ask him for one." That, at least, was true. "While I was ill I hardly managed to get any sleep at all. That's all that's the matter with me. A couple of weeks of early nights will work wonders."

"Not if you starve yourself to death. Come on, put down that brush and get your coat. You've wasted nearly ten minutes of my lunch hour already."

The little French restaurant across the street from the Pellini gallery was noisy and crowded, bustling with the usual lunchtime trade; businessmen, office workers, ladies straight from their shopping sprees in the nearby London stores carrying ribboned hat boxes and gift-wrapped packages as they struggled to their seats through the press of people. As the two girls edged their way behind the waiter to one of the few vacant tables, Evelyn nervously glanced around her and back again the way they'd come, and when they sat down she went on looking toward the door, fidgeting awkwardly with her gloves and then the menu.

"Is something the matter?"

"No. No, of course not. I just thought I saw someone I knew, that's all."

Helene glanced at her copy of the menu.

"I'm starving, aren't you? Grilled sole looks good . . . I love the way they do it in here. But I think I'll just have it with the salad on the side, and skip the potato and dressing. Got to watch my figure."

"I'll have the same." Evelyn caught the waiter's eye and beckoned him over.

"Shall we splash out and have a glass of wine with it? Just to wash it all down. Better make it red; for you, anyway. Isn't red wine supposed to have more iron in it than white? You need something to perk you up."

"I don't really care what color it is. You choose."

The waiter disappeared into the ever-moving throng with their order, and they sat there as they waited for the meal, watching the mass of chattering, raucous people, to Evelyn like a huge, rambling canvas by one of the French Impressionists, alive with vividness and light and color. Monet or Renoir or Gauguin would have found much to paint here. To Helene, the scene in front of them was just a busy restaurant interior at lunchtime.

She reached out a hand and touched Evelyn on the arm.

"Look. I know it's none of my business, but . . . is it . . . him? You know. The man you were involved with a while back . . . the one you told me about. You seem so on edge and preoccupied lately . . . ever since you got back from being ill . . . that I just . . . well . . . wondered." A worried note crept into her voice. "You haven't done anything silly and started seeing him again, have you?"

Reluctantly, Evelyn turned from the scene of din and clatter around them, and looked at her.

"No, of course not. I told you. I'm done with all that. For good." Not quite a lie. She hadn't started seeing him again because she had never stopped seeing him to begin with. She glanced away again, hastily, so as not to meet the other girl's eyes. "I wish the waiter would hurry up with our order. I don't want to be late back." Being late back meant staying on to finish past half past five, being late back to the apartment, and precious time lost in working on the copy of the Giorgione Venus, and time was running out. And she already felt tired, very tired. All she wanted to do was to lay her head down on the table and close her eyes.

Helene picked up a newspaper someone had left on the seat, unfolded it, and scanned the front page.

"Oh, God. Not the Spanish Civil War again. Why the hell can't these reporters write about something else? Something cheerful for a change. It's always all gloom and doom." She turned the page. "Two million still out of work. Rumblings of unrest in Europe. I think they enjoy churning out this stuff, just to make everyone else feel guilty that they've got a roof over their head and a job to go to. Don't you think so? Mind you, when you think that a man with a wife and family to support who's unlucky enough to be out of work only gets forty-seven and six a week dole money, it does make me feel grateful. Just imagine. Four people living on little more than I get just for myself." She paused while the waiter came up with their plates. "Poor devils. They probably never get the chance to even look at a meal like this."

"The world's always been divided into two halves . . . the haves and the have-nots . . . it isn't fair, but it's a fact of life. And there isn't very much that we can do about it, even if we wanted to." No, nothing was fair. She loved Jack Neville, but he was trapped in a marriage to a woman who didn't. Everywhere people were living in misery and poverty, while men like

Robert De Braose could spend fifteen thousand pounds on a painting to hang above a door in his daughter's house where nobody would ever see it.

Slowly, she picked up her knife and fork, suddenly finding that she had little appetite for the food in front of her.

"You know what you need?" Helene stopped eating and sipped her wine. "A good holiday. A complete break, away from it all. Studios, paintings, London . . . the whole lot. Didn't you tell me once that you had family somewhere in the Channel Islands? Well, why not drop them a line and arrange to spend some time with them over there? It'll do you the world of good . . . and you won't even have to fork out for a hotel."

"What's left of my father's family still live in Jersey, yes. But I can't go there."

"Oh? Why not?"

"I wouldn't be welcome. My grandparents never forgave my father for marrying outside the island, and although I've kept up a correspondence with my aunt Blanche for years, ever since my mother died, there's never been anything in any of her letters to indicate that they've had a change of heart."

"But that's crazy! Anyone'd think we were still living in the Middle Ages . . . Dame Agnes Paston and all that. What business was of it of theirs who he wanted to marry . . . it was his life, not theirs. And in any case, it's not your fault. How can they blame you?"

"They hated my mother and I'm her daughter. It's as simple as that. I can't make them want me. My grandfather died years ago . . . not long after my father was killed. But my grandmother never came to his funeral and she never sent a single word of sympathy to my mother. Just a wreath of flowers. She's never attempted to have any kind of contact with me from the day I was born . . . I've no reason to think that anything's changed now."

"What has she got for a heart? Half a stone of reinforced concrete brick? Her own flesh and blood. What about blood being thicker than water and all that?"

Evelyn managed a wan half-smile. "I doubt if she's ever thought of me as her own flesh and blood. I'm just another persona non grata, like my mother was. All because she was born outside the island and earned her living as a nightclub singer. I think my father's people thought that any girl who did that kind of work was nothing more than a loose woman."

"You're kidding?"

"No, I'm not." Evelyn pushed away her half empty plate and leaned back in her chair. "They blamed my mother for everything. For him stopping in London. For never going back again. Even for the accident when he died. But by all accounts he was only too glad to have got away from Jersey."

Helene looked dumbfounded.

"But how can they blame her for all those things? I mean, it's ridiculous. Even if he hadn't met her, chances are he'd have stayed in London anyway. How can they say it was her fault that he didn't go back or that he was killed in the car crash? Was it because she was driving?"

"No. She wasn't even there. But they considered that if he hadn't left the island he'd never have been driving a car that night and he'd still be alive. As for him never going back . . . he always wanted to, Mother said. Not to live . . . but to take her there and let them meet her. My grandmother wrote and told him that he'd always be welcome, but that she'd never receive my mother. He answered that unless she did, he wouldn't set foot on the island again. And that was that."

"Does your grandmother have any idea that you and your father's sister are exchanging letters?"

"I don't know. I suppose she must. I always address all my letters to Blanche at the house in St. Ouens, and she always answers them. We've never made any secret about writing to each other. If my grandmother had wanted to put a stop to it, I'm sure she would have done it a long time ago."

"Everything you've told me makes me agree even more with what Napoleon is supposed to have said about relatives . . . keep as far away from them as possible." She glanced at her watch, then waved a hand in the direction of the nearest waiter. "We've got time for a coffee if you want one."

"Yes, why not?"

The restaurant was gradually beginning to empty of its occupants, the noise and chatter and the clattering of cutlery and plates had died down. Evelyn let her eyes wander from table to table, then beyond the windows to the busy street outside.

If only she was far away from here. If only she could get up and walk out, back into the past before any of the things that were complicating her life had ever happened. If only Jack Neville had never married. If only he had met her first and not Laura De Braose. If only she could turn back and begin all over again.

"Why, look at this . . .." Helene's voice broke into her thoughts, bringing her sharply back into the present. "Some businessman in Milan is threatening to sue the president of Delacroix Art Syndicate . . ." She glanced up briefly from her newspaper. "You've been commissioned to do a portrait of his daughter, haven't you?"

"What was that you said?" Helene's voice seemed to be coming from a long way away. She felt cold, invisible fingers up and down her spine.

"I said, some businessman in Milan is threatening to sue the president of Delacroix . . . oh it's about some painting . . ." She looked back at the newspaper and began to read from it. "'The buyer, who wishes to remain anonymous, is reputed to have paid the Delacriox Art Syndicate a six-figure sum for the sixteenth-century Italian masterpiece, which a spokesman for Delacroix confirms was dispatched to its destination more than six weeks ago . . . and Delacroix officials are looking urgently into the apparent disappearance of the painting, which, although heavily insured, is an irreplaceable example of the work of the fifteenth-century Italian artist Giorgione da Castelfranco, who died before he could complete the painting' . . . bla bla bla . . . 'left unfinished in his studio, it was finished by Titian after Giorgione's death in 1511, probably of the plague.'" She refolded the paper and put it back on the seat. "Oh, well, it'll give Lloyd's underwriters something to think about, won't it? Serve Robert De Braose right. He rang up the gallery once and wanted to speak to Guy Pellini . . . I've never spoken to anyone so rude. I'd have given anything, except my job, to have been able to put the phone down on him."

"Can I have that newspaper?"

"Why, what for? Evelyn, is something wrong with you? You've gone as white as a sheet!"

"I . . . I've come over a bit sick, that's all. Maybe I ate the meal too quickly . . ."

"But you've hardly touched it . . . here, have a glass of

water." She beckoned to the waiter for their bill. "If you're going to be sick I'd better get you into the ladies'. Come on."

"No. No, I'm all right. Really. I'll be fine in a minute. But I don't want to make you late back. You go on ahead and tell Mr. Pellini that I'll be a few minutes late . . . please." She fumbled in her handbag for her purse, and handed Helene her share of the bill.

"Are you sure you're all right?"

"Yes, yes. I'll be fine." She lashed around in her mind for something else to say. "It's just that I've been burning the midnight oil trying to get that portrait done in my own time, and after a hard day's work it isn't easy to come home and start all over again . . . I've been skipping meals to cut corners . . . you know the kind of thing you do when you get behind in something . . . and today is the first time I've eaten a proper meal. That's all."

Helene stood up and began pulling on her gloves. "You really shouldn't push yourself like this, Evelyn. It isn't worth it. And no one can work day and night without suffering for it in the end, I don't care who they are. Let bloody De Braose wait for his daughter's picture. Anyway, must rush." She bent forward, gave Evelyn a swift peck on the cheek, then disappeared from the restaurant into the crowds outside. The instant she'd gone Evelyn paid the waiter and grabbed up her coat and bag.

"Is there a telephone here I could use?"

"Yes, miss. There's a booth over there."

It was already occupied. She walked up and down, agitatedly, fidgeting with her gloves, looking every few seconds at her watch and then at the stout, middle-aged woman inside the booth. Just as she was about to tap on the glass and ask her how much longer she was going to be, the woman replaced the receiver and came out.

"It's a bad line, dear," she said, as she walked by. "I could hardly hear what they were saying on the other end. There's another box ten minutes up the road . . . better to use that."

Evelyn smiled nervously. "I haven't got the time. My call's urgent. And someone's bound to be using it anyway." She dashed into the booth, pulled the folding door closed behind her and with shaking hands fumbled inside her purse for change. Then she lifted the receiver and dialed Jack Neville's office number.

She'd never dared to telephone him at work before. It was too risky. Too dangerous. All outside calls to the Delacroix building went through a switchboard, and not even the president's telephone line was 100 percent private. The switchboard operator, a secretary, any one of them might pick up another telephone and listen in. But she was much too frightened to wait until he contacted her next . . . and that might be several days or even several weeks. Her heart was hammering while the bell at the other end rang. Then the line clicked and crackled, and Evelyn heard a woman's voice.

"Delacroix Art Syndicate . . . can I help you?"

Evelyn swallowed.

"Would you please put me through to Mr. Neville?" She clutched tightly at the receiver. At the other end there was more clicking and crackling on the line, then a momentary silence followed by a woman's voice.

"Mr. Neville's office. Who's speaking, please?" His secretary, no doubt.

She took a deep breath and leaned against the side of the booth for support. "My name is Evelyn Tregeale. Could you put me through to Mr. Neville, please? It's very urgent." No, that was a mistake. It might sound suspicious. She added, quickly, "I've been commissioned to paint Mrs. Neville's portrait, and I need to check something with him."

There was a few seconds' silence, then the voice said, "One moment please and I'll connect you." In the background Evelyn could hear the sound of a buzzer, then the noise of someone else picking up a receiver. Finally, the voice she knew so well.

"Jack! Thank God you're there!" She closed her eyes and leaned forward, then the words came tumbling out in a torrent, one on top of the other. When she paused for breath he said, coldly, angrily, and so abruptly that she was startled, "I told you never to ring me here!"

"What else could I do? For God's sake, Jack, when she read out about the painting from that newspaper I was scared out of mind!"

"Stop talking. Don't say another word. Look. I'll handle it. OK?"

"But Jack, it said—"

"I don't give a damn what it said. And the only thing I ever believe in the newspapers is the date! Just listen. I want you to ring off as soon as I've stopped speaking. Then ring Pellini. Say you've come over dizzy and you're taking a taxi back home. Say you're going to see your doctor and you'll let him know when you're well enough to go back to work. Understand?"

"Jack, I can't—"

"Stay in the flat. I'll try to wind things up here as soon as I can, and I'll call by this evening and tell you what's happening." She tried to speak but the line buzzed and crackled so badly that her words were lost; the woman had been right. It wasn't a clear line. From what seemed a long way off she caught his last words.

"Evelyn? Just do exactly as I say, and everything'll be all right. And as soon as you get in get working on that picture. It's got to be finished quickly." Without saying goodbye he hung up.

Slowly, she replaced the receiver and rested her head against the side of the booth to try and compose herself. Her whole body was shaking, her palms were wet and clammy. For a few more minutes she stayed where she was, then she pushed back the folding door of the booth and walked through the restaurant to the street outside.

As Jack Neville put down his receiver the door of his private office shot open and in came Robert De Braose. He slammed it behind him.

He never knocked before entering anyone's office. He was president of the Delacroix Art Syndicate and to him manners and the ordinary courtesies between colleagues only applied to Other People. He was a self-made man who'd bought a one-way ticket to South America when he was nineteen, and who'd returned, fifteen years later, almost a millionaire.

Nobody had ever found out how he'd made his money and he never let on; but he'd bought himself shares in a multitude of burgeoning companies and tripled his fortune, then married a well-connected socialite heiress before going into the business that really fascinated him, buying and selling fine art. He'd founded the Delacroix organization twenty years before and made it one of the foremost powers in the art world, and he had never looked back since.

Beauty meant nothing to him. If a painting was worth twenty-five thousand pounds then it had to be more beautiful than one which was only worth ten. And he always got what he wanted, at whatever price, even if it meant riding rough-shod over everyone else to do it. It was his personal boast that nobody had ever succeeded in getting the better of him either inside the auction room or outside it, and he'd successfully turned ruthlessness into a fine art. Invariably, he'd made enemies; but there were so many of them that even he had lost count.

He knew everyone who was anyone; just by picking up the telephone he could get things done that to anybody else would have been virtually impossible, and he ruled his self-made empire with a rod of iron that he never hesitated to bring down on the head of anyone who was human enough to make even the simplest of mistakes. He bullied. He manipulated. He outmaneuvered. He crushed, ruined, and destroyed with a single-mindedness that was almost mechanical. But there'd been the inevitable price to pay. Though he had hundreds of acquaintances and was invited everywhere, he had no real friends . . . and there were only three loves in his life. Power, money, and his only daughter.

Jack Neville noticed that his face was blood-red with anger and he was carrying a bundle of the day's newspapers under one arm. He strode over to the desk and threw the lot of them at him.

"Take a look at those! Go on, take a good look!" Slowly, Jack Neville leafed through them. "It's a plot. Against me. To discredit me and the whole organization in one blow. You can bet the American consortium's behind all this bad publicity . . . Delacroix outbid them at the Canaletto auction in Paris six months ago, and ever since then they've been waiting, plotting some kind of way to get back at me for being smarter than they are! This dirt's it. Paying those scandalmongering bastards in Fleet Street to print this bullshit that Delacroix's got so big it doesn't even remember where it put an Italian Old Master worth well-nigh a hundred thousand pounds!"

"It's OK," Jack Neville said, the story he'd carefully concocted and rehearsed for several weeks past clear in his mind. "I've dug down as deep as I can go and I think I've found out what's really happened."

"*Think* you've found out? Sonny, you're not paid to think! You're paid to *know!*"

"All right. I know. More or less. It's the only thing that *could* have happened to the painting, unless it's been stolen en route. Which you say isn't possible because of security—"

"Every work of art I dispatch to a client is insured up to the eyeballs and I pay for round-the-clock security to surround it for every minute of the journey, from the second it leaves this building or any other Delacroix building until it arrives at its destination. And this is the first time in twenty years one of my pictures hasn't turned up where and when it should!"

Jack Neville opened a large book on his desk and flicked through the pages. "I've got here the complete list of every painting that was crated up and dispatched on the same day as the Giorgione Venus . . . here, see for yourself. More than thirty. And going to thirty different destinations all over the country and the world. It's obvious what went wrong. The people responsible for dispatch have sent it to the wrong destination, and until it arrives there and can be checked, we can't do a thing. All we can do is telephone Milan and explain what's happened, be profusely sorry, and say whoever's responsible'll be severely reprimanded, and so on. We'll issue a statement to the press and they can put it out in their next editions, and in a week the whole thing'll be forgotten." He made a pretense of looking through the newspapers to avoid De Braose's eyes. "Who was it that said today's news is tomorrow's fish and chip paper?"

De Braose's pale, steely eyes nearly bulged out of his head.

"Forgotten? In a week? Something like this? A mistake that threatens my organization's credibility and makes me look like a laughingstock, a man who employs people that mislay priceless paintings as casually as if they'd mislaid their false teeth? No way. You get me names. By the end of the day or first thing tomorrow morning at the latest . . . you hear? I want to know who was responsible for this fucking cock-up and I want to know fast. Severely reprimanded, my arse! Everyone involved in this fiasco gets fired. And with no references." He was interrupted by the sudden ringing of the telephone.

"It's your secretary," Jack Neville said, handing him the receiver. "On the private line."

De Braose snatched it from him roughly.

"What is it?" A pause. "Right. Tell her I'm on my way down. And get my chauffeur to bring the Rolls round to the front entrance." He banged down the receiver so hard that the whole desk shook. "My little girl, downstairs in reception. I promised to have lunch with her today and then go on with her to Mainbocher's for the fittings for her new ballgowns . . . now I'm more than twenty-five minutes late!" He stalked over to the door, then glanced over his shoulder before going out and slamming it harder than when he came in.

"Their names. All of them. On my desk first thing tomorrow morning."

In the sudden silence of the room, Jack Neville leaned back in his winged swivel chair and closed his eyes. His head was throbbing. He badly needed a drink. He'd thought out every single detail of what he planned to do, over and over again, until it was as smooth and clear in his mind as a route map that had been pressed flat and creaseless in a laundry. Nothing could go wrong. He'd covered his tracks so well that even a man as cynical and astute as Robert De Braose wouldn't discover what he'd done until it was too late. And by that time he planned to be far away. It was a shame that innocent people would have to lose their jobs . . . through no fault of their own. He regretted it. But it couldn't be helped. He needed scapegoats to buy him a few weeks more precious time, while he completed his plans for his escape. And, besides, in this world it was dog eat dog. Seven years working for Robert De Braose had taught him something.

He picked up his telephone and dialed for an outside line. Set the wheels in motion. Go through the pretense of finding out what De Braose had asked for but what he already knew. He glanced at the clock on the opposite wall. They'd lunch late, spend at least two hours at Mainbocher's, and then, most likely, drop in at the Ritz for afternoon tea. He had at least four hours, then, after a swift, short appearance back home just for the look of it, the rest of the evening to spend with Evelyn. He could tell Laura that he was working late for her father, and neither of them would ever think to question it. Besides which, he knew De Braose was taking her to the theater that evening, then on to the Embassy for supper afterward. He smiled.

At the other end of the line the bell was ringing. Then someone answered.

6

"Jack, I'm frightened. The worry of it's driving me out of my mind. I'm a nervous wreck; people are beginning to notice. I jump when they talk to me. I can't eat. I can't sleep. When I came home this afternoon from the restaurant and telephoned Pellini, my hands wouldn't stop shaking."

He took her in his arms and kissed her hair, then stroked a single, bright red strand back from her face. She was beautiful. Very beautiful. And he wanted her. But it was no good like this.

"Listen . . . stop this. Calm down. It's not like you. You must get a grip on yourself, Evelyn. Remember, it's hard for me, too. But I've already told you there's nothing to worry about . . . I've got it all worked out and under control. So trust me. Just put everything out of your mind except one thing . . . getting that copy of Giorgione's Venus finished as soon as it's humanly possible." He smiled. "Come on, how about showing me how much progress you've made?"

"If I work nonstop I can do it in another week or ten days."

"Ten days? You're sure no longer?"

"I'm working on it as fast as I can!" she burst out, near to tears. Sleep. All she craved was sleep. "I'm so scared somebody will call unexpectedly and find it here, I have bad dreams about it. I toss and turn. I jump if the phone or the doorbell rings. Jack, I just can't go on this way for much longer."

"But it won't *be* for much longer. Look. I've brought a bottle of Scotch with me. Let me pour us both a double . . . it'll make you feel better." He guided her into one of the big armchairs, then went over to the other side of the room. As she sat there with her head in her hands and her eyes closed, Evelyn could hear the clink of glasses and the sound of liquid being poured into them, then his voice again.

"You know I hate putting you through all this, piling on the pressure this way . . . but I've had no choice, I explained all about the consortium to you in the beginning. And it isn't just that they want to see how multitalented you are . . . and that's rare, believe me. But they were telling me that there's a special, fast-growing market for copies of Old Masters, that they're especially anxious to get in on." He came over to her and handed her the drink. "There's a vast section of the new affluent all over the world who could never afford a real original of any of the great artists, but who'd be delighted to buy a painting that neither they nor anyone else could tell from the real thing. They'd know it wasn't, of course, and that would naturally be reflected in the sale price. But it's a rapidly expanding section of the art market that the Americans want to capitalize on as soon as they can." He gulped down his whisky. "I'm surprised my father-in-law's never explored it. After all, there aren't many pies he doesn't have a finger in."

Evelyn put her drink aside untouched.

"Jack . . . that newspaper article. And there were more, on the front pages of others . . . I saw them on the newsstand on my way home . . ."

"Stop worrying. You know what newspapers are, what they don't know they'll make up. And mostly they do. It's all press speculation because De Braose hates the whole of Fleet Street and he'll never issue statements unless it's necessary. Now listen to this. I've convinced him that the people in crating and dispatch have sent the painting to the wrong destination, and he's bought it. No, hear me out. It'll take weeks before anything can be done because of the number of works of art he ships abroad, some of them as far afield as South Africa and Brazil. By then I'll have got the picture recrated and sent off— by air—to Milan. The buyer'll stop screaming his head off and threatening to sue Delacroix, the press'll shut up and forget the whole affair, and everything will be OK. And we'll be off to New York on a one-way ticket . . . satisfied?"

She leaned against him. He had taken off his jacket and as she slid her arms around his neck, she could feel the warmth of his body through his shirt. She suddenly felt less afraid, less tense.

"How long can you stay?"

"Oh . . . till half six or seven. Then I'll have to put in an appearance at home, just in case Laura or her father get suspicious. He's taking her to the theater tonight and then on to a supper club with some of her friends . . . I'll simply leave a message that I'm calling back at the Delacroix building to sort out a list that he wanted for tomorrow morning, and I'll cover myself because the night porter will see me arrive and then leave again. But instead of going back home afterward, I'll come here to you."

"Supposing someone on your staff at the house let slip that you didn't get back again till late? They won't believe you were working on until that time of night . . . and the night porter will remember what time you left the Delacroix building."

"Yes. But all I have to say is that I went straight from Delacroix to a restaurant and had a late meal by myself. No one will ever be the wiser."

"Will your wife be back before midnight?"

"When she goes to the Embassy she never gets back before two A.M. And I mean never."

Evelyn's face brightened. It had been a long time since they'd spent any real time together. He was always in a hurry; checking and rechecking his wristwatch; after he'd made love to her he'd smoke a cigarette and then say, apologetically, "I'm sorry, but I really have to be going," and then dress, kiss her quickly on the cheek, and then rush downstairs to his car and drive away. Many times after he'd gone she'd lie there, turn her face into the pillow and cry, but there was never anyone to hear her.

Now she could smile. She looked up at him, all her love in her eyes, and wound her fingers in his thick, wavy dark hair.

"Don't ever leave me."

Laura Neville slammed the car door, pulled her mink cape further around herself and rushed up the steps to the front of the house, the long, glittering train of her flimsy evening gown sparkling in the moonlight. She rang the bell impatiently, then walked straight past the maid who had opened the door.

"Good evening, Madam . . ."

"I'm not stopping. Stay by the door," she called back over her shoulder as she went up the stairs. "I went out in such a hurry that I forgot to take something with me. Damn!" She disappeared at the turn of the stairs.

She opened her bedroom door and switched on the light. The maids had already drawn the curtains and lit a small fire in the grate to warm the room, and the light from the flames reflected across the thick pile carpet and the satin-draped bed.

She went over to her dressing table, opened one of the drawers, and took out a small bundle of snapshots tied with ribbon, then put them into her evening bag. As she turned round to go out again something on the opposite side of the room caught her eye.

Her husband's jacket lay over the back of one of the chairs, and on the darkness of the cloth, sparkling and glinting as it caught the light from the fire, lay a single red hair.

7

She opened her eyes. Daylight, creeping through a chink in the curtains, stole in a single bright shaft across the floor and onto the canvas propped up on the other side of the room. It lit up only the eyes in the face; those cold, steely, hostile eyes she remembered so well from their first, solitary meeting.

She'd caught their expression exactly; the stark look of jealous antipathy that had emanated from that face as she'd painted it was reproduced in such startling clarity that it might have been a photograph.

For a while longer she sat there, leaning against the bed head staring at it . . . the last morning she would ever have to wake up and come face to face with that hated portrait of her lover's wife. Today it was being delivered to Robert De Braose's house.

As she sat down on the long settee and began to brush out her long, wavy red hair, she thought of him, sitting at the top of his self-made empire, manipulating, pushing, scheming, moving men around at his whim as if they weren't real people at all, just pieces on a chessboard. She imagined him behind his desk, gold pen in hand, writing out a check with her name on it, just as he did with countless others. His price for services rendered.

She lay down her hair brush, made herself morning tea, then switched on her radio set and hummed the Irving Berlin tune

56

that the orchestra was playing while she dressed. Today was a special day. In twenty days' time she'd walk out of this apartment with Jack Neville to catch the flight bound for New York, and never enter it again.

An hour later, on the twenty-minute walk to work in Bruton Street, she wore a smile as brilliant as the morning's sunshine.

The instant she opened the door of Guy Pellini's office and went inside she knew that something was wrong.

As usual he was seated behind his desk. As usual a tray of reports and papers lay there in front of him, ready to be looked over. But the expression in his eyes as he glanced up and looked at her was not usual; there was no smile, no greeting. He stared at her as if she were a stranger. Her own smile died on her lips.

"I couldn't get a taxi for love or money this morning," she said, still hesitating inside the open doorway. "So I had to walk from my flat carrying this . . ." She held up the finished canvas of Laura Neville, devoid of its protective cloths and brown paper wrappings. "Still, it wasn't heavy. More awkward than anything else. People kept walking straight into me." Still, no response from the man behind the desk. "Well . . . I'll take it to the packing room, shall I?"

Slowly, Pellini turned his head and glanced across the room. It was then, as she followed the direction of his eyes, that she saw for the first time he was not alone.

There, on the edge of one of the armchairs in the far corner of the office, sat a man. And his eyes were the same cold, hostile, steely eyes that looked out from the painting she held in her hands.

"Miss Tregeale?" He spoke before Pellini could. "Do you have any idea who I am?"

"I think so." Her heart began to hammer wildly. But outwardly she somehow kept calm. He had every reason to be here, after all; he was the president of Delacroix Art Syndicate and Delacroix often did business with the Pellini gallery; he'd commissioned her to paint a portrait of his daughter, and Pellini would have told him it was finished, and was being delivered today. Why else should he have come here in person if not to collect it?

Yet the way in which he was looking at her told Evelyn that

the real reason he'd come had nothing to do with either. For the first time in her life, she knew what it was to feel fear.

"I'm Robert De Braose," he said, not taking his eyes from her face. "And I've come here to show you something that just about every Fleet Street journalist would give his eye teeth to look at." Slowly, he heaved his bulky frame from the arm of the chair and went over to two large canvases that were shrouded in heavy, gray sheets. With a flick of his wrist, he pulled them away, and there, side by side but so identical she was unsure at this distance which of them was the original, were the two paintings of the Giorgione Venus.

All color drained from her face.

"Pellini," she heard De Braose's harsh voice speak from what seemed a long way away, "would you mind leaving us for a short while?"

It was an order and not a question. Guy Pellini got up from behind his desk and went silently toward the door; he gave her one single look as he passed her by. It might have been contempt; it could have been pity. Then he went out and closed it behind him. And Evelyn was left alone with her tormentor.

"Right, you underhanded little bitch," De Braose said, in a soft whisper that was more terrifying than any shouting match could ever have been. "Before I tell you what I intend to do about you and that no-good bastard you've been sleeping with behind my little girl's back, let's hear what you've got to say about what you've done!"

She was all alone. There was no escape from him, no way to hide from those cold, hostile eyes that burned with hate and resentment for her. She was trapped with nowhere to run to. And there was nobody to help her.

She took a few faltering steps toward Pellini's desk, found the thick, solid edge of the wood and hung on to it to stop the shaking in her hands. Somehow, she found her own voice.

"What is it that you think I've done, Mr. De Braose?"

The last thing he'd ever expected her to do was to stand up to him. Nobody ever did. Nobody ever dared to. For a few brief seconds, he was completely taken aback for the first time in his life.

This wasn't the way he'd planned the confrontation; this wasn't the way she was supposed to be. He wanted to see her crushed. Cowering, crying, humiliated. He wanted to see fear in her eyes. To see her plead and then grovel. But most of all he wanted to see her punished for making a fool of him and for daring to be desired by the man the De Braose power and money had bought for his little girl.

When he spoke his voice rose to a shout.

"What have you done? You want to know what you've done? You make yourself an accomplice to the crime of stealing a priceless work of art from my syndicate . . . and then forging it . . . while you fornicate with my daughter's husband whenever he can find the time to sneak into your bed behind her back . . . *and you ask me what you've done?*"

She winced under the onslaught of his words. She stood there, numbly, fighting down the lump in her throat and the tears that were stinging like ammonia at the backs of her eyes. He made it sound so cheap, so sordid, so trivial, the love between them that men like him and women like Laura Neville could never experience or understand.

Somehow she fought back the tears and found her voice.

"I love Jack Neville and he loves me. And I've never stolen anything in my life."

"Oh, is that a fact? So he stole the painting and you didn't. That leaves us with just forgery and adultery."

"I made a copy of the picture, yes. Because he asked me to. Because he'd met someone from an American art consortium in Brussels when you sent him there who was looking for a British partner to join them, and an artist who could work in their reproduction department. Jack knew how much that would mean to both of us, and when he explained it all to me, I agreed." Her voice got stronger. "As for adultery . . . isn't it less immoral for a man to go to bed with a woman he's really in love with than it is for him to go bed with a wife that he doesn't love at all?"

"Why, you brazen little slut!"

"It's the truth . . . whether you like it or not. He doesn't love your daughter. He never did . . . he told me so. And when I saw her for the first time that day at the house I understood why." Visions of that morning in the vulgar, over-gilded hall came back to her, and she shuddered with distaste. "She's as cold, and hard, and arrogant as you are. A real chip off the old block!" His mouth fell open. "Somebody who thinks that all you have to do to be a lady is to put on a mink coat and a diamond necklace, or that wearing a dress that cost more than a man's wages for a whole year makes her better than anyone else. Somebody who thinks that everyone else in the world is just there to be used, or exploited, or bought." She paused. "And whose father only has to open his checkbook and write in it to buy her what better women can have for nothing. A man's real love. Yes, you bought your spoiled daughter the husband she wanted, didn't you? But neither of you got the bargain you expected. Because love is one thing in this world that nobody can buy. Least of all a man like you."

His face had turned a deep, ugly purple. His eyes bulged from their fleshy sockets, like chinks of colored glass. For a moment she thought he was going to hit her.

Instead, he pointed a shaking finger toward the two paintings behind them.

"You know what I could have done to you for this? For being party to what that bastard did, for daring to insult me and my little girl? You, a penniless little nobody who'll never be any more than you are now. And shall I tell you why? Because you're a fool." Spittle appeared at the corners of his mouth and trickled down one side of his chin. "You think love is worth more than anything. You think it's worth more than power or money or position . . . but you're wrong. And I'm going to prove to you how wrong you are, and also that you're a fool." He walked over to the paintings. "Brilliant. I'd even go as far as to say you're so talented that it amounts to genius. Not even I know which of them is which . . . and I won't, not until one of my experts back at the Delacroix building has come over to take a look at them. You know why he wanted you to do this?" His mouth turned up at the corners in an unpleasant smile. "You swallowed all the lies he told you, of course. Well, you love him, don't you? And he loves you, didn't you say?"

"He borrowed the original so that I could make a copy for the American consortium to look at, that's all! He held it back from shipment for a few weeks longer . . . not because he intended to steal it or to pass off my copy as the original to them or anyone else!"

"The American consortium never asked him to join them or to show them your painting. Yes, that's right. He met one of their representatives in Brussels at one of the business cocktail parties, sure enough. As he met representatives from half a dozen other countries who were there. But your forgery was bound for quite another destination. The real buyer in Milan.

Your darling Jack Neville planned to sell the real Giorgione Venus to an unnamed art collector in Brazil . . . known to the South American dealer who he also met that night in Brussels . . . someone who couldn't care less how he got hold of it or where it came from, so long as he got his hands on an original Old Italian Master, unique of its kind. By the time the forgery was discovered by the genuine buyer—if it ever was—he reckoned to be far away with you on the other side of the world. And because we don't have an extradition treaty with Brazil, the law couldn't even lay a finger on him."

"I don't believe you!"

Slowly, De Braose reached inside his suit pocket and took out two tickets. Then he held them up so that Evelyn could see them.

"Two one-way airline tickets. To Brazil."

Woodenly, she stared at them. Then she covered her eyes with her hands. She was too stunned to cry.

"If I want to, all I have to do is pick up that telephone and call the police. And destroy you both." She looked up through her fingers as if she were looking through the bars of a cage in which he'd trapped her, at those cold, hostile, steely eyes. They taunted her. Laughed at her for her innocence and naiveté. "Don't think I don't want to do it. Don't think I'm not going to because I feel sorry for you. Or because I believe you're nothing more than an infatuated, ignorant little fool . . . nothing would give me greater pleasure than to grind both of you underfoot and crush you as I'd crush a beetle." He went over to Guy Pellini's desk and pulled out the chair. "You know why I'm not going to? Because of my syndicate's credibility and reputation, and because of my little girl's good name.

"If any of this ever went further than this room, we both know what'd happen, don't we? There'd be a scandal so big that every enemy I've ever made'd grab it like a bone and sink his teeth into it like a bulldog. The papers would have a field day. My organization's international standing'd be dragged through the mud, and my little girl's name'd be bandied about from one end of society to the other as if she was a rotten music hall turn. And that's one thing I'd move heaven and earth to stop from happening." He sat down in Pellini's chair behind the desk. "Get this straight. I don't give a damn about you or that no-good bastard my daughter's married to. He's not my flesh and blood; and if I'd had my way, she'd have chosen one of the viscounts or earls who were running after her, and got herself married into the aristocracy instead of wasting herself on someone like him. But there you are, he was the one she wanted and he was the one she got. Now he's shown his true colors, she can see him for what he is." He folded his arms. "Divorce is out of the question . . . I'm not having her dragged through the courts and made a social outcast of, or it being made common knowledge that the man she married cheated on her with another woman. She's been through enough humiliation already. So let me spell out to you what's going to happen." They stared at each other across the floor. "There are two choices. And I've left it up to Jack Neville to decide."

"I don't understand."

"It's simple. He can either stay with my daughter, or go with you. No one would ever be the wiser, whatever happened. There are dozens of well-known, respected couples in society—even royalty—who stay married to each other but live entirely separate lives . . . no stigma attaches itself to them as long as they're reasonably discreet. No washing dirty linen in public. Only divorce and scandal shut doors. So I gave him the choice. Stop with Laura and continue to enjoy the style of life my money has given him ever since he married her . . . but never see you again. Or take these airline tickets and go with you to Brazil . . . without a penny." He smiled. "I don't think I need to tell you which one of those options he chose."

She opened her lips to speak, but no sound came out.

"You're quite a bastard, aren't you?" she whispered.

"Just a good judge of character." He reached inside his suit and pulled out a leather case. "My checkbook. The thing you profess to despise." He lay it open on Pellini's desk and began to write.

"I don't want your money!"

He got up. "I'm not giving you any. And this isn't a gratuity." He came over to where she was standing and stuffed the check into her pocket. "I commissioned you to paint my little girl's portrait and you've painted it. This is for services rendered." He picked up a paper knife from Pellini's desk and slashed the canvas from top to bottom. "But I wouldn't have anything you've touched hanging in my daughter's house if it was the last picture on earth.''

He picked up his hat and overcoat from one of the chairs and walked past her to the door. She pulled his check from her pocket, tore it in half, and threw it on the ground at his feet.

"Take your blood money with you when you go. I wouldn't take a penny from you if I was starving in the gutter.''

He gave her one pitying glance before he went out.

"Before long I reckon that's just where you'll be.''

8

She didn't realize that Guy Pellini had come back into the room until he spoke. Woodenly, she turned round to face him, her eyes full of tears. There was no reproach in his expression, only a dull, solemn look that almost told her what he was going to say. But she could only stare at him, helplessly.

"Evelyn . . . I'm sorry." He glanced beyond her to where the two canvases of the Giorgione Venus stood, side by side. "Whatever he says, I'll never believe that you were capable of doing anything you believed was wrong. I know about Jack Neville . . . he told me." She turned away her head. "I'm not making any moral judgments. What you do or what you've ever done in your private life isn't any of my business; I've only ever been concerned with your ability." He hesitated, as if he'd come, inevitably, to the hardest part he had to say. "I don't want to lose you. I don't even know how I'm ever going to replace you . . . because the talent you have is in a class of its own. But De Braose hasn't given me any choice. And he's far too big for me to fight with on my own. I couldn't survive and neither could my business if I tried." He looked down at his hands, awkwardly. "If it's a question of money . . ."

"No. No, thank you. I can manage." She went to the door and opened it, wondering how she ever would. She looked back at him. There was much she longed to say, but suddenly she was tongue-tied. And suddenly nothing seemed to matter anymore.

She went on out into the street, leaving a chunk of happiness and memories from her life inside. The door was closed and locked. And Robert De Braose had thrown away the key.

She caught sight of him at the window of his chauffeur-driven Rolls Royce, parked in the side street beside the back entrance of the gallery, and as she came down the steps she saw him make a sign to the driver, and it came forward, glinting silver-blue in the sunlight, then glided to a halt almost at her feet.

Instinctively, she knew that he'd been waiting there, deliberately, until she came out, for some twisted reason of his own. To gloat, maybe to check if Guy Pellini really had dismissed her. Then, as she glanced through the back window of the car, she at last understood why.

Sitting there, between his wife and Robert De Braose, was Jack Neville. And as she gasped with surprise, then called his name, he turned away his face and the car went on, leaving her standing alone on the edge of the pavement.

She ran on and on, blindly; dashing away the streaming tears, banging into people as she went. She ran across roads, ignoring cars and buses as they honked their horns or screeched to a grinding halt in front of her, deaf to shouts of abuse and protest from their angry drivers. When she reached her apartment door she pressed against it, panting and crying both at once; then she fumbled in her handbag for her keys, hardly able to see the lock through the wall of tears.

When she'd let herself in she flung herself full length onto the settee and sobbed her heart out.

Helene Morgan found her there, hours later, still crying.

"Evelyn, you left your door open with the key still in the lock! Anyone could have walked in!"

"I don't care!"

"Evelyn, please . . . I want to help you . . ."

"If you want to help me just go away and leave me alone!"

"No, I won't go away." Helene knelt on the floor beside the settee and put a hand on Evelyn's shaking shoulders. "Look. Pellini told me you'd had to leave because of some trouble with Robert De Braose, and I came straight here as soon as I'd finished work at the gallery. Not to pry. Please, don't think that.

But if you need someone to talk to, or if I can do anything . . ." she squeezed her hand. "Whatever's happened, I'll understand. And I'd never breathe a word of it to a soul, I swear it."

Slowly, Evelyn drew herself up and leaned against the back of the settee. She wiped her nose on the back of her sleeve. She looked at Helene, then at the ground. What did it matter? Nothing mattered anymore. He was gone. He'd turned away his face from her, and left her standing there, alone. As long as she lived she'd never forget how he'd turned away his face when she'd called to him.

Slowly, she began to speak, and she kept talking until the whole of the story had been told.

"Evelyn . . . why didn't you tell me this before? In the gallery that day . . . in the restaurant, even. I would have understood. You could have trusted me. After I read out that article in the newspaper about Delacroix and the missing painting, I sensed some kind of change in you. But I didn't know why or what it was. If only you'd confided in me then."

"And what would you have done? Told me not to be a fool."

"He used you, Evelyn."

"Yes, I know he used me. Now. Looking back I can see it all. But in the beginning you only see them through a cloud . . . and when the cloud blows away and you see them as they really are, it's too late to turn back." She stared down at her hands. "I was only aware of how much I loved him. How much I thought he loved me. I believed he loved me. I believed he wanted me. I believed that he wanted us to be together. Just because he said so." She closed her eyes. "Dear God . . . how she must be laughing at me!"

"You mean his wife?"

"Yes." She looked at Helene with huge, sad, tear-filled green eyes. "She can laugh now, can't she? Because she's beaten me. She's won. He's still with her, in spite of everything he said, in spite of everything he told me. When De Braose gave him the choice of staying with her or going to me, he took the easy way out."

For a few moments neither of them spoke.

"You won't believe this," Helene said at last, "not yet. Not until the pain's gone and the wounds he made have healed. But I think you've had a lucky escape from him. Think about it. If a man loves a woman and has the chance to be with her, would he choose to stop with a wife he doesn't feel anything for, tied to her for the rest of his life like a dog on a chain? I know I wouldn't, if I was in his place. I couldn't bear it. If he's willing to do that, if he's willing to make a sacrifice of you and his own happiness, then he isn't worth crying over."

"Yes, in my heart I know that. But tell me how I stop myself from crying."

"It's easy for someone else to say. I know that, because I've been there. That man I told you about . . . do you remember? Well, I thought my heart would break when I found out he was married. I wanted to shut myself away and never be with people ever again. I wanted to curl up and die. And I was full of bitterness and hate. I used to lie awake at nights, torturing myself, imagining him in bed with her. But if I hadn't been able to let my thoughts run riot I'd have bottled them up inside and driven myself insane. There was so much violence in me, it scared me. But you have to confide in someone, you have to let go. Otherwise all that hate and resentment ends up by poisoning you, not the other woman. I can laugh now, when I think back to it. But when it was happening to me it was hell on earth."

"Is he out of your system?"

"If you mean can I think about him without hurting any-more . . . yes. But I haven't forgotten about him. I don't think I ever will . . . or that I could even if I tried to. It was the first time that I'd ever been in love, and that's something that I don't think you ever forget about, even if it came to nothing. As mine did. It hurt, yes. It hurt like hell. And I've never cried so much then or since. But it taught me something. About men. How naive and cruel they can be, without even meaning to." She sighed. "And after you've slunk away to lick your wounds, they'll go sneaking back to their boring wives as if nothing had ever happened. You're left on your own. Angry. Bitter. Thinking of all the time you've wasted that you'll never get back again, all the other chances you've let go by. And for what? A dead end and a broken heart."

Evelyn managed a weak smile.

"Thanks for being here. It helps, hearing that."

"That's what it was meant to do. And I didn't only come here to help you dry your tears. You need more than that. You have to start thinking about what you're going to do."

"That's one thing I can't answer . . . because I don't know myself. Except that De Braose will make sure that no one in London—or anywhere else for that matter—would risk giving me work as an artist ever again. He's closed the doors and thrown away the key. I can't fight that." Things that she couldn't even begin to think about came crowding into her mind all at once. "I've got to be punished, kicked back down again to where I belong. I stole away his little girl's prize toy and he wants revenge. For her. For himself. To show me how powerful he is. I'm not so stupid as to believe that getting me dismissed will satisfy him. He wants to drive past a doorstep in his big Rolls Royce and see me scrubbing it, on my hands and knees."

"Well, he won't. Because you won't be here." Helene gripped her arm. "The way I see it, there's only one thing for you to do. Go to Jersey, to your father's family."

Evelyn's face showed only astonishment.

"But that's the last place on earth I could ever go to! You know why. I told you what happened when my father left the island and married my mother. They turned against him. They wouldn't even acknowledge her. Or me, for that matter. Even when he was killed and my mother wrote to them and told them, the only one who answered her was Blanche. My grandmother refused to even attend his funeral because my mother would be there. Can you imagine what would happen if I just turned up, case in hand, on their doorstep, begging for a roof because I had nowhere else to go?"

"For Christ sake . . . you're her son's child! Her own flesh and blood! Do you really think if it came to the crunch she'd turn you away? You know what old people are like, Evelyn . . . they're proud. Stubborn. They cling to old morals and old habits. But they're still human. Have you ever thought that your grandmother might be longing for you to make some kind of contact with her, but that she's got too much pride to make the first move herself? No, I didn't think you had. Well, it's true. And another thing you've overlooked. If she was so much against you why has she let her daughter Blanche go on writing to you for all these years? Think about it."

For a long time Evelyn was silent.

"Look, I'll help you compose the letter. You don't have to tell her all the details about why you've got to leave London.

Living on an island in the middle of nowhere all her life I doubt if she's ever heard of Robert De Braose or the Delacroix Art Syndicate. You've got to write that letter, Evelyn." She stared into her dull, swollen eyes. "You don't really have any choice."

"You *bastard!*"

"Laura—"

"Stay there, right where you are. Don't come anywhere near me! Just take everything that belongs to you out of this room and move it into one of the other bedrooms. I don't give a bloody damn which one. Just so long as it's as far away from me as possible!"

"If you feel that way why did you go along with your father's idea that I stop with you?" Jack Neville's voice was bitter. "What's the matter? Worried that your idle society friends might start gossiping behind your back?"

"Shut up! And get out of my room! This is my bedroom, you hear me?" She picked up a pair of shoes that belonged to him and threw them across the room. "Go and think about your red-headed little slut! Because that's all you'll ever be able to do from now on . . . think about her." Tears of rage filled her eyes and she dashed them away with the back of her hand. "My God, what a fool you took me for! You were playing around, right there under my nose, and I didn't see it! Except that night when I came back because I'd forgotten something, and found one of her hairs on your jacket! Even then I didn't want to believe it. Part of me even couldn't, not when the evidence was staring me bang in the face! If I hadn't told Daddy and he hadn't had you followed, I'd never have known. My God, how I hate you! And that cheap little bitch!" Suddenly, her control snapped and she began to cry. "How the pair of you must have laughed together, thinking you'd got me fooled! And how many times did you come back here and climb into my bed after you'd made love to her, you bastard!" Her voice rose to a scream. "Do you know what kind of a hell you're putting me through?"

"Laura, for Christ's sake!" He came across the room to where she was, took hold of her wrists and shook her. "Do you want the whole house to hear!"

Furiously, she shook herself free, then hit him a stunning blow across his face. "Get your filthy hands off of me! Go away, get out of my sight! Every time I look at you all I can see is you and her, together in bed. And I want to be sick!"

Slowly, he walked away again toward the door. He bent down and picked up the shoes she'd thrown there.

"You really want to live like this? You think we can? Going on, day after day, living under the same roof, being seen together on your empty round of theater and parties and nightclubs, making out to other people that everything's the same as it ever was, when underneath your pathetic little masquerade you're seething with jealousy and hate! What did you really want me back for, Laura? Tell me the truth. Was it because you and your father can't bear the thought of anyone else finding out what really happened . . . or because you can't bear the thought of me being happy with another woman?"

She glared at him, wild-eyed, all the meanness and vindictiveness of her character alive in her narrow face.

"Daddy gave you the choice . . . and you chose. Her or me. And we both knew exactly which choice you'd make . . . because you can't live without my father's money and what it can buy you." Her thin, pale lips turned up at the corners in a cruel, triumphant smile. "What did I really want you back for, Jack? Because when something belongs to me I never let it go. And I never intend to let you go, either."

PART TWO

JERSEY

9

Through the same cloud of seasickness that had descended on her the moment she'd first stepped aboard the boat, Evelyn watched the Jersey coastline and St. Helier harbor draw slowly but ever closer into sight, while all around her other passengers swarmed up on deck, chattering, laughing together, pointing toward the shore ahead, ignoring the pale, solitary figure who stood apart from them, leaning over the boat rail with shaded eyes.

As the boat began to lose speed, she stayed where she was, staring uncertainly toward the quay with its mass of bobbing, anchored craft, and the multicolored moving dots beyond that were human beings. Somewhere among them would be Blanche Tregeale, waiting to welcome the niece she'd never seen, the only child of the woman her mother had never stopped hating and the brother she'd idolized and lost.

Slowly, Evelyn opened her handbag and took out her last letter, together with the only picture of her aunt she had. It was curious about the photograph. Though she'd asked Blanche to send her a recent picture so that she'd have no difficulty recognizing her when the boat landed, Blanche had never sent one. But maybe there was a good reason why she hadn't. Maybe she didn't even have one. Maybe she hadn't been photographed in a long while. Maybe she'd meant to send one but forgot. It hardly mattered now. It was scarcely likely that anyone else in the waving group of people standing on the quay would resemble that beautiful face that looked up at her from the dog-eared picture in her hand.

She felt a little less sick now. As the boat moved slowly through the calm water and into the harbor, she stared in front of her at the unfamiliar buildings and the landscape beyond them, wondering how her father had felt when he'd left his native island for the last time . . . not knowing, then, that he was destined never to return. And now here she was, more than twenty years later, coming back to them in his place.

As she picked up her single suitcase and waited to go ashore, all the misgivings that she'd fought down before and on the journey came surging back, sharp and clear, and her heart lurched and began to beat faster. Would everything be as she'd imagined; would her grandmother forget what had happened in the past and accept her, as a Tregeale, into what was left of the family? Would she be happy here, would she be able to forget Jack Neville and everything he'd meant to her? Would she be able to erase all the ugliness that scarred her memory of those last nightmare weeks back in London? The scene with De Braose, Pellini's last look, standing alone on the edge of the pavement outside the gallery, when she'd called out to Jack Neville and he'd turned away his face? Maybe. As the boat docked and the gangplank was lowered, she edged her way slowly forward, jostled all around by the crowds of passengers as they all made their way onto the quayside.

She let them go past her. Putting down her suitcase, she scanned the faces on the quay for Blanche's, without success. She stood back. She waited, anxiously, while the crowd grew smaller. She watched as people smiled and greeted each other, and then went off toward the town, or climbed into waiting cars and drove off in the opposite direction.

She looked at her wristwatch. She glanced back toward the boat, uncertain what she should do if no one came to meet her. She could find a telephone somewhere in St. Helier, or take a taxi to the house. She hesitated, looking anxiously around her. Then, from a large, old-fashioned car that was parked some way along the road beside the quay, she saw a tall, uniformed man walking toward her. She stared at him.

"Miss Evelyn Tregeale?" the man said, as he came up.

"Yes, I'm Evelyn Tregeale."

He removed his cap and she suddenly realized what he was.

"I'm Mrs. Tregeale's chauffeur." He smiled. "She sent me to meet you from the boat." He glanced down at the single piece of luggage she had brought with her. "May I take your suitcase to the car?"

"Th—thank you, yes, if you would." Puzzled, she stared toward it, and saw that it was empty. "My aunt was meant to meet me here . . . is something the matter?"

"I understood from Mrs. Tregeale that Miss Blanche was indisposed. That's why she wasn't able to come. Shall we go?"

"Yes. Yes, of course." She followed him to the waiting car and climbed inside. "I hope it's nothing serious . . . when I didn't see her on the quayside, I was worried."

He glanced at her in the mirror.

"I'm sure it's nothing serious, miss, since Mrs. Tregeale never sent for the doctor. One of Miss Blanche's sick headaches, I believe. She seems to get a lot of them, so I understand."

"Oh?" Blanche had never mentioned the malaise in any of her letters. But then most people wouldn't. Sick headaches were unpleasant but scarcely something anyone would make a point of writing about. Evelyn lay back on the seat, looking from the car window as the car made its way through the streets of St. Helier, then gathered speed as they left the town behind.

Everything seemed strange to her. Different, smaller, unfamiliar. Like being suddenly in some far-off, distant land, not a small island less than eighty miles from the English mainland. She glanced at the chauffeur's rigid back and tried to strike up a new conversation.

"It's a beautiful place, Jersey." She glanced out at the countryside as they sped by. "Is it like this all over the island?"

"Oh, yes, miss. Lots of granite. That's what always strikes people from the mainland when they come here for the first time . . . granite cliffs, granite castles, granite churches, granite farms, granite everything. And all colors, too. Red and orange, blue and gray. Up in the north, if you ever get to go to that part of the island, it's much higher ground . . . great, rugged precipices there on the coast, with a honeycomb of caves, some of 'em more than four hundred feet high . . . then the land slopes down, till it reaches the sea level down in the south. You'll find mostly every kind of scenery here, even though the whole island's no more than nine miles by five, plenty to look at . . . sandy beaches, little streams, forests, coves . . . and some kinds of plants and flowers that you don't get on the mainland at all, on account of it being much milder here in winter." He chuckled, half to himself. "That's what the tourists like, the warm weather. Hardly ever get snow here, you know."

"No, I didn't know." So many things Blanche Tregeale had left out of her letters. "Do you get many English tourists in Jersey?"

"A fair number. and from other places, too. France, mostly. We're nearer to the French coast than we are to England."

For several minutes there was silence.

"Is it a long drive to the house from St. Helier?"

"Not too long, miss. The house lies halfway between Sorel and the Mourier valley, in St. John's parish." Their glances met briefly in the driving mirror. "To my mind, it's the most beautiful spot on the whole island . . . the house stands in half a dozen acres of its own ground, so you don't get many people coming around who aren't meant to be there . . . and yet, if you want to, you can get to any other place on the island in no time at all, by car. And you've got the finest scenery in Jersey. Forest, countryside, and cliffs. You'll see for yourself if I'm not right."

"Were you born on the island?"

"Yes, miss. An' I've worked for Mrs. Tregeale for the last fifteen years."

The house came upon her suddenly, when she was least expecting it, through a cluster of gigantic shrubs and trees, startling her with its size and rugged beauty. Instantly she sat forward on the edge of her seat.

It was nothing like the house of her imagination. Like dozens of smaller houses that they'd passed on the drive from St. Helier, it was built of massive granite blocks, a central building flanked by two wings and an ancient granite tower, the outside half covered by some kind of climbing vine that Evelyn had never seen before. Beyond the house she could see more trees, and a wild, rambling wilderness of a garden filled with bushes and shrubs not yet in flower. As the car drew slowly to a halt outside the massive, iron-bound front door, there seemed no sign of life from within the house itself. There was no movement behind any of the many windows. No one opened the door and came out to greet her. Solemnly, the chauffeur helped her from the car, then carried her suitcase up to the front door and deposited it on the step. Evelyn turned to him.

"Is anyone at home?"

"Why, of course, miss. Just ring the bell there an' somebody'll come." He touched his cap and went back to the car while Evelyn watched him. He restarted the engine, then it moved forward and out of sight behind the house.

For several minutes she stood in the strange, eerie silence. Then she glanced up at the windows above. Some were slightly open, but no sound came from the rooms inside. On the far side of the house, the two uppermost windows were tightly shut, and their curtains drawn all the way across.

She looked all around her. At the old tower, toward the gardens and the woodland beyond, then back the way they'd come toward the road, hidden from sight by the thickness of the shrubbery and trees. Then, her heart in her mouth, she took hold of the bellcord and rang it.

For several minutes nothing happened. Then, just as she was about to reach for the bell a second time, she heard movement on the other side of the door and at last it creaked open; but instead of her aunt or her grandmother, she found herself face to face with a pale, fair-haired girl about her own age.

"Oh . . ." She picked up her suitcase. "I'm Evelyn Tregeale." She held out her free hand. But although the other girl smiled nervously, she stepped back a little and did not take it.

"Yes, miss. Mrs. Tregeale and Mrs. de Corbiere've been expecting you." She took another step backward and Evelyn went inside, into a cool, dark hall that smelled old and musty, like a church. "I'm Jeanne Le Bon, miss." Another nervous smile. "My mother's the housekeeper here." She picked up Evelyn's case and led the way along a wide, dark, picture-lined corridor, talking as she went. "I'm afraid you'll find the place a bit quiet at this time of day . . . Mrs. Tregeale, she always has a lie-down in her room after lunch, and most of the servants have the afternoons free, unless there's extra work to be done, or guests in the house. Mrs. de Corbiere had to go into St. Helier, and Miss Blanche is asleep upstairs . . ." She hesitated. "So I'm afraid there's nobody to do for you except me."

"That doesn't matter. I'm used to seeing to myself." The idea of having servants seemed quaint to her. "My aunt's asleep upstairs, you say?" She remembered what the chauffeur had said. "When the boat docked and I didn't see her at the quayside, I was worried . . . the driver told me that she'd been taken ill."

Jeanne Le Bon went on walking ahead of her.

"Yes, poor Miss Blanche. One of her bad headaches." She set down the suitcase at the bottom of the stairs. "I'll get Etienne or Jean-Louis to carry this up to your room, miss . . . if I show you where it is now, you can get settled in." She began to lead the way up the big, wide staircase. "All the rest of your things arrived a few days ago. I wanted to unpack them for you and hang them away, but Mrs. de Corbiere said we'd best wait till you got here before we touched anything."

"Mrs. de Corbiere?"

"Miss Julia that was. She'll be sorry that she wasn't here to meet you when you arrived . . . but she did have some business to see to in town for Mrs. Tregeale, that couldn't be put off, my mother says. But she'll be back soon enough, I shouldn't wonder." They reached the top of the stairs, went along a wide landing and stopped outside one of the many doors.

"What a beautiful room." Evelyn followed her inside, her eyes moving rapidly from one side to the other, taking in antique furniture, china, pictures. The largest, hung high above the marble mantlepiece, riveted her attention. "I never knew my grandmother collected paintings . . . the house is full of them. And they're all originals." She went closer to the canvas and studied it with expert eyes. "Did she buy this Watteau or has it always been in the family?"

Jeanne Le Bon lay down the suitcase on the bed. "As far as I know, miss, all the pictures have been in the family for donkey's years." She went over to the window and opened it. "There, that'll give you a nice breath of fresh air. Not that the room hasn't been well aired already . . . Mrs. de Corbiere was most particular about that. But the rooms on this side of the house trap the afternoon sun, and if you don't open the windows they can get a bit stuffy. Mrs. de Corbiere wanted everything to be right for when you arrived." She glanced around her. "Well, I'll leave you to settle in now, miss. Can I bring you some tea? You must be thirsty after traveling all that way from the mainland."

"That's kind of you. But I really don't expect to be waited on." She laughed. "You see, I'm not used to it. When I lived in London I had a flat and I did everything for myself. Washing, cooking . . . all that sort of thing. If you show me where the kitchen is, I can make some for myself."

Jeanne Le Bon looked shocked.

"Oh, no, miss! You can't do that! Mrs. Tregeale'd have a fit if she found out! None of the family ever go down into the kitchen, except Mrs. de Corbiere when she comes to look over the menus with my mother."

Evelyn was amused at this totally different way of life. "Does it really matter that much? I mean, would it really be so terrible if I made my own cup of tea?"

Jeanne Le Bon looked back at her, awkwardly.

"To Mrs. Tregeale and Mrs. de Corbiere it would, yes. And my mother'd have my guts for garters! They wouldn't like it, even, if they knew I was up here talking to you." Evelyn looked astonished. "I'm not exactly one of the house servants . . . I help my mother in the kitchen, and go with her to the market or to St. Helier for one thing or another . . . and I type letters for Mrs. de Corbiere if she wants me to. She taught me on an old machine Mrs. Tregeale bought, a couple of years ago. I enjoy doing that. But my mother says we all have our place, and we should never step out of it." She jumped, suddenly, as the sound of a car drawing to a halt down in the courtyard broke the stillness. "Oh! That'll be Mrs. de Corbiere back." She moved away toward the open door. "I'd best go down and let her know you're here."

"Jeanne!"

"I must go, miss . . . but I'll fetch up a tray for you. Then I'll give you a hand to unpack your things." She was gone before Evelyn could say another word.

She went to the window and looked down into the courtyard, but it was empty now. Then she went over to the dressing table. A set of hair brushes and combs had been laid out in a neat line on the polished top, and she picked up one of them, then sat down on the stool and looked at her reflection in the mirror.

Her face was still pale, though the seasickness had left her now, and the bright lipstick she always wore served only to heighten her unusual pallor. Her hair was still tousled and windswept from the boat. Unpinning it, she let it fall around her shoulders in a bright, glossy cascade, then began to brush it with hard, vigorous strokes. As she did so, another face appeared behind her in the mirror, and she sat there, rooted to the stool, the brush in her hand suspended in midair.

"You know who I am?" said the woman in the open doorway.

Slowly, all her anxiety and nervousness returning, Evelyn got up from the stool and put down the brush.

She was tall and elegant, striking but not beautiful. Her thick, black hair was swept upward into a chignon, and her cold, light eyes bored into Evelyn's face.

"You're my aunt Julia?" Uncertainly, she got up and held out her hand; the hand that took it was cold and dry. Julia de Corbiere's thin lips turned up almost imperceptibly at each corner of her mouth. Not quite a smile. "So. *You* are my brother Gilbert's daughter?" She stared at Evelyn openly, bold almost to the point of rudeness. "Well. I must say you don't look much like him. I suppose you take after your mother." There was a sarcastic note to her voice and Evelyn took an immediate dislike to her.

"Most people who knew her say I have her coloring."

"Obviously. There have never been any redheads in the Tregeale family." She glanced at the suitcase on the bed. "Did Jeanne tell you about the trunks that arrived for you a few days ago? Mother had them put in the old tower."

"Yes, she did, thank you. I hope they're not taking up too much room. Most of the things are my working materials . . . paints, spare canvases, brushes . . . I did mean to write and let you know that I was having them sent on, but I left in such a rush that there just wasn't time."

"We already found that out for ourselves when I came to London to see you."

Evelyn stared at her, unable to believe her own ears.

"*You* came to London? To see me? When? Why?"

"I would have thought that was obvious, after the letter you wrote Blanche. Naturally she showed it to Mother the moment she received it, and of course Mother showed me. She was extremely concerned about you . . . when you wrote it you must have been in a highly emotional state. You gave no details about what had happened, except to beg Blanche to ask Mother if you could come to stay with us on Jersey . . . and since in all the years you and Blanche have been writing to each other you'd never even suggested such a thing before, we realized that whatever had happened must have been something very serious . . . I can see by your face now that it was." Evelyn looked away. "Mother considered it unthinkable that you should make the journey here all alone . . . she sent you a telegram telling you that I would be traveling to London to bring you back . . . but when I arrived your flat was empty and nobody seemed to know where you were. Clearly, you'd left before the telegram arrived and I was too late."

Evelyn's heart began to beat faster. Had Julia unwittingly discovered the truth she was so desperate to keep hidden? Dumbly, she stared back at her, trying to read what lay behind those cold, hostile eyes, but failing.

"When I made inquiries, it appeared you'd left the flat the week before we arrived, and we got back to Jersey expecting to find you already here . . . but there was only your brief note to Blanche, saying you were arriving from the mainland today."

"After I left the flat I stayed for a few days with a girlfriend. Just to sort myself out before I left London for good."

"I see. You might have let us know and saved me the journey that I could have well done without making."

"I'm sorry. I just didn't think. And I never dreamed that you'd come all the way to London just to look for me. There was no need for you and Blanche to go to so much trouble on my account."

"Blanche didn't come to London with me. I took Jeanne, as a maid."

"Oh! I see. I misunderstood you . . ."

"You seem very sure that you'll never want to go back again." The sarcasm had come back into her voice. "I find that hard to believe. In fact, I don't believe it. From what I saw of London, it's another world, compared to life on Jersey. You'll soon find that out for yourself. And I doubt you'll be able to adjust to the way we live here."

The last thing Evelyn wanted was to be reminded of London, the life she'd left behind her. There was too much to remember that hurt too much.

"I don't ever want to go back to London."

For a moment they looked at each other. Then, before Julia could answer, Jeanne Le Bon came back into the room, carrying a tray. She knocked on the open door.

"Jeanne will fetch you up anything you might want," Julia

said, preparing to leave. "And she'll unpack and hang up your clothes. Give her anything that needs pressing, and she'll see to it."

"But I can do all that for myself . . . I don't expect anyone to wait on me."

Her aunt looked at her as if she'd taken leave of her senses. "You really do have a lot to learn, Evelyn. Ladies don't unpack suitcases . . . or press their own clothes." She spoke across Jeanne Le Bon as if there had been only the two of them in the room. "Tea is at five sharp in the downstairs living room. Please don't be late. As you'll soon find out, Mother is a stickler for people being punctual."

"Will I see Blanche then?"

Julia de Corbiere's lips curled upward, almost a sneer. "I doubt if you'll see her before tomorrow. If then."

Evelyn stared at the empty space where she had been.

"Was it something I said?"

"Oh, no, miss . . . that's just Mrs. de Corbiere's way . . . though it's hardly my place to say so." She began to pour Evelyn's tea from the ornate silver pot. "Do you take sugar, miss?"

Evelyn sat down on the edge of the bed and eased off her high heels. "Look, Jeanne . . . I don't want to sound patronizing . . . but you really don't have to keep calling me 'Miss.' Whatever the house rules are here . . . I'd much rather you just call me Evelyn. To tell you the truth, all that formality just makes me feel uncomfortable."

Jeanne put down the teapot and stared at her.

"Oh, miss . . . I couldn't do that . . . really I couldn't! Whatever would Mrs. Tregeale and Mrs. de Corbiere say? And my mother . . . why, she'd give me a right talking to, I can tell you! Say I was well and truly stepping out of my place."

Evelyn sighed.

"OK. The last thing I want to do is to get you into trouble . . . but let's compromise, shall we? When we're alone you call me Evelyn." She smiled when Jeanne hesitated. "Please."

"All right, miss . . . Evelyn."

She took the cup of tea gratefully and sipped it.

"You didn't mention before that you'd accompanied my aunt all the way to London."

"Oh, well, I didn't like to. It wasn't my place to say." She laughed. "Mrs. de Corbiere was in a right old fury when we got there and found you'd already gone. Not that I ought to say so, I suppose. But it was such a thrill for me, going to London . . . when Mrs. Tregeale first told me that Mrs. de Corbiere'd be taking me with her as her maid, I just couldn't believe it. I was so excited that I never slept for three nights." She smiled. "To tell you the truth, I didn't want to come back."

"All that glitters isn't gold, Jeanne."

"Oh, I know that. But it was so . . . different. So big, so bright, so busy. And so alive! It was like a dream, being there, right in the middle of it." She hung her head. "I felt so guilty when we got back because for the first time in my life I was discontented . . . because it was so quiet and dull here after living in the middle of all that noise and color . . . I daren't tell my mother . . . but I've never felt that way before."

"And you can't understand why I've left all that behind me and come here to Jersey?"

Jeanne Le Bon's pale face reddened.

"Oh, no! It's none of my business to wonder anything of the sort."

Evelyn got to her feet and wandered across the room. She stopped at the window and gazed absently out of it. "I felt that way about London, once. Until I found out that all the glitter is just a facade." She could feel Jeanne's eyes on her. "Anywhere can be beautiful when you're happy. Happy within yourself. But happiness is like a thin, brittle sheet of glass . . . it takes very little to shatter it into pieces that you can never put back together again." She turned back into the room. "You can still be lonely in the biggest crowd, believe me. I was."

"Will you stay here for good, then? Here, on Jersey?"

"I don't have any plans to go back."

There was a moment of silence.

"I know it's not my place to say . . . but after living in a place like London, you'll find it very different here . . . for one thing, it won't be easy just living under somebody else's roof when you've been independent . . . not that I meant to criticize Mrs. Tregeale . . . but that beautiful flat that you had . . ." She stopped speaking almost abruptly, as if she suddenly felt that she was saying too much.

"You and my aunt were inside it?"

"When we got there and no one answered, Mrs. de Corbiere

went and found the janitor . . . but he was only a relief, and didn't know if you'd left for good or were coming back again. He unlocked the door for us so that we could wait inside. After a while Mrs. de Corbiere went out to try to find the gallery where Miss Blanche said you worked, and I stayed behind in case you turned up." She smiled. "I couldn't help standing there in the middle of that big, light room, and imagining what it would be like to live there. When somebody rang the door-bell, I half jumped out of my skin!"

Evelyn's heart suddenly began to race.

"Who was it?"

"He didn't give a name and I was so startled I didn't think to ask. When I told him that I wasn't even sure you'd be coming back at all, he just thanked me and went away."

Evelyn held her breath.

"Can you tell me what he looked like?"

"Oh, just ordinary. I don't even think I'd recognize him again if I saw him."

Evelyn's heart stopped racing. No woman would ever describe Jack Neville as ordinary. But something else that Jeanne Le Bon had said was still worrying her.

"Did my aunt Julia find the Pellini gallery?"

"She was gone a long while. But when she came back to your flat she only said that she hadn't found you, and that we'd be going back to Jersey a few days later."

"I see."

"I could tell she hated London! And there was me, exactly the opposite! Imagine, me, never off the island in the whole of my life, riding about with Mrs. de Corbiere all over the city in taxis! And the driver opening the door for me to get in and out . . . I felt like a duchess, truly I did! And the hotel where we stayed, too . . . it was like wonderland." In her rush of enthusiasm she had momentarily forgotten the bridge between herself and Evelyn; she, the housekeeper's daughter, Evelyn, granddaughter of the mistress of the house. "Mrs. de Corbiere was never one for keeping late hours . . . so when she'd gone up to her suite for good, I put on my best clothes and went out by myself . . . I felt so daring! All those crowds! And the noise and bright lights! I didn't have the courage to walk far, just in case I got lost and Mrs. de Corbiere found out about it . . . but I was longing to . . ." her eyes held Evelyn's. "If only we could have stayed there for longer . . . tell me what it was like for you . . . what it was like really living there all the time."

Evelyn smiled, a little sadly.

"I was just another ordinary working girl leading just another ordinary life. Nothing special. Nothing different from the kind of life any other working girl might live in any big city. I just got glimpses of the way other people lived, now and then . . . as you did when you were at the hotel." Unwillingly, she thought of De Braose and Laura Neville. "Rolls Royces driving along Piccadilly and Mayfair. Chauffeurs opening doors for people outside Ciro's or the Embassy Club. Crowds spilling out of the theaters late at night, the men in evening suits and top hats, the women in fur wraps and expensive gowns. That's all part of London, yes. But only a little part. Underneath all the glitter that you read about in the society columns, there are other things. Things most people don't want to see or even think about. Umemployed men walking up and down the streets with placards on their backs, pleading for work; slums, like Bethnal Green, where families of five or more are all crowded together in one room; and young children with dirty faces and filthy clothes, sitting about on the pavement waiting for their mothers to come home from some soul-destroying job scrubbing other people's floors for a pittance, just to try and make ends meet. Whatever you feel about living here, I can tell you that any one of those would give their eyes to change places with you."

"I never realized . . . that's awful . . . of course, we never saw anything like that."

"No. Most visitors never do. That's the trouble. People who do see it tend to be shocked at first, then shock dissolves into apathy." She went over to her suitcase and opened it. "When I was very young, and my mother didn't have much money . . . I used to wonder what our life would have been like, if my father hadn't died when he did . . . so many 'if onlys.' Thinking on what might have been . . . it doesn't do any good, really. I always swore that I'd never set foot on this island after the way the Tregeales treated my mother . . . and yet here I am, cap in hand." In her sudden flood of unexpected emotion she'd almost forgotten Jeanne's presence, forgotten that she was only the housekeeper's daughter and that she, the granddaughter of the mistress of the house, should never say any of these things. It wasn't right. It wasn't proper. But the

misery from the aftermath of her doomed love for Jack Neville,
everything that had cost her, crowded in upon her, pushing out
all else. She longed to talk, to exorcise the guilt and pain. "I
suppose everyone in the house knows why I've never been here
before? About my father?"

"Well . . . it's common knowledge, mostly, about why
Mrs. Tregeale's son never came back. He married outside the
island and they never forgave him for it. From what little my
mother's told me, Miss Blanche had a letter from you a while
back, asking if you could come to Jersey to get over some
trouble or other. As Mrs. Tregeale was agreeable, I should
think that she's decided the time's right to forgive and forget.
For the sake of the family."

"I wish I could believe that."

"She's only human, you know. And it must have hurt her
when your father died. They both idolized him."

"So did my mother."

"I can understand why you feel bitter. I know I would, too,
if I was in your place. But you see . . . there's a special kind
of bond within island families, a bond that's difficult, maybe
impossible, for outsiders to really understand. Your father
broke it, you see . . . he went against everything they
believed in and they couldn't come to terms with that. I'm not
trying to make excuses for them. I don't even think they were
right to do what they did and pretend his marriage didn't happen at all. That was wrong. And it seemed cruel and stubborn.
But they never stopped loving him, I know that . . . my
mother said that for a whole year after he died, Mrs. Tregeale
wouldn't wear any color but black."

"When he was killed in the car crash she never wrote a
single line of sympathy to my mother. She never answered any
of her letters. She sent a wreath, but she never came to his
funeral . . . because she knew that my mother would be
there. She must have known what hell my mother was going
through, because she'd lost her own husband not long before
that." Evelyn stared down into the suitcase, battling with her
agitation. "That's why I was so reluctant to come here, after
everything that had happened. And I wouldn't have come, not
if there'd been any other way out . . . but there wasn't." For
an instant Robert De Braose's, then Jack Neville's face, flashed
across her mind. "It's not something I can talk about. Not

yet." She looked up into Jeanne's face. "But when I can, I think I'll be able to trust you to understand."

The other girl smiled. Yes, I like you, Evelyn thought.

"Thank you for saying that. Let me help you with these things."

She had always imagined how their first confrontation would be, and now she was about to find out. As she walked slowly and steadily down the wide staircase into that musty-smelling hall, she could hear their voices in the distance, what they were saying not quite audible through the thick oak of the drawing-room door. For a moment she hesitated outside, her hand poised above the door handle. Then, taking a deep breath, she straightened her clothes, smoothed back her hair, and then went in.

It was not a bright room. And for a moment she found herself blinking in the gloomy light. Then her eyes traveled to the very end of the room, where she could see her aunt standing beside a huge, old winged chair. And there, in the chair, her cold, imperious blue eyes looking at Evelyn in a long, unblinking stare, sat the woman who had turned against her only son, repudiated her mother, and never recognized her as a true Tregeale.

"Come closer, so that I can see you," said her grandmother.

Slowly, Evelyn walked toward the figure in the winged chair, in a silence so stark that she could hear the sound of her own breathing.

Then they were face to face.

"Red hair and green eyes," said the woman in the chair in a harsh, bitter voice. "You've inherited her color hair and eyes. My son's hair was black and his eyes were blue."

"Her? You mean my mother? Since I'm her daughter it's hardly surprising that I look like her," Evelyn answered steadily, determined not to be cowed by her grandmother's hostility. "What a pity you never knew her. You would have liked her." From behind the huge chair, she saw her aunt flinch.

"Well. You certainly have your father's defiance. He was the only one of my children who would ever dare to speak back to me."

"I wasn't speaking back to you. Just stating a fact." For a long moment they looked at each other. In the haughty, fine-boned features Evelyn could see traces of her grandmother's lost youth, a handsome face rather than a beautiful one, with piercing blue eyes and gray hair that had once been dark and luxuriant. There was no warmth in her face. The almond-shaped eyes were bright and alert, but not with any softer feelings for the granddaughter she had spurned until now.

"So. You wrote from London and asked if you could come to Jersey to live . . . for urgent personal reasons . . . they were your exact words, were they not? And here you are." She shifted herself in the chair. "Now, before we have tea, I expect you to explain what exactly those reasons were that brought you here."

"You never answered my letter."

"You received my decision through Blanche. As you've received every other piece of information about your father's family on this island for the past seven and a half years . . . since you never troubled to communicate with me before now—when you want something—you can scarcely expect me to abandon the principles of a lifetime and do likewise."

"I'm sorry, but that isn't fair. Or true. My mother wrote to you many times . . . but you never replied to a single letter. And when she died I wrote to tell you as well as Blanche." She looked her grandmother straight in the eyes. "If you ever sent me a word of sympathy, I never received it."

There was a long silence while each woman took stock of the other. Then Julia de Corbiere's voice sounded from behind the big wing chair.

"Mother . . . shall I pour tea?"

Frederica Tregeale gave her a perfunctory glance, as if she had almost forgotten her presence.

"Yes. Yes, Julia, pour the tea." She looked back at Evelyn. "Well . . . you'd best sit yourself down. Over there, where I can look at you." Evelyn sat down. "There's much I shall want to ask you . . . and that I shall expect you to answer. That can be done later, after dinner, in private . . . since you show a marked reluctance to speak of your London troubles here." There was a short pause while she turned to take her cup from her daughter. "Did you have a good journey?"

"I was seasick through most of it." Evelyn took her tea and sipped it. "When the boat reached St. Helier and I couldn't see Blanche, I was afraid something had gone wrong. Then your chauffeur told me." She put down the cup. "Isn't there anything the doctor could give her to help her?"

"Nothing at all helps her but to lie down in her room with a cold compress over her eyes and the curtains drawn."

"I noticed that the curtains of one of the upstairs rooms was drawn across as I got out of the car today. Is that Blanche's room?"

"Yes, that is Blanche's room. When she suffers from these headaches she can't bear to see the light."

"She never mentioned that she suffered from bad headaches in her letters."

"That doesn't surprise me," said Julia de Corbiere, sitting down beside her mother. "Blanche has always shown a remarkable facility for covering up things she doesn't wish to recognize." She and Evelyn stared at each other for a moment. Then Frederica Tregeale spoke again into the strained silence.

"Well. Blanche tells me that you've worked at an art gallery in London for the last several years . . . as an expert restorer. What do you intend to do with yourself here?"

"What I've always done . . . paint. I couldn't live without painting, it's part of me, just like seeing or breathing. To try to live without doing it would be like trying to live with one of my senses missing . . . it's far too important to me to ever give up. I just couldn't." She searched for understanding in the two cold, impassive faces, but found none. "When I was working at the gallery in London, I more or less worked to a regime that they set out for me, on canvases that they'd acquired for exhibition or for a special client . . . I rarely found any time at all to do what I really wanted for myself . . . now I can. I'd love to start work on a life-size posthumous portrait of my father . . . that's something I've longed to do for years . . ." They both went on staring at her. "I'd have to do it from photographs, of course . . . and that's much more difficult than doing it from life. I have a few pictures of him, none of them are very good quality . . . certainly not up to studio standard. That's where I thought you might be able to help me . . . I suppose you must have quite a collection, taken before he went away."

"We have some, yes. After dinner you can go into the library and Julia will get them out for you."

"I'd really appreciate that."

"But is it possible to paint somebody's portrait just from

looking at a photograph? A black and white photograph? I've never heard of it being done before."

"I've painted from photographs before, yes. I did a sketch, a long time ago, from the photograph that Blanche sent me of herself, and I always wanted to use the sketch as a basis for proper painting . . . and when I worked in the gallery in London, I did a watercolor of a well-known society hostess, just as a sort of experiment, and the gallery liked it so much that they exhibited it." Deliberately, she made no mention of the other paintings, of the launching party that Guy Pellini had held for her. Too dangerous. Her eyes moved on to Julia, wondering how much she'd managed to find out from the staff at the gallery. "I like to try new ways of presenting different ideas I've had of my work, and painting well-known people from photographs is a special challenge . . . I did a whole series of sketches of the duke and duchess of Windsor."

"*That* woman! I would have thought you could have found a more worthy subject for your talents than a scandalous, scheming, twice-divorced adulteress who almost brought the whole monarchy into disrepute! Hers is not a name I ever wish to hear mentioned in my house, Evelyn . . . and I'll thank you to remember it. The king's abdication was nothing less than an act of sheer moral cowardice . . . it shocked and saddened everyone on this island . . . as I've no doubt it shocked and saddened his subjects everywhere else. Not to mention his long-suffering family and the rest of the world."

Evelyn looked at her, appalled. "How can you say that? How can you call a man a moral coward for standing by a woman he loves and refusing to let people dictate to him what he should do? How many other men—let alone kings—would have had the guts to do what he did?" She could feel her cheeks beginning to burn. "Whether she was divorced or not— and she was the innocent party in both cases—what difference does that make? She loved the king and he loved her. Her first husband was a drunkard who used to beat her; her second husband was having an affair with another woman. Was she supposed to stay married to either of them, just because it suited the Church of England and the British government? Everyone has the right to be happy, whoever they are or whatever they are. And nobody else has the moral right to interfere. Or to pass judgment on something that isn't even their business."

"You seem to forget—like the vast majority of young people today who think nothing matters but their own pleasure—that marriage is a sacrament, entered into by two people for life . . . it isn't some game that either can duck out of when they grow tired of their responsibilities to each other. Whatever faults a man or woman may have, there is no excuse for them to forget their marriage vows, or their duties to each other. The king was the head of the Church of England, and it was to him that people looked for an example. How could he justify himself to his government or the nation at large for taking for his wife a woman who had two husbands still living? The very idea was unthinkable."

"I'm sorry, I can't agree with you. I don't believe that people should be expected to stay tied for the rest of their lives to someone they no longer love, and who no longer loves them." Bitterly, thoughts of Jack Neville and De Braose's daughter echoed through her mind. "To expect anyone to do that is just inhuman."

"I can see you have a lot to learn . . . like most of the younger generation. You think romantic love is everything because indulging in its fantasy gives you the excuse you need to pursue a life of selfishness. When the king turned his back on his country, his family, and his duty, he could no doubt do do so with a clear conscience because he told himself it was all 'for love.' Just as your father did."

Evelyn jumped to her feet, her throat tight with rage.

"That's a lie! He loved my mother and he married her, despite everything you tried to do to stop him! You tried to make him choose between his family and her, and because he chose her you never forgave him. Or her. You ostracized him. You wanted to punish him for loving someone you didn't approve of!"

"Julia . . . will you please leave us?" There was a short silence while Julia de Corbiere got up, gave Evelyn one single, dark look, then went out of the room. Behind her, the door clicked softly. "Well, you certainly believe in speaking your mind. That at least indicates to me that if I ask you a straight question you're likely to give me a straight answer. So we'll start right now, shall we? I intended to speak to you after dinner about why you really came here . . . but I think we might as well have it out right now." She watched Evelyn's reaction carefully. "Since you clearly approve of your father's ill-advised marriage against the wishes of his family, and express yourself so emotionally about the duke and duchess of Windsor's conduct, I begin to wonder whether the true reason you left London in such a hurry was you found yourself in a similar situation. Urgent personal reasons, your letter said. I shall be most interested to hear what they were.''

For a moment, Evelyn hesitated. "As I said, they were personal. And if you don't mind I perfer them to stay that way.''

"You were involved with a man?"

Without looking toward her grandmother, Evelyn went across to the other side of the room, near the window. She sighed. She stared out across the courtyard and to the lawn beyond it.

"Yes, I was involved with a man."

"You were in love with him?"

"I wouldn't have been involved with him if I hadn't been."

"But he didn't love you?"

"Yes, he did love me."

"Then why didn't he want to marry you?"

Slowly, Evelyn turned back to face her.

"He couldn't. He was married already."

"I should have guessed. So. You were having a love affair with another woman's husband?"

"It has been known to happen," Evelyn answered dryly.

"You knew he was already married? Or did he lie to you?"

Evelyn ran a hand through her hair.

"I didn't know for sure, not at first. Although to be honest, I suppose I half guessed it. I just didn't want to believe it, that's all. It hurt too much. But nobody like him would still have been a bachelor . . . unless he was homosexual . . . which he wasn't! He was too successful and too good-looking not to have been snapped up by some woman or other. When I found out the truth for certain it was too late. I loved him too much to have the strength to break it off. And it just went on from there.''

"Until his wife found out, you mean? And, no doubt, confronted him with his adultery. Having had his way with you, he had no further use for you . . . am I right? He abandoned you. And you packed your bags and came here to me.''

"It wasn't like that!" Evelyn's voice rang out, passionately.

How could she even begin to explain to a woman like Frederica Tregeale what had been between her and Jack Neville? There seemed no point in even trying to. "His father-in-law was a very powerful man in the art world. That was how we first met. When his wife found out she went running to him, and he told Jack that if he ever saw me again, he'd ruin him. He meant what he said."

"And your lover chose a life of comfort rather than a less certain mode of living with you?"

Evelyn walked slowly back to her chair and leaned against the back of it.

"Yes." The single word held unspeakable pain.

"So much for love. But that leaves one question still unanswered, Evelyn. Why you decided to come here to Jersey. You could have gone on living in London. That was where your work was. And all the people you knew. Even if you felt you couldn't stay there after what had happened, in case you came face to face with your ex-lover . . . there are plenty of other places in England that you could have chosen . . . had you wished. Which leads me to believe that although you've told me part of your story, you have yet to tell me the whole of it."

Evelyn looked up into her face, into the cold, bright blue eyes, and knew that she could never lie to her.

"His wife's father came to see me, too. He told me that if I didn't go away he'd see to it that I was sorry. And that I'd never get work in any sphere of the art world again. I had no choice. And nowhere to come except here."

Frederica Tregeale nodded her head, slowly.

"That leaves me with one last question. Had none of this happened, would you ever have written that letter and asked to come here?"

For a moment Evelyn hesitated.

"I don't know. I don't suppose I would have."

"That at least is an honest answer. But you'll forgive me if I object to being used as a convenience . . . a port in a storm, as the saying goes . . . even by my own granddaughter. Under the circumstances, you can hardly expect me to welcome you with open arms."

"You don't want me here?"

"I didn't say that. But I want to make very clear to you that while you're welcome here as a member of this family, I ask you to remember that this is my house and that I shall expect you to do me the courtesy of conducting yourself by my rules." She leaned back in the big chair. "Yes, I did disapprove of your father's marriage. Time hasn't changed that. He allowed himself to be seduced by another way of life, a way of life that I could never accept as suitable for my son. And in marrying your mother he turned his back on his obligations to his family, and on the young woman we considered to be eminently more fitted to be the wife of the only son and heir of one of the oldest and most important families on this island. But of course I can never make you understand that. It would no doubt be a waste of time trying to . . . no fault of yours. You weren't brought up, as your father was, by that particular code of conduct and morals. That he broke it knowingly and willingly was part of the reason why I could never accept his marriage. Yet as angry as I was, and as deeply as he hurt me, I forgave him. That was my duty as his mother."

"Did it mean nothing to you that he and my mother were in love with each other?"

"That is where you and I must beg to differ, Evelyn. I was brought up to believe that one obeyed one's parents as well as respected them, that duty and obligation are the ruling forces of our lives. You think that love for someone—however immoral or unsuitable that someone might be—matters more than anything else . . . am I right? Would I be correct in thinking that if your married lover had been prepared to leave his wife for you, you'd have welcomed him with open arms? Yes, I thought so. That is a way of thought that I could never accept."

"You think it's more moral to be miserable living your life with somebody you don't love?"

"I didn't say that. But can you tell me in all honesty that you would have felt no guilt had this man left his wife and lived with you?"

"Yes, I can say it. I never felt one moment of guilt when I was with him. I loved him and he loved me. I still love him." She could feel the hot tears, stinging painfully at the backs of her eyes. There was a lump in her throat. "I shall love him as long as I live, in spite of everything. His marriage was a dead marriage. There was nothing there, least of all love. He never loved her." The lump in her throat grew bigger, making it harder for her to swallow, but she forced out the words. "Her father bought him just like he bought everything else for his rich, spoiled little girl. But whatever he gave him he could never make him love her."

Her grandmother looked at her almost pityingly.

"In my view you're well rid of him." Getting up from the big winged chair, she handed Evelyn a beautiful, white, lace-edged starched handkerchief. "Time is a great healer. Sometimes the only healer we can ever have."

Evelyn looked up at her through the haze of tears.

"You despise me, don't you? You don't really want me here at all?"

"That isn't true. You're a Tregeale. My son's flesh and blood. Where else should you be but where you belong?"

10

She lay there in the pitch darkness, tossing and turning. However hard she tried, sleep continued to elude her. Strange, after her emotion-charged day, the sea trip, the scene with her grandmother, the strained dinner downstairs, at which no one had spoken more than a dozen words. She turned over once more and willed herself into sleep. Then, just as her eyelids were growing heavy at last, the faint sounds of a woman weeping pulled her back again into wakefulness. She sat up.

There was no mistake. Far away along the corridor the weeping grew louder. Getting up she put on her satin dressing gown and went quietly from her room.

The passage outside was in total darkness. Slowly, feeling her way along the wall, she made her way toward the room from which the crying came.

It was the fourth door along from her own; from outside, the fourth set of windows from the main front door . . . the windows she had glanced up to from the courtyard and noticed that their curtains had been drawn all the way across. Blanche Tregeale's room.

For a moment she hesitated, still listening. Then she tapped lightly on the door.

"*Blanche?* Blanche, is that you?" There was no answer. "Blanche . . . it's me, Evelyn. Can you hear me?" She tapped on the door for a second time, more loudly. "Blanche, are you there?"

The crying had grown louder, become almost a pitiful wail. But there was still no response from inside the room. Taking hold of the handle, Evelyn turned it . . . but the door was locked.

For a few moments she stood there, wondering what to do. The whole house was silent. Then, reluctantly, she made her way back to her own bedroom. She turned on the bedside light and sat down on the bed. Should she try to find Jeanne? Should she go and wake up her aunt?

She went on sitting there for several minutes more. The crying had ceased. Everything was quiet again. She climbed back into bed and lay there with her eyes closed. Then, so suddenly that the noise made her jump out of her skin, a piercing scream rang out, followed by wild, hysterical sobbing. As she threw back the covers and got quickly out of bed for the second time, she heard a door slam somewhere, then the sound of footsteps rushing past her door.

She ran out into the dark corridor outside and along the landing, to find the door of Blanche Tregeale's bedroom wide open, and as she looked inside she covered her mouth with her hand to stifle a gasp of shock and surprise.

The room was a total shambles. Tubes of lipstick and boxes of face powder lay scattered across the floor. A broken glass and half its contents littered part of the carpet. An empty bottle lay on its side near the dressing table, where the large mirror had been covered over with a sheet. And there, slumped across the unmade bed, lay Blanche Tregeale, her face hidden by a tangle of dark, matted hair. As she lay there whimpering and sobbing, Julia Tregeale leaned over her, shaking her violently.

"Be quiet! *For God's sake be quiet!* Do you want to wake up the whole damned house?" Suddenly, she became aware that they were not alone, and as she swung round to look behind her came face to face with Evelyn. For a few seconds they stared at each other. Then Julia Tregeale shoved her sister aside and got to her feet.

"That's right. You're not seeing things. She's drunk. Dead drunk. She's been drinking ever since yesterday, long before you came. That's why she wasn't there to meet you off the boat. Why she didn't come down for tea or dinner last night.

She couldn't. She was so intoxicated that she couldn't even see straight!''

"But I don't understand!"

"It's very simple. Blanche is an alcoholic."

Shock and surprise gave way to anger.

"Why the hell didn't someone tell me the truth? Why did you lie and say she was suffering from headaches? All of you! Did you think I was so stupid that I'd go on living in this house and never find out what was really wrong with her?"

Julia Tregeale took Evelyn by the wrist and pushed her backward away from the door. "Go back to your own room and go to bed! Don't come here meddling in things that don't concern you!"

"Take your hands off of me! You and my grandmother might hate my guts and me yours, but Blanche is someone special. She was the only one who stood by my father when you all turned against him! She was the only one who wrote and sent my mother flowers when he was killed in the accident, the only one out of the whole lot of you who really cared what she was going through! And she's the only Tregeale who ever cared anything about me. That's why I'm here."

"You're here because it suits you! Because your married lover left you high and dry and went crawling back to his wife . . . and you had nowhere else to run to! Mother told me the whole story . . . did you think she wouldn't?"

"If Blanche hadn't been here I wouldn't be either. Whatever you think." She pushed Julia Tregeale aside and forced herself past her into the room. Gently, she tried to raise Blanche's head.

"It's no use! Can't you see you're wasting your time? She won't be sober for hours!"

"If you know she can't stay away from drink, why the hell don't you see that it's kept locked up where she can't get at it?" Furiously, Evelyn stooped and picked up the empty bottle from the floor. "This is whisky! Ninety proof! And you stood by while she drank down the lot! What are you trying to do to her? Kill her?"

"Don't you dare speak to me like that." Her aunt's voice had gone deadly soft. "You come here, straight out of the blue . . . you haven't even been here for a day, and you think you have the right to start preaching to me about what's best for my sister. *My* sister." She snatched the bottle out of Evelyn's hand. "You'd better learn something before you've lived in this house for much longer. And remember it. Everyone under this roof lives by Mother's rules. That includes you. Mother chooses not to lock the spirits away from Blanche . . . shall I tell you why? Because she must learn on her own to be strong enough to resist them. By taking the easy way out and hiding every bottle in the house, we're not helping her at all. Her struggle isn't against the drinking. It's against her own feeble self-will."

Evelyn could hardly believe her ears.

"And you think that's the kind thing to do? That pushing blatant temptation right in her face is going to cure her? My God, I think you're all mad!" She sat down on the bed and tried to roll Blanche over onto her side. Groaning, whimpering, the strained, dark-circled eyes gazed up at her, without recognition, the face itself not recognizable as that of the bright-eyed, beautiful girl in the photograph Evelyn had brought with her.

"You little fool!" whispered Julia Tregeale. "She doesn't even know who you are!"

Evelyn jumped up and rushed from the room.

"Where are you going?"

"Where do you think? To ring for a doctor! She needs help. Proper help." She went to the telephone on the other side of the landing and picked up the receiver. "And I intend to see that she gets it!"

"Put that phone down." Julia Tregeale rushed after her and banged her hand down on the receiver. "I forbid you to use it."

They stared at each other in open hostility. Then, slowly, Evelyn withdrew her hand.

"Very well. If you won't let me use this one, I'll ring from the telephone downstairs. I saw one earlier, on the sideboard in the hall." She ran down the stairs.

At the bottom she felt for the light switch and turned it on. Then she went to the telephone and picked up the receiver. But as she began to dial for the operator, the line suddenly clicked and went dead.

At that moment she glanced up and saw Julia Tregeale standing at the top of the staircase, a loose lead in one hand. She held it up.

"You won't get through, Evelyn. Not tonight. As you see, I've pulled the telephone wire out of the wall. By the time someone has gone into St. Helier in the morning to report it out of order, Blanche will be sober again. And you'll have no more need to trouble yourself about her."

"*You!*"

"I suggest you go back to bed. And leave Blanche alone. The only way for a drunk to get better is to sleep it off. Goodnight."

For a long while after she had gone, Evelyn sat there on the bottom of the stairs with her head in her hands, wondering what to do. There seemed little point in going back to see Blanche until the morning when the effects of her drinking bout had worn off. Even less point in waking up anyone else. With cold anger, she turned out the light and went back upstairs.

It was a long time before she slept.

She was awake before anyone else in the house, even the servants. Getting up, she went along the corridor to the bathroom to wash, then back to her bedroom to dress. The sky outside her window was still not quite light when she drew her curtains and sat down in front of the dressing table mirror to brush out her hair.

It was unfashionably long, down to her waist, and for working at Pellini's she had always worn it up, twisted into a chignon or French pleat, or coiled into some other self-created style. Only for Jack Neville had she worn it loose, tumbling down her bare shoulders and her back, and often he'd brushed it for her, while she'd sat, naked and cross-legged on the bed, and they'd laughed together. For a brief, painful moment his face appeared in the mirror behind hers. Then she closed her eyes, willing him away, and when she opened them again saw only the sad-eyed reflection of herself.

She couldn't remember how long she sat there, with the bright morning sun stealing through the windows and lighting up her hair like a cloak of fire. But all at once she heard a tap on her door and when she answered it opened, and in came Jeanne Le Bon holding a tray of toast and tea.

Their eyes met and held in the mirror.

"Why didn't you tell me the truth about my aunt?"

"Evelyn?"

"Please. I thought we were friends." Evelyn turned round to face her. "Don't lie to me. Don't pretend that you don't know what's going on. Because I know that you must." She got up, pushing her mane of hair back from her face. "I realize you kept it from me to spare me the unpleasantness and shock of finding out after all this time . . . but there's no need to hide it anymore. I found out the truth last night. That my aunt Blanche is a drunkard."

Slowly, white-faced, Jeanne put down the tray.

"Evelyn, I'm sorry . . . I would have said something if I could. But it wasn't my place to tell you what was really the matter with her. If I had Mrs. Tregeale would never have forgiven me."

"Who else knows?"

"Besides your family? My mother, of course. And me."

"None of the other staff?"

"I doubt it. And if any of them ever guessed they'd never breathe a word outside. They know they daren't. This is a very small island and news—good or bad—travels fast. If Mrs. Tregeale sent them packing for gossiping . . . without a reference . . . they'd never find another job on Jersey for love or money. None of them would ever dare risk that."

"How long has she been drinking?"

"I don't know exactly. About five years or so, I guess. She didn't drink much at first. I don't think anyone really began to notice it . . . until it started to get a grip on her. She doesn't do it all the time, don't think that. She might go for weeks, even months at a time without going over the edge . . . but then something happens to upset her and she'll drink anything she can lay her hands on."

Evelyn flinched, thinking of the beautiful, bright-eyed, smiling face of the treasured photograph, the face that no longer existed.

"What made her start?"

"I can't answer that. I don't think anyone could . . . maybe not even her. It just happened."

"Nothing ever just happens. There has to be a reason."

"If there is then you'll have to ask her what it is."

The door to Blanche's bedroom was unlocked now. From inside, Evelyn could hear the sound of someone moving around the room, and she hesitated for a moment before knocking. Then she tapped lightly on the door and went inside.

To her astonishment, though the sun was bright outside the windows, no curtains had been drawn. The sheet that had been draped over the dressing-table mirror last night was still there, and all the lights were burning. But the debris of lipstick tubes and broken glass had been cleared away from the carpet, the bed had been neatly made. And there, standing in the middle of the floor looking at her, was Blanche Tregeale.

She bore no resemblance whatever to the sobbing, whimpering, intoxicated woman of last night, with dull, lifeless eyes and tangled hair. The face that she saw now was almost the face of her photograph; slightly older but still strikingly beautiful; calm, assured, perfectly made up. Her wide blue eyes were bright. Her black hair gleamed in the artificial light.

For a single moment she stared at Evelyn. Then her mouth curved into an excited smile that lit up her whole face.

"It's you! It's really you! Evelyn . . ." She came toward her, holding out her hands. "But you're so beautiful . . . I knew you would be. Much more than your pictures."

"Blanche . . ."

"You know who you look like? Dolores Costello . . . You're just like her, really you are. You've heard of Dolores Costello, the American movie actress? Wait . . ." She rushed over to a case on the floor and began to rummage through it, feverishly. "I've got a picture here of her . . . where is it? Yes, here it is." Excitedly, she held it up. "See? See how much you look like her? She was married to John Barrymore, you know . . . you've heard of the famous Barrymores? But she wasn't happy with him . . . she had to run away because he was so jealous of her . . . did you know that? I've read all about it. Here, I've still got all the magazines . . ." She went on rummaging through the case. "I keep them all in here, you see . . . Mother doesn't approve of me reading movie magazines . . . if she knew I still had them she'd make me tear them up and throw them away. But I like to read about other people's lives . . . famous people, that you read and hear about in the newspapers and on the radio . . . but Mother doesn't approve of that. She doesn't approve of the kind of lives they lead."

"Blanche . . ." Awkwardly, Evelyn stared down at the photograph in her hands. "It's so good to meet you at last. After so long. After all the letters you wrote me, I felt I knew you already."

"Yes, yes, I felt that way about you, too. And your mother. If only I'd met her. If only Mother had relented and let Gilbert bring her home. I wanted to meet her so much . . ." She looked away from Evelyn and back into the case, crammed with yellowed magazines and newspaper cuttings, and bundles of old photographs tied together with faded ribbon.

"Gilbert sent us all pictures when he got married . . . where are they now? Mother never kept the ones that he sent to her and Daddy, and Julia tore hers up. I saw her. But I still have all mine." She pushed aside the bundles. She picked up a stack of magazines and put them on the floor beside her while she continued rummaging through the rest of the things. "I can never find anything when I want it . . . there's so much here . . . but I know his pictures are here somewhere . . . this is where I keep all my special things . . ."

"Blanche, it doesn't matter . . . you can show me later if you like. And I brought all my own photos with me so that I could show you . . ."

Blanche stopped what she was doing.

"You brought photos? Of Gilbert and your mother? Oh, I'd love to see them! You must show me. All of them. I have so few, you see." Suddenly, she put her hand to her head. "But it's Sunday today! Oh, God, I'd forgotten . . . it's Sunday. And I'm not ready."

"What is it? What's wrong? What's so special about Sunday?"

"Church. We have to get ready for church. It's Mother and Julia, you see. They always go. Mother says it's a duty for all of us. She makes me feel as if I have to. Even the servants have the morning off to go to church." Frantically, she began to bundle everything back into the case. "We must hurry." Nervously, she glanced up at Evelyn. "Quickly . . . you'd best go back to your room and change . . . Mother won't approve of you wearing that. Not for church. I like it, though. It's so smart, and elegant. Did you buy it in London? I expect you did. You won't find clothes like that over here, even at La Riche in St. Helier."

"But, Blanche—"

"I must hurry . . . Mother expects us to go down to breakfast on Sundays already dressed for church. We always leave the house directly afterward, you see."

"But I've too much to do . . . I still have half of my luggage left to unpack."

Blanche locked the case and pushed it back beneath the bed.

"You don't know Mother very well, do you? Well, you will when you've been here a bit longer. But let me warn you now that one thing she won't let anyone get away with is missing church on Sundays. It's a ritual with her. It's always been. Even when Daddy was dying and she couldn't leave him, she'd sit in his room and read to him from her Bible . . . and most of the time he was too ill even to hear what she said."

"Has she always been this way?"

"She says it's a duty. For all of us. She was just brought up that way. Church every Sunday. I hate it. All those people, sitting there in the pews, staring at me as we walk by to our pew. Watching. Whispering behind their hands. At least Mother's sincere. She goes because she thinks it's right, because it's the Christian thing to do. Half of them go for other reasons. To watch one another. To gossip. They pretend to be friends, then they just go back home and talk about everyone else. Hypocrites. That's what it's like, living on an island as small as this one. You can't get away from them. You can never get away. They're always there, watching, trying to find out what you're doing or where you're going. They haven't got anything better to do."

There was a pause. There was no mistaking the sad note in her voice.

"Are you happy here?"

"It's my home," Blanche answered, without looking at her.

"That wasn't what I asked."

"I don't know any other way of life. I don't suppose that I ever will, not now."

"Have you . . . have you ever been married? You never told me in your letters and I never really liked to ask . . . I didn't want to pry."

"No," Blanche answered, almost harshly. "No, I've never been married." She half turned away and looked out of the window, as if she couldn't meet Evelyn's eyes. "Julia was, a long time ago . . . but he died in France. He used to travel there a lot, on business. And then he got taken ill somewhere near Dijon one summer, and he never came back. I don't think Julia would ever get married again."

"She didn't have any children?"

"No, no children. Can you imagine Julia with a child? She doesn't like children. She never has." She turned and looked back at Evelyn. "Don't ever ask Julia about him, will you? It . . . it isn't something she likes to talk about."

"No, of course I wouldn't. I wouldn't dream of it. And I wasn't prying, don't think that. I was just curious, that's all." A pause. "Not so much about Julia, but about you. You're so beautiful . . . and yet you've never been married . . ."

Blanche looked away to hide the expression in her eyes.

"Being married isn't everything . . . that's just a myth. Living happily ever after . . . that only happens in cheap novels and women's magazines." She glanced back at Evelyn again. "Besides, on an island this small, there aren't that many men available. None that'd ever interest me, at any rate." She smiled and took Evelyn by the hand. "It's getting late. We'd best go downstairs if we don't want to upset Mother. She'll forgive you almost anything except being late for church."

The only sound in the big, old-fashioned dining room was the deep, slow ticking of the longcase clock. As they opened the door and went inside, the two women at the refectory table looked up, coldly, and glanced from one to the other. In the background, by the big sideboard, two servants in white pinafores and starched caps were waiting to serve the food from a line of massive, silver-domed tureens.

"You're both late," Frederica Tregeale said, with a glance toward the clock. "And on a Sunday morning . . . when coming down to breakfast on time is especially important because we have to leave promptly in time for church." Her eyes rested on Blanche. "Evelyn can be forgiven, since she only arrived yesterday and isn't familiar with the way we do things here. But for you, Blanche, there is no excuse."

"I'm sorry, Mother. I overslept." She took her place at the table opposite her sister, eyes downcast. But Evelyn stayed standing where she was.

"It wasn't Blanche's fault, it was mine. I kept her talking upstairs and we forgot the time. Besides which, I hardly ever eat breakfast, thank you. Just coffee. Or tea."

"That would explain your complete lack of thought for those of us who do eat breakfast. And are sitting down here waiting for you," said Julia, acidly.

"I'm sorry. I didn't realize. I just thought you'd start eating whether I was here or not."

"That isn't the way we do things here. Meals are served at

precise times of the day, when every member of the family is expected to be seated at the table ready to begin. No meal is ever started until we are all present." Her grandmother made a sign to the servants and they brought the domed tureens over to the table and set them down. "If you don't want anything to eat, Evelyn, might I suggest that when you've had your tea you go back upstairs and change into something a little more suitable . . . if you please. A tight-fitting open-necked dress is hardly appropriate apparel for worship in a church."

"It's real silk, Mother," Blanche said, with barely suppressed enthusiasm. "Evelyn bought it in London—"

"Be quiet, Blanche." She helped herself to bacon from the tureen. "I can see for myself, thank you very much. But what is considered suitable in London is not suitable for Sunday church in St. Helier."

Evelyn cleared her throat and kept her temper.

"I was going to ask you if you'd excuse me this morning. I still have most of my packing to get through, and my trunks and crates that you had moved into the tower. If you don't mind, I'd rather get on with that than go to church. In any case, I haven't been inside a church for years, anyway. To start going now would seem a bit hypocritical."

There was a shocked silence.

"I see."

"I'm sorry if that offends you . . . I didn't mean it to. And I'm not an atheist or anything like that. When I was a little girl, my mother always made me kneel at the foot of my bed every night and say my prayers. And I think I can remember going to a carol service once or twice, a long time ago when I was still at school, with some friends of mine from class. But that seemed different. Other than that I've only ever gone for weddings, or christenings, things like that . . . and of course when my mother died . . . times when I felt a real need to be there." The memory came back, swift and sudden, like a long-lost book falling open at a forgotten page. The dark, windy winter's afternoon, the rain falling around her. Standing there in the dank, cold, musty-smelling church, her eyelids swollen, biting back the tears, mouthing the words of a prayer. Walking away alone, the graveyard path strewn with dead twigs and leaves that blew about her feet. "I've always thought that going to church is something you should decide about for yourself, and not be made to." She felt Julia's cold, hostile eyes resting on her, and she looked back defiantly, remembering last night. "Anyone can go to church once a week and playact at being holier than thou. I think what we do every day when we don't go to church is more important. True Christians don't have to publicize what they are."

"How dare you speak to Mother like that!"

"Sit down, Julia. Evelyn has a point. I'm sure there are many people in the congregation each week who would fit that description more than accurately. But I don't happen to be one of them."

"I didn't mean to imply that you were."

"Of course not." One of the servants came across to where Evelyn had sat down and poured her tea. "Blanche tells me that some of the crates that arrived here for you contain paintings. Is that true?"

"Yes. I brought most of my work with me." She sipped the scalding hot tea gratefully. "I could have sold it, I suppose . . . although that would have taken quite some time . . . but I thought if I brought it with me I might sell it here. Are there any galleries in St. Helier?"

"Very few, I'm afraid. Though the biggest, Tostain's, is owned by friends of ours whom we've known for many years." She paused while she buttered a slice of toast. "I've invited them, and several other people, to dinner tomorrow night. The invitations are of a few weeks' standing . . . but it'll be good for you to meet them. Maybe afterward you can show them some of your work. I'm sure Peter Tostain would be pleased to sell it for you, for his usual commission. And of course he can always keep you well supplied with any materials you need. He has regular consignments from London and Paris."

Evelyn's eyes lit up.

"That would be wonderful! I'll look forward to meeting him." A sudden thought turned her stomach over. "Does he . . . has he a lot of dealings with any of the big London galleries?" The blot on the horizon. Beneath the table she clutched her hands together, praying he'd never dealt with Guy Pellini or Delacroix.

"I couldn't say, you'd have to ask him about that. But I do know that although he goes every month or so to Paris, it must be years now since he was in London."

Inwardly, Evelyn breathed a sigh of relief.

"It's a matter of distance. Here on Jersey we're a lot closer to the French coast than we are to the mainland of England." Frederica lay down her knife and fork and sat back in her chair. "While we're talking about your work, there's something else I meant to say, yesterday. As you intend to go on painting, you might as well turn the old tower into a studio. It's never been used for anything except a storeroom for things that we don't have room for in the house. Rather a waste, I always thought. But it has two floors that could be put to good use if they were thoroughly cleaned. And the top one, I'm told, has a good north light . . . a perfect working place for an artist."

"If you're sure . . . I'd love to turn it into a studio . . . I could clean it out myself . . ."

"Scrubbing floors is hardly a fitting task for a lady. But if you really want to do it . . ." Frederica shrugged. "At least nobody can call you idle." She got to her feet. "Well, I must speak to Martha about lunch. Blanche, go upstairs and fetch your coat. Jean-Louis will be bringing the car around for us any minute. I won't be late."

The instant she'd left the room Julia turned on her sister.

"Yes. Hurry back upstairs and get your coat, little sister. And while you're about it, wipe that filth off your face . . . unless you want to be a laughingstock. At your age you ought to know better than to plaster it with makeup that makes you look twice as old as you really are!"

"That isn't true!" Blanche's face crumpled, tears sprang into her eyes. "You spiteful bitch, you know it isn't true!"

"Go and look at yourself then!"

For a moment the two sisters faced each other across the big table. Then Blanche burst into tears and ran out of the room.

"What the hell are you trying to do to her?" Evelyn was on her feet. "Last night. Now. You can't wait to put her down! Does my grandmother know about this? If not, you can bet your life I shan't hesitate to tell her!"

"Tell her *what?* You think she'd listen to your petty little tales, a stranger who hasn't been inside the house for five minutes? Don't overestimate yourself, Evelyn. You might have the name Tregeale. But you're nothing more than an interloper to me. If it'd been my choice and not Mother's, you wouldn't be here at all!"

"Well, I am here. So you'd better get used to it!"

"And you'd better stop pandering to my sister's vanity!

That's right. Vanity. All her life, ever since she was a little girl, it's been her weakness. Now she's getting older it's become an obsession!''

"I don't have to listen to this!''

"You saw for yourself what it's done to her, you saw the disgusting state she was in last night. So blind drunk that this morning she couldn't even remember! Is that a sight you're likely to forget in a hurry? No, I didn't think so. But it'll answer a question for you. Why she drinks and why she can't stop drinking. Because it helps her to blot out the one fact she can't live with. That she's losing her looks and there's nothing she can do about it!''

"You're jealous of her, aren't you?''

"Jealous? Of someone as pathetic as my sister?'' There was a mocking ring to her voice now. "Why don't you get back to your painting and keep your nose out of things that don't concern you? Better still, go back to London and stay there!'' She slammed the door after her.

For a moment Evelyn stayed where she was, standing against the table, hands gripping the chair back, fighting down her rage. Then she went upstairs and found Blanche.

"Don't cry. Don't, Blanche.'' She put her arms around her shoulders. "Don't let her get to you this way. Can't you see . . . that's just what she wants you to do?''

"Please . . . go and tell Mother I can't come to church . . . not with my face like this.'' She looked up, swollen-eyed. Her mascara had run and made two ugly black smudges beneath her eyes, and the tears had made rivulets in the powder on her face. She caught sight of herself in the mirror and covered her face with her hands. "I'm so ugly. She was right. I can't let people see me like this . . . they'd laugh. They would, they'd just laugh!''

Evelyn shook her.

"Listen to me. Don't talk that way. There's nothing wrong with you. Nothing wrong with your face. Julia's so jealous of you she'd say anything to hurt you, don't you realize that?''

Blanche sank into the nearest chair and put a hand to her head. "One of my headaches is coming on . . . I can feel it . . . it always starts this way . . . a dull, throbbing pain, right across my eyebrows.''

"I'm going downstairs to get you a glass of water and some aspirin. Wait here.''

"It won't do any good. Nothing does." She got up from the chair and threw herself full length on the bed. "Evelyn . . . when they've gone . . . get me a drink. It's kept in the cabinet in the dining room, on the lefthand wall. Anything, I don't care what it is, but just get it."

"No, I won't. That'll just make it worse." She ran down the stairs as fast as she could and caught her grandmother in the hall. Martha Le Bon was helping her on with her coat and hat.

"Is Blanche ready? We're already five minutes late."

"She can't come, she's too upset." Evelyn looked through the half-open front door to the courtyard outside. The car was already there, with Jean-Louis standing ready and waiting. "I'm afraid you'll have to ask Julia what happened." She glanced toward Martha, hesitating, unwilling to say more in front of a servant. "Blanche has got one of her headaches coming on and she needs some aspirin. I told her I'd fetch it for her."

Frederica Tregeale sighed. "Martha will see to it." She started to draw on her gloves. "I can't stop and discuss it now, we'll miss the start of the service."

Evelyn watched her go outside, then step into the back of the car. A few moments later, the drawing-room door opened, and Julia came out of it. She glanced coldly at Evelyn; then, as she passed, she exchanged a single look with Martha La Bon.

"If you'll tell me where the aspirin is kept I'll take it up myself," Evelyn said. They looked at each other. It was the first time they had had anything to do with each other since she'd arrived at the house yesterday, and Evelyn wondered how a girl as pretty as Jeanne could be the daughter of this plain, sour-faced woman, with her dull, expressionless eyes and coarse peasantlike features. All they had in common was their pale eyes and hair.

"No need to trouble yourself, miss," Martha said, in her heavy, flat voice. "I'll go and see to Miss Blanche."

"I'd rather do it myself, if you don't mind."

A moment's hesitation. "Just as you like, miss. I'll go down to the kitchen and send Jeanne back up with it."

"Thank you."

On her way back upstairs with the water and aspirin, Evelyn wondered what it was exactly that she didn't like about Martha. But there was no name for it.

• • •

"Please . . . don't let in the light. Please draw all the curtains."

"Lie down then, and swallow these." Evelyn went over to the windows and pulled the heavy curtains across, blotting out the strong, bright sunlight. "You brought this headache on yourself, by letting Julia upset you." She came over to the bed and sat on the edge of it. "Why do you let her do it to you? Has she always been this way?"

Blanche pushed the aspirins into her mouth and gulped down a mouthful of water.

"She's always been a bully, if that's what you mean. Ever since we were small. Ever since I can remember. When we were children Gilbert used to protect me . . . and Daddy . . . but when they weren't there she always used to pick on me or get me into trouble. I suppose because she was the oldest, because I was Gilbert's favorite sister, because I was Daddy's favorite girl . . . then, when we grew up and Gilbert went away, then Daddy died, everything changed. There was no one there to take my side anymore. If Julia was hateful and I told Mother, Mother would say I was just telling tales. And Julia always won." She put the water glass back on the bedside table. "Even when we were grown up, she always treated me like a child. Her harebrained little sister. She'd talk across me at dinner and ignore me when I spoke. She used to hate it when we were young and people invited us to dances or garden parties, because the young men always used to flock around me while she was left standing there with no one. I knew she really resented that, but it wasn't my fault. Often, I'd pretend I'd twisted my ankle so that I'd sit the dances out and make her feel less like a wallflower. But that made her resent me even more."

"But surely your mother must know the truth."

"She's always been closer to Julia than she ever has to me . . . I don't really know why . . . perhaps because I was closer to Daddy when he was alive . . . in an odd way I think Mother resented that as much as Julia, because she thought he spoiled me . . . and of course she didn't approve of that." She lay back and closed her eyes, then reached out and lay her hand on Evelyn's arm. "I'm so glad you're here, Evelyn. I don't feel alone anymore. I feel like part of Daddy and my brother has come back." She opened her eyes for a moment. "You have Gilbert's eyes . . . not the color, but the expression. If only I could have seen him again."

"You would have liked my mother. She would have liked you."

"I longed to come to London when she wrote and said he'd been killed. I begged Mother to let me go . . . even if she and Julia refused to come. But she wouldn't relent. It wasn't that she didn't love him . . . Gilbert was always Mother's favorite. She idolized him. But she isn't a person who ever shows her true feelings . . . whatever happens. I know that makes her seem cold and callous to you . . . but it's the way she's made, the way she was brought up. Duty and principles first, love second. She longed to go to his funeral but she wouldn't allow herself to, because that would mean breaking her own principles and recognizing his marriage. I could never be like that . . . love always came before anything else with me."

Evelyn heard the taut note in her voice.

"Were you ever in love?"

A long silence before she answered. "A long time ago, when I was very young . . . but I don't want to talk about it." Her pain-filled eyes rested on Evelyn's face. "You were, weren't you? In London. And it went wrong. That's why you really wanted to come here. You never said. But I knew. I could tell. I could read between the lines in your letter, and I guessed." A pause. "Did you love him very much?"

Evelyn nodded, slowly. "But he didn't love me enough. He chose to go along another path." She hung her head. "He was married, you see . . ."

"Evelyn . . ." Blanche's hand tightened its grip on her arm.

"It's all right . . . I'm just getting over it now. At least I think I am. I hope I am. But it still hurts me when I think about him, when I look back and think about all the times we were together. I can't seem to erase any of those . . . I keep remembering things he said, things we did. I try to fight it but it's no use, it's still too raw."

"Did his wife find out? Is that what happened?"

"Yes, she found out. Then she went and told her father. He was the head of one of the biggest art syndicates in the country, and he threatened to break Jack—and me—if we ever saw each other again. I hated him at the time, but I suppose I can't blame him. After all, I hurt his daughter. He wanted to hurt me back. And they both wanted revenge.''

"If he didn't think your love was worth fighting for, then he isn't worth crying over."

Evelyn gave a small, bitter little laugh.

"Someone else said that to me, too."

"It's true. Easy for other people to say, though. I know that." A few moments of silence between them. "Does Mother know?"

"She got it out of me, yes." A wistful smile. "As you can guess, she didn't approve . . . how could she? An affair with a married man! The penultimate sin, to someone of her upbringing and generation. Second only to murder. Of course, she thought I was to blame. It's always considered the woman's fault, isn't it? Serves me right, for touching something that didn't belong to me. I played with fire and I got burned. Rough justice and no sympathy."

Blanche's eyes rested on her face, seeing the hurt beneath the brave facade.

"I hope he got burned too."

11

The two men lay back in their big leather winged chairs, their conversation momentarily halted while a club steward replenished their half-empty glasses with brandy.

The club was almost deserted at this time of the afternoon—too late for lunch and too early for dinner—and what men there were either were immersed in their newspapers or had dozed off in the relative quiet and warmth of the club lounge.

"So . . . you're off back to the States to have that wrist of yours checked up on . . . then back here again and off to the Channel Islands?"

Ross Klein took out his cigarette case and flicked it open. "That's the idea. Whether it'll all work out that way or not . . . who knows? Certainly not me. Certainly not the way things are looking on the international scene. None of us can afford to ignore them anymore, much as everyone around here'd like to." A brief, impish smile. "Present company excepted, of course." He held out the cigarette case and his companion took one from it. "If there is going to be a war . . . and I'm one of those who reckon there will be . . . it's going to happen pretty soon. Wham. Then everyone who's been going around trying to make themselves believe that Hitler's really a nice, patriotic little guy will have the real truth staring them in the face. No country rearms itself at the rate Germany's been doing it for the last—how many years?—without there being a sure-fire reason behind it." He took a cigarette for himself and put away the case. "He made his aims and ideals clear enough in his own book, *Mein Kampf*. It's just that most people never bothered to read it."

Ray Lytton smiled. "Consider me guilty too. But then when you're just a general dogsbody at the Foreign Office you don't get much time for serious reading—a quick flick through *The Times* or the *Daily Mail* is all I seem to manage these days—but then, even if the whole British cabinet had read it, from Chamberlain down, do you really think they'd have taken what he wrote literally?"

"I guess they wouldn't have . . . most of them are far too dumb." He took out his lighter and lit his friend's cigarette, then his own. "They don't want to believe that war's been a strong possibility ever since the German National Socialist government rose to power . . . like most of the guys you've got running the show over here, they stick their heads in the sand like ostriches the minute something comes along that they don't like the look of. They think that if they ignore something for long enough, it'll just go away."

"All except Churchill."

Ross Klein smiled.

"Churchill's half American."

It was Ray Lytton's turn to smile now.

"Trust you to say that!"

"Well, it's true . . . most people forget. He isn't just the son of Lord Randolph Churchill, he's 50 percent a Jerome. You British should be grateful for that 50 percent. I reckon that before long you're sure as hell going to need it."

"And you should be grateful that this space is half empty at this time of day. And that anyone likely to overhear you is also likely to be stone deaf as well."

They both laughed, they both sipped their brandy.

"I'm sorry. But it's just the way I see things. Your government's been crazy to turn the other cheek while Hitler's been ranting and raving and Germany's been rearming faster than any country with peaceable intentions would ever think of doing. What they really intend to do, ultimately, couldn't be plainer. They haven't exactly made a big secret of it. And it isn't just Churchill who's been giving out warnings that have fallen on deaf ears. I seem to recall your Lord Weir protesting about the British army being sent abroad as far back as '36. What was it he said? Something about how useless it was sending more and more of the army abroad when it was going to be needed right here . . . in particular a strong navy and a real powerful air force for home defense. But then, hardly anyone who ought to have listened to what he said ever did." He stubbed out his cigarette in a nearby ashtray. "As it is, you've let the Krauts get away with goddamn murder."

"Remember the old fable about the race between the hare and the tortoise? The hare got more than a head start, but he still didn't win."

"The hell that's gonna break loose sooner or later is a far more serious business than what happened in some fairy tale."

"You don't think very much of the British, do you, Ross?"

"Oh, you've gotten me all wrong. I have the greatest respect for the British. And I like them. It's just the guys you've elected to run the show that I don't think much of. With a few exceptions." He took out another cigarette and lit it. "You know, you sure have a strange brand of democracy over here . . . the people elect a government to do what they want, and then the government goes ahead and does just the opposite. That's a crazy way to run anything, let alone decide the fate of several million men, women and children."

"Most of those several million are more like the government they elected than you might think. Almost none of them even want to think that we might be dragged into another war. And that includes me."

"I thought you were a realist. Isn't it plain common sense to take a mad bull by the horns and throw him, before he gets the chance to throw you? And if ever I saw a mad bull, it's Adolf Hitler. Have you seen the way that guy performs on the newsreels?"

"The German people seem to like what they see. And hear."

"That's what worries me."

There were several moments of silence between them while they finished their brandy.

"Turning to another subject . . . tell me about your plans."

"Oh . . . first of all I have to go back home and get this wrist checked up on. It feels OK to me now, but if it isn't 100 percent, there's no way they'll let me fly planes until it is. Stands to reason. Either way, I half promised to call in on my kid sister's friends on Jersey for a few weeks, before I'm recalled. I like to keep even a half promise if I can."

"It's a nice place to be, the Channel Islands. Peaceful. Secluded. Great scenery and beaches. Much warmer than here on the mainland, more often than not!" They both laughed. "But if your pessimistic predictions come true . . . well . . . they could find themselves anything but peaceful and secluded. The islands are far closer to the French coast than they are to the mainland of Britain. Certainly close enough for the Germans to cast a beady on, if they had a mind to. Far enough away from the immediate protection of our navy or air force to give the British government one big head-ache. As far as I know, if the worst came to the worst and war were declared, the islanders would find themselves in a pretty unenviable position. The proverbial meat in the sandwich. The only home-based form of defense they have is their own militia, and they're hardly equipped to deal with the kind of air attack Germany's capable of carrying out. I hate to think about it, even, but if Jersey and Guernsey were ever bombed from the air, both islands would be reduced to rubble in a matter of minutes."

"That's partly why I'm going out there. I was hoping my sister's friend and her family would consider leaving Jersey and coming back to the States for as long as need be. Just in case."

"You think they'll listen to you?"

"Maybe they have more sense than the people on the mainland."

"Maybe they'll just think you're a pessimistic, cynical Yankee who wants to uproot them from their nice, quiet, tranquil little home."

Ross Klein laughed.

"Since I was raised near Houston, Texas, I don't think anyone'd call me a Yankee . . . and I wouldn't be trying to persuade them to come back with me if I didn't think it was urgent that they seriously consider it." He ran a hand through his thick, dark straw-colored hair. "One thing's for sure. If your government can't even handle the tiller of its own ship, or decide which direction to turn it in, then God help all the people on those islands!"

"That's where ignorance is bliss. None of them know what's really going on."

"And you think that's good? You English are just plain

crazy! You've gotten the whole of National Socialist Germany rearming to the teeth without anything to throw back at them when they strike, a policy of disarmament that's been limping around on crutches since 1919, and a prime minister with less backbone than a garden-pond newt . . . and you don't think you have anything to worry about?"

Ray Lytton shifted in his chair. A vague smile hung about his lips. "You know, you seem very touchy lately, Ross. Ever since you got here, in fact. Not having girl trouble, are you?"

"I don't know any English girls. I haven't been here long enough to meet any."

A smile from his companion.

"We'll soon fix that. How about it? That's why you've been so bad-tempered lately. I should have known! It's not good to go without female company for more than twenty-four hours—and you're talking to an expert."

"I'm supposed to be on sick leave!"

"A cracked wrist wouldn't stop me. I could do it with one hand tied behind my back."

Ross's lips turned up at the corners in a ghost of a smile. "You don't say?"

12

The door of the old tower creaked open, stubbornly, letting in a flood of daylight from outside that spread a vast, mellow-gold carpet over the dank, gloomy interior, and both girls went inside, looking around them. They shivered.

"God, it's filthy!" said Jeanne Le Bon, pulling her cardigan closer around her shoulders. She wrinkled her nose. "And it stinks! Look at the cobwebs on the ceiling! I shouldn't think this place has been cleaned out for years."

"Maybe that's why my grandmother offered to let me use it," Evelyn answered with a wry smile.

"If the old main house hadn't been built onto it, it would have been pulled down years ago."

"Oh, I don't know. I think it's got character. Let's take a look upstairs."

"Mind how you go. There isn't even a rope to hang on to on the way up . . . I remember that much. And those narrow little steps are steep, too."

Carefully, they made their way upward to the turret room, stopping every so often to look back the way they'd come.

"I wouldn't fancy falling down there."

"Me neither. Maybe that's why my grandmother was so eager to give it to me. Wishful thinking."

"Oh, no, Evelyn! That isn't true!"

119

"Just a bad joke. My sense of humor isn't all it could be these days." Out of breath, they reached the top.

"When all's said and done, you're the only real Tregeale left. The last of the line. That's more important to Mrs. Tregeale than you can ever realize. I mean it. The family name means more to her than almost anything else."

"Except perpetuating the grudge she's always held against my mother. And transferring it to me. She's accepted me into the family, yes. But not into her heart. When she first set eyes on me, she didn't see her long-lost granddaughter, just a replica of my mother. I could see it in her eyes."

"You're still the daughter of her only son. He was always her favorite, you know. Mother told me that, a long time ago."

"I'd rather she accepted me because she wanted to. Not because she feels it's just her duty. That makes it all meaningless."

They stood there in the bare, circular, strange-smelling room, surprised by the contrast between the gloom of downstairs and the bright light above.

"If she'd really cared about my father she would only have wanted him to be happy."

Jeanne leaned against the thick gray stones of the wall and gazed from the window. "I know it's difficult, maybe even impossible, for you or me to really understand the way another generation thinks. How they reason things out. How they behave. It's like Queen Mary and old King George and Edward, all over again . . . have you ever thought of that? Mrs. Tregeale is just like Queen Mary, right to a tee. She was brought up on a rigid, uncompromising diet of discipline, meals served on the chime of the clock, and told to put duty and all that kind of thing before everything . . . especially before personal feelings. They have a lot in common, don't they, when you sit down and think about it? They both had sons they idolized and then the same sons went off and married women they didn't approve of. A complete conflict between two sets of values, with both sides thinking that their way is right." She hesitated a moment before going on. "I know you'll find it hard to believe this, but I'm sure that she really cares for you very much. It's just that being the kind of woman she is, she'll probably never tell you."

"I wonder why my grandfather ever married her."

"She was very beautiful, by all accounts, when she was a

young woman. That's something else my mother told me. And you'll have seen her portrait in the house."

"A man doesn't marry someone just because he likes the look of the packaging, surely? There has to be more. Otherwise he might as well buy a painting, or a beautiful sculpture, and simply look at that. Looks are a facade we all hide behind . . . but when you have to live with someone, day after day, you can't keep up a pretense. I wonder if they were ever really happy?"

Jeanne was silent for a moment.

"It's a kind of unspoken rule, here, on the island. Like marries like. The sons of important Jersey families marry the daughters of other important Jersey families, and vice versa. Woe betide anyone who thinks he can kick over the traces and get away with it. It's tradition. Which would explain why they were so hard on your father when he decided that he wasn't going to follow in their footsteps and toe the line. No doubt they'd got somebody already picked out for him."

"My grandmother said as much." She started to laugh. "She had all his life mapped out for him, and then he went and married my mother . . . a London nightclub singer! How she must have seethed when he wrote to tell her that!" She came over to where Jeanne stood, and they both looked out together onto the courtyard below and the garden beyond. "But I'm so glad he did. That he didn't give in. That he had the strength of character to do what he really wanted. My mother was so in love with him." She glanced toward the house. "Julia doesn't like me, she made that plain enough straight away! She doesn't even think I have the right to be here. An interloper, she called me. To my face. Well, at least she didn't bother to hide what she really felt. I suppose I ought to respect her for that, in a strange sort of way." She thought back to the scene in the dining room, the bitter words they'd exchanged last night. "But she was so hateful to Blanche that I can't."

"Oh, Mrs. de Corbiere's always been a bit strait-laced. It takes her ages to really accept people, Mother could tell you that. She thinks the world of her . . . I see that surprises you. But when Mrs. de Corbiere was small, my mother had charge of her. Brought her up, almost, you might say. In those days, Mr. and Mrs. Tregeale did a lot of traveling, mostly to do with his business, and the children were left at home here on Jersey. Since she was that much older than Mr. Gilbert and Miss

Blanche, she was too old to be looked after by their nurse, so my mother looked after her." Jeanne smiled. "There's always been a special bond between them, even after Mrs. de Corbiere got married and left the island for a while. Mother still calls her Miss Julia whenever she talks about her, even now." Evelyn recalled the knowing look that had passed between them in the hall, and understood.

Jeanne came away from the window.

"Well, I'd best be getting back to the house now, if you're sure you can manage on your own for a while . . . there're so many things to get done on Sundays. Some day of rest! Mrs. Tregeale has got me to sort out all the old papers in the big attic, and I'm not even halfway finished yet. There's no electric light up there, you see, so I have to do it with a lamp. No wonder I'm getting a squint! Then I have to cycle down to the village and find out why they didn't deliver the newspapers today." Her smile faded a little. "Not that there's likely to be anything cheerful in them worth reading, if last week's are anything to go by. When I went shopping in St. Ouens a couple of days ago and stopped by one of the newsstands, the headlines scared me stiff, I don't mind telling you."

"All the talk about another war, you mean? Yes . . . it scares me too. But however much we want to ignore it it just won't go away if there's any truth in it. You know the old saying, no smoke without fire." She lay back against the stone wall, sighing loudly. "Ever since the German National Socialist government came to power and made Adolf Hitler chancellor, they've been rearming at the rate of knots . . . and though I'm the last person in the world to have any understanding of the machinations of politics, you can't tell me that they don't have some aggressive purpose behind all that. Only a fool would think otherwise."

"People only see what they want to see, don't they? But if it did happen . . . oh, God! I can't even bear to think about it. What would we do here, more than a hundred miles from the British mainland and hardly any proper defenses to speak of? It makes my blood run cold." She came away from the window and began to pace the bare flagstone floor. "Why the hell can't countries live in peace?"

"Ordinary people have been asking that same question for the last few hundred years!"

For a moment Jeanne was quiet.

"If—if anything did happen . . . I mean, if the unthinkable happened and a war was declared . . . would you leave Jersey? Would you go back to London?"

Jack Neville. Robert De Braose. Loneliness. Disgrace. She looked at Jeanne Le Bon.

"Never."

13

She stood in front of the full-length mirror, holding the black taffeta evening gown against her body; she stepped back, then forward again. She turned right, then left, loving the silken swish of the material as she moved. But, finally, she lay it down on the bed and went to her wardrobe for something else. No. It was too soon, yet. Too soon for her to be able to wear that black gown, the gown she'd last worn for Jack Neville; maybe she could never bring herself to wear it again. He was still too close, too much a part of her for her to be able to easily forget. And maybe she never could.

She kneeled there on the bed in her underclothes, hugging herself, trying not to give in to the temptation that racked her so many times, to imagine he was there, that it was his arms and not hers that were there around her. If she closed her eyes and willed herself back again, she could hear his voice, whispering, close to her ear, the voice that sent tingles down her spine and set her pulse leaping. Jack. Jack.

Against her will she thought of what he might be doing now. With De Braose and his daughter, at the theater. At Ciro's, dining or gambling at the Embassy Club, then back to the great, lavish, over-gilded museum that could never be a home, just a gold cage for the captive bird that the rich man had bought for his daughter. Who'd never set him free.

124

She was almost grateful when Blanche knocked and came into the room, chasing away the painful memories and the bitter regrets. If, if.

She forced back the tears that had come into her eyes.

"Blanche! Your headache's better!"

She came in and closed the door.

"I've been looking for you. Jeanne said you were busy unpacking your canvases and paints over there in the old tower. Could I have a look at some of your work later on? I'd love to see it. And how a real artist works. How long does it take you to finish a single painting?"

Evelyn picked up the black taffeta gown and hung it away again. "Oh . . . it depends. On the size of the canvas, how much detail you have in the picture. All artists work in different ways. Some paint a little each day; then they go back and look and study and criticize what they've painted. If they're like me, they start a new painting and find that they just can't stop working until it's finished. It's an urge, a fire that consumes you, and you can't put your brush down, not even to eat or sleep. Like a fever, almost, it won't go away until it's run its course. Me, I'm all or nothing!"

"I'm not good at anything!"

"I can't believe that."

"Here . . . I brought you these. You wanted more photos of Gilbert, didn't you? For the portrait you're going to paint of him. The ones Julia found for you were all taken from the same angle . . . these are better." She smiled at them as she looked down at them. "I can remember all these being taken. And here are some of the three of us with Daddy." Evelyn took them. "You'd have loved Daddy. He was so kind, so gentle. So full of life. Just like Gilbert was. I couldn't believe it when he died. Couldn't believe that he was gone, and that he'd never come back again." She swallowed. "Everything changed then. This wasn't a happy house anymore. No fun. No laughter. It seemed more like a tomb than a home. I'd walk through it, through the rooms where he'd been. I'd walk by myself in the garden where we used to walk together on summer evenings, and I'd sit there on the seat he'd made under the big tree all by myself, trying to will him back again. But he was gone."

"That's how I felt when my mother died." She remembered afresh that winter's afternoon, with the rain falling and the twigs and leaves blowing in front of her as she'd walked alone from the little church. "There was no one else. I was suddenly all alone. It was as if somebody had closed a door and locked it, then thrown away the key. I was too stunned and too miserable even to cry. It was weeks before I could cry. And when I started to, I couldn't stop." She looked back at the photographs. There was a tall, dark-haired, striking-looking man, with two dark-haired, striking-looking children, one on each knee. "Is this him with you and my father?"

"Yes, that's Daddy with Gilbert and me. It was taken one summer at St. Aubin's Bay. That's one of the island's best-known beauty spots . . . not so far from here. You should take a picnic lunch one day and go up there to do some sketches. The views are breathtaking. There're so many things to paint on the island . . . even though it's so tiny, you'd never get tired of seeing them."

"I can't see Julia here."

"She probably took the picture. She'd have been old enough, then. There's one photo here with all of us, though." She leafed through the pile and brought one out. Evelyn stared down at it.

"She's standing apart from the rest of you."

"It's funny, but she was never very close to Daddy. Or us. She was always more Mother's girl. And Martha's. Martha practically brought her up."

"Yes, Jeanne told me."

"That's why Martha has never liked me very much, I suppose. I think she thought that Daddy spoiled Gilbert and me, and left Julia out. I know Mother thought that. Julia and I have always been so unalike, you see. Ever since we were children." She smiled. "It was Daddy I took after. Gilbert used to say that I was so different from her and Mother, that it was almost as if I wasn't Mother's at all! I was born in Switzerland, did I ever tell you? Daddy took Mother for a holiday there, after one of his business trips, and they liked it so much that they decided to stop there for a while. They came back again to Jersey when I was three months old."

"No, you never told me that."

"We had a nanny then, and she looked after me and Gilbert. When we were older, Gilbert used to joke that the nurses had given Mother the wrong baby in the Swiss clinic . . . and we'd both laugh!" She suddenly caught sight of some boxes on the floor. "Records!" Her blue eyes lit up with excitement, like a child's. "Evelyn . . . you brought all these from London?"

"Yes. I brought my wind-up gramophone, too. But that's over in the old tower, waiting to be unpacked. It's too heavy for me to bring over."

"It doesn't matter! There's a wind-up gramophone in Daddy's old room!" Down on her hands and knees, she looked through the pile incredulously. "Oh, how he would have loved these! Josephine Baker. Jessie Matthews. Artie Shaw. Mother didn't approve of any of those, I can tell you! So Daddy used to go to his room and play them, and I'd go with him to listen."

"She doesn't approve of *music?*"

"Only classical. Or singers who have private lives pure as the driven snow. She nearly had a fit when Daddy played Josephine Baker singing a Cole Porter love song in French! Just because she'd read somewhere or other that she'd danced almost in the nude in Paris, in some American revue. She was scandalized. She didn't approve of Jessie Matthews, either, because she was involved in a divorce case with Evelyn Laye and Sonny Hale. Mother said she was nothing more or less than a husband-snatcher . . . but Daddy didn't agree with her. He said nobody could help falling in love with someone else, whether they were married or not."

"And what did Artie Shaw do that upset her?"

"Got divorced a few times. And divorced people, as you've probably guessed, are top of Mother's blacklist. If any of her friends went through the divorce courts, she'd never invite them into this house again. Yes, it's true." Blanche picked up a pile of the records. "Mother won't ever compromise on any of her principles. No matter what." Evelyn followed her to the door. "Come on, let's play some of these before they come back from church!"

"But how long is that likely to be?"

"Oh, at least another couple of hours. After the service they always stay to talk to the vicar, and anyone else they know." Suddenly, there was a banging noise from overhead, and they both looked up. "What's that, for heaven's sake?"

Evelyn remembered something that Jeanne had said.

"It must be Jeanne, up in the attic. She said something about havng to sort out trunks of old papers for your mother."

Blanche frowned.

"I didn't know anything about it."

"She's been helping me to sort out everything I brought with me from London, ever since I got here yesterday." Together, they reached the door of Roland Tregeale's room. "After that sea trip, and then the scene with your mother, I was grateful for a shoulder to lean on. And to be able to talk to a girl of my own age." She smiled, so Blanche wouldn't feel slighted. "I'd been longing to talk to you the whole way here. Then when Jean-Louis told me you'd been taken ill and were lying down, it was a bit of an anticlimax."

"My cursed headaches . . ."

Even now, close as they were, Evelyn couldn't bring herself to talk about what she'd seen that first night. She changed the subject. "So this was my grandfather's room?"

"Yes . . . just the way he left it. He was very ill at the last—it was his heart. And there were other things, the doctors told Mother. But he never complained. Never grumbled when he was in pain. I loved him even more for that, because it was agony for him, even to make the effort to speak." A far-seeing look came into her eyes. "Mother had a special bell fitted in here, so that if he needed anything, all he had to do was to ring, and we'd hear him . . . but on the night he died, Mother had people downstairs for dinner. If she hadn't had guests, one of us would have come up here to sit with him. Julia and I used to take turns, to help Mother. But when everyone had gone and I came up to kiss him goodnight, he was dead." She dashed away her tears on the back of her sleeve. "He looked so peaceful, lying there. But he was gone. Gone forever. And he'd never look at me and smile again. I cried myself to sleep that night."

"You loved him very much, didn't you?"

"I still do. Even though he's gone and he'll never come back." She looked down at her hands. "I'd like to believe that when you die, it isn't the end, that there's something else, something waiting that's so wonderful and perfect that none of us can ever begin to imagine what it's like until we're there. Heaven, I suppose Mother would call it. Somewhere the Church tells us about. The place we'll all go to if we're good. It sounds so simple-minded, doesn't it? Like telling children that if they're good on Christmas Eve Santa Claus will bring them lots of presents. Maybe we never do grow up. Maybe we can never stop believing that there are really such things as miracles."

"You mean you don't really believe it?"

"I can't answer that because I don't know what I believe, not really. I know what I'd like to believe . . . what I'd like to happen . . . to go somewhere where nobody ever grows old, or gets ill; somewhere where you're happy all the time, and nothing can ever hurt you. A place where all the people you've ever loved are gathered together, and you can just be there with them for ever and ever." More tears welled up into her eyes. "Often, when I can't sleep, I lie and think about my brother . . . about Daddy . . . about things in the past. If only there was some way I could make them come back again."

For a moment Evelyn didn't answer.

"If I had a wish . . . I think it would be to have no past at all."

She stared around her at the walls of the old, musty-smelling stone church, curiously like the inside of the ancient tower back at the house, at the rows of unfamiliar faces. The lighted candles on each side of the velvet-draped altar, the stained-glass windows, the mellow, gentle light on the flagging and the ancient pillars. She mouthed the words of the hymn they were singing, but without thinking or feeling about them. As she glanced distractedly across the aisle she noticed a tall, dark-haired, good-looking man watching Blanche and her. Their eyes met and held for a moment, and then he smiled.

"Who is he?" she heard herself whisper to Blanche. Blanche glanced up, fleetingly, from the pages of her hymn book and her eyes followed Evelyn's.

"Philip Le Haan. Mother's lawyer. Or advocate, as we call them in Jersey. The Le Haans have handled our legal affairs for years. Philip took over from his father just before Daddy died." She glanced nervously toward her mother at the other end of the pew, in case she saw them talking.

"He hasn't taken his eyes off you," Evelyn said.

Blanche fell silent. Her eyes moved back to the pages of her hymn book and Evelyn's went back to Philip Le Haan. He smiled again and she smiled back. As she made herself look down again into the open pages of her hymn book, she noticed that Julia was watching them. She looked abruptly away.

Outside in the porch, when the service was over, he disengaged himself from the group of people he was with, and came over to them.

"Blanche!"

"Oh, Philip!" She turned toward Evelyn. "This is my niece, Evelyn Tregeale . . . she only arrived in Jersey yesterday, from London." Smiling, they shook hands.

"So, you're Gilbert's daughter?"

"Yes, that's right."

"Then I'm delighted to meet you." He glanced back at Blanche. "You weren't in church this morning. I missed you."

"I didn't feel up to it, to tell the truth. I had a bad night and I woke up with a splitting headache. Mother didn't grumble for once. Besides, Evelyn had only just arrived and it seemed rude to leave her all alone in the house on her first day, with just the servants." They exchanged glances. "Of course, neither of us could manage to get out of the evening service. You know Mother!"

"Yes . . . indeed I do." His eyes were still on Blanche's face. "So. I shall look forward to seeing you two ladies tomorrow night, at Frederica's dinner party. I'll be at the house early, by the way, to go over the draft she wanted me to make of her new will."

"We'll see you then, Philip." Blanche looked back into the church, where she caught sight of her mother and sister, disengaging themselves from a small group of people. Philip Le Haan smiled at them both and then walked away, swallowed up in the press of people standing outside the church.

"He's nice," Evelyn said, staring after him.

"Yes, he is. I've always liked Philip. But Mother doesn't think he's as good a lawyer as his father was, mostly because he doesn't always agree with everything she says."

"That's probably why she doesn't like me. Is the only reason she's asked him to dinner that he sees to the family's legal business?"

"Oh, I wouldn't go as far as to say that. Between you and me, I think Mother enjoys a good argument with someone, whoever it is. The trouble is, she always thinks she's right. But Philip's the perfect dinner guest for any of the hostesses on the island, because he's a bachelor. Most of them seem to be perpetually short of spare men."

Evelyn's curiosity had been aroused.

"Has he lived on Jersey all his life? Was he born here?"

"Yes, but he was educated in some public school in England. That's why Mother always thinks of him as an outsider, even though the Le Haans have lived on the island for years. His father was a great friend of Daddy, in the old days. But he died a couple of years before Daddy did." They walked on outside together, toward Jean-Louis and the waiting car. "Do you know what Daddy used to say? That old age is realizing how many of your friends you've outlived."

Evelyn threaded her arm through Blanche's as they reached the lych gate.

"Yes, that's true. It isn't only the good who die young."

Jeanne Le Bon wiped her aching eyes on the back of her hand, then picked up the lantern and set it down on one of the big, heavy, dust-caked trunks that were stacked along the sloping walls of the attic.

It was growing dark outside now, making the dim glow from the single lantern seem even brighter than before. She stood up among the old chests and boxes, the broken crates that had once held pictures, the piles of yellowed newspapers and mildewed books, and looked toward the tiny, narrow door, not three feet high, built into the wall at the far end of the attic. Slowly, picking her way through the old debris, she went toward it.

The old lock was thickly rusted, its key long lost. Reaching into her apron pocket, she pulled out a ring of keys, and, with great patience, tried every one. But none fitted.

There was no handle to the tiny door. She put her weight against it, then pushed. But it stayed fast. Gritting her teeth, she pummeled the wood with both fists. Then she paused, as from the courtyard below she heard the unmistakable sound of an approaching car.

Putting the bunch of keys back into her pocket, she went back the way she had come. Then, standing tiptoe on one of the heavy boxes, she peered out of the grimy, tiny skylight in the slanting roof. Far below, she could see the tall figure of Philip Le Haan get out of his car and walk up to the front door. She climbed down, wiping her dirty hands on her apron.

She picked up the lantern and made her way back down the steep attic staircase, and then downstairs to the hall. She glanced at the clock as she passed. Too early for any of the other guests to be arriving yet. The Tregeale sisters and Evelyn would still be upstairs, in their rooms, dressing for dinner. But from the other side of the drawing-room door, Jeanne could hear the unmistakable voices of Frederica Tregeale and Philip Le Haan.

Glancing all around her, she moved closer. Then, listening carefully, she lay her ear to the door.

"You've just come back from Paris, then?" Julia said. She smiled at Louis Tostain. "It's so many years since I was there, I expect it's changed out of all recognition, like most big cities."

"There was one big difference from when I was there last year, and I must admit it came as quite a shock. Ever since the beginning of the year the entire city has been preparing itself for war, as if a conflict with Germany is more or less inevitable." Across the table, Evelyn saw her grandmother's face stiffen with disapproval of the subject. "Everyone's been issued gasmasks—although practically nobody knows how to put them on—and beds of begonias have been planted over bomb shelters under the Champs-Élysées. There's no music, no dancing, and no movies after ten o'clock, and people apparently dine early at Maxim's or at the Coupole. It's unbelievable. But Paris is in bed and asleep by midnight." His face showed an expression of surprise. "You must have read something about it in the newspapers. They've been full of nothing else for weeks!"

"I canceled the newspapers," said Frederica Tregeale. "And I certainly have no intention of reordering them until they cease to fill their pages with nonsense about war and other alarmist trash." Her voice was like ice. "All this talk about war is pure speculation. And I refuse to pay for a newspaper that prints speculation and not facts."

"But you can't ignore what's going on in the outside world, Frederica," Philip Le Haan said, into the momentary awkward silence that followed her outburst. "Just canceling your newspapers because they tell you something that you don't want to listen to won't make the reality of an almost inevitable war go away. A fact doesn't cease to be a fact simply because it's ignored."

"The facts as I interpret them are that certain people get pleasure from spreading ridiculous rumors that scare ordinary citizens out of their wits. And I refuse to listen to them. What purpose has the German government in starting a war? The whole idea's absurd. No country wants war. And you can't tell me that they do."

"Governments have never needed very much in the way of reasons for starting wars in the past, and they don't need very much now, or in the future. Ever since Hitler's rise to power nobody can be blind to the fact that the German National Socialist government's policies have become more and more aggressive. They've been casting a greedy eye over all the little countries around them and it doesn't take much imagination to guess what they're thinking."

"Oh, I hate all this morbid talk about wars!" said Margaret Le Fevre. "For goodness' sake let's talk about something else."

"What would happen here on the island, Philip, if war were declared?" Evelyn said, ignoring her aunt's warning glance. "Is Jersey under direct control of the War Office administration in London?"

"That's a little complicated to answer. Legally speaking, Jersey is a self-contained bailiwick, responsible for its own administration and its own laws, all entirely independent of the government in the United Kingdom. We have our own lieutenant-governor and commander-in-chief, who's the personal representative of the Crown, and the official channel of communication between the island governments and the government in the United Kingdom. While the islands owe allegiance to the British sovereign, strictly speaking they're outside the British Parliament.

"But to answer your question as best I can, Channel Island men have been exempt for centuries from service in the armed forces of the Crown, but they've never sheltered behind that right. On the contrary, many islanders volunteered during the First World War, and when the United Kingdom introduced conscription, the States here immediately followed suit. If war were declared now, exactly the same thing would probably happen."

"But how the hell could we defend ourselves?" said Peter Tostain before Evelyn could ask another question. "We haven't got the equipment, we haven't got the means to sustain our food supplies for more than a few months at most! We're wide open to attack from France by air and sea. And much too far from the British mainland to be protected by the navy or the air

force. Besides which we have no strategic value whatsoever."
Two bright red spots appeared on his cheeks. "I can see what'll
happen; I can see it coming a mile off! They'll just forget about
us! We'll be left to get on with managing as best we can."

Philip Le Haan finished his glass of wine. He glanced
around the table. "The islands might be of no military impor-
tance to either the War Office or the German forces . . . but
the capture of them would be their first conquest of British soil
and of great propaganda value. That's something you've both
overlooked."

Frederica Tregeale looked at him, outraged.

"I think this morbid conversation has gone quite far enough!
The very idea of Jersey or Guernsey being captured is perfectly
ludicrous!"

"Unfortunately it isn't. On the contrary, it's a very real
possibility."

"I don't accept that, Philip. And I'll thank you to confine
your conversation at my dinner table to more suitable subjects
in future. Otherwise I see little point in including you in future
invitations." Stony-faced, she rose from the table. "Julia.
Ring for the coffee and port to be served in the drawing room."
Philip Le Haan and Evelyn exchanged glances. "Peter.
Margaret. Shall we go?"

Peter's son, Louis Tostain, was quickly at Evelyn's side,
helping her from her chair, and as they walked side by side
from the room, they began a lively discussion about Renaissance artists. In front of them, Julia glanced back toward
Blanche, who was smiling up into the face of Philip Le Haan.

"You're looking very beautiful this evening," he said,
giving her his arm. "But then, you always do."

"Thank you, Philip. It's kind of you to say so."

"I only speak the truth."

She smiled. "I thought that was what lawyers always did."

Evelyn sat down and eased off her high-heeled shoes. She
felt tired tonight, without understanding why. Perhaps it was
the combination of the sultry August heat, evaporating into the
sudden chill that seemed to descend with the fall of darkness.
Maybe the strain of the last few hours, trying to make
conversation with her grandmother's guests, afraid of introducing subjects that she knew would be disapproved of, on edge in
case somebody might ask an awkward question about her past,

had taken their toll of her. She had never felt this weary in London. And it wasn't even half past eleven.

She unpinned her long hair and began to brush it out, slowly and rhythmically. Then she got up and went over to the window to draw the curtains, and suddenly stiffened. She screwed up her eyes, closed them, then opened them again. No, she wasn't seeing things in the dark. There, halfway along the drive, a bag slung over one shoulder, was the shadowy but unmistakable figure of a man.

All her tiredness left her. Her breath came in gasps. Her heart beat faster, her whole body shook. And then she was seized with a wild, almost unbearable joy. Turning from the window she ran out of her room and down the stairs as fast as her legs would carry her, toward the front door.

The servants had already locked and bolted it. With shaking hands she fumbled with the key and then the double bolts before she could frantically pull it open. Then, barefoot, her long hair streaming behind her in the night breeze, she ran out of the house and along the drive toward him, breathlessly shouting his name.

Blanche sat down on the stool in front of her dressing table and unclipped her diamond earrings. Then she replaced them in her jewelry casket and began to brush her hair. Behind her, the bedroom door suddenly came open.

"Julia!" Their eyes met in the mirror.

"Stay where you are."

"I . . . I thought you'd gone to bed. It's nearly midnight."

Nervously, she half turned round. Ever since she'd been a child, for as long as she could remember, she had never felt at ease in her sister's presence. To avoid her eyes she went on brushing her hair in the mirror.

"What is it? What's wrong? Why are you looking at me like that?" The hand holding the hair brush began to shake.

"You wore too much powder and too much lipstick tonight, Blanche." The door clicked shut. "Don't you remember what I told you about that?"

Blanche swallowed.

"I . . . I don't think I did." She glanced at her reflection and saw nothing wrong with it. "Philip said—"

"Can't you see he's laughing at you? *Laughing!*" Her cold eyes held Blanche's in the mirror. "They all were. I could see it. Every one of them. And pitying you. *Pitying you.* Poor Blanche! I could almost hear them thinking out loud. She's terrified of being old."

"No!"

"Poor Blanche, so young and pretty once, trying to hide her face beneath those layers of cosmetic muck . . . because she can't bear to admit the truth of what she sees in the mirror!"

"That isn't true." There was a break in her voice. A tear welled up in one corner of her eye and ran down her cheek. "Why are you saying these things to me?"

Julia came closer, her harsh voice a low-pitched hiss, like that of a poisonous snake. "I'm saying them to you because I'm the only one who'll ever tell you the truth . . . none of the others would dare to, because they all feel sorry for you. Yes, that's right. You're an object of pity. Any woman who is incapable of growing old without even a modicum of grace is to be pitied. And you are growing old, Blanche. You can't cheat nature. It moves on, despite everything you try to do to hold it back. You can never fight it, it's too strong." She grasped both sides of her sister's face in her cold, dry hands and thrust it forward within inches of the mirror. "Look at yourself! Go on, look! In four years you'll be forty. *Forty!* You can't bear it, can you? You can't face it. Not unless you can go running to the nearest bottle and drink yourself senseless to blot out the truth. You've always been weak. Weak and vain. But you'll never be young again. Every morning when you wake up and go to this mirror, you'll see that I'm right. Every day there'll be deeper hollows under your eyes, every day a new line that wasn't there the day before, until the face you see now no longer exists."

Desperately, Blanche tried to wrench her face free, but her sister's hands held her in a grip of iron, pushing the flesh of her cheeks forward so that she looked like a fleshy, grotesque gargoyle. The face that stared back at her now was the face of someone she did not know.

"Stop it! Please, stop it."

"Whatever you do, you'll never turn back the clock. That beautiful face will soon be gone—gone, Blanche. No man will ever turn and look twice at you, ever again. That hurts, doesn't it?"

All the fight had gone out of her. Julia let her go, then stepped back, while Blanche slumped forward onto the dressing-table top, knocking everything on it aside, her body shaking with sobs. There was a light tap on the door and Julia answered it without turning round.

"Come in, Martha."

Martha Le Bon came into the room, carrying a tray covered with a white cloth.

"I brought it like you said, Miss Julia."

"Good. Put it down there." She went over to the tray and picked up the bottle and the glass that were on it. "Do you have the strength to resist this?" Slowly, she put them down beside Blanche on the dressing table. "You want a drink, don't you, Blanche? You want one so badly . . ." She turned away, but hesitated when she reached the door. "I wonder what Daddy would say if he could see you now?" There was a mocking tone in her voice. "I wonder if he'd still be so proud of you." Then she and Martha were gone.

Sobbing, Blanche sank from the stool onto the floor, clutching her face, her hair hanging down around her shoulders. She stared at the bottle through her sticky, tear-stained fingers, then shut her eyes and turned away her head.

Her whole body shook. Though the embers of a small fire burned in the grate and warmed the room, she could not stop shivering. She looked back again toward the bottle, fighting with herself. One glass. Just one glass. To calm herself. To steady her nerves. To stop her limbs and hands from this violent shaking. One glass, and then no more.

Unsteadily she groped her way toward the dressing table from the floor. She pushed back her hair from her eyes and stared at her white, tear-stained face in the mirror. Where the light shone down she could see deep, dark hollows beneath her eyes, the eyes that seemed to belong no longer to her, but to some other, alien woman she was unable to recognize. Her face was marked with mottled patches of color, where her face powder had been dissolved by the tears, and mascara stains clung to the skin beneath her eyes. Frantically, she put up her hands toward the mirror to blot out the reflection that she saw. Then she grabbed the bottle of whisky and fumbled wildly with the top to open it.

He came toward her out of the darkness, and for a single moment she held her breath. Above them, the moon had slid out from behind the barrier of clouds and the light suddenly fell upon his face.

"I . . . I'm sorry," Evelyn stammered, taken aback. "I thought for a moment . . . that you were someone else."

"I wish I had been. And I envy him, whoever he is." He smiled what could have been Jack Neville's smile and held out his hand. "You must be the most beautiful girl on the island." The moon was right overhead now, lighting his face and hers. No, it had been no trick of the light; he was so like him, so very like him that it hurt. Her heart lurched as she reached out and took his hand.

"I'm Evelyn Tregeale."

"My name's Richard Mahone. And if you're a Tregeale then I must have found my way to the right house." Slowly, they began to walk back along the drive together. "I must apologize for arriving on your doorstep so late. In fact, the truth is I'm not even expected. To cut a long story short, I only arrived on the island from St. Malo a few hours ago . . . and as soon as I'd checked in to a hotel in St. Helier, I decided to take a look up here."

"I still don't understand."

"I meant to take a taxi, of course. But there didn't seem to be any about. I was one of the last passengers to get off the boat, and everyone in front of me seemed to have bagged them first. Patience isn't one of my virtues, I'm afraid. So I thought that after being stuck on board that boat for the last few hours, a bit of exercise wouldn't do me any harm. That's when I decided to take a walk up here. Trouble was, I didn't realize just how far it was."

Evelyn stared up at him through the darkness.

"You walked all the way from St. Helier?"

"In the morning I'll have the blisters to prove it."

"But how will you get back again? I doubt if you'll get a taxi at this time of night . . . it isn't London, I'm afraid."

"The same way as I got here, I suppose." He smiled the smile that went straight through her. "Serve me right, won't it, for not having the patience to wait until the morning to come out here. I daresay nobody ever killed themselves through walking."

They had reached the front door.

"Whether my grandmother's still up or not, I couldn't let

you walk back! It's more than five miles into St. Helier. You'll have to stay the night."

"I'd hate to impose on anyone's hospitality," he said, holding the door back for Evelyn to walk through first. He suddenly glanced down and noticed her bare feet. "My, you did run out in a hurry!" There was a gentle teasing note in his voice. "You forgot to put on your shoes."

Evelyn glanced down, too, and laughed. When she looked up, Jeanne Le Bon had come up the stairs from the kitchen below and was staring at them.

"Oh, Jeanne! I thought you'd gone to bed. Do you happen to know if my grandmother or my aunt are still up?"

"No, I don't," she answered abruptly; then turned and ran back down the stairs.

"What's the matter with her?" asked Richard Mahone, and Evelyn shrugged her shoulders.

"I don't know. It isn't like her to be so offhanded. Here, this is the drawing room. My grandmother usually sits and reads awhile by the fire before she goes up to bed. She might still be here."

She was. As they knocked and went inside she looked up from the Bible she had open on her lap, and stared as strangely at Richard Mahone as Jeanne had.

Before Evelyn could explain, he'd gone over to her chair and offered his hand. He smiled at her.

"Mrs. Tregeale . . . please, forgive me for turning up in your home like this, without any warning, without even being invited here first . . . and at this time of night, too," he smiled again. "But I've looked forward to coming to the island for so long, and meeting you. You see . . . although my name is Mahone—Richard Mahone—my mother was born here. And she told me that her eldest sister was one of your greatest friends." He moved closer to her. "My mother's name was Diana Sorel."

Evelyn, forgotten on the other side of the room, stared toward her grandmother and saw something that she'd never thought possible. The cold, stony face broke into a genuine smile.

"Diana Sorel? You're Diana's son?" Incredulous, she leaned foward on her stick and stared at him. "I can scarcely believe it! A Sorel back on Jersey after all these years! The

whole family left the island, more than thirty years ago . . .
Diana couldn't have been more than ten or eleven years old
then . . . she was the youngest. Violette Sorel and I went to
school together."

"Yes, my mother told me that."

"But why haven't I heard from any of them for all these
years?"

His smile faded a little.

"The dead can't write letters, I'm afraid. After they'd gone
to Kenya, after my mother had married, a fever swept through
the plantation and practically wiped everyone out. Some
tropical virus or other, brought into the house by one of the
black servants."

"Dear God!"

"My parents took me and went to live in Cape Town, South
Africa, and we lived there until I was seven or eight years old.
When I was thirteen, my mother died with cancer. We were
living in France then, near Bordeaux. We'd gone there because
the doctors told my father that she needed a better climate.
Cape Town never really suited her . . . her health seemed to
go rapidly downhill year after year . . . I think it was that
heat that got to her. And the dust. There was always so much
dust . . . but we couldn't leave because my father was a
mining engineer for one of the big companies and he was
earning good money. After my mother died, he went back to
South Africa while I stopped on in France. Then I got the news
that he'd been killed in an underground explosion at one of the
mines . . ." He paused for a few moments. "They never
managed to recover his body."

"Poor Diana. But at least she was spared that! And you. You
were left all alone to fend for yourself as best you could?"

"There was the money my father left me. A tidy sum. I
invested it in one thing and another, and it's kept me going
pretty well up till now. Of course, I've never led an idle life. I
wasn't brought up to do nothing for a living. I've had various
jobs, trying to find something that suited me, something
worthwhile. I'm still looking." He gave her another charming
smile. "I'm really looking for an interesting business to invest
in . . . I'll probably find something when I eventually go to
Paris. But I've promised myself for so long that I'd come back
here, to where my mother was born . . . I didn't feel that I
wanted to put it off for much longer. She always told me that

I'd love the island. And she was right. The moment I caught sight of the shore as we came into the harbor, then as I stepped off the boat, I felt that I belonged. Do you know, I've never felt that way before."

"I can't tell you how happy I am that you're here, Richard. And I insist that while you're in Jersey you stay in this house, as our guest. Wait until I tell my daughter Julia . . . she was only fourteen or fifteen years old when your family left the island—1909, it must have been—she used to play with your mother as a little girl, did you know that?"

"We have so much to talk about!" Again, the charming smile. "But it's late and I've intruded too much already. I was telling Evelyn, your granddaughter," he flashed her a glance, "that when I got off the boat I left all my luggage except this bag at my hotel in St. Helier . . . if I could use your telephone and get hold of a taxi . . ."

"Nonsense! You'll do no such thing. A son of Diana Sorel staying in a hotel when we have this great house, two parts empty? Never. Besides, you're not in Paris now, young man. You won't get a taxi or any other kind of transport on the island at this time of night for love or money."

"Someone else told me that," he said, smiling across at Evelyn.

"Very well then. It's settled. Evelyn, go and find Martha. Tell her to make up the bed in one of the guest rooms. And be sure to tell her to use the good linen." She lay back in the big winged chair and studied his face. "You know, you definitely have your mother's eyes. In the morning, Jean-Louis or Etienne will drive back with you into St. Helier, and you can pick up your luggage at the hotel." She tugged on the bell rope. "Now . . . what do you say to a glass of my best French brandy for a little nightcap? Or, better still, a little celebration? After all, no Sorel has been on Jersey for more than thirty years!"

He sat down in the chair opposite her.

"How can I ever thank you?"

Evelyn went down into the kitchen to look for Martha Le Bon, but only Jeanne was there, warming milk in a pan over the big stove.

"Evelyn!"

"I was looking for your mother . . . Jeanne? Are you all right? You seemed so strange, earlier on."

For a moment she looked flustered.

"Oh . . . that . . . oh, I'm sorry! It was just that—well, I was so shocked. Stunned, really, to come up the stairs and then see him standing there. A complete stranger, at the front door, at this time of the night! And you with all your hair loose and no shoes on!"

Evelyn stifled a yawn.

"He stunned me, too."

"What do you mean?"

"I was just about to get undressed when I noticed someone walking up the drive in the darkness. I'd gone to the window to draw the curtains and that's when I saw him. But from that distance, in the poor light, he looked like someone else. That's why I ran downstairs to meet him, without waiting to put on my shoes."

"You thought it was someone for you?"

"For a moment . . . I could have sworn . . . it's crazy, isn't it? I really thought he'd gone and defied them all and come here to find me and take me back."

"You mean the man you were involved with in London?"

"Yes. Of course in my heart he never would, but they're so alike . . . even the way he smiles is the way Jack used to smile at me. It's almost uncanny." She rubbed her tired eyes. "Grandmother's invited him to stay in the house because he's the son of someone she used to know who left the island over thirty years ago. Do you know something? I've never seen her this way before. I've never seen her look pleased, or happy ever since I came here. And I've never seen her really smile. Not really smile, as if she meant it. But tonight, when he told her who he was, he seemed almost to cast a spell over her. I'd never have thought that was possible."

"You would if you'd known what she thought of the Sorels. My mother's often talked about it." She took the pan from the stove and poured the milk into a tall cup. "Why, she idolized the Sorel sisters, Mrs. Tregeale did. They were bridesmaids at each other's weddings . . ." Her voice trailed away as the back door opened and Martha Le Bon came into the kitchen. "Oh, there you are, Mother. Mrs. Tregeale's got an unexpected guest for the night, and we're to make up a bed for him in one of the empty guest rooms. Best linen. Fresh towels. Do you want me to do it?''

"You can help me," Martha answered, gruffly, her pale eyes on Evelyn. "That way we'll get it done quicker." As one of the housemaids came down into the kitchen, she turned on her irritably and shouted something in patois. On her way back upstairs, Evelyn asked herself why it was that she'd taken an instant dislike to Jeanne's mother. There seemed no real reason that she could think of, other than it was obvious that because Martha was so close to Julia, by the same token she had made up her mind that anyone Julia disliked, she disliked also. No doubt she despised Blanche and regarded Evelyn as an unwelcome intruder, Tregeale or not.

The light was still showing beneath Blanche's door. No sound came from inside the room, and for a few moments Evelyn hesitated, wondering if Blanche had been so tired that she'd fallen asleep before turning out her bedside lamp. She knocked and listened, but there was still no answer. When she tried the door handle, she found that it was locked.

"Blanche? Are you in there?" Her voice rose in alarm. "Blanche, are you still awake?"

Blanche never slept with her bedroom door locked, unless something was wrong, something she couldn't even bring herself to think about. But she had to. Fighting down her rising panic, Evelyn hammered frantically on the door.

"Are you all right? Blanche, please answer me!"

She turned and ran back along the landing and down the stairs. Past the drawing room, through the half-lit hall, back down again to the kitchen stairs. At the bottom she almost collided with Jeanne and Martha Le Bon, coming up the same way.

"Jeanne! Something's wrong with my aunt, I know there is! I've been banging on her bedroom door but I can't make her hear me!"

"But it's gone midnight. She'll be asleep by now."

"No, you don't understand." She struggled to get her breath. "Her light's still on and the door's locked from the inside. She'd never lock herself in unless something was the matter, I know she wouldn't!" She looked beyond Jeanne to her mother. Of course, Martha Le Bon knew about Blanche. "Martha, are there any spare keys to her bedroom door?"

There was no expression on the flat, peasantlike face. "Not

a spare key in the house, Miss Evelyn, savin' to the front and back an' the old stable block where they keep the gardenin' things. But you've no need to upset yourself, take it from me. I was up in Miss Blanche's room not more'n half an hour since, takin' her her jug of water for the night. She was half asleep then. Must have laid down on her bed and dropped off without turnin' off her light. Wouldn't be the first time she's gone an' done that."

"Are you sure she was all right?"

"Right as rain, miss. Sittin' brushin' her hair, she was."

"She hadn't been drinking?"

"Drinking, miss?"

Evelyn exchanged glances with Jeanne.

"Come off it, Martha, you know what I mean. You don't have to pretend. I saw her drunk the first night I got here, and my aunt Julia told me that she is an alcoholic." Martha just went on staring at her. "Her door was locked that night. That's why I'm so sure something's wrong now."

"You're making a mistake, miss."

"Can you be sure that she wasn't upset when you saw her? That there wasn't a bottle in her room?"

"If there was, then I'd have seen it. And gone and told Mrs. de Corbiere or Mrs. Tregeale." She gave a rough nod of the head toward Jeanne. "You'll have to excuse us, Miss Evelyn, we've got Mrs. Tregeale's guest to see to." Jeanne went ahead and her mother followed. "The Missus won't like it if his room's not ready, an' it's gone midnight now. They won't be downstairs talkin' much longer." She went on up the stairs.

In the pitch blackness, Blanche groaned and rolled over onto her back, holding her throbbing head with both hands. The light had been on, hadn't it, when she'd taken that last drink? Why was it out now, why was the whole room in darkness? She didn't remember turning it off herself . . . had someone else done it for her? But how could they, when the door was locked from the inside? She remembered locking it, she remembered turning the key and then staring at that hollow-eyed, tear-stained face that bore no resemblance to her own, in the mirror, and then unscrewing the top of the whisky bottle, and drinking, drinking . . .

She reached out a hand and found the switch to her bedside lamp. She pulled herself up and leaned against the carved wooden bedhead. She glanced down at the floor and saw the empty bottle, lying on its side, the spilled whisky a dark stain on the carpet. She stared at it. She remembered falling over and knocking it down, so that half of it had wasted . . . Water. Water. Her mouth was dry. Her lips felt cracked. She looked for the jug. There it was, lying near the empty bottle, itself empty on the floor. So she had knocked that over, too.

Wincing with the pain over her eyes, she groped her way out of bed and felt for her dressing gown. Then she unlocked the door and went out, unsteadily, holding her hands against the walls. She felt dizzy. She stopped, and screwed up her eyes . . . Why did they hurt so much? Halfway along the landing she hesitated, hearing the sound of voices. Steadying herself against the wall, she looked back. At the other end of the long corridor she could see a light from beneath the door of one of the empty rooms. She rubbed her eyes again. The light was still there. Slowly, holding on to pieces of furniture as she went, she made her way toward the light, and the sound of the voices.

They were hushed voices, but voices that held anger. She could not hear what they were saying. As she came closer to the door of the room, her elbow brushed against the small table and sent the vase on top of it crashing to the ground. Falling to her knees, she tried to gather up the pieces with shaking hands. When she looked up, the light beneath the door had disappeared and the voices were silent.

She blinked. She rubbed her eyes again. Had she imagined she had seen the light and heard the voices? Had she imagined it as she imagined so many things?

Evelyn. Where was Evelyn? She groped her way back along the wall and fell against Evelyn's bedroom door. She turned the handle and stumbled inside, falling over a footstool.

A light suddenly came on, then she heard the sound of Evelyn's startled voice.

"Blanche!" She leaped out of bed and knelt on the floor beside her. "Blanche, what is it? Are you ill?"

"No, no. I'm all right . . . but I . . . I saw a light . . . voices . . ."

"Blanche, come and sit down." She pushed back the curtain of dark hair from the strained, pale face, and her heart sank. She could smell the traces of whisky on her breath. "Have you been drinking?"

"My water . . . my jug of water . . . it's all spilled, it's all over the floor . . ."

"Blanche . . . what happened tonight? Before I went to bed I knocked on your door because your light was still on . . . but you didn't answer. I kept banging on the door but you didn't hear me. Blanche, are you listening to me? I went back downstairs to see if I could find a spare key, and when I came up again your light was out."

Blanche stared into space.

"I don't remember . . ."

Evelyn got up and poured her some water from her own jug. "Here, drink this. Blanche, can't you remember anything? Did Martha bring you up a tray? *Did she bring you whisky?*"

Blanche turned her head and gazed at Evelyn with heavy-lidded eyes.

"I can't remember . . . just the light, just now . . . and the voices." She put her head in her hands. "Did I imagine that, too?"

"What light? What voices?"

"The light under the door . . . in the empty room at the end of the passage . . . they were talking. Arguing. I couldn't hear what they were saying . . ." She swigged down the rest of the water. "But I couldn't have seen it, could I? No one's used that room for years."

Suddenly, Evelyn understood what she meant.

"You mean the big guest room down the corridor, the room next to the room that used to belong to your father?"

Slowly, Blanche nodded.

"There is someone in there. Yes, he came tonight, not long after dinner. He's stopping here while he's on the island. His family left here, a long time ago; they used to know you."

Evelyn got to her feet and tried to help Blanche up. Somehow, she had to get her back to her room without waking anybody. For everyone's sake, she had to cover up what was going on, at least while Richard Mahone was a guest in the house.

When they reached Blanche's room she helped her back into bed and covered her with the blankets and eiderdown. She knelt and picked up the fallen water jug. Then her eyes fell on the empty bottle, lying on its side, half hidden by the frilled valance on the bed. As she leaned over to pick it up, she felt the damp patch on the carpet where the liquid had soaked through. She touched it, then smelled the tips of her fingers.

There was no mistake about it, it was whisky, not water. But how had Blanche got hold of the bottle, if Martha Le Bon had been telling the truth? True, the cabinet where the spirits were kept in the dining room downstairs was never locked; she remembered only too clearly what Julia had told her. But if Blanche had helped herself from there, when could she have done it? She had gone upstairs to bed before anyone else, soon after the dinner guests had left, and when Evelyn had seen the light beneath her door she must have still been inside, as the door was locked. And, if she wasn't drunk then, why had she never answered when Evelyn had called out to her?

Slowly, Evelyn got to her feet and glanced at the figure in the bed. She was asleep now, her dark, glossy hair stretched out across the whiteness of the pillow.

For a moment Evelyn stood there looking down at her. Then she turned off the bedside lamp and went quietly out.

She hesitated outside the door of her own bedroom, looking down at the empty whisky bottle in her hand. Then she closed her door softly and went on down the stairs.

When she reached the bottom she paused and listened. The whole house was silent, except for the ticking of the clocks. Going into the dining room, she felt her way inside and closed the door behind her before turning on one of the lights.

The spirits cabinet was on the other side of the room. She went to it and opened it, and her eyes moved quickly over the assortment of bottles inside. Then they halted, fastened on a single bottle of whisky that bore the words *Special Reserve*. She remembered that there had been two bottles left in the cabinet before dinner, when she'd come into the room and seen Etienne, one of the servants, taking sherry from the cabinet for her grandmother's guests. The distinctive label, black and bright red, had for some reason stuck in her mind. Everyone had drunk wine with their dinner, and only port and brandy had been served afterward, with the coffee. Therefore it stood to reason that there should still be two bottles of the special reserve whisky left in the cabinet now, unless one of them had been removed after the guests had gone, by someone in the house. And that someone could only have been Blanche.

The only question remaining in Evelyn's mind was, When? Blanche had been the first to go upstairs when the guests had left, and if she'd come back down again, Evelyn would have seen her. Except . . . if she'd come down to the dining room and taken the whisky back upstairs during the few minutes that Evelyn had been out of the house, when she'd caught sight of Richard Mahone.

Why had Blanche done it? She'd seemed so normal, happy, during the whole of the evening; vibrant, even. Laughing, talking gaily to the Tostains and Philip Le Haan. What could possibly have happened in the space of an hour, between the time when everyone had left and the time that Evelyn had gone back upstairs and found her locked inside her room? She could not even begin to guess.

It was a question only Blanche could answer and Evelyn knew that it would be useless to ask her. Because the answer would be the same answer she'd given her tonight. "*I can't remember . . .*"

14

The next morning she overslept. When she got downstairs, breakfast was half over and Richard Mahone had already gone back into St. Helier to collect his luggage from the hotel. There was no sign of Blanche. Only her grandmother and Julia were seated at the long table. They both looked up at her.

"Well, so here you are." Gone was the smiling, animated face of last night, when she'd talked and laughed with the son of her old girlhood friend. "An hour and a half late to the table. Well. You certainly don't do things by halves, do you?" She paused to sip her tea. "You might at least make the effort to get down here on time when we have a guest staying in the house."

Evelyn closed the door behind her.

"I'm sorry. It wasn't intentional. I don't usually oversleep." She held up the empty whisky bottle that she'd found in Blanche's room last night. "But I didn't get to bed till this morning. Because of this."

"Where did you get that?"

"From Blanche's bedroom."

Frederica Tregeale put a hand to her forehead. Julia's face showed nothing, not even surprise.

"She's started drinking again."

"You already knew that, didn't you? Julia told me so, the

149

first night I got here, when her crying and whimpering woke me up and I got out of bed to see what was the matter. She said that you wouldn't lock the spirits away because you thought Blanche should learn to have the strength to resist them. Well, that hasn't done her much good, has it?''

"Give the bottle to me."

Evelyn did as she was told. "When I went up to bed last night there was a light showing under her door, but it was locked from the inside. That scared me. I went back downstairs to ask Martha if she had a spare key, but she said she didn't. I couldn't tell you. You were still talking to Richard Mahone, and I knew he'd be the last person you'd want knowing. I went back to my own room and tried to sleep. Then, a couple of hours later, Blanche came staggering in and woke me." She ran a hand through her hair in her emotion. "I could tell by her breath that she'd been drinking again. When I helped her back to her own room, I saw her water jug and this whisky bottle, lying on the floor, both empty. She must have knocked them over herself by accident . . . and thank God she did! Most of what was in here was spilled out onto the floor. I can't even bear to think what state she'd have been in if she'd managed to drink the whole lot!''

Frederica heaved herself up from her chair.

"Julia. Tell Etienne to bring me the key to the spirits cabinet. From now on it will be kept locked . . . and the key will stay with me, in my handbag. *My God!*" She gripped the edge of the table so hard that her knuckles turned white. "I might have known she couldn't stay sober. I might have guessed that as soon as my back was turned she'd go running back to the bottle. God above knows why she does it . . . I doubt if she even knows herself. Maybe what Julia said is right, that she can't face the fact that she isn't young anymore. I don't know . . ." Wearily, she rubbed her eyes. "I find it almost impossible to believe that any woman could turn to drink because of something like that."

"It's true, Mother. You know it's true!"

"If you'd locked the spirits up when she first started drinking she wouldn't be suffering now!"

Julia sprang up, furiously.

"Blanche suffering? Well, that takes the cake! Are you trying to blame us because she's a bloody drunk?''

"*Julia!*"

"I'm sorry, Mother. But I can't stay and listen to this!" She went out, slamming the door behind her. Her footsteps echoed, then died away.

For a long moment they looked at each other. Then Frederica spoke at last into the awkward silence.

"You must forgive Julia . . . but her anger comes from her concern for me. She knows what a strain Blanche's drinking has put me under, more so because I feel that somehow I'm to blame, that in some way I've failed in the way I brought her up . . . and Julia hates to see me upset this way. I've always been much closer to her than I ever was to Blanche. She was always her father's girl."

"Maybe that's part of the reason she started drinking in the first place. Because she felt that you were rejecting her for Julia . . . sibling rivalry. Maybe this is the only way she has to get your attention." She hesitated, trying to choose her words with care. "I'm not judging you. I'm not saying you're to blame, please don't think that. I don't have any right to. I've made too many mistakes of my own to criticize anyone else for theirs. But I feel very close to Blanche. I care about her more than I care about anything else. When there was nobody else and I found myself all alone, her letters were the only thing that kept me going, and I can't bear to see her like this, destroying herself. I realize you don't want anyone else to find out that she drinks, but for her own sake and your own peace of mind, don't you think that she ought to have some kind of help? A doctor who can find out what's wrong?"

"I've already thought about that, yes. But I decided against it. I wonder if it would really do any good. After all, consider this. When all's said and done, the only person who can help Blanche is herself. If she doesn't want to get better, no doctor and no treatment on earth will make her."

"So you're just going to go on doing nothing . . . except to turn a blind eye?"

"That isn't true, Evelyn. And you know it. I've done everything in my power to stop her drinking, all to no avail. I put her on trust not to touch the spirits cabinet, and she's broken her word to me. I'd hoped that it wouldn't come to this, locking up everything as if we had a thief in the house, but after last night I can see I have no choice."

Evelyn nodded, slowly.

"If you went upstairs and talked to her, I'm sure that would mean more to her than anything."

"Yes, perhaps you're right." She came over to where Evelyn stood and paused. "Perhaps I should have done it a long time ago . . . then maybe none of this would ever have happened." She opened the door. "By the way, you made a great impression on the Tostains last night. And so did the paintings you brought with you from London." She spoke haltingly, almost with difficulty, as if praising someone was a thing she had never been used to. "When I saw them for myself, I must admit that they impressed me, too. I hadn't realized how talented you are."

"Thank you."

Frederica could not quite smile at her. "I'll be going up, then." Another pause. Another moment of awkwardness. "Richard has gone back into St. Helier to collect his luggage from the hotel. He probably won't return for some time. But when he does, please don't mention any of this business about Blanche. I'd hate him to know . . ."

"No, of course not. I wouldn't dream of it."

When her grandmother had gone, Jeanne came looking for her.

"Oh, there you are! There's been a phone call for you. Louis Tostain rang from the art gallery in St. Helier and asked if you'd ring him back. He said something about one of his father's canvases being damaged in the consignment from Paris. They thought you might be able to help."

Louis Tostain. She had enjoyed talking to him and his father last night. And if she went into St. Helier to see him, there was the possibility of running into Richard Mahone.

Blanche's problems, Julia's hostility, the scene with her grandmother, had all built inside her and unsettled and upset her. She felt she needed to get away.

"Yes, of course. I'll telephone back right now."

"Father would pay you, of course," Louis Tostain said, watching her as she stood there, head to one side, examining the canvas with an expert eye. "And of course the full going rate. Not many of the paintings we buy need this kind of detailed attention, but Father was very taken with it and he thought it was a good bargain. A small dealer, in a tiny studio gallery just off the Rue de Boulogne . . . do you know Paris very well yourself?"

"Hardly at all." Paris. Just a name to her, a memory that hurt. She recalled, too vividly for her own peace of mind, how she'd felt that day when Jack Neville had told her he was going there with his wife. Resolutely, she made her mind go on. "I'd love to go there, of course . . . no doubt anyone could spend months on end, just strolling around, discovering new things. There must be so much unknown talent in those little back-street studios."

"Talking of talent, your own work shows a great deal of talent. Are you working on anything now?"

She made herself smile. The unpleasant scene with her grandmother had left her nerves frayed and raw. But she had to act normally, as if nothing had happened.

"I'm afraid the country air has made me temporarily idle. It's not like me usually. I've been meaning to start painting again almost since the day I got here. Of course, it's taken some time to turn the old tower into a working studio . . . it was so full of dust and cobwebs I was beginning to think we'd never finish cleaning it out."

"That was a truly brilliant idea of your grandmother's, suggesting you make a studio up there. Have you got all the equipment you need?"

Evelyn went on studying the painting to avoid his eyes. He was so nice, so polite, so kind. But her instincts told her that his interest in her went beyond her painting, and she didn't want that. Her life was far too unsettled and complicated already, even if he'd been her type, even if she'd managed to get Jack Neville out of her system.

"Yes, I have. I brought my own things with me from London. And there was already an old table up there, which Jeanne and I scrubbed down, and a big cupboard where I can store most of my things." She walked away from him and began to look around the picture-covered walls. "Of course, I was worried that the damp up there might be a problem, but I think that's just because there's never been any proper heating in the building. But they've managed to dig out a couple of oil stoves that I can use, and when they've been cleaned up the studio should be ready for me in a day or two."

"I'm looking forward to seeing it," he said, a little too eagerly for comfort.

Nervously, Evelyn smiled. She made a pretense of looking at her watch.

"Is that the time? Really, I ought to be going. I still have some shopping to do."

Outside in the street, she stood for a moment to get her breath. Then she crossed the square and made her way toward La Riche department store. She needed some face powder, a new lipstick, and some perfume as a present for Blanche. But just as she'd selected the goods and handed them to the salesgirl behind the counter, a hand appeared over her shoulder holding a five-pound note.

"I'll pay for those," said Richard Mahone.

She spun round, startled, too surprised to see him to protest.

"You're the last person in the world I expected to see in here!"

He smiled. "And you're the last person in the world I expected to see buying cosmetics." He took his change from the salesgirl and handed Evelyn the package. "You're far too beautiful as you are to need any artificial embellishment."

"Thank you." They began to walk away from the counter side by side.

"Oh, don't thank me . . . I've got nothing to do with it!" There was a short pause. They smiled at each other.

"I thought you'd be back at the house by now. Did you pick up your luggage?"

"First thing this morning. But there were one or two things I wanted to do in town and I rather fancied having a look around the place, after everything my mother told me about the island." As they went out into the street again he stopped and looked around him. "I wonder if it's changed much since she knew it? I suppose it must have done. Most places do, if you go away and come back again."

"Will you take a ride out to see the house where she lived when the family lived here?"

He shrugged, seeming almost evasive. "I'd like to see it, certainly. But your grandmother was telling me that strangers live there now . . . I mean, complete strangers, not even islanders. Some English tax exile and his American wife. I shouldn't think they'd appreciate it if I just turned up and expected them to give me a guided tour. Foreigners hardly ever do."

"They're hardly foreigners!"

"Your grandmother's description of them, not mine."

She nodded in understanding.

"Yes, I can imagine."

"So . . ." he checked his wristwatch. "Time's getting on . . . almost one o'clock. How about us having a spot of lunch together somewhere or other? Jean-Louis was telling me that there's a marvelous place where they serve French food just over on the other side of the square. Will you join me and make my day?"

It was the second time he'd surprised her.

"Well, I . . . yes, I'd love to. But we'll both be expected back at the house for lunch."

"All taken care of. When I sent Jean-Louis back in the car with my luggage, I told him to give Mrs. Tregeale a message from me—that I'd be having lunch in town today. All I have to do now is find a telephone somewhere and ring through to tell her that you're joining me. There's bound to be a phone booth in the restaurant." He winked at her and she started to laugh, softly. "Well, how about it?"

"If it's a choice between eating with my grandmother and Aunt Julia or eating with you, then there's only one answer I can give. Yes, thank you. I accept!"

"I hope that was meant to be a compliment."

"It certainly wasn't meant to be an insult." She had realized several minutes ago that he was flirting with her, and she was surprised to find that she was enjoying it. "One condition, though."

"Anything!"

"You make the telephone call to my grandmother."

Blanche pulled back the net curtains and leaned forlornly against the window, staring out into the deserted courtyard and beyond it to the gardens. A strong wind was coming up now, and the sun had vanished behind the clouds. She could just glimpse the faint steely glimmer of the sea beyond the distant line of the trees, and she imagined how the fast-moving tide would be rushing into the bay, cutting off the path back to the safety of the clifftops, crashing against the craggy boulders and rocks, drenching them with its wild, foaming spray. She remembered walking there, long ago, arm in arm with her beloved father, laughing together, sharing jokes, taking photographs with the old box camera, spreading their picnic lunch on a tablecloth beneath the trees. She remembered how they'd played games, how one of them would have brought a ball to play catch and piggy-in-the-middle with Julia and her brother Gilbert. Gilbert. Gilbert. Whom she'd loved and missed very much.

Julia had not often joined them, she remembered. Julia, who had always sat apart, a book laid open on her lap, sitting reading while the three of them played and shrieked with laughter.

She pulled the curtain back further. There in the distance she could see the gardeners, down on their hands and knees, weeding the vegetable patches, going back every now and then to fill the wheelbarrow with grass clumps and leaves. Outside the old stable block, long converted into a garage, she could see Jean-Louis and Etienne, sleeves rolled up, washing and polishing the cars.

Slowly, she came away from the window and began to look about the room, the room that had once been her father's, the only room in the great, brooding house where she felt a flicker of her old happiness. She walked over to his bed and sat down on it, then stretched out her hand and touched the pillow. If only she could bring him back. If only he were here now. If only he hadn't died and left her all alone. Alone in the house she'd grown to hate; alone with Julia, alone with her mother, the mother who had always seemed curiously distant from her, growing further and further away as each year went by. Only Evelyn's sudden appearance had made life bearable again.

She had a wild longing to hear Evelyn's music again, the kind of music her father had loved and played with her and Gilbert on his own windup gramophone. The music her mother and sister disliked and disapproved of. Another wedge between them.

Her head still ached dully from last night. Only traces of memory remained of the evening. Evelyn's bright, happy laughter. Philip Le Haan's smile. Then she had said goodnight and come up here. She could recall half undressing, then sitting down in front of the mirror to brush out her hair. The rest of what happened was only a blur. Julia coming into the room—had that been a dream or had it really happened? Sighing, she sat down on her bed and buried her face in her hands.

Then someone knocked on her door.

"Blanche?"

It was her mother's voice and immediately her whole body stiffened. She got up as Frederica came into the room.

"How are you feeling now?"

"Tired. My headache's worse. I think I'll draw the curtains again and lie down."

"Do you really think that will do any good?"

"I'll take some more aspirin."

"Swallowing tablets isn't the answer to the problem, either. In your heart I think you know that too."

Blanche stared at her mother.

"I haven't a problem. All I want to do is lie down. I'm tired, I didn't sleep well last night."

"Blanche . . . I know what happened. Evelyn told me. You've started stealing from the spirits cabinet again, and I won't stand by and watch you destroy yourself. I don't know why you do it . . . I've never understood. I know it's more my fault than yours because in the beginning I believed that ignoring it would somehow make it go away. I suppose that was incredibly naive of me." She went on, each word more difficult to say than the last. "I've thought about this a great deal, and about what I can do to help you. Apart from keeping the spirits locked up so you can't touch them, there isn't very much." She hesitated. "Blanche, I think you should see a doctor."

Blanche's blue eyes suddenly came alive with something like rage.

"This is Julia's doing, isn't it? It's not your idea at all! She wants to get rid of me because she hates me! She always has, ever since we were children." Her voice grew louder and more unsteady. "She'd love to find some doctor who'd say I was losing my mind, and have me locked up in one of those places—what do they call them? Sanatoriums. Sanatorium my eye! That's just a polite word for the bloody madhouse!"

"Blanche!"

"Well, I won't see a doctor! I won't let anyone lock me up and throw away the key! I won't, do you hear me?" Tears started to run down her cheeks. "If Daddy were here, he'd stop you! He'd see through your little game!"

"Blanche, all this is just in your mind." Frederica came toward her, but Blanche recoiled. "Please, Blanche . . . all I want to do is help you."

"Don't touch me! Don't come near me! I don't need you!" The tears ran down into her mouth and she dashed them away. "You never loved me. Nobody ever loved me except Daddy and Gilbert . . . and they're both gone."

Before Frederica could do or say anything more, there was a rap on the door and then Martha's voice.

"Mrs. Tregeale? Are you in there, ma'am? Telephone."

There was a sudden silence, broken only by the sound of Blanche's loud, labored breathing.

"Coming, Martha. Tell whoever it is to hold the line." She moved away, slowly. "Blanche . . . please. Try to pull yourself together. We have an unexpected guest staying in the house who arrived last night . . . the son of an old friend. I don't want any scenes or to find you drunk while he's here. I beg of you." She turned and went out of the room. Blanche stood staring at the door long after she was gone.

Liar. Hypocrite. Didn't give a damn. Never had, never would. Julia was her favorite, always had been, always would be. Julia had told her so, and she had always seen it for herself. Julia had told her all the things her mother had said about her, behind her back. Julia always enjoyed telling her the truth, especially if it hurt. Truth never hurts the teller, and that was a saying that was in itself a truth. Her mother had never loved her. Julia said so and she knew that it was true.

But nobody was going to send her away, not ever. She wouldn't let them. Not to one of those big, white clinical buildings with their long, shiny corridors that smelled of disinfectant and rooms like little cells with thick, thick doors that were always kept locked, night and day. Never, never. She'd kill herself sooner.

She'd tell Julia that, too.

"I know what you're trying to do to me. And it won't work."

Her sister glanced up, disdainfully, from the accounts ledger that lay open on the library table in front of her.

"Well, well. So you're back on your feet at last. Slept off the bottle of special reserve that you drank yourself senseless with last night?"

"I'm as sober as you are!"

"That certainly makes a change!"

"It was you who sent Mother upstairs to see me, wasn't it? All this talk about getting me to see a doctor is your idea!"

The corners of Julia's thin lips curled upward in a sneer. "Your mind must still be addled from all that booze, sister dearest. What you do is of no interest to me whatsoever. I couldn't care less if you drink yourself silly seven nights a week. Or whether you see a doctor or not." She looked down again to the long columns of figures in the ledger. "As far as I'm concerned, you're a hopeless cause."

Her calmness only enraged Blanche further.

"You sly bitch! Do you think I believe that? Mother would never have suggested the idea unless you put it into her head first! You want to get rid of me, don't you? You want to get me locked up in one of those places for crazy people that you told me about!"

Julia's hard eyes narrowed to slits in her face.

"Whether you want it or not, Mother will have her way in the end. And when the time comes, I promise you, I'll be right behind her backing her to the hilt!"

Something in Blanche suddenly pulled taut, then snapped. Through a pounding, hot mist that made her head swim round and round, she felt herself rushing toward her tormentor at the table. Then she grasped Julia by her clothes and shook her, violently.

"I hate you! I hate you, do you hear me? You'll never send me away from here. *Never.* This was Daddy's house and I'm never going to be made to leave it!" She thrust her backward into her chair with so much force that it almost overturned. Then she burst into tears and ran out, fighting down the loud sobs of impotence and rage. Outside, she leaned for a moment against the closed doors, her eyes shut. Desperately, she longed for a drink. Any drink. Anything to blot out that sneering, self-righteous face, the face she hated and feared. She ran out into the corridor and along it to the dining room. Empty. Too late for any of the servants to still be cleaning. Too early for them to come and set the table for dinner. She closed the door behind her and went over to the cabinet where her mother kept the spirits.

She stood there for what seemed a long while, staring at it. Then she knelt and opened it.

Her hand stretched out, fingers shaking, toward the nearest bottle. Beads of sweat stood out on her forehead. Then she heard the sound of voices and laughter in the hall, and she shut it quickly and staggered to her feet again just seconds before the door came open and Evelyn, followed by a young man, stood there on the threshold of the room.

"Blanche! Come and meet somebody!" She turned to the young man behind her and he smiled. "This is Richard Mahone."

"Hello!"

"I'm pleased to meet you." Nervously, she came over and they shook hands. "I'm sorry I didn't manage to see you at breakfast. I'm afraid I—I overslept."

"So did I," Evelyn said. Blanche noticed how her eyes were sparkling as she looked at her companion. "And then Jeanne came and told me that I'd had a phone call from Louis Tostain and he wanted me to drop by his father's gallery in St. Helier. I'd just left him and gone into La Riche for one or two things, and banged right into Richard. We had lunch together at . . . what was the name of the restaurant?"

"La Rozel."

"We had lunch there, instead of coming all the way back. Blanche, the food was exquisite. The chef was French. You and I must have a day shopping in St. Helier next week, and I'll treat you. You'll love it!"

The palms of Blanche's hands were sticky with perspiration. She made herself smile.

"You must be Mother's special guest who arrived last night. I'm sorry I wasn't up to meet you."

"My fault." He smiled his charming smile. "I had no right to turn up on your doorstep at that hour. Luckily, everyone seems to have forgiven me."

"Are you staying here long?"

"I'll go when your mother wants to throw me out!" They all laughed. "Well. I'd better go upstairs and get changed. Won't do to come downstairs again with a creased dinner jacket."

"We'll come too," Evelyn said brightly. "Oh, that reminds me, Blanche. I've brought something back for you."

"Evelyn, you shouldn't have."

"What's wrong? Don't you like it?"

"Well, yes, I . . . of course I like it." She looked down at the bottle of perfume in her hands. "But it's so expensive, I feel guilty even accepting it."

"Oh, nonsense. I wanted to buy you something that I knew you'd like. If you prefer another brand don't feel afraid to say so. I can change it next time I'm in St. Helier."

"No! No, I love this. Who wouldn't love Chanel?"

"That's what I thought." Evelyn sat down and eased off her high heels. "It felt wonderful today, getting out, going around the shops and the department store. Not quite like London, but then the town has a charm all its own, something I never expected to find, really." She looked down at her hands. "Right up almost until today, I felt homesick. Silly, isn't it? Everything that happened to me in London, everything I was running away from, didn't seem to make any difference. I missed it. The traffic, the shops, the people. All the familiar sights and buildings. Theaters. The rush hour . . . most of all I missed Jack. Losing him has been harder for me to accept than anything else. I tried to stop myself thinking about him, reminding myself that everything between him and me was done and finished with. That I'd never see him or hear from him ever again. I fought with myself. I tried to push him out of my mind. I tried to come to terms with the fact that if he'd really cared about me, he wouldn't have let them keep us apart. And up till now I'd failed." She looked over at Blanche. "Until today. Do you know that while we were having lunch together, I actually forgot about Jack . . . I never thought of him once. And when I did, on the way home, it didn't hurt anymore. It really didn't hurt."

"You're falling for him, aren't you? I can see it coming a mile off."

Evelyn laughed.

"Oh, it's too soon. We only met yesterday!"

"How long did it take you to fall for Jack Neville?"

Evelyn nodded, slowly, and smiled.

"Point taken. My hands started shaking the first time I set eyes on him. Then the rest of me followed!"

"Does he intend to stay in Jersey long?"

"He didn't say exactly what his plans were. Only that he wasn't in any rush to get back to where he came from. Like everyone else around here except grandmother and Julia, he thinks a war with Germany is pretty well inevitable, and if that does happen, it'd be safer for him to stay here than go back to France."

"But the Germans wouldn't invade France—they couldn't. They'd never cross the Maginot Line."

"That's not what Richard thinks. Hitler's got the entire population worked up to fever pitch, feeding them with talk about a new German empire in Eastern Europe and Russia, controlled by a 'master race,' and saying that Germany didn't really lose the war in 1918, but that they were betrayed. He's playing on the people's sense of injustice over the terms of the Treaty of Versailles, and everything he's done since he rose to power has got full popular support—rearmament, the reoccupation of the Rhineland and annexation of Austria. Christ knows where it'll all end! Richard bought three editions of all the main newspapers today after we'd had lunch, just to see if there'd been any further developments."

"I hope Mother doesn't get to see them."

"Whether she does or not, she just can't go on pretending that nothing's happening in the outside world."

"She's been doing that ever since I can remember. It was one of the things that used to irritate Daddy so much." Blanche went over to the window and stared out into the courtyard below. "Evelyn . . ."

"What is it?"

A moment's silence and hesitation before she spoke again.

"Evelyn . . . what happened to me last night? Did I—did I drink too much?"

Evelyn paused, fighting to find the right words.

"You'd had some whisky . . . just a drop. Enough to make you giddy. I don't know where the bottle came from, but you'd knocked it over onto the carpet and most of what had been in it spilled out."

Blanche put a hand to her head.

"I don't remember . . . I don't remember touching any whisky."

Evelyn put an arm around her.

"Did something upset you before you went to bed? Did anything happen?"

"No, I . . . I don't think so. As I said, I can't really remember." She grasped Evelyn's hand and squeezed it so tightly that it hurt. "Mother came up after you left. She wants me to see a doctor, but I won't, Evelyn. I won't do it. It's just an excuse, an excuse to get me sent away. Don't let them send me away to one of those places . . . please . . . don't let them do it."

"But a doctor could help you, make you understand why you have to keep drinking. It's only when you find the answer to that, that you can help yourself to stop."

Blanche stared at her.

"I thought you were on my side."

"I am on your side. I care about what happens to you. About what you're doing to yourself. Blanche, you have to face it sooner or later. You have a problem with drinking and you're the only person on this earth who can do anything about it."

"Julia told you that, didn't she? She told you I was a drunk!"

A long moment of silence.

"She didn't have to tell me anything. I saw it on the first night I came here, for myself."

Blanche broke away from the shelter of her arm, and covered her face with her hands.

"I didn't have too much to drink . . . just a couple of snorts, that's all. Brandy, to settle my stomach and help me to sleep. I can't sleep without it, you see. Not for a long time. But I can't take it. It makes me dizzy, then sick . . . and then I pass out."

Evelyn suddenly remembered her grandmother's words. *The only person who can help Blanche is herself.* If she refused to admit that she couldn't stop drinking once she started, how could any of them hope to help her stop? And there was no time to talk now.

"Blanche . . . if you have trouble getting to sleep, try something else. Sleeping tablets, a glass of hot milk . . . the doctor will prescribe something for you."

Blanche hung her head.

"Yes . . . yes . . . that's what I'll do. But I don't have to see him, do I? You could ring him up and say what's wrong. Then you could collect the prescription from him when you go into St. Helier." She glanced up, with still-bloodshot eyes. "You'd do that for me, wouldn't you? Please, Evelyn . . ."

Evelyn patted her hand.

"Yes, of course I will. You know I'd do anything to help you."

• • •

Back in her own room, Blanche stared from the window into the darkness outside. It was growing darker sooner now, each evening drawing in closer than the one before, and pulling the curtain aside she could see her own reflection in the glass.

One moment it was the reflection. The next, her sister's appeared behind it in the open doorway.

"You're not dressed for dinner. Remember we have a guest." Julia came inside and closed the door behind her, then leaned against it. "You didn't show yourself at breakfast. If you don't come down for dinner, he'll begin to think that something strange is going on."

"He'd be right, wouldn't he?"

"And what exactly do you mean by that?"

Blanche turned away from the window and faced her.

"You know very well what I mean. What do you want, Julia? What have you come here for?" She felt anger rising in her. "And next time, knock first, will you? This is my room. *My* room. The only place in this damned house that I have any privacy!"

"The only place where you can get drunk without anyone finding out!"

"Get out!"

"Mother sent me to tell you something and I won't go until I've said it. She's decided to keep the spirits cabinet locked, at least while Richard's here. You've brought enough shame on the family in the past, she doesn't intend to let you bring any more on us by getting drunk and letting him see what you really are. And she told me to warn you about something else, too. No more vivid lipstick. Do you understand?"

Blanche laughed, bitterly.

"You can't bear it, can you? Even now. Even when between you you've done everything in your power to destroy me? To destroy what I am, what I once was. You've always hated me, haven't you, Julia? Because Daddy loved me best . . . because I was always prettier than you . . ."

Julia's eyes narrowed. The truth still hurt. But what hurt and angered her even more was that Blanche, weak, drunkard Blanche, could still see through her.

She looked past her sister to the big photograph of their father that stood on the mantelpiece, Blanche on one knee with her arms around his neck; Gilbert on the other. There was no sign of her anywhere in the picture, and that was the way it had always been. Julia, serious, solemn, reserved Julia, always the odd one out. She had adored him. Longed for his love, longed for his attention, longed for him to sweep her up into his arms the way he did Blanche and hug her to him. But he never did. She recalled, bitterly, the birthdays and Christmases, when he'd given Blanche the gifts that she herself had longed for. The china dolls, the pretty dresses, the dainty satin shoes with bows. For her the initialed pen case, the leather satchel, the fitted writing box. Even when he was dead, Blanche was still the one who attracted everyone's attention.

She remembered the parties and the garden fetes and the charity balls, where the moment her sister came in sight, everybody would turn to stare at her, because she was so beautiful. She remembered the young men crowding round, begging her for the next dance, clamoring for her attention, while Julia had stood forgotten and alone. Even now, despite the misery of her life, despite her lapses into drunkenness, Blanche was still striking. It was the unfairness of it all that dug into her as deeply as a knife edge. Oh, God, how she hated her!

"I don't have time to stand here and argue with you, Blanche," she said coldly. "Just remember what Mother said. And if you're thinking of sneaking down to the wine cellar after everyone has gone to bed, forget it. Martha's been instructed to lock it up and hide the key." She turned and went out.

"You're a naughty boy, Richard. I see you've been buying newspapers in St. Helier."

Across the table, Blanche and Evelyn exchanged glances.

"Evelyn did mention that you'd stopped having them delivered to the house, yes. But I like to keep abreast of what's happening in the wicked world outside, I must admit."

"If it's factual reporting that you're looking for, you won't find it in any of the papers you bought today. Truth is the last thing their editors are concerned with."

"You mean about the war?"

"As far as I am aware, there is no war. Only scaremongering nonsense put about by those who ought to know better."

He smiled his easy smile.

"Of course, you're quite right. They have to exaggerate and frighten us half to death—after all, that's what sells more newspapers. Even if there is a war with Germany nobody's going to bother about us. We're far too insignificant."

"Do you really believe that?" Blanche said, ignoring the warning look from her mother at the far end of the table. "Philip Le Haan thinks that if war does happen—and he thinks some kind of confrontation is inevitable—then we'll be right in the middle of it."

"Lawyers are always pessimistic," Julia de Corbiere said, coldly. "And Philip more than most."

"That isn't true!"

"I don't know why you bother to invite him to the house, Mother. He irritates me and exasperates you."

"Only because he tells you things you don't want to hear!"

"Be quiet, Blanche." Frederica Tregeale turned and pulled the bell rope behind her chair. "We'll have coffee in the drawing room. Richard . . . I've got out all my old photo albums for you." She smiled at him. "It brought back many wonderful memories for me, looking at those pictures of Violette and your mother."

"I can't wait to see them. Forgive me for staring, but that necklace you're wearing, I seem to have seen it somewhere before. I've never seen anything so beautiful. Even in Cartier's windows in Paris."

"These? The Tregeale emeralds." She touched her throat with her hand. "One of my late husband's ancestors, Maria Josepha Tregeale, is wearing them in the Hoppner portrait that hangs on the stairs. That's where you've seen them."

"Of course!"

"They've been in the Tregeale family for more than 250 years—quite some time! They're passed down to the wife of every male Tregeale on marriage . . . that's when my husband gave them to me."

He went on staring at them in admiration.

"They must be very valuable. I hope you have them properly insured."

"They are extremely valuable, yes. And virtually unique. As you know, emeralds are rarely perfect. But each stone in this necklace, and the bracelet and coronet that go with them to make up the set, was selected for its purity and flawlessness of color. Of course all my jewelry is insured, my husband insisted on it. But in practice there was no necessity to do so. Crime is almost nonexistent on the island."

"I find that incredible."

"Incredible maybe, but true. This isn't London. Or Paris. The island police hardly have anything to do, other than direct the traffic. We get some petty pilfering, of course—children stealing the odd apple or two from one of the stalls in the market place, a few light-fingered foreigners who come over during the tourist season to help in the hotels or provide extra manpower with the tomato and potato crops, but that's all."

"You're very lucky over here."

"I like to think so." The servants came in to clear the table and she got to her feet. "Coffee in the drawing room, then?"

Richard Mahone smiled and came to stand beside Evelyn. "It's such a warm night, have you noticed? Even though we're nearly into the first week of September. Would you mind if we sat out on the terrace and had ours?"

"No, of course not. You can look through the albums when you come in again. We'll see you later, then." They went out of the room one by one and Evelyn followed him through the open french windows onto the terrace.

"Nobody but you could have got away with that!"

He laughed, softly.

"It seems I have a lot to thank the Sorels for, yes."

Evelyn sat down on the stone seat and he sat down beside her. "She seems almost like a different person, since you came here. It's incredible, really." She gazed out over the moonlit gardens. "When she's with you, anyway. To the rest of us she's just as sharp as she always was. Well, almost. Though I didn't think so when I first arrived, I think she has a heart somewhere or other. She just doesn't believe in showing it." She turned toward him. "But Sorel is a magic word around here these days."

"Is that the only reason you're glad I'm here?"

Despite the cool breeze, her cheeks began to burn and tingle. She looked away in front of them, to hide her confusion and conflicting emotions. The past was still too real to her, too raw. She wasn't ready to trust a man again, to confide what she felt.

"Evelyn?"

She stared ahead of her, without speaking. By the lights from the house she could see part of the distant flower beds, a statue in the grotto, the stone sundial beside the pond.

"It must seem very dull here to you in Jersey, after living in

Paris. I know it did to me when I first came from London. Have you thought any more about how long you'll stay?"

"Nowhere could be dull where you are." He reached out and lightly touched her hand. "And I don't have any plans to go back yet, no." A pause. "Tell me about your painting. Your grandmother said that you were using the old tower as a studio. If you don't have objections, I'd love to come and watch you sometime, if that won't put you off what you're doing."

"No. No, of course not. Come when you like." She tried to smile. "I want to start working on a portrait of my father; it's something that I've always longed to do, but with my job in London I just never found the time."

"Where did you work in London?"

Her heart missed a beat and began to race wildly.

"A man called Guy Pellini . . . he owned the gallery where I worked as a restorer."

"Never heard of him." He laughed. "You'll have to forgive me, I'm afraid, but I'm totally ignorant of everything to do with the art world, though I appreciate something beautiful when I see it." The touch of his skin on hers took away her breath. Quickly she drew away her hand as if he had burned it, a sudden sense of panic rising in her. He was too close, it was too soon. If only she hadn't come out here alone with him. If only she'd stayed inside . . .

"Did he really hurt you that much?"

She stared at him. "Has my grandmother been telling you my business?"

"Nobody told me anything. Except you. Nobody needed to." He took back her hand and held it tightly between the palms of his own. "I could see that someone had hurt you. Was that the real reason you left London and came here to the island? To get away from what happened, to try to bury part of your past?" She looked down at their clasped hands without answering. "That first night when you ran out of the house toward me, thinking I was somebody else . . . that was the first clue you gave me. Then there were the other little things . . . I noticed them all because I notice everything about you . . . the way you can't quite meet my eyes when I look at you and you know what I'm thinking . . . the way you just pulled away your hand, even though I know you didn't want to." He tightened his grip. "I understand how you feel, Evelyn . . . please believe me. Trust me. Whoever he was and whatever he did you ought to forget about him. Because any man who could turn away from a girl like you isn't worth wasting breath on."

Slowly, she raised her eyes to his face. She moved her free hand as if it had been frozen and put it on his, the feeling of warmth from his skin both a comfort and a delight. How good it felt to hold hands with a man again. A man she wanted, a man who she knew wanted her. And Jack Neville had gone at last, a ghost finally laid to rest.

"But . . . you don't know me. You don't know anything about me at all."

She felt his arms sliding around her waist, she felt her whole body moving toward him.

"I already know everything I need to."

Above them, overlooking the terrace, a curtain moved in the window of one of the empty bedrooms. And a pair of cold, hostile eyes watched as he kissed her.

"You didn't come back for your coffee," Frederica said, her eyes resting first on Evelyn's face and then on Richard Mahone's. "It's cold now. Do you want me to ring for some more?"

He smiled at her and went over to the silver tray.

"No; no need to bother them down in the kitchen at this time of night. The pot still feels warm." He glanced over his shoulder and winked. "Shall I pour you some, Evelyn?"

She smiled at him and nodded. Their hands touched as he handed her the cup. "Have Julia and Blanche gone on up to bed already?" She could feel her grandmother's questioning eyes resting on her, as if she knew. But how could she, how had she guessed what had happened between them?

"Blanche has. Julia went upstairs for something or other a while ago."

"It's not like Blanche to go up without saying goodnight."

"I'd have thought you'd been here long enough to realize that nothing Blanche ever does is predictable." As she spoke there was a sudden crash above them, followed by a piercing scream. They jumped to their feet both at once.

"Christ Almighty, what's that?"

"It's Blanche!" Running from the room, Evelyn fled along the corridor and up the stairs, Richard Mahone after her. Jeanne and some of the servants had rushed up from the kitchen below. A few steps from the top, Evelyn caught sight of Blanche, her face covered with white cream, trying to shake herself free from her sister's grasp.

"Blanche, for God's sake control yourself!"

"Blanche! Blanche, what is it? What's happened?" As Evelyn reached the landing, Blanche twisted herself free and ran to her.

"My face, my face! It's burning! Please, Evelyn, help me . . . my skin feels like fire!"

Evelyn looked at her. Beneath the layer of cream, her face was covered with huge, angry blotches. She grabbed her by the wrist and pulled her along the passageway to the bathroom. Then she grasped a flannel, soaked it under the cold tap, and wiped her face clean. "What is this stuff? What have you been doing to yourself?"

Blanche began to cry uncontrollably.

"I . . . I was getting ready for bed . . . I didn't have any cold cream left . . . so I went into your room to borrow some of yours." She sank onto the stool beside the wash basin, her whole body shaking. "I just took a little bit . . . only a little bit. I didn't think you'd mind . . . but as soon as I put it on my face, it started to burn."

"Blanche, it's all right. Keep still. It's all off now." She rinsed out the basin with hot water, then put in the plug. "Here . . . wash your face with ordinary soap and water . . . then I'll put some Vaseline on it. The rash will all be gone by the morning."

"Are you sure? Are you certain it will? Evelyn, I won't be scarred, will I? Not my face!"

Julia de Corbiere suddenly appeared in the doorway.

"She wouldn't tell me what was wrong . . . she just kept screaming something about her face burning. I didn't know what she was talking about."

"You could see the red blotches all over her skin, couldn't you?"

"She wouldn't let me help her. I tried to help her but she was hysterical!"

"Look . . . just go away. Please. Just go downstairs and tell them everything's all right." She handed Blanche a clean towel, then helped her back to her room. "Did you bring the jar of cold cream back here?"

"Yes." Blanche suddenly caught sight of her reflection in

the mirror. "No . . . no!" She started to scream and claw at her face. "My face . . . Evelyn . . . my face . . ."

"It's all right. Don't look. It's just a rash. You just have some sort of allergy to the perfume in the cold cream, Blanche. Stop it." She took her by the shoulders and pressed her down onto the bed. She ran back into her own room and fumbled in a drawer for a jar of Vaseline. Then she ran back again and smoothed a thick layer of it over Blanche's inflamed cheeks. "You're lucky it didn't stay on your skin for very long. There. It'll feel sticky and unpleasant, and make a mess of your pillow, but it'll get rid of that red rash." She went over to Blanche's dressing table and picked up the jar of cold cream she'd bought that morning at La Riche. Slowly, she unscrewed the top and sniffed it. A strange, sour odor that burned her nostrils and made her eyes water rose up to her, and she held it away from her face quickly.

"What is it, Evelyn? Is there something wrong with it?"

"I—I don't know. It doesn't smell like ordinary cold cream. It has a strange smell. Yet it's the same brand that I've always used." She screwed the top back on the jar. "One thing's for sure. I'm taking it back to La Riche first thing tomorrow morning and complaining to the manager." She went over and put her arm around Blanche. "Are you all right now? Shall I help you into bed or do you want to just sit here awhile? Shall I fetch you a book, or a magazine? I've got some, in my room. I bought them today when we were in St. Helier."

Blanche managed a weak smile.

"Yes, I'd like that. It's so long since I've read a magazine. Mother's never approved of women's magazines. She says they're just trivial, rubbish . . . but I like them."

"I'll fetch them for you."

Later, back in her own bedroom, Evelyn sat for a long while staring at the jar on her dressing table. Baffled. Confused. Unable to understand. Even when she'd undressed and got into bed, she found that it was impossible to sleep. Then she heard a soft tapping on the other side of her door.

"Blanche? Is that you?" She put on her bedside light and went over to the door. But when she opened it, Richard Mahone was standing there, not her aunt. "Richard!"

"*Shh!*" He put a finger to his lips. He smiled at her. "I had to see you. Can I come inside for a moment?"

"What is it?"

He slid his arms around her waist.

"I tried to sleep." A teasing note came into his voice. "I lay on my left side, I lay on my right side. I turned this way and then that. I even tried counting sheep. But you know what? I couldn't think of anything except you."

"Richard . . ." She stifled a laugh and tried to push him away. "You must go . . . my grandmother . . ."

"She told me she was hard of hearing."

"Don't you believe it! She hears just what she wants to hear. If she thought that I'd let you into my bedroom after knowing you for just two days . . ."

"Two days, two hours, two years . . . what difference does it make, Evelyn? There was something special between us, right at the beginning, you know that." The teasing note had gone from his voice and his eyes were serious now. She looked up into them, the blue-gray eyes that had reminded her so painfully of Jack Neville's that first night they'd met. But not now. "Do you really care that much what she thinks?"

"I care about how she'd make it sound . . . and she would, if she found out. She'd make me feel . . . cheap. Shameless. Easy. She'd say that I'd thrown myself at the first man who came along, just as she'd expect any daughter of my mother to do . . . the cheap nightclub singer who stole away her son! And I couldn't bear that!" She sighed. She began to pace around the room, distractedly, while he stood there. "Oh, I can't expect you to understand—how could you? She's put on an act for your benefit ever since you got here. All the smiles and charm, getting out her old albums to show you pictures of your mother—Julia, too. When I first came here all I got was a dressing down and a lecture."

He caught hold of her hand and pulled her toward him. "Evelyn, why are we even discussing them at all? They aren't important to me. I came here to meet them, yes, because they knew my family, because your grandmother used to be a special friend to my mother. I had some time on my hands, I was curious, I wanted to take a look at the island where my mother came from and see the old family home . . . that's all. But when I met you, everything changed. I couldn't just pack my bags at the end of my stay and go back to where I came from." He paused. "When I do go I want to take you."

"Richard!"

He reached out and unpinned her hair. As it fell down

around her shoulders to her waist, he wound his hands about it, and then buried his lips in the softness of her neck.

"Do you really think I'd be here if that wasn't true?"

Suddenly, she stiffened and drew away from him, her green eyes wide with fear.

"What was that? Did you hear it?" Her heart began to beat faster. "There's someone outside, on the landing. I heard the floorboards creak."

"Evelyn . . . everyone in the house is asleep . . . there's no one there!"

"I tell you I heard a noise."

Impatiently, he went over to the door and opened it several inches, and they both peered out. Somewhere a clock was ticking. The corridor was empty. The landing beyond was dark and silent.

"Satisfied?"

"I'm sure I heard someone. Footsteps."

"Maybe there's a family ghost."

"Not that I know of."

He closed the door, then turned the key in the lock. For a moment they stared at each other. It was so long since she'd been with Jack Neville, so long since she'd felt the delicious warmth of another body against hers, that she had almost forgotten what it felt like to make love with a man. She tried to speak, but no words came. She could only hold out both her hands, dumbly, like a blind woman, and wait for him to come to her.

"I want you, Evelyn," he said.

In the darkness, Blanche tossed to and fro, restlessly, murmuring, locked in fitful sleep. The dream was real, vivid, and terrifying. Sweat had broken out along her forehead in little glistening beads. Her dark hair was damp against the pillow.

They walked side by side, hand in hand. She looked up at the tall, dark, handsome man beside her, and laughed and smiled. On the other side of him she could see her brother, Gilbert, a red ball under one arm, laughing and pointing to the seagulls that circled above them ahead, near the summit of the cliffs. The sun was bright overhead and the sky was blue, like her father's eyes, and then he stooped and picked her up, and she threw her arms about his neck and kissed him. But then suddenly the sun had vanished, and she was alone there on the clifftop. She looked around her, shading her eyes, but she was all alone.

A house loomed in front of her. A tall, dark house with shuttered windows and endless stairs that echoed eerily when she stepped upon them. And then she looked up and into the cold, hostile eyes of the sister she hated and feared.

"No . . . please, no! No, Julia. Don't do it. Please, don't do it! Don't lock me in the dark again!"

There was blackness all around her, there was no way out. Frantically, she sobbed and screamed, she put out her hands and tried to feel her way in the lightless, airless room but there was no window, no escape.

She lay there on the cold, bare flagstone floor, crying, shivering, clutching her arms about her body to keep warm. Then through the unrelenting darkness, she heard her sister's whispering voice.

"He's dead. He's gone. He'll never come back now. There's only me. Me. and I mean to punish you. Punish you. Punish you . . ."

She woke, seconds later, still screaming.

Bathed in sweat, she clutched at the bedclothes to stop her hands from shaking. She ran a hand through her half wet hair. Above her, where the ceiling was, she could hear strange, unfamiliar sounds, as if somebody was walking overhead. Screwing up her eyes, she stared upward.

For a moment there was silence. Then, more softly than before, she heard the sound of footsteps once again.

She sat up in bed, rubbing her eyes. She shook her head, in case she was not awake but still dreaming. Suddenly she heard a voice, coming from somewhere up above. Then another.

She put her hands to her ears, then took them away again, but the noises above her and the voices were still there. This was not part of that hateful, haunting dream; the voices and the sounds were real.

Pushing back the bedclothes, she got to her feet and went over to the door. She opened it a few inches and pressed her ear to the crack. It made no sense. The attic did not extend as far as the bedrooms on the north side of the house . . . yet the sounds came from directly overhead.

She stood there for a few moments longer. Then, when silence fell once more, she closed the door and went to sit on the edge of her bed. Had she been dreaming after all? Surely everyone was asleep? It had all been in her imagination. Yet it had seemed real, like the dream, very real . . .

She went over to her mirror and stared into it. Her face swam, a pale oval in the semidarkness, a face shiny with Vaseline and only faint touches of the ugly, flaming rash of the night before. Timidly, she reached out her hand and touched one side of it with the tip of her finger.

It would be all right. Evelyn had said it would be all right. Evelyn was telling her the truth. Evelyn was the only one who had never lied to her.

She poured herself a glass of water from the jug and drank it down. Then she got back into bed and lay her head down on the Vaseline-stained pillow.

The house was quiet, the noises had stopped, and the voices she'd thought she heard were silent now. The nightmare had passed away, until the next time.

Fitfully, she slept.

15

Her heart missed a beat when she suddenly caught sight of him ahead of her, on his way through the hall to the front door. She stopped and held on to the banister rail for a moment, to steady the shaking in her hands.

He turned and saw her.

"Good morning!"

"Richard, where are you going?"

"Just into St. Helier for an hour or two. I'm driving myself." He smiled the smile of last night, the smile that turned her to jelly. "I've already told them I'm skipping breakfast, and that I'll probably grab a bite of lunch in town. Good food's wasted on me this early in the morning, anyway."

"Can I come with you?"

"Sorry, not allowed. I want to get something special and I don't want you to see it. Not until later."

"But I can wait in the car."

"No deal. Be a good girl and do as you're told." He winked at her. "I'll be back before you know it."

She ran after him.

"Richard, wait! I have to go into St. Helier. I was going anyway. I have to take that jar of cold cream back to La Riche . . ."

"It can wait."

"No, it can't! You didn't see what that stuff did to Blanche's face."

"All right. I'll settle for a compromise . . . OK? I'll get the car out and you run back upstairs and fetch the jar of cream. I'll take it back and complain to them myself. Besides, it's better that way. They'll take more notice of a man."

Evelyn nodded. "I suppose you're right." He smiled and squeezed her hand. "But I so much wanted to be with you all today . . . and I thought we could . . ."

"Evelyn . . . I said I wouldn't be long." He blew her a kiss with his fingertips, and went on outside into the courtyard, jingling the car keys in his hand.

"What will I do while you're gone?" she called after him.

He looked back over his shoulder.

"The same as you'd have done if I'd never come here at all."

She hesitated outside the dining room, then let her hand fall slowly from the handle of the door. On the other side she could hear her grandmother's voice, talking sharply to one of the servants, and she turned away.

No, it was no use, she couldn't face it. Not now. Not yet. Not after the happiness and elation of last night. She couldn't face sitting at that absurdly long table, mumbling Grace, the silence between them all broken only by the monotonous ticking of the clock, or the occasional word.

What an anticlimax this morning was to the joy of last night! The forlorn, oppressive stillness of the house when he wasn't here to bring it to life with his smiling and his laughter was almost unbearable. She had to get out. She had to go somewhere, anywhere. She had to escape from it before it overwhelmed her and crushed her.

In the early hours after he'd left her and crept back quietly to his own room, she'd lain awake, too excited and happy to sleep, reliving it, savoring it, planning what they'd do together today, and the days afterward until they left. A drive in the car around the island, for one last look. A picnic in the cove on the white, sandy beach of St. Clouet's Bay. Arm in arm, walking in the woods above the clifftops, watching as the waves crashed across the rocks far below. They'd take a camera and take photographs of each other, and then he'd sit still, on a giant rock or against one of the trees near the summit of the cliffs, while she sketched him, battling with the strong sea breeze that would try to blow the pages of her sketchbook from her hand.

Her eyes fell on the telephone on the other side of the hall, and she felt guilty. She should have called Louis Tostain back by now, should have made arrangements to go back to the Tostain gallery and work on the painting he had showed her yesterday . . . but somehow she couldn't bring herself to do it. Not now. Later. Tomorrow. Perhaps the day after. Maybe there wouldn't be time to do it after all.

She went down the steps into the kitchen, hoping to find Jeanne alone. But instead Julia was there going over the menus with Martha Le Bon, and Jeanne was peeling a dish of potatoes in the big sink. They all looked at her. Was it her imagination that they all stared at her in a different way, even Jeanne?

"What are you doing down here at this time of the morning?" her aunt said, coldly. "You'll be late for breakfast, and you know how Mother will react to that." Had they been alone she would have retorted, "Not in front of Richard, she won't. She's far too cunning." But she could scarcely speak to her aunt like that in front of the servants—not that she'd ever thought of Jeanne as one. But Martha Le Bon was different.

"I don't want any breakfast, thank you." She smiled toward Jeanne. "I wanted to ask Jeanne if she could find me a basket to pack some food in, and a flask. I thought I'd walk up the cliffs and then make my way down into St. Clouet's Bay, to do some sketching. It's so long since I did any real work. I want to get started again."

Jeanne put down her knife and started to speak, but Julia de Corbiere stopped her with a glance.

"Jeanne's busy now. She has work to do."

"I know that. I don't expect anybody to wait on me. But if she can tell me where the baskets are kept I can get one myself."

Martha Le Bon looked at Evelyn with her pale, expressionless eyes, then back at Julia. "It's all right, Mrs. de Corbiere. Jeanne can finish the vegetables later, if Miss Evelyn's in a hurry to get off." Was that a hint of sarcasm in her voice? Evelyn couldn't be sure.

"Thank you. I'll go and see if Blanche is all right after what happened last night. She wasn't up when I came down."

"Do as you please."

• • •

She was relieved to find the kitchen empty except for Jeanne when she came back downstairs, her pencil box and sketchbook tucked into a leather satchel underneath her arm.

"I didn't get you into any trouble just now, did I? I didn't expect anyone else to be down here."

Jeanne smiled.

"No, of course not." She went over to the small hamper sitting on the table. "There . . . I've made up some sandwiches and a flask of coffee. Oh, and I put in some fruit as well. I hope it won't be too heavy for you to carry, what with your other things. It's quite a steep walk up to the clifftop, you know."

"Oh, I'll be all right, thanks. A bit of exercise will do me good."

"You couldn't have picked a better day. Even though we're into September now, the sun's hot on the wall outside. Oh, before I forget . . ." She fished in her apron pocket and pulled out a piece of paper. "I've made you a map of the best way to get down into the bay, and I've marked where I think you'll find the best spot to do your sketching. See." Evelyn looked over her shoulder. "This little part of the cove is a real sun trap, not many people who aren't local know about it. You hardly ever get any tourists down there, and it's cut off from the strong breeze that usually comes off the sea at this time of year."

"Oh, thanks, Jeanne." She folded the map in half and tucked it into her cardigan pocket.

"One more thing. You ought to start making your way back to the cliff path before the tide comes too far in. It's very fast in the bay, and it can be very deceptive if you don't know about it. If you leave it too late, you can be cut off on the rocks, and it's such a lonely spot that even if you got into trouble and tried to shout for help, there'd be nobody around to even hear you. You must take your watch."

"I've got it on. And I've checked it's right and wound up. Besides, I'll probably start back well before four or five. Don't worry."

"How was Miss Blanche after last night? When we heard her screaming . . ."

"The rash is still on her face, but only faintly. Thank goodness. It couldn't have happened to anyone worse than

Blanche. She won't even come downstairs until it's gone, or take my advice and see the doctor in St. Helier."

"Mrs. de Corbiere came down and told Mother it was something to do with a jar of cold cream. Is that true?"

"That's the only thing it could have been, yes. She'd run out of her own and borrowed the jar from my bedroom. But as soon as she'd spread it over her face, it started smarting and burning her skin. That's when she panicked and screamed, though I can't blame her. The rash was pretty bad last night. And if the cream had stayed on for longer it might have been worse. It smelled strange, too. Sort of acidy. When I unscrewed the top of the jar it made my eyes water. Maybe she just has an allergy to the perfume they use in that brand, I don't know. I'd only just bought it that morning. Richard had to drive into St. Helier for one thing and another today, so he offered to take it back to La Riche for me and complain to the manager."

"A good thing, too." Jeanne turned to pick up the hamper from the table; then she stopped, frowning. "Why, that's odd . . ."

"What is it?"

"I could have sworn—I could have sworn that I fastened the strap on this basket. Now it's undone." She opened it up and looked inside. "Everything's there, just as I packed it. Sandwiches, flask, fruit." She shrugged her shoulders. "Perhaps I did leave it undone." She rebuckled the strap and gave it to Evelyn. "Oh, well . . . here you are. Have a good day. And take care!"

"I will." She smiled as she went up the kitchen steps. "See you later."

The walk was much longer and the cliff path much steeper than Evelyn had thought. The sun was hot overhead. Several times she stopped, put down her basket and her artist's satchel, and sat down on the grass for a few moments' rest. She could smell the fresh, salty odor of the sea, and could hear it in the distance, far away from the little sandy beach in the cove and the bare, seaweed-strewn rocks.

When at last she reached the summit of the cliff and peered cautiously over it to the cove below, the sheer drop almost took away her breath. Reaching into her cardigan pocket, she took out Jeanne's carefully drawn map and studied it.

To her right, by a small clump of trees, there was a wide,

natural staircase hewn from the granite slope, which would take her down safely to the sand below, the rocks around it near the bottom bare and dry with the warmth of the sun. Only later, when the tide rushed into the cove, would they be covered beneath the rising waves.

Slowly, carefully, balancing her satchel in one hand and the picnic hamper in the other, she made her way down to the tiny strip of beach, then picked a path toward the secluded cove across the rocks.

Jeanne had been right. There was hardly any wind blowing in from the sea at the sheltered point she had marked with a cross on her map. Breathing in the sharp, bracing, sweet sea air, Evelyn spread the small rug she'd packed into her satchel and got out her pencil box and her sketchbook, then lay it on her lap.

It was a long time since she'd created anything, since she'd even held a brush or a pencil in her hand. Too long. Not since she'd come here from London. She'd neglected so many of the things that had always been important to her, and she felt guilty.

The sun seemed warmer overhead when she'd covered several pages with her sketching, and she checked her watch. Still only half past two. Closing her sketchbook, she put away her pencils and unfastened the leather strap on the picnic basket. Jeanne's sandwiches tasted good. She ate a little of the fruit, then took out the flask and cup and poured herself some coffee.

It tasted slightly bitter as she sipped it. But she was thirsty and drank it all. Unlike Jeanne not to make it with enough sugar. She put the top back on the flask and began to repack the basket, then her satchel, her movements gradually becoming slower as a strange, heavy tiredness settled over her. She rubbed her eyes, then yawned. It was the extraordinary warmth and brightness of the sun overhead that was making her feel so sleepy; and she'd had little sleep last night.

The side of the huge rock behind her felt comfortable and warm. Leaning back against it, she smiled and closed her eyes.

The first thing she became aware of the moment she awoke was that she was shivering and her feet were wet. As she opened her eyes and stared with disbelief at the incoming tide, she realized that she had fallen asleep and that the only way

back to the clifftop had been cut off by the fast-rising sea.
Desperately, she leaped to her feet, grasped her belongings,
and stumbled back across the shingle to the foot of the cliffs
behind her, but there was no way she could escape. All around
her the towering walls of granite rose forbiddingly upward
toward the sunless, cloud-strewn sky, a sheer drop from top to
bottom, enough foothold only for birds. The way she'd come
down to the cove from the summit above, the huge natural
staircase hewn from the cliffside itself, was already swirling
with the treacherous, foaming, incoming tide. And she
couldn't swim.

She was too petrified to cry. She screamed out for help, but
she knew that there was no one to hear her. Jeanne had said so.
Jeanne had warned her about the danger of leaving the cove too
late. Now she was trapped. Now she was going to die. Flinging
down the basket and rug, she struggled as best she could over
what remained of the biggest boulders, slipping and sliding as
she tried to hold on to them, her voice lost in the roar of the
wind and the sea. Dragging herself desperately to the highest
one, she clung with aching arms to the slimy surface.
Suddenly, a huge wave rushed toward her and crashed
mercilessly over the boulder, soaking her to the skin and
knocking her helplessly into the sea.

Ross Klein slowed the car, then pulled onto the grass verge
near the foot of the cliff path near the sea. He was longing for a
cigarette. He turned off the engine, took out his cigarette case
and lighter, then lit up. After a few moments he glanced
casually from the window, at the wind bending the branches of
the nearby clump of trees, then beyond them to the edge of the
summit, where the cliffs dropped to the cove below. It was too
late to walk there now; his hosts had mentioned that while St.
Clouet's Bay was one of the less known beauty spots on the
island, the fast-rising tide swept through it within half an hour,
once it was on the turn. By now the tiny strip of beach would
be under water.

But he didn't want to go back yet. He wanted to walk. He
wanted to think. Getting out of the car he slammed the door
shut and began to make his way up the steepening path toward
the clifftop. St. Clouet's Bay had a great view, they'd told him.
Pity he hadn't even remembered to bring along his camera.
When he reached the top he walked slowly along the edge of it,

marveling at the panoramic, breathtaking view he'd half expected, then paused and leaned against a tree to finish his cigarette.

That was when he saw it. A sudden movement among the rocks and waves, a flash of vivid red. Then, so faint and weak that he couldn't be sure he'd heard it at all, a far-distant voice. He threw down his half-finished cigarette and came closer to the edge of the precipice, eyes straining toward the thicket of rocks half submerged beneath the waves. Then he saw her.

The sea had swept her toward the last remaining clump of boulders, and she was desperately trying to cling to one single jagged edge, fighting against the waves that kept rolling back and over her, drenching her, smashing her body against the wall of rocks. He could see by the way she clung there, like a flimsy strand of seaweed, that she must have been in the sea for some time, and was rapidly getting weaker.

He shouted. He waved. He shouted again, not even sure that she could either see or hear him. Then he ran back down the clifftop path toward the car, flung open the trunk and grabbed the single length of towing rope he'd remembered had been in there. As fast as he could he ran back the way he'd come toward the trees and tied one end of the rope around the thickest trunk, then threw the other over the edge of the cliff. It reached only three quarters of the way down, only enough if he could swim out to her and bring her back to where the huge natural staircase submerged beneath the rising tide met the foot of the cliff, then somehow haul her to safety. There was no more time to think. Tearing off his jacket and shoes, he dived into the sea and swam as hard as he could toward her. As she suddenly twisted her head round and caught sight of him the expression on her face was something he'd never forget as long as he lived.

"Swim toward me!"

"I can't swim!"

Another wave crashed over them and she cried out as the salty spray drenched her and stung her eyes.

"Hang on, I'll be there!"

"Help me, please . . . help me!"

It took him another ten minutes to reach her on the rocks, and she was so cold and frightened that he had trouble in getting her to let go her grip on them. "Come on, hold on to me! It's OK. I'm here."

"Oh, God, the waves are so high!"

"Hang on. That's it. Let the rock go . . . let it go, baby . . ." He spat the salt water out of his mouth. "Hold on to me as tight as you can!"

"I can't . . ."

"Just do what I tell you and it'll be OK."

The sea was too strong, even for a good swimmer, to get back to the rocks at the bottom of the cliff face without having both arms free to swim against the tide; there was no way he could swim and hold her at the same time. She had to hold on to him herself or they'd both be swept out to sea.

"Don't let go. Whatever you do, don't let go, OK?"

She was too exhausted and afraid to answer, but he felt her arms gripping him around the waist, and he swam back the way he'd come as best he could with the dragging weight, screwing up his stinging eyes, spitting the sea water from his mouth. When at last he reached the bottom of the cliff where the rope hung, it was another fifteen minutes before he could get hold of it with both hands. "Hang on tight. Don't let go now!"

"My arms," she wailed, starting to cry. "My arms are aching so!"

Gritting his teeth, he put one arm around her waist and clung to the end of the rope with the other. Only one question left— would the rope hold? Beneath him he could feel the rocks that, when the tide was out, formed a wide, natural staircase from the summit of the cliff to the beach below, and he heaved himself and the shaking girl onto the step above.

Panting, using all his strength, he helped her up each step behind him, using the aid of the rope, until they got to the topmost part of the rocks where the incoming tide had yet to reach. Then, with one last pull, he tugged her and himself to safety at the summit of the cliff. Gasping, exhausted, they both fell onto the grass where Evelyn burst into tears, sobbing and trying to thank him both at once.

"If you . . . hadn't seen me . . . the waves . . . swept out to sea . . . Oh, God!"

"Hey, come on, honey . . . it's OK. You're safe now. That's terra firma you can feel right there! Let's get into the goddamn car before we both catch pneumonia, huh?" He got to his feet and helped her to hers, then he picked her up in his arms and carried her down the cliff path to the car parked below. When he'd bundled her inside and gotten in himself, he grabbed a rug from the back seat and draped it round her. Then he leaned forward, closed his eyes, and rested his dripping head on the steering wheel.

There was silence between them for several minutes; then, slowly, he turned his head toward her and looked at her. She was shivering, saturated; her green eyes, green as the strands of seaweed that clung to her soaking hair, looked enormous in her pale face. Sitting there, with her long fiery hair hanging around her shoulders and over the blanket like a mermaid, she looked like a tired, frightened little girl. He felt both sorry for her and angry with her.

"What the hell were you doing down on that goddamn beach, for Christ's sake? Don't you know how fast the tides come in around here? What d'you think you were trying to do . . . get yourself killed?"

A tear welled up on the corner of her eye and ran down her white face.

"Please don't shout at me . . ."

"I'm not goddamn shouting at you, you crazy little broad, I'm asking what the hell you think you were doing down there? And you can't even goddamn swim!"

"I came here to sketch . . . to sketch the cove . . . I knew about the tide. I was told about it. I was going to pack away all the things I'd brought with me and leave before the tide started to come in again. But I . . . I suddenly came over so drowsy that I just couldn't keep my eyes open. The next thing I knew, I'd woken up and the sea water was right up to my feet." She buried her face in her hands. "When I looked round and saw there was no way back again, I didn't know what to do. I just panicked."

"That figures." He turned on the engine. "You OK now?" She nodded. "OK. Let's get you back home so you can get the hell out of those goddamn wet clothes."

She looked at him. "But you're soaked through, too!"

"I'll live."

She looked down at her clasped hands awkwardly.

"I don't know how I can ever thank you . . ."

"The best way you can thank me, baby, is to never do a fool thing like that again. We got a deal?"

She tried to smile. He drove the car back onto the road.

"You give me directions. I don't know the way around this island too well myself."

Pulling the rug closer around her body, she pointed out the way she'd come. "You're American, aren't you?"

"You noticed."

"Are you here on holiday?"

"You mean am I here on vacation? Not exactly." He felt guilty for the brusque way he'd spoken to her a few minutes before. "I'm sort of on sick leave, from the United States Air Corps . . . cracked some bones in my arm and wrist and they don't seem to want to get better as quick as I want them to. Goddamn bones. I feel fine." He took one hand off the wheel and flexed the wrist before putting it back on again. "All set and ready to get back to my plane . . . trouble is, the squadron doc has other ideas. No 100 percent, Klein, no flying. Not fair on all the other guys. All the gold bars in the First National Bank won't make him change his mind."

"How long have you been a pilot?"

"Since I was a raw, rookie nineteen-year-old kid . . . nearly nine years back." He laughed, showing white, even teeth that seemed even whiter against his sunburned face. "Boy, did they work the ass off me in those days! When you first join up, they put you through so many physicals that at the end of the day, you're asleep before your head touches your bunk pillow. I know I was." He shifted down gear to take a sharp bend in the road. "After the first physical they put you through intelligence tests, then on to a classification center, where there's more physicals and more intelligence tests . . . then, if you get through all that you go on to a battery of psychomotor tests, with an analysis of hand-eye-foot coordination—how you respond to those dictates whether you end up a potential pilot, navigator, or bombardier."

"Where did they send you after all that?"

"On to preflight school, to start the first phase of real training. For pilots it was called ground school. The other guys had their own kind of specialized training. We had physical training, drills in military discipline, conditioning, and then classroom studies in calculus and physics. All in nine weeks flat."

"You must have been exhausted."

"You bet. But you can't let up—or you're out on your ass. Anything less than 100 percent effort isn't good enough. After preflight training, all the cadets who've made the grade are sent on to learn the real stuff, how to handle the controls on real planes. When you've done eight hours of instruction you're ready to fly solo. The guys who don't learn quick enough are soon eliminated . . . I reckon that nine out of ten wash out somewhere along the way, most of them in primary. I guess I was just lucky to make it.''

"You've very modest."

He didn't answer. "I went on to basic flying school after that, to the big, heavy planes that they use there. When I first got a look into the cockpit of a BT-13 it looked like the Grand Canyon full of alarm clocks! But after seventy hours of formation flying and night landings, I reckoned I was getting there. That's when you're ready for fighters and bomber planes. B-17s, P-38s . . . You name it, I've flown it. By the end of the year the designers'll have brought out a whole lot more. Long-range, four-engined bombers, twin-engine airplanes for backup on ground attack. Marauders and medium-range bombers. When we pitch into this goddamn war that's coming, we're as sure as hell going to need all the best planes we can get."

"You really think there'll be a war?"

He glanced at her, then looked back to the road in front of them. "Why, don't you?"

"I hate to even think about it."

"So do most people, but that won't stop it happening. The goddamn Krauts are spoiling for a fight and if they start one we'll be ready for them. No question."

"But if they do declare war it isn't anything to do with America."

"Who says? We're natural allies. Sooner or later we're going to be in there, side by side. It's only a question of time. If someone picks on your best pal or your kid brother, what's the first thing you do? Bust their goddamn head in. Stands to reason."

There was a long silence, broken only by the noise of the car's engine.

"Are you . . . planning to leave the island soon?" Evelyn heard herself ask him. He answered without looking at her.

"I came here to persuade some friends to go back with me to the States . . . looks like I was wasting my time, they won't budge. But I reckon to be moving on in a week or so, yes. I have to get back for another checkup on how my bones are mending, and a full-scale physical. No pass, no flying until I do." There was a pause. "What about you? You live here all the time or are you just on a vacation from England?"

"I came from London a little while ago. My father was born here and his family home is still here. He's dead now."

"That's tough."

"When my mother died I decided to come to Jersey for good." Not quite accurate but it would have to do. She could hardly tell him the truth word for word. She looked down at the floor of the car. "I'm not doing very well, so far . . ."

"I wouldn't say that. We all make mistakes. Hopefully once we've made them we don't do it again." He smiled at her and she felt her face flush, unexpectedly. "You're very pretty." The flush grew hotter, and she tried to drag her eyes away from his face, but failed. "You haven't told me your name, yet. Mine's Ross Klein."

"Evelyn Tregeale." Suddenly she felt self-conscious. She pushed the wet strands of loose hair away from her face. "I must look a mess . . ."

"You look real cute to me. Like a mermaid, with all that seaweed threaded through your hair." She wondered if he was teasing her. "If you think you look a mess now, I'd sure like to see you when you're not."

She suddenly thought of Richard Mahone and last night, and felt guilty without understanding why.

"Are you married?"

"No. Are you?"

Silently, she shook her head.

"You said you lived in London, a while back. Must have been something wrong with all the guys there, to let a girl like you slip through their fingers." She could feel his eyes looking at her, and her cheeks grew hotter still. "Maybe we could meet somewhere before I go back . . . could I take you to dinner somewhere?"

She hesitated, wanting to say yes.

"No, I'm sorry, I can't. You see I—"

He slowed the car as she pointed to the entrance to the drive. "You're already tied up with some other guy, and I'm leaving soon. That's OK. I understand. No big deal." He fell silent. Then he drove so fast along the winding drive that she had to cling to her side of her seat to steady herself, and he braked so hard when they reached the courtyard in front of the house that she cried out as she felt herself jerked toward the windscreen. He didn't apologize.

"So long, then."

"Thank you so much . . . I can't tell you how grateful I am for what you did."

"No sweat. I'd have done the same for anyone."

She suddenly remembered that she still had his rug draped around her, and she started to take it off. But he shook his head.

"Keep it. Just do yourself a favor, will you, baby? Learn how to goddamn swim." He drove off in a cloud of dust without looking back. He hadn't even said goodbye. She watched him until the car had disappeared from sight around the sweep in the drive. Then she turned and ran into the house and up the stairs to her room, sobbing as she went. Within seconds, Blanche, then Jeanne, had burst into her room after her.

"Evelyn!" They both cried out simultaneously.

"Dear God!"

"Evelyn, what's happened? You're soaked to the skin!"

"Please, help me get out of these wet clothes."

Jeanne ran over to the wardrobe and pulled out her dressing gown, Blanche rushed to the nearest bathroom for a towel.

"Evelyn, your hair's full of seaweed!"

Crying, still shaking, she managed to blurt out the whole story. They rubbed her down, helped her on with her dressing gown, then wrapped the towel around her dripping hair.

"Everything was lost in the sea. The rug . . . the picnic basket . . . all my sketches . . . Jeanne, I'm sorry."

"For God's sake, Evelyn! Do you think any of that matters? Thank God you got back safely!"

"I don't know what happened." She clutched at her head. "I just—I just couldn't stop myself from falling asleep."

"I'm going straight downstairs to get you a cup of hot, strong tea. With a nip of something in it to calm you down." Jeanne ran out and Blanche sat down and put her arms around her.

"If he hadn't seen me, Blanche, if he hadn't just happened to come along . . ."

"Stop it. Don't even think about it." Blanche squeezed her hand. "It's all over. You're back, here. Safe. Look. I'll go and tell Jeanne to make you a hot-water bottle. You can go straight to bed. If you're hungry Jeanne'll bring you something up here on a tray. All right? When she comes back I'm going straight downstairs to tell Mother."

Undressed, Evelyn let Blanche help her into bed. Then she remembered something. "Isn't Richard back yet? He's been gone all day." A terrible, sudden thought. "Do you think he's all right?"

"Of course he's all right. He phoned up an hour or so ago, Jeanne said, to let us know that he'd be back in time for dinner. Come on, let me help you get that hair dry. There's so much of it." She began to rub it briskly with the towel. A few minutes later Jeanne reappeared, holding a tall mug of steaming tea.

"Stay with her, will you, Jeanne? I'm going to tell Mother what's happened."

"Ross! You're soaked through!"

"Tell me something I don't know," he answered dryly. "You mind if I grab a hot bath before I put on dry clothes?"

"No, of course not, but . . ."

"I just saved some crazy girl from drowning, out there in the bay." He went on upstairs, apologizing as he went for the dripmarks on their carpet.

"St. Clouet's Bay?"

"That's the one."

"Who was she? How did she get there?"

"Same way as everybody else does, I guess. Except that she fell asleep before the tide came in. When she woke up the sea was all around her and she couldn't get back again." He opened the bathroom door. "Wouldn't mind a double helping of your husband's Scotch when I get out of here."

"Yes, Ross, but—"

He went inside and turned on the taps.

"Need a hand with those wet clothes?"

"Thanks, David."

"So who was this girl?" asked David. "Not a local girl, that's for sure. It's common knowledge on the island how strong the currents are in the bay. And how fast the tide is when it's coming in."

"She said she knew that. That she'd been told. Said she'd gotten so drowsy that she couldn't keep her eyes open." He shrugged, pulled off the last of his wet gear and got into the bath. He lay back and sighed. "Christ knows what would have happened if I hadn't picked that moment to stop the car and take a walk along the clifftop to have a cigarette. She couldn't even swim."

"Did she say who she was?"

"Yep. On the way back. Evelyn Tregeale. She's come over from London to live in the family house. She was too shook up to say very much else, so I did all the talking." He described the drive back from the bay. "It was a big place. Kind of creepy. Couple of miles back along the coast road."

"That's it, that's the Tregeale house."

"Is the name supposed to mean something to me?"

"One of the oldest families on the island. Well off, too. The old man was an art collector . . . just his widow and two daughters left living there, now. There was a son, but he left Jersey years ago and settled in England. He was killed in some automobile accident."

"She must be his daughter, then. She said her old man was dead. And her mother, too. That was why she'd come to live on the island. Seemed like a fish out of water, to me."

There was a knock on the bathroom door and then it opened, and a woman's hand appeared, holding out a large glass of whisky. "I won't look if you're not decent."

"I don't mind if your husband doesn't." He reached out to take the glass from her, and then winced.

"Ross, what is it?"

"My goddamn wrist!"

"Ross, no!"

He held it out, grimly. "I felt something go, just a little, when I was hauling that Tregeale girl out of the water on the rope, but I didn't even want to think that I might have twisted it and put it back to square one again. Looks like I don't have any choice now." He pulled a face. "It's goddamn ironic, isn't it? In a few days I'm supposed to be starting back for the States again, to have the base quack tell me it's all healed up and I'm OK to go and rejoin my unit. Today I do some crazy girl a good turn, and put it right back to where it was more than three months ago!" He took a swig of the whisky. "Someone up there sure as hell don't like me!"

"You saved her life!"

"Oh, sure . . ." He lay back in the soapy water and closed his eyes. "I'd do it all over again, tomorrow, even though to begin with I was real mad at her . . . she was so good-looking I couldn't stay mad at her for long." He opened his eyes again. "If you can find me the number, I guess I ought to phone the house, a little later on, and find out how she is. It's only polite."

"Why don't you go over there and see for yourself?"

"No can do. I asked her out for dinner sometime, before I go back, and she said she couldn't. Some other guy in the picture." Another swig of whisky. "I guess that shouldn't have surprised me. She's too pretty to not have every guy on the island chasing after her, let alone one." He reached over to the side of the bath and picked up the soap. "Hey, that reminds me, David . . . I gave her your car rug to keep herself warm. I told her she could keep it."

"That was generous of you."

They were suddenly interrupted by his wife, shouting to them as she rushed breathlessly up the stairs.

"Ross! David! I've just turned on the radio! The Germans have invaded Poland!" She put her head around the bathroom door. "Britain and France have ordered total mobilization."

They both heard the sound of the two cars drawing up at the front of the house at the same time, and exchanged glances. Blanche put down her supper tray, then went over to the window and pulled aside the curtain.

"Richard's back!" She frowned. "And Philip's here." She glanced over her shoulder at Evelyn, who was propped up in bed. "We weren't expecting him. I wonder what he wants at this time of night?"

"I want to know why Richard's been gone all day!"

"I'll go down and find out."

One of the servants had opened the front door, and the two men burst through into the hall, Richard Mahone shouting at the top of his voice. He suddenly caught sight of Blanche, halfway down the stairs.

"Hitler's invaded Poland! We heard it on the radio in St. Helier. Those bloody Krauts have overrun the whole country and practically wiped the Poles out!" He rushed into the drawing room leaving Philip le Haan standing in the middle of the hall.

"Philip? Philip, what's happening? What's going on?"

He came toward her. "It's true. The British and French

governments insisted that the Germans immediately withdraw all their troops from Polish soil . . . but of course they refused. As of now we're mobilizing for war."

Blanche came down the remainder of the stairs, her face white and drawn.

"But what does it mean? To us, here? How will we be affected?"

"That's something we can only wait to find out. I've no doubt that when the news spreads all over the island, there are bound to be some people who'll start to panic. That's human nature. But though there's been a general mobilization for war, that doesn't mean that things are going to start happening tomorrow."

"Philip, I'm frightened." She looked up at him in mute appeal, desperately seeking reassurance. "Will they drop bombs on us?"

He placed his hands squarely on her shoulders.

"Of course not. Whatever action Britain and France take, none of the Channel Islands can take any active military part, other than releasing all our able-bodied young men for active service in British regiments. Last April the Home Office proposed delegating to the States of Jersey and the Royal Court in Guernsey the power to make our own defense regulations if the need happened to arise, but complete demilitarization of all the islands seems to me the only sane thing we can carry on doing. What defenses we do have would be completely inadequate for any long-term purpose."

There was still fear in her eyes.

"Oh, God . . . if only Mother had stopped behaving like an ostrich with its head in the sand and not canceled our papers, forbidden everyone to turn on the radio to listen to the news . . . maybe this wouldn't have come as quite such a shock."

"Everyone was hoping against hope, whether they read the newspapers and listened to the Home Service or not. And no doubt a lot of things have been going on over the past months that none of us outside the bailiff's office will ever even know about." He put his arm round her and led her into the dining room, where a heated debate was already going on. "All any of us can do for the moment is to keep as calm as possible."

"That won't be as easy as it sounds."

"To think that the government has dragged us into this!"

shouted Frederica Tregeale, leaning forward on her stick. Her throat was tight with rage. "After nearly five years of world war from 1914 to 1918, you'd have thought they'd learn their lesson, wouldn't you? You'd have thought that they'd have enough playing their little game of toy soldiers with the lives of innocent young men! But oh, no! They just can't learn from their own stupid mistakes! Germany walks into Poland and they all get up on their high horses and start demanding that they turn round and walk straight back again. They just can't mind their own business. And now they've put Jersey at risk because of their cursed meddling in other countries' affairs! These islands will be nothing more than the meat in the sandwich!"

"Bloody Krauts," Richard Mahone said. He took out a packet of cigarettes and lit one, unnoticed in the furor.

"You reckon the Krauts'll be casting their beady eyes over in our direction?" Richard Mahone said, dotting his cigarette ashes into one of the empty glasses nearby. "I heard rumors a long while back that if there was going to be any big trouble on the international front, Hitler would use the Channel Islands as a convenient base for his operations against mainland Britain." He suddenly remembered the things he'd said previously, and added, "Of course, I didn't really believe that at the time, but what do you think about it?"

"I'd say it was a very strong possibility that we could ultimately find ourselves occupied, maybe it's even inevitable. But as I've just said to Julia, all we can do is to wait and see."

"Occupied? By the Germans?"

"I'm afraid we have to consider that possibility very seriously, Julia."

"I don't believe it!"

"You mean you don't want to believe it. That's what the last three prime ministers said about war. They didn't want to believe that, either. And look where their pussyfooting around has got all of us! We've found ourselves at war with them without having a fraction of their military power to fight back with! We can barely rake up enough weapons to defend ourselves, let alone France or Poland! As for what pathetic defenses we've got here on Jersey . . . they wouldn't ever be enough to protect a wooden fort in a child's game of toy soldiers!"

"As usual, you're being far too pessimistic!"

"That's what the last three prime ministers said to Winston Churchill!" With increasing difficulty, Philip Le Haan controlled his anger. "But he's been proved right about Germany, hasn't he? And now they've got to listen because the truth's staring them in the face. He wasn't being pessimistic, he was being realistic!" He went toward the door. "Well, I've said what I came over here to say. Blanche . . . I'll ring you later."

"I'll see you out."

Only Richard Mahone said goodbye to him.

"Well," he said, lighting another cigarette, while the two women stared at him. "Now the fat's really in the fire!"

"Richard? I didn't realize that you smoked."

"Oh . . . er . . . yes." He held the packet out toward Julia. "Want one?"

"No! Certainly not, thank you."

"Nobody smokes in this house," said Frederica Tregeale as he puffed out a cloud of blue-gray smoke. "I've never permitted either Julia or Blanche to have cigarettes and I certainly don't intend to begin now. Of course, with a guest, and a man, the situation is entirely different. So long as you don't smoke at the table."

He smiled at her. "Of course not." He glanced around the room as if he'd just realized somebody was missing. "No Evelyn? Where is she? Up in that old tower of hers, painting a picture?"

Julia and her mother exchanged a glance.

"There was an accident today at the cove in St. Clouet's Bay . . ."

He got to his feet, frowning.

"What kind of accident?"

"She went to the cove to do some sketching and got cut off by the tide. If someone hadn't come along and seen her she'd have been—she'd have been swept out to sea."

He stared at her, appalled.

"What the hell happened? How to Christ did she get cut off by the tide?"

"She told Blanche that she felt very drowsy. That she fell asleep and when she woke up again the water was all around her. She was trapped. And she can't swim. But even a strong swimmer would have trouble getting back from the spot where she was to the bottom of the path near the cliffs when the tide's coming in. The currents in the bay are the fastest and the most dangerous anywhere around the island."

"Bloody hell! She could have been drowned!"

"Yes, she could have. And it would have been entirely her fault. Jeanne warned her about the tide, about the danger of leaving it too late before she started to make her way back. She even drew a detailed map. I may sound harsh but it's no less than the truth. She endangered not only her own life, but also the life of the young man who rescued her."

He frowned again, more heavily.

"Who was he?"

"Evelyn was in such a state of shock when he brought her back that she didn't say. All Blanche could get out of her was that he was an American."

"An American? Here, on Jersey?"

"Americans do come here occasionally, though we don't get many."

Impatiently, he stubbed out his cigarette.

"I'll go up and see how she is straight away."

She was sitting propped up in bed, her fiery hair dry now, brushed and spread out across the pillows. At the foot of the bed Blanche sat reading aloud a newspaper cutting that she had clearly gotten from Philip Le Haan.

"I hear you've been swimming today," he said, standing there in the frame of the open door. She stared toward him. Her green eyes lit up.

"*Richard!* Oh, Richard! Where have you been all day?"

"Hey! Get back into bed! None of that sprinting around. Doctor's orders." He winked at Blanche. He went to the side of the bed and sat on it. "Christ, Evelyn . . . when they told me downstairs what had happened . . ."

"I was lucky."

"What the hell did you go there for? If that Yank hadn't turned up on the clifftop and seen you in the sea, you wouldn't be here now!"

"I don't need reminding about that."

"Why did you go down to the bay, dammit?"

"Because I wanted to do some sketching of the cove . . . because it was a beautiful day . . . because I didn't know how long you'd be gone and I wanted to fill in the time . . ."

"If I hadn't gone into St. Helier none of this would have happened, would it? It's all my fault!"

"No!"

"Yes it is. And the bloody irony is that the most important reason I went there was to do with you. I never dreamed you'd go wandering off. I thought you'd stay here, and work on your father's portrait in the old tower . . ."

"If the weather hadn't been so glorious, I would have. But it seemed such a sin to stay cooped up indoors when the sun was shining."

Cautiously, he glanced toward Blanche. If only she'd go, if only they could be alone together, as they had been last night.

"Richard . . . I want to try to forget about it . . . I know that's easier said than done . . . if only this other news hadn't come right on top of what happened to me today, I think I could bear it, but it's just what I've been dreading, what all of us have been dreading." She reached out and gripped his hand. "I can't stop thinking about what it's all going to mean . . . for all of us . . ."

"Bloody Krauts!"

"Philip said he was having drinks with Coutanche later tonight." Blanche lay down the newspaper cutting on her lap. "He said he'll ring through as soon as he gets any more news."

"Coutanche?"

"The lord lieutenant. As soon as the news about the German invasion became public, he must have got on to London to see if there were any specific instructions."

"But I thought the islands were both self-governing? That they were completely independent of the British government and Parliament?"

"Normally, yes, we are. But this is different. For a start, hundreds if not thousands of people are going to want to be evacuated. Especially the British who are here only for tax reasons. Like the Shermans, who bought the old Sorel house near St. Helier, for instance. I can't see them staying . . . particularly since his wife is an American citizen." Her eyes rested on Evelyn now. "Maybe she's related in some way to that American you met today?"

"Maybe."

"Whatever . . . do you really believe in this mass panic and rumor about evacuating? I don't. The Germans'll be so busy overrunning Europe that they won't bother us, a handful of little islands in the middle of no-man's-land, stuck halfway between England and France. What have you got here that could be of any use to the Krauts? Potatoes, tomatoes, and a few flowers. That's not the sort of stuff they're after. Hitler's got bigger fish to fry."

"Why did all this have to happen? Why?" Evelyn wailed.

"Why does any war happen? Ambition, greed, someone falls out with someone else or wants something they haven't got but somebody else has . . . the Krauts have been itching to pick a fight with somebody or other ever since Hitler got into power, and the Poles are just what they've been looking for to start the whole thing off. Small, antiquated army, minimal resistance. A real walkover."

Frederica's voice called Blanche from downstairs, and she got up and went out, kissing Evelyn on the cheek as she passed. As soon as they were alone, Richard Mahone shut the door and took her in his arms.

"Evelyn . . . if only I'd put off going into St. Helier this wouldn't have happened to you . . . how can you forgive me?"

"You can't say that! There's nothing to forgive."

"I can and I do. I feel responsible."

She lay back against the pillow and looked at him.

"It doesn't matter. You're here now."

A moment of silence.

"Tell me about this American."

She smiled. "He was nice. You'd have liked him. He knew how shocked and shaken I was after he pulled me out of the sea, so when he drove me back home he kept talking, I suppose to try to keep my mind off what had happened. And it worked. He told me all about how they train their pilots in the U.S. Air Corps . . ." She thought back. "And it fascinated me."

"What would he know about it?"

"That's what he is, a pilot in the Air Corps."

"What's he doing over here, then? He's a long way from home base, isn't he?"

"He said he'd come to Jersey to see some friends of his. To try and persuade them to go back with him to the U.S.A., because of the threat of another war."

"So he's on leave, then?"

"Sick leave. He cracked some bones in his arm and wrist, and until he's passed fit again, they won't let him fly."

"If he climbed down that bloody cliff face and then back up it again with you as well, he can't be that sick! Sounds to me like he fancied a holiday, and decided to skive off for a while!"

"Richard, that isn't true! He didn't strike me as being that kind of man . . . quite the opposite. He was upset that the injuries hadn't healed as quickly as he thought they should, and that he couldn't get back to his plane. Besides, only men who were 100 percent dedicated would go through the kind of training he's been through. He told me that it's so tough that only one man in ten makes the grade."

"It sounds to me as if he was trying to impress you. Well, that doesn't surprise me. Typical Yankee. None of them can resist showing off, especially in front of a woman. They'll flirt with anything in a skirt, everyone knows that!"

"It wasn't like that."

He got up and went over to the window. Dusk was falling now. He opened the skylight and lit a cigarette.

"Did he say when he's leaving Jersey?"

"In a few days' time. That's all he said."

Another silence.

"Don't try to tell me he didn't ask you for a date!"

"He asked me if he could take me out to dinner one evening, before he goes back, yes. But I told him that I couldn't."

"Was that because of me?" For the first time, he smiled.

"Yes, of course it was. But you've misunderstood. He asked me out of politeness, nothing else. Just the same as if . . . as if someone like Philip Le Haan had asked me to dinner. It was just a gesture, that's all."

He came over to the bed again and sat down, then took her hands in his and kissed them.

"I'm sorry, Evelyn. I'm just angry with myself. Angry because I wasn't there when you needed me. But promise me something and promise me now . . . that you'll never go down to that bay again, unless there's someone else with you. Even then I don't want you to."

She leaned against him.

"I promise." She looked up into his face, for a swift, fleeting moment seeing traces of Jack Neville there, and then they were gone again. "Now tell me . . . why were you away for so long?"

"Because I wanted to bring you back a present, and it took me all day to find the right one." He reached into his pocket and brought out a long, velvet-covered box. "Here . . . this is for you."

Slowly she took it from him and just as slowly she opened it, almost as if she could not bear to. There, on a bed of milk-colored satin, lay a necklace of gold and pearls.

"Richard, it's beautiful." She reached out and touched it with the tips of her fingers. "But you really shouldn't have . . . it must have cost so much . . ."

"To give and not to count the cost . . . I always remember that line, from a prayer we used to say at school . . . about the only thing I bothered to remember."

"I can't wait to wear it."

"Not tonight, you won't. You need rest. And your grandmother's telephoned the doctor, Blanche said, just to make sure you're OK."

"But I'm all right now. I don't want the doctor . . . I was badly shaken, that's all."

"No arguments. Better to be safe than sorry, you know that."

Suddenly all the events of the day seemed to crowd down upon her, and she clung to him, as she'd clung desperately to the foam-drenched rocks in St. Clouet's Bay. She leaned against him, eyes closed, arms around his neck. If only they could stay like this. If only they were a thousand miles away. She felt stifled by the smallness of the island, her grandmother's strictness, Julia's hostility; the war was creeping closer and she was suddenly afraid.

"Richard, please . . . let's leave here as soon as we can, while there's still time. Let's go away from this place!"

He held her away from him, at arm's length.

"Hey, what's this? What's the big rush? I'm here with you."

"You don't understand. It's got nothing to do with you. I just want to leave, to go away. Anywhere. Wherever you want to go, I'll go with you. I don't care where it is." She had a fleeting vision of the German bombers, blitzing Poland. "We could go back to France. Where you used to live before. Or England, if that's what you want."

"No, Evelyn. It isn't what I want. Don't you understand? When the Krauts start flexing their muscles and looking for a follow-up to Poland, France and England are going to be right in the front line. Whatever part of them you go to. You're forgetting something, aren't you? England and France will be at war with Germany.''

"But I don't feel safe here."

"You're wrong to feel that way. Take it from me. We're safer here on Jersey than we'd be anywhere else."

"But Philip said that thousands of people will want to be evacuated! If that happens, why can't we go too?" She paused and gave him a hard look. "You don't want to go, do you?"

"It's not a question of what I want. It's a question of what's best for us. Both of us, in the long run. Let's keep our options open . . . let's play it by ear and just wait and see." He took hold of her hand and lifted the necklace from its bed of satin. "We could start by seeing how this looks on that beautiful neck." He smiled the smile that warmed her straight through. "Lift your hair, so that I can fasten it." She did as he asked her, and the touch of his skin on hers made her whole body tingle. "There . . . it was made for you."

She looked at him for a long while, no longer seeing the reflection of Jack Neville that had haunted her. Now, she could stop running away, because there was no longer anything to run from.

"I'm not staying in bed. I want to get up." When he started to protest she silenced him. "No, I'm all right now. But I'll go mad if I just lie here, thinking. I want to get dressed and do some painting. Real painting. It's too long since I worked, and that's bad for me."

"But your grandmother's phoned up for the doctor to come out and take a look at you. He won't be very pleased if he gets here and finds you on your feet as if nothing's happened."

"The best way for me to forget what happened isn't to lie here, where all I have to do *is* think. When I'm painting, Richard, I can forget everything else." She took some clothes from her wardrobe and lay them over the back of a chair. She smiled at him. "But only another artist could really understand that."

It was cool and silent in the old tower, and her footsteps echoed as she walked across the floor, then climbed the winding staircase to her studio at the top. She stood there, looking all around her.

It seemed different now, since it had been scrubbed and cleaned out, with her trunks of oil paints and brushes, piles of old sketchbooks stacked on top of one another, and her easel set up by the light of the open window. Holding up the lamp she had brought with her from the house, Evelyn walked over to it and stared down at the preliminary sketchings of her father that she had left propped up against the wood. His wide, light eyes looked up at her from the paper, and she found herself smiling. Then, carefully, she set down the lamp on an old chest of drawers and sat down with a sketch pad on her lap. For a few moments she paused, biting the end of her pencil. Then, with meticulous detail that was as clear in her mind as if he were sitting beside her still, she drew a profile sketch of Ross Klein. When she'd finished it she went over to the chest of drawers and took out a single sheet of writing paper, and wrote two words on it, then signed her name.

First thing tomorrow, she'd cycle down to the post office in the village and mail it to him, a keepsake to take back with him to America.

That made her feel happy, somehow.

16

"I haven't seen much of you these past few months. Not since you finished your father's portrait and the restoration work on my father's painting."

Evelyn went on glancing through the pile of old prints, uneasily, trying to avoid his eyes.

"I'm sorry, Louis. I've been working in my studio in the old tower most days. And once I get a brush and palette in my hands I don't find it easy to stop. Old habits die hard."

"I wanted to ask you if you might care to come to dinner one evening. I could collect you in my father's car and bring you back again afterward . . . either we could eat at the house, or I could take you somewhere in St. Helier if you'd rather."

So, at last, he'd raked up enough courage to ask her what she'd been dreading ever since they'd first met. Desperately, her mind flailed around for an excuse, something that seemed plausible but not a deliberate snub that would hurt his feelings.

"There's no need to go to all that trouble." She gave him a quick, nervous smile. "You've already been invited to dinner with us. I heard Julia going over the menu last night with Martha Le Bon. I'll see you then."

He was standing too close to her and she moved away.

"I was thinking more along the lines of you and I having dinner together, without anyone else." From the corner of her eye she could see his hand coming toward her and she quickly put her hand into her pocket.

"I can't think where Jeanne's got to. Ten minutes, she said. She must have got caught up in a queue, somewhere or other. I just hope that people don't start panic-buying, because of all this threat of an invasion . . ." She went over to the window and stared from the shop, her eyes searching the busy street outside for some sign of Jeanne Le Bon. If only she'd hurry. If only they hadn't agreed to split up and meet here later, Jeanne would have been with her now and this wouldn't be happening to her. She could feel him moving closer to her and she began to panic.

"Do you think the Germans will invade Jersey?"

"I hope not. But all the indications are that an occupied Channel Islands is inevitable. Think about it. Nobody ever dreamed that the German army would cross the Maginot Line, or do half the things that it has ever since war was declared. Nobody likes to think the worst, but facts have to be faced even if we don't like the reality of them. Admittedly, we haven't got any spectacular strategic advantages, other than being conveniently near the British mainland—if you can call eighty-odd miles convenient—but to capture the islands would be a tremendous boost to the Nazis for their propaganda value." There was a hint of impatience in his voice and he moved close to her again. "Oh, let's forget about the war for a moment, Evelyn . . . just tell me that you'll—"

"Oh, look, there's Jeanne!" Never in her life had she been so relieved to see anyone, except Ross Klein that day many months ago. "I'm sorry. I really must go now, Louis . . ." But as she reached for the door handle he caught her by the arm.

"You haven't given me an answer."

She turned and faced him. Reluctantly, she forced herself to look him in the eyes, knowing there was no way now that she could bluff herself out of this one. As Jeanne came into the shop, she took a deep breath and decided to tell him the truth.

"I can't accept, because I'm going to marry Richard Mahone." She couldn't tell which of them was more stunned, Louis Tostain or Jeanne. They both stared at her. "We haven't told anyone about it, not yet. It didn't seem to be the right moment, not with the war and the island being put in a state of

alert. But you might as well know now as later on." She
paused, to let her words sink in. "I'm sorry, Louis."

"I—I owe you an apology. I had no idea . . ."

She smiled, so that he wouldn't feel slighted.

"You've done me a favor. Now I can't put off telling
everyone back at the house, can I?"

She and Jeanne walked along the pavement for several
moments before either of them spoke.

"When did he ask you?" Jeanne said without looking at her.

"A few days ago. We haven't told anyone yet because I
know everyone except Blanche will disapprove. And it's never
quite seemed to be the right moment." She glanced sideways
at the other girl. "You're surprised, aren't you?"

"I could see that he was really keen on you, almost from the
beginning," Jeanne said, in a voice more nearly normal. "A
blind man could have seen that." They walked on a few paces
further. "Why do you think everyone else will disapprove?
Your grandmother treats him almost like a son . . . even
Mrs. de Corbiere gets on well with him. He has that way about
him that could win over anybody."

"Not many people approve of wartime marriages," Evelyn
answered bluntly. They crossed the square, side by side. "I
suppose I can understand why. Men get called up. They get
injured, disabled, killed. In the last war a whole generation of
women were left widows, God knows how many of them with
children to bring up on their own. That's the first thing my
grandmother will think of. And say to my face."

"But it isn't really anything to do with her. You're both over
twenty-one."

"True, but we're living in her house and that makes a
difference."

"I don't see why."

"Oh . . . maybe I'm seeing obstacles where there are
none. I don't know. Richard and I have talked it over a hundred
times, and he's set on staying here. He says it's safer than either
England or France, because of the bombing. Maybe he's
right." She thought for a few moments. "I tried telling him
that there are lots of places in the country where we could go, if
we see about getting a passage back within the next few weeks,
but he says that my grandmother will think we're deserting the
family, and be hurt. And then there's Blanche. I don't think I
could bear to leave her behind even if I wanted to."

"I agree with Richard. You're far safer stopping here. And you're with your family. Besides, I think Blanche needs you. If you ever left the island for good, I'm sure she'd fold up, emotionally. Except for a few lapses, since you came here she's been almost a different person."

They stopped walking. People milled and jostled all around them.

"Do you really think so?"

"Even my mother remarked on it." Jeanne smiled, a little tight-lipped. "Maybe you've just been too busy with other things to notice."

They caught sight of Jean-Louis, up ahead, standing by the car with the door ready and open.

"What do you think Mrs. Tregeale will say when you tell her?"

Evelyn laughed, remembering the expression on her grandmother's face when she'd first told her about her affair with Jack Neville.

"Most likely that I can't get married in white."

Blanche took down the evening dress from its hanger inside her wardrobe and held it up against herself in the mirror. Then she carefully laid it down on the bed, came back to the mirror, and stood staring at her reflection for a long while.

Slowly, hesitantly, she touched one side of her face and then the other. She moved closer, then stepped back a few paces, frowning. Was it a figment of her imagination, a trick of the light? Beneath the surface of her smooth, pale skin did she only fancy that she could see traces of the rash that had temporarily disfigured her many months before? She began to sweat. Her heart beat faster. The palms of her hands felt wet and sticky, beads of perspiration stood out along her forehead.

She felt sick. Dizzy. Her whole body began to shake as if she had palsy. Where had she read that sometimes, rarely but it was still possible, rashes were apt to reappear at will in certain people, triggered by stress?

She swallowed. She picked up her hand mirror and went over to study her face by the light at the window. No, nothing that she could see. Not now. Yet, a moment ago . . .

Downstairs the big hall clock chimed. It was getting late. She must hurry. She must be ready in time. She felt unsteady on her feet. She went over to her dressing-table stool and sat down, then buried her face in her hands. She needed a drink. Just one. Only one. Even a glass of weak wine would do. To steady her nerves. To stop the shaking in her legs. They would all be ready, soon, waiting for her downstairs . . . she had to get dressed. Philip . . . she had to look her best for Philip . . .

She tried to pull herself together, steel herself to meet them, she had to go down for Evelyn's sake. She owed it to her. She wanted to be there and see her happy, happy because she was in love with Richard Mahone. He'd be good for her, after Jack Neville. He'd take care of her. He'd let nothing hurt her. Damn the Germans. Damn the war.

She looked up at her reflection again through her fingers. *You wish it was you, you, you! Then you could escape!* From all of them. From this house. From all the hateful, evil memories that haunted you . . . but you're trapped, trapped, and there's no way out except the bottle . . .

Her door suddenly opened, so quietly that when she saw her sister's reflection in the mirror, she cried out.

All at once, she started to shake again, uncontrollably.

"I didn't hear you knock!"

"I don't need to knock in my mother's house." She closed the door and leaned against it. "Well, what's this? Nearly half past seven and not even dressed?"

"I'll be ready in a minute!"

"Why, Blanche, your hands are shaking." A cold smile. "What is it? Got the hankering for another drink?"

"I don't want a drink!" Abruptly, she turned her back on Julia.

"Don't bother lying to me. I know you too well, remember? Not to worry. Although Mother's been keeping the drinks locked up, she'll have to open the cabinet this evening, so that Etienne can serve the guests." A pause. "By the way, she keeps the key hidden in her handbag, if you're interested."

"Go away."

Their eyes met and held in the dressing-table mirror. Julia looked past her yet again to the big photograph of their father, Blanche on one knee, Gilbert on the other. No sign of her, Julia, anywhere in the picture; nor in any of the many others that lined the mantelpiece and shelves above the bed . . . Julia, without her brother's charm or her younger sister's sparkle. Oh God, how she hated her!

Outside, down in the courtyard, they both heard the noise of the approaching cars.

"Better put on plenty of powder and paint tonight, Blanche. Hide those little wrinkles. Can you see them, there, all under your eyes? I noticed them from here." She smiled, coldly. "Make the most of what you've got while it still lasts."

Tears sprang into Blanche's blue eyes, and she spun round to confront her. But she was gone.

Evelyn had noticed long before they all sat down to dinner that Blanche had had more than enough to drink. Where she'd gotten it from was still a mystery. Before anyone had arrived the spirits cabinet had been locked, and when Etienne had brought out the bottles that would be used during the course of the evening, her grandmother had relocked the cabinet and put away the key.

Blanche wasn't herself tonight, even aside from the drink. Ever since she'd come down from her room, almost reluctantly, she'd sat away from everyone else, even from Philip, sullen-faced, eyes downcast, staring at the floor, her hands moving in her lap. Evelyn had noticed that every time Etienne or one of the maids passed by her with a tray of drinks, she'd taken one and downed it in a single gulp.

"Richard, I'm worried about Blanche." They moved out onto the stone terrace through the open french windows, away from the groups of chattering guests. "There's something wrong. I know there is."

He shrugged his shoulders.

"Maybe she's not as overjoyed as you seem to expect her to be about us."

"What do you mean by that?"

"Well, it stands out a mile, doesn't it? She's nearly thirty-seven, never been married, never even been with a man in her whole life as far as you know, because her mother wouldn't let her off the leading strings to have a fling. And now here you are, years younger, with a past behind you that she'd probably give her eye teeth for, and about to marry me. Think about it. She's not had much of a life, has she? And what the hell has she got to look forward to? Growing old in this bloody house, us gone, left behind with her bitch of a sister and her tyrannical mother, both as sour as vinegar!"

"Richard, for God's sake! I've never seen eye to eye with

Julia, but my grandmother isn't that bad . . . just hopelessly old-fashioned and set in her ways. Most old people are."

"Oh, come on, Evelyn! I know there's no love lost between you and them. Even a fool can see that. Not that it bothers me. I'm only here because of my mother and I only stayed on because of you. No other reason. The old lady is the piper and she's got the lot of you jumping up and down, dancing to her tune. The servants are all terrified of their own shadows, except Martha, and she bullies Blanche like a first-former at public school. Julia—she's just a chip off the old maternal block!"

"I know all that. But I'm not talking about any of the others, I'm talking about Blanche. She's different. She isn't like them. And there's always been a special relationship between us, even before I came here. I told you how we'd been writing to each other, ever since my father died."

"Maybe. But surely you must have noticed how strange she's been, ever since we told everyone we were getting married? You'd have to be blind and deaf not to!"

Evelyn stared at him, hardly able to believe the implication of his words.

"You think Blanche is jealous? Of *me?*"

"Not of you. Of what's happened between us. She probably curses the day I turned up here."

Evelyn was silent for a moment.

"I must talk to her. Later, when they've all gone home. I'll make her understand that nothing's changed between us, whether I'm married to you or not."

He threw down the cigarette he'd been smoking and stamped on it. When he spoke his voice was oddly harsh.

"Do what you like. But if you ask me you'll just be wasting your time."

From the far end of the table, Evelyn watched Blanche, eyes glazed, food in front of her untouched, another full wine glass in her hand. She was sitting between Peter Tostain and Margaret Le Fevre, and every time either of them tried to include her in their conversation, Evelyn noticed that she made no response, except to drink her wine.

She glanced toward the head of the table and her grandmother; then across it to Julia, but neither of them had even noticed Blanche. Evelyn lowered her voice.

"Richard, she's drunk already. We've got to do something!"

"Let sleeping dogs lie. Or should I say sleeping bitches! Everyone's too busy talking about the Krauts to notice she's had a skinful."

"People are panicking, yes," said Peter Tostain, putting down his knife and fork. "But after Coutanche addressed the crowds in Royal Square, they realized there was nothing to be gained by losing their heads. Rumor's been the worst enemy so far." He cleared his throat. "We should all stay put, no matter what."

"Only a certain breed of rat would even dream of abandoning the ship in the face of the Germans!" Julia said sharply.

"You can't blame people for wanting to look after number one." Richard Mahone sat back in his chair and sipped his wine, nonchalantly. "After all, it's only human nature!"

"I think you'll find that the vast majority of true Jersey-born people will follow the lord lieutenant's example and refuse to run in the face of the enemy. Your mother would have agreed with that."

He looked sideways at Evelyn, and winked.

"My mother and the whole Sorel family, come to that, did a bunk and left the island . . . and there wasn't anything to run away from, in those days. One man's meat is another man's poison, and all that." He ignored the look of outrage on her face. "It's all very well to stand up in the square making speeches. But when food and all the other things we take for granted now are in short supply—and remember electricity and gas are bound to end up being rationed, too—it'll be every man for himself and the devil take the poor bastards at the back of the queue!" He drained his wine glass, completely oblivious to the shocked faces around the table.

"Richard. Please." Frederica looked at him as if she was seeing him for the first time. "There are ladies present, myself included. Would you please be kind enough to remember that this is my dining room, not the mess of an army barracks."

Stealing a sideways glance at him, Evelyn saw him struggling not to smile.

"My apologies, ladies all."

Frederica sat stiffly in her chair. "We all know what occupation is likely to mean, for all of us. But there's a lot that we can do to help ourselves, before it's too late. I for one shall make sure that we have at least a year's supply of tinned foods stored away down in the cellar. And plenty of firewood for when the coal runs out. We have our own chickens, and a two-acre vegetable garden." She glanced round the table at the others. "If we start acting now we can at least make sure that we don't have to suffer any more than necessary."

Margaret Le Fevre looked over at Julia.

"I expect you're thankful that your poor husband never lived to give you any children, Julia. I know I would be, in your place. I only thank God that my sons are grown up!"

There was a sudden guffaw of laughter from Blanche, slouched in her chair at the far end of the table. She swigged back the last of her wine, and then staggered to her feet, swaying, clutching the empty glass in her hand.

"Thankful? Thankful that he never gave her any children . . . well, that's rich!" Her glazed, bloodshot eyes rested on her sister's shocked face. "He never gave her any because he couldn't stand the sight of her, let alone the touch . . . isn't that right, sister dearest?" Her body rocked with drunken laughter. "Why don't you stop play-acting and tell them all the truth? That he preferred men in his bed to any woman! That's why he left you and went to live in St. Malo, wasn't it? And why you and Mother had to make out that he was always away on business! Some business!" She hiccupped. "He went there because the French turn a blind eye to things that would have everyone up in arms over here!" They all stared at her, horrified, stunned into silence. "Go on, tell them what really happened, Julia! He didn't die of a heart attack . . . he died of some venereal disease! *Rectal syphilis*, his death certificate said. And he spent the last five years of his life living with a sixteen-year-old boy!"

"Shut up!" Tears of humiliation and rage sprang into Julia's eyes. "Shut up, you drunken bitch! There's more than a few skeletons that I could drag out of your cupboard, if I didn't have more respect for Mother!"

"Julia!" Frederica was on her feet. "Blanche! Both of you, leave this room at once. *How dare you!"*

Julia pushed back her chair and rushed out of the room. Blanche burst into tears and ran out in the opposite direction, while the others stayed in their places, too shocked and embarrassed to speak. Only Evelyn stood up.

"I'll go to her."

• • •

"*Blanche!* Blanche, open the door. Please. It's me, Evelyn."

"Go away!"

"Blanche, let me come in. I must talk to you!"

"Go away and leave me alone!"

Slowly, sighing, Evelyn reluctantly moved away from the door. It was pointless. Useless to try to reason with her. She was upset, unstable. She'd drunk far too much. Only when she was ready would she unlock the door and talk. And that could be hours or it could be days.

Evelyn went back downstairs, but not into the drawing room with all the others. She wanted to walk by herself in the garden. She wanted to be alone, without even Richard.

As she walked out of the now-empty dining room onto the stone terrace, she glanced up at the windows high above her on the north side of the house. Even from here she could hear the faint sound of sobbing.

But there was nothing she could do.

The two women stood side by side outside the bedroom door, listening to the muffled crying coming from inside. Then Julia turned round to her companion and held out her hand.

"She won't open it. The spare key, Martha?"

"Yes, Miss Julia." She took it from the ring in her hands and gave it to her. Julia fitted it into the lock and turned it, and the door swung open.

Blanche was lying there on the floor, slumped against the side of the bed. Her dark hair was falling into her eyes. Her eyes were bloodshot and hideously swollen from crying. She stared at them, then backed away like a cornered animal.

Her sister strode over to her, brandishing a stick, while Martha Le Bon leaned back against the door, barring her escape.

"*Get away from me!*"

Julia stood above her cowering body, then slapped her so viciously across both sides of her face that she cried out and fell backward, holding up her hands to protect herself.

"You disgusting little bitch!" Julia hit her a stinging blow with the stick. "You dare to do what you did tonight, down there, in front of all of them?" She hit her again, even harder. "You dare to open your filthy drunken mouth about Pierre?"

Chest heaving, blood running from the wound on her cheek, Blanche tried to drag herself out of reach.

"It was true! Everything I said was true and you know it! You knew what he was long before you ever married him!" She dashed away the blood with the back of her hand. "But you didn't want to marry a proper man, did you? As you didn't want me to marry anyone at all! You're so twisted inside with jealousy and hate that all you care about is trying to wreck other people's lives! And what a fine job you've made of it. You married a pervert and turned me into a drunk!" The amount of wine she'd had during the evening had made her giddy, and she clutched at her throbbing head. "But you can't take away what I've had, can you? And you can't look at me without hating me for it, because once, I really tasted happiness!" She struggled to get her breath. "And that's something you'll never know about for as long as you live!"

Julia's cold eyes narrowed to slits. For a moment she was speechless with rage. Then she hit Blanche so hard across the mouth that the rings on her fingers split her lip, and blood spurted.

"You shameless little whore!" Trembling, she slowly backed away from the shaking, sobbing heap crumpled like a discarded blanket on the floor. "I curse the day that you were born, do you hear me? You should have been smothered at birth!"

She left her there in the semidarkness, still crying and whimpering, the brief, violent outburst of defiance spent. Outside on the landing, she turned to Martha Le Bon.

"For God's sake go and mix up some stuff to give to her. If Mother or Evelyn come upstairs and hear her, you know what that means."

Martha nodded without speaking. Good Martha. Loyal Martha. Martha, the only one in her life whom Julia could ever trust. It had always been that way, when her parents had left her behind whenever they went away, and Martha had treated her like her own. No blood bond could have been closer than theirs was.

"I must go down, in case anyone suspects."

Martha hesitated on the landing.

"The other one's already been up here, poking around. She'll come back, if I know her."

"Evelyn? She'll be too busy with her precious Richard!

Besides, if the door's kept locked she can't get in, can she? Nor can anyone else." There was a noise from somewhere downstairs and they both stopped to listen. Nothing. "I'll keep Blanche's key myself . . . so even when she's sobered up tomorrow, she won't be able to let anyone inside even if she wants to. And Mother'll just think she's stolen another bottle and drunk herself stupid." She bit her lip, frowning, her face almost ugly in the dim light. "I'll make her pay, Martha. I'll make her pay for what she's put me through."

PART THREE

THE ORSINI
MADONNA

17

Slowly, the car turned the corner of the square and drew to a halt outside the old Norman church, where a small crowd was already beginning to gather. Passersby, catching sight of Evelyn inside the car with her bridal gown and white veil, stopped to smile and stare.

She was surprised to find that, now she was here, she was nervous. There were butterflies in her stomach. Her throat felt tight and dry. Every now and again as Philip Le Haan spoke to her, she could only nod a reply. When Jean-Louis got out and opened the door of the car for her to climb out, she could feel her legs turning to jelly, and she clutched at Philip's hand.

"All right, Evelyn?" He smiled at her, and she tried to smile back.

"I will be when it's over."

"Oh, you don't mean that! You'll savor every minute of it!"

She glanced around nervously at the fast-growing crowd. "I wish we hadn't told anyone, then nobody would have been here."

"They'd have found out anyhow. Everybody loves a wedding and they always will."

Behind them, the second car had drawn up, and as she stood uncertainly on the pavement, holding Philip Le Haan's arm, she could see her grandmother, face expressionless, sitting there behind Etienne, between Julia and Blanche.

"Shall we go on into the church?"

"Yes . . . I'm ready."

Her long train rustling behind her, she walked forward with him and through the tall arched door.

Organ music was playing softly in the background beyond the half-closed door, as they waited in the dim, musty-smelling porch. Then as it changed suddenly into the wedding march and the sound filled the crowded church, she walked slowly and a little unsteadily still toward the altar on Philip's arm, clutching her simple bouquet of Jersey summer flowers.

As she passed by the packed rows of people standing in the wooden pews, they turned round in their dozens to stare at her, and she flushed and lowered her eyes to the faded red carpet beneath her feet.

When she glanced up again, she could see the huge vases full of flowers standing at each end of the altar, and there, smiling at her, at the foot of the altar steps near the waiting vicar, stood Richard Mahone.

As she reached his side and he took her by the hand, she had one fleeting glimpse of Blanche, sitting there in the front pew between her mother and sister like a sad, pale ghost, her dull blue eyes glazed and full of tears.

They burst from the church porch out into the bright June sunshine, laughing, hand in hand, shielding their faces from the sudden hail of dried rose petals and rice. As she linked her arm through Richard's and waited for the photographs to be taken, she busily brushed the debris from her hair and dress. Then it was all over.

As they walked toward the car through the smiling, cheering little crowd of well-wishers, Evelyn tossed her bouquet into the middle of a group of giggling girls, and as they reached the car where Jean-Louis was waiting to help them inside, she turned to gather up her sweeping train. Then she stopped, abruptly, as she caught sight of a face watching her from across the busy square.

She remembered him at once—how could she ever forget the face of a man who'd certainly saved her life? Nor could she even if she tried, for it kept coming back. For a split second she saw the rocks and the waves crashing over her, then the sight of him, swimming against the tide toward her. Raising her hand she waved to him and smiled, and he smiled back. Then she ducked her head, gathered up her trailing gown and climbed into the car, Richard a few paces behind her. But when she turned to link her arm through his, she saw that he was frowning.

"Who the hell was that you were waving and smiling to?" For a moment his unexpected anger took her aback.

"It was the American who rescued me from St. Clouet's Bay! I wonder why he's come to back to Jersey?"

"Whatever he's come back for is nothing to do with either of us," he retorted, irritably, and told Jean-Louis to drive on.

Affectionately, Evelyn reached out and lay her hand on his. But he did not take it.

Ross Klein stood on the edge of the pavement on the opposite side of the square, watching until the car had disappeared from sight. Then he turned away, strolled back the way he'd come, whistling, hands stuck into his trouser pockets. So, the crazy girl he'd pulled out of the sea over at St. Clouet's Bay had gone and gotten herself married. What an irony that he should be standing right opposite the church when she came out of it. Another minute and he'd have walked on past, another minute and she'd have gone. It was the flaming hair, lit up like a torch by the bright strong sunlight, that had made him turn and look again. And, sure enough, there she was.

He hoped she'd be happy. Hoped she'd gone and taken his advice and learned to swim. He hoped she wouldn't go off on any more crazy expeditions on her own in dangerous places. But whoever her husband was, he'd certainly picked himself a real looker.

He went on walking, staring into shop windows but not seeing them, knocking against people around him without apologizing. When he reached the spot where he'd parked his friend's car on the other side of the square, he kicked a stone out of his path, angry without knowing why.

He thought of her as he'd seen her that day, sitting beside him in this very same seat. Shaking, soaked to the skin, with the car rug wrapped around her, long hair dripping, her green eyes enormous in her pale face.

He got into the car and turned on the engine. On the journey back he drove too aggressively and too fast, ignoring the honking horns and fist-shaking of the other drivers. But, what the hell? Everyone moved too slowly around here anyhow.

The car sped out of the town and on into the countryside, the sun still bright overhead, the fields peaceful and green, wildflowers blowing in the gentle breeze beside the road. But try as he might, he still couldn't shake off his unaccountable feeling of depression.

He swerved suddenly to avoid a cyclist too far out in the middle of the road, cursing under his breath.

The sooner he was out of this goddamn place the better.

"How about a bit of swing to liven things up, eh? Hey, Etienne! Go and root out Jean-Louis wherever he is, and get him to help you bring down the gramophone from upstairs." He helped himself to a glass of white wine from Etienne's tray, then turned to Evelyn. He raised the glass in the air. "This is to you, Mrs. Mahone! Now go and fetch some of those records of yours and let's have some real music!" He raised his glass in the direction of the other guests who had come back with them from the church. "Might as well enjoy ourselves before the Krauts come marching in!"

"Records?" said Frederica Tregeale, looking from Richard to Evelyn suspiciously. "What records are you talking about?"

He winked at her.

"The ones she and Blanche play upstairs every time they can get out of going to Sunday church! Didn't know that, did you, Frederica?" He started to laugh. "Well, to coin a phrase: I've well and truly blown their cover, haven't I?"

Frederica gave Evelyn, then Blanche, a long, cold, unsmiling look; then she turned her back on them and began to talk to the Tostains.

"Richard . . . for God's sake! What did you tell her that for? You know what she'll do now, don't you? Take it out on Blanche!"

"Blanche doesn't really seem to be with us one way or the other just lately, if you take my meaning. So it hardly matters, does it?" He swigged back the rest of the wine and then plonked the empty glass onto the nearest table. "Ever since that night when she had a skinful and spilled the beans to all your grandma's pals that Julia's dearly beloved was a nancy boy, she's been slopping around the place like a sleepwalker.

Maybe a bit of swing'll liven her up." He helped himself from a silver salver piled with sandwiches. "Oh, come on, Evelyn! I'm only kidding!"

"I don't like you when you behave this way," she answered, upset by his sudden hard, flippant manner. "Ever since we got back from the church, you haven't been acting like yourself at all." She ran out of the room and up the stairs, angry with him. This was the other side of him that previously she'd only glimpsed, now and then, before it had disappeared again, so quickly that she'd barely noticed it was there. The sudden harshness, the unexpected flash of cynicism, the sarcastic quip that bordered on callousness. Yet he could be, and almost was, exactly the opposite. Sensitive, thoughtful, demonstrative.

He was the only man she'd ever met who truly understood her. She could tell him things about the past, and herself, that she could never quite bring herself to confide to anybody else, not even Blanche. Tonight, when all the wedding guests had gone and they were alone in bed, Evelyn had decided to tell him about Jack Neville and the forged Giorgione Venus.

Kneeling to pull out the heavy case of records from beneath the bed, she felt guilty for responding to his tactless words with anger. And today of all days. He was right about Blanche, she admitted that. It was true that ever since that night when she'd gotten drunk and made an exhibition of herself, she'd stayed almost constantly in her room, not even coming down for meals but having Jeanne or Martha take food up to her on trays. She'd kept her door locked more often than not. And no matter how many times Evelyn had tried to make her come out again, Blanche had never once responded to her knocking.

But there was something else, too. More worrying. More noticeable than her curious withdrawal from everyone since that night. The strange, almost vacant look in her eyes. The slowness of all her actions when previously she'd been so quick and sharp. The way she'd gazed absently at Evelyn as if she was looking at a stranger.

"Need any help with anything?" said Richard's voice from behind her, so suddenly and unexpectedly that it made her jump.

"Richard!" She got to her feet with the records in her hand. "You scared the life out of me!"

"I can't do anything right today, can I, my love?" He strolled into the room and took the records out of her hands.

"I'm beginning to wonder if you're sorry that you married me at all."

"Don't say that, it isn't true!" She came toward him, hands outstretched like a supplicant, her green eyes pleading. "I love you, Richard. And I'm not sorry about anything that's happened between us!"

"Except that you don't like what I said about Blanche?"

"It was the way you said it. The way you mocked her because of what she is. If you'd had to live on this island, in this house, for the last thirty-seven years with Julia and my grandmother . . . wouldn't you hit the bottle too?"

"So what was there to stop her packing up and leaving?"

"That's easier said than done. Where could she have gone . . . the only family and friends she's ever had are here on Jersey. How could she have earned a living? She's never been taught to fend for herself."

"With her looks and figure I'd have thought she could have earned plenty, anywhere."

"Richard!"

He hung his head in mock sobriety.

"Joke, of course. And one in my usual poor taste. I stand chastised." He dumped the records on a chair and took her into his arms. "Don't fight with me, Evelyn. Not today. Not now." He kissed her, and she slid her arms around his neck.

"I wish we could be alone. I wish everyone else would go away."

"They can't stay forever."

"Ross! Have you just driven back from St. Helier?"

"Yep." He got out of the car, slammed the door and walked toward the front door. "Why, what's up?"

"We've heard reports that German aircraft have been seen, circling high above the town, near the harbor and Springfield sports ground, where the air raid shelters are." Caroline Sherman followed him through to the living room, twisting her hands nervously together. "Didn't you see anything?"

"Nope." He sat down in a chair and picked up one of the newspapers. "I was looking in front of me, not up over my head."

"And come back with a bee in your bonnet?"

"Not that I can feel," he answered, laconically, flicking over the pages without reading them.

"David'll be back any minute. He walked over to the Fourniers' house to see if they'd heard any more news."

"Why should they have heard any?"

"Ross, what's the matter with you? You're like a bear with a sore head!" She sat down opposite him. "Look. I know what this is all about . . . it's me, isn't it? You're mad at me because I refuse to leave David and go back to the States. We had this out last time you were here, and what I decided then hasn't changed, and it won't. Ross, David's my husband and I belong here with him, no matter what. I won't leave unless he leaves too."

"He's as goddamn crazy as you are."

"I know you mean well. I know you can't understand why he won't leave and I can't. But apart from all his business interests, it's a matter of principle. This is our home now, for better or worse, war or no war. And no German army is going to force us to move out."

"Amen." He went on flicking through the pages of the newspaper mechanically, without looking at them. "So I'm wasting my time on the pair of you. So your minds are made up. So when I leave this time I won't bother to come back. OK?"

"Ross . . ."

"End of discussion. David's back." He glanced up. "Sorry I wasn't back in time with your car. I got held up in town. Or, I should say, that goddamn little pipsqueak of a place that you crazy islanders call a town."

David Sherman looked at his wife and she shrugged her shoulders. "That doesn't matter. It's only a couple of hundred yards to the Fourniers' house. Janet Fournier said that they're taping all the shop windows in St. Helier to prevent flying glass."

"Can't say I noticed myself."

"Some of the people who were desperate to get away on the British evacuation ships got left behind on the quayside, they heard. When they finally trudged all the way back home with their luggage, they found the whole place had been looted from top to bottom, even the coal that was left outside in the bunker."

"Real neighborly."

"David, that's terrible! How could anyone do something like that?"

"There's no morality in war, baby."

"But this was done by their own people! And that's even worse! *My God!*"

"To quote . . . you ain't seen nothing yet!"

Caroline Sherman gave him one more exasperated look, then she turned toward the door. "I'm going to make some coffee. Do something with him, will you? He's been this way ever since he got back from St. Helier."

For a long moment neither of them spoke. Then David Sherman took out a cigarette and lit it.

"Something got to you?"

"Nope."

"You and Caroline have words?"

"No more than usual. She says she won't leave and I said she's just as crazy as you are."

"We told you we'd decided to stay last time you were with us. Nothing's happened to change our minds."

"No sweat. It's your neck."

There was another long silence.

"Fournier was saying that they've been stacking up more sandbags along by the harbor, and by the first aid post. You see anything new while you were there?"

"I certainly saw something I never expected to see, yes."

"What do you mean?"

"Oh . . . that crazy Tregeale girl I pulled out of the sea a while back. I was right about her. She's certainly crazy." He gave a short, hard laugh. "You know what? She was coming out of the church opposite the big square . . . in a wedding dress. Can you figure that? The goddamn Krauts are overrunning half of Europe, not a stone's throw from your back door, and she goes and gets goddamn married! That's one crazy dame!"

"Did you speak to her?"

"Like I said, she was coming out of the church on the other side of the square. She saw me, though. She smiled and waved . . . then she got into a car and that was that."

Caroline Sherman came back with a tray of cups.

"We'll miss you when you go back." She smiled. "Promise you'll write, though?"

"I'm a lousy letter writer, didn't my sister ever tell you? Besides, I'll be too busy flying planes."

"But we're not in this war yet. You think that might change?"

"You better believe it. Guys I've talked to—who're in a position to know more than I ever could—reckon it's just a matter of when, not if." He got up. "Mind if I pass on the coffee? I think I'll just go take a walk outside." He left the house and strolled off into the garden, head down, hands in his pockets, looking around him but seeing nothing. Only the sun lighting up the long, loose hair that he ached to touch, the expression in her eyes as she'd recognized him. Try as he might, somehow he couldn't get her out of his mind.

"What is it, Evelyn? What is it that you want to tell me?" He stopped undressing, tie in one hand, shirt buttons undone to his waist. She still sat there on the bed, in the long, white satin nightgown that had been a wedding present from Blanche.

"Something that happened before I met you. When I lived in London."

He half laughed as he finished undressing, barely stopping to pause.

"For Christ's sake, Evelyn . . . this is our wedding night . . . can't it wait till the morning?" He sat down, pulled off his trousers and pants, and went over to where she was. He took her chin in his hands and, leaning toward her, kissed her long and lingeringly on her lips. To his surprise and irritation, she did not instantly respond. He drew away from her. "OK. Tell me. What's so bloody important that you've got to make a confession now? And if it mattered that much to you, why the hell didn't you tell me before?"

She hung her head for a moment, before looking up at him again. "I wanted to tell you before. I wanted to tell you a long time ago . . . it's just that I couldn't." She fought to find the right words. "I suppose I was afraid that you'd despise me, that it might make a difference to things between us. I suppose I didn't have the courage . . . and it never seemed to be the right moment."

He looked back at her steadily. Then he reached out and took her hand. "So now is. And I'm listening."

18

Blanche's bedroom door was unlocked; Evelyn could hear her moving about inside. But when she tapped lightly, then more loudly on it, there was still no answer. She opened it and looked around it into the room.

"Blanche? Can I come in?"

"Yes, of course. I didn't hear you."

She was sitting in the middle of the floor now, the large case that she always kept hidden beneath the bed open in front of her, piles of photographs spread on her lap and across the carpet. She held one up.

"I've been searching for this one everywhere . . . see, it's a picture of Gilbert with your mother. He sent it to me . . . did I ever tell you that? He sent one to Julia and Mother, but they tore theirs up." She sat there, gazing down at it. "I miss him so much. I miss him so much that sometimes I just can't bear it."

"Blanche . . ."

"He was so like Daddy . . . so like him. Here, look at this one." She rummaged feverishly in the suitcase. "This is a photograph of Daddy, taken when he was young—you can see the likeness, can't you? Here . . . you can keep it. I've got others. Go on, take it."

"Blanche, is everything all right?" She knelt on the floor

beside her. "You've seemed so . . . distant . . . for the past few months . . ." She let her voice trail off, not quite knowing what it was that she really wanted to say. It was the drink, of course. Little by little it was slowly destroying her. She thought of the photograph she'd cherished, the photograph Blanche had sent of herself that she'd treasured for so many years, the photograph of a young, bright-eyed girl who no longer existed inside this pale, glazed-eyed imitation, a tragic shadow of what she'd once been. It brought a lump to her throat.

"Blanche, is there anything I can get you? Some hot milk to help you sleep before you go to bed?"

Slowly, her dull blue eyes looked away from the picture and rested on Evelyn's face. "Hot milk? Martha always brings me hot milk."

"I know that . . . but I'll get it for you tonight." She smiled. "I won't be long." She got to her feet and went out of the room, hesitating in the doorway to look back. Blanche was still sitting there, as if she was in a trance, staring at the crumpled, dog-eared picture, holding it in her hands as a small child might clutch its favorite toy. The lump still in her throat, Evelyn turned away.

She could hear Martha's voice among the others' as she passed by the drawing room, but she went on down into the deserted kitchen, where the first thing she saw was Blanche's tray in the middle of the table, the tall beaker standing on it, ready for the heated milk. It was already in a saucepan, sitting on the hotplate beside the stove, and Evelyn picked it up and carried it over to the table. But as she poured it into the beaker, she hesitated, then frowned. Coming from the milk was the same strange, undefinable odor that she remembered from the flask of coffee that she'd drunk, that afternoon at the cove. Slowly, she dipped the tip of her finger into the liquid, then tasted it; as she did so Jeanne's words came back to her in a sudden flood. *I could have sworn I fastened the strap on this basket . . . now it's undone . . .*

Suddenly, she heard the slam of a door from upstairs, then footsteps. Grabbing up the beaker she ran over to the big sink and threw away the milk, then she ran the tap to flush away every trace of it. She found a dishcloth and scoured out the saucepan. She knew where they were kept. Shoving it away at the back of the cupboard, she took out another one, almost identical, then refilled it with fresh milk from the big jug in the pantry. She rinsed out the beaker and dried it.

As the slow, heavy footsteps came down the kitchen stairs, Evelyn was standing back at the stove, stirring the saucepan of milk.

"Mrs. Mahone!"

She half turned her head.

"Oh, it's you, Martha." Deliberately, she kept her voice casual and light. "I just came to say goodnight to Jeanne," she lied, "I haven't seen her since we left for the church . . ."

"She's gone on to bed, miss."

"Well, it doesn't matter. I'll see her in the morning. I saw the tray and the beaker on the table, and this sitting on the hotplate, so I thought I'd save you a job and take it up to my aunt. It's on my way." She came away from the stove and poured the fresh milk into the beaker, watching Martha's face from the corner of one eye. Was it just her imagination or did she seem unusually agitated and ill at ease? She took the saucepan back to the sink and began to wash it out.

"Leave that, miss. One of the girls can do it in the morning, when they do the stoves."

Evelyn picked up the tray and carried it toward the steps.

"Goodnight then, Martha."

Once inside her own bedroom, she paced up and down, clenching and unclenching her fists, impatiently waiting for Richard. When he finally appeared she banged the door behind him and drew him into the middle of the room.

"Evelyn . . . what the hell's got into you?"

"Listen to me." She ran a hand through her mane of hair and lowered her voice. "It's my grandmother. And Martha. I think . . . I think they're trying to . . . to do something to Blanche."

"What?"

She told him about the milk. "It's not just that. The flask of coffee I took with me in the picnic basket that day. It had the same peculiar smell and taste. Richard," she clutched his arm, "I'm sure it had something in it. Something to make me so drowsy that I just couldn't stay awake. That's what Blanche has been like, ever since that night when she got drunk . . . you said it yourself! She goes about like a zombie. Don't you see? They're giving her the same drug that one of them put into that flask of coffee for me! Don't ask me why. I don't know the answer to that; or the reason that they're giving it to Blanche, because I don't know the answer to that, either. But do you realize what this means?" She stared into his eyes, urgently. "Whoever put that stuff into the flask that day knew where I was going, and about the danger from the tide." She hesitated for a moment. "And if that American hadn't come along and seen me, I wouldn't have come back at all! Richard . . . somebody wants to kill me!"

"Oh, for Christ's sake, Evelyn!"

"How can you say that? You can't get away from the evidence!"

"OK. Where's this bloody milk that smells and tastes weird? Let me take a look at it!"

"I told you I threw it away! What else could I do . . . I heard Martha coming . . ."

"Who the hell in this house would want you out of the way? And for what reason? Come on, Evelyn, I'm tired. Let's go to bed. You've been reading too many Agatha Christies."

"No, Richard, listen to me! I know something's going on here. I've felt it since I first came to the house."

He turned away and started to take off his shoes.

"All right. So someone wants you out of the way. Whom have you got to be suspicious of? Your grandmother? OK. Give me one good reason why. If she didn't want you here she wouldn't have let you come in the first place. Julia, maybe? What motive could she possibly have? Or Martha? For God's sake, Evelyn, the woman's just the housekeeper! She hardly says two words to you all day long! Or to Blanche, for that matter. She just sits closeted in that bloody musty-smelling morgue of a library, going over the insurance valuations for every cup, spoon, and saucer in the bloody house!"

"You don't believe me, do you?"

"I think you're letting your imagination run away with you." He finished undressing. "Think about it. The night before you went to St. Clouet's Bay, you spent with me, and unless you've forgotten we didn't do very much sleeping. Of course you felt drowsy the next day. I did. In fact it was as much as I could do to keep my eyes on the road!" He reached out and pulled her onto his lap. "It was sunny, you were out in the fresh air . . . no wonder you fell asleep."

"All right. If I'm wrong about that then what about Blanche?"

"To be honest, ever since the first time I saw her she looked as if she was in a trance. Some days she's just worse than others. You know that—you've been here much longer than I have!"

Evelyn sighed, and leaned against him.

"I'm sorry, I suppose you're right."

Gently, he stroked her hair.

"You don't want to stay here, do you? Well, I don't, either. It was OK at first, but I'd rather we were on our own. The thing is . . . if it wasn't for this war everything would be so simple. But it hasn't worked out that way."

"People are still leaving on the boats. There's still time to go . . . Richard, why can't we?"

"We've been through all this a dozen times before. I told you why not. This is the safest place to be. Evelyn, the Krauts have overrun half of France and the Luftwaffe'll bomb the hell out of the RAF and every city and military target it can get to on the mainland. All we can do here is to sit tight, keep our heads down, and hope it won't last too long."

"It scares me so much . . . the thought of them coming here . . . what will it be like, what are they likely to do to us all?"

"Oh, it won't be that bad, if we all do as we're told and say Heil Hitler! Besides, half the stories you hear about the German atrocities are probably mostly propaganda anyway. They usually are."

"There's no smoke without fire!"

"This is a bloody war, Evelyn, not a game of bloody croquet on the manor house lawn!"

"But all the stories about the work camps in Germany and Poland . . ."

"Bloody rot. More war propaganda. Just like in the last war, when they were saying Krauts ate babies! Only morons believe that kind of stuff!"

She pressed her lips against his face. She slid her arms around his neck and closed her eyes. She was tired of talking, tired of arguing. She wanted him as she'd never wanted him before, even more than when they'd first made love, even more than on their wedding night when she'd told him everything about London and Jack Neville. There were no ghosts between them now.

"Richard . . . if only we could be far away from here . . ."

He pulled her down beside him and lay over her. He gazed down into her face.

"No more talking, Evelyn. Not another single word."

Slowly, he undressed her and tossed her clothes into an untidy pile on the floor. Her new silk dress, stockings, her brassiere and panties of black crepe de chine. Then his lips moved lightly and expertly over the warm softness of her skin, and he felt her body suddenly come alive in his arms. He reached out and began to stroke her, gently, then he bent his head toward her and kissed her thighs, her breasts, her nipples, her lips. Her long, loose, luxuriant hair was damp, her eyes were closed.

More roughly, he grasped her with both hands and as his fingernails dug deeply into the tender flesh of her shoulders, her green eyes opened and stared at him, desire jostling with alarm.

"Just tell me," he said scarcely above a whisper. "Just tell me if it's as good as when you did it with Jack Neville . . ."

19

Though it was coming into early evening, the June sunshine was still bright overhead, and Evelyn walked along the still-busy square, wheeling her bicycle, staring around her at the shuttered shops and taped windows of town houses. Every now and then groups of people would pass her, their belongings in tow, on their way to the harbor, still hopeful of finding a boat that would take them back to the mainland before the inevitable occupation.

The past few weeks had been fraught with chaos and confusion, panic, fear that had rapidly spread like forest fire. Shops had been closed and shuttered, bars and cinemas closed; stray dogs had been shot by the hundreds and cattle turned loose. There had been a run on the banks, cars had been abandoned on the jetty, and a rumor spread that Alderney had been completely evacuated. Thousands of people had lined up at the town hall to register their names for embarkation, but such was the disorganization that the next day people who had registered were bundled onto the boats indiscriminately with those who had not, while hundreds more waited on the quays in the glaring sun with their weeping, hungry children for twelve to twenty-four hours before they were taken aboard an available boat: small boats, mail boats, coal boats, and potato boats, anything that could hold human beings and sail. Those who managed to get away could look forward to a sea journey of anything from six to twenty-four hours, without food or water.

"Bloody fools," Richard had said to her once as they'd driven by on their way back to St. Ouens. "If they had any sense in that empty cavity between their ears they'd realize that all they're doing is jumping out of the frying pan into the fire . . . serves them bloody well right! I've got no sympathy with rats that break their necks trying to abandon a ship that isn't even going to sink. Gutless bastards. No one in his right mind would choose to go to a place where they're nothing more than a sitting target for Kraut bombers, which is just what they'll be. All those of us who're clever enough to stay have to do is to mind our P's and Q's and pretend to love Hitler, and we'll hardly notice the change!"

Evelyn had turned away and gone on staring from the car window, alienated by his sudden callousness. Had he subtly begun to change, little by little, over the past few weeks, or was it just her imagination? He'd become inexplicably less affectionate, more irritable, more critical of everything she did. Though she'd wanted to get into St. Helier today to see if Peter Tostain could stock her up with new brushes, canvases, and oil paints before they became rare or even unobtainable, he hadn't offered to drive her in, and instead she'd come by bicycle. Yet the backlash of panic and pervading fear wrought by the constant threat of German invasion had left its mark on plenty of others besides him. Martha was more morose and surly than ever. Jeanne had become sullen and introverted, scarcely answering when spoken to.

Evelyn continued to walk along, wheeling the bicycle at her side, until she reached Trinity Street, then she turned at the corner and made her way toward the harbor, and the home-bound road. The sun seemed to shine more brightly than ever in a blue, cloudless sky, and she paused and adjusted the brim of her hat to shield her eyes from the glare. Then, suddenly, she caught sight of him, standing away in front of her near the jetty, leaning against a wooden post, hands in pockets, staring out to sea. Almost at the same time as she first saw him, he turned his head and recognized her. Then he smiled. Leaning her bicycle against a nearby wall, Evelyn ran toward him. Then she stopped abruptly in her tracks.

Suddenly, there was a deafening, terrifying scream of noise

above and all around them, as the dark shapes of airplanes swooped out of the sun, then a tremendous explosion as the first bomb fell, followed by a lightning hail of machine-gun fire. Everyone in sight ran for cover, half of them mowed down like skittles by the bombers' guns, blood spurting horrendously in every direction. In the split second between the first bomb falling and the machine-gun fire, Ross Klein ran toward her and pulled her down beneath a nearby cart loaded with hefty barrels.

"Keep your head down! Don't look up!" He held her tightly against himself, covering her shaking body with his own. As she sobbed with terror while the planes swooped and the guns set fire to everything in sight, he cradled her head in his hands and whispered against her ear. "It's OK, baby . . . it's OK. I'm here. Hold on to me."

"Oh, God! They'll kill us! We're going to die!" Clinging to him, trying to blot out the terrifying screaming of the guns, Evelyn buried her face in his chest, the warmth and strength of him giving her comfort, negating her paralyzing fear. After what seemed an eternity, he said, breathing a sigh of relief, "It's all clear, baby." He took hold of her hand and squeezed it. "Goddamn lousy Kraut bastards!" He rolled over onto his back and peered out from beneath the edge of the cart. "You OK?"

They were lying side by side, her hand still clutched tightly in his. Slowly, she turned her head toward him to nod; then relief from the tremendous fright made her burst into tears. He gathered her into his arms and rocked her to and fro.

"Cry all you want to, baby. That's it. Let it all out. Shh . . ." She could feel him stroking her hair, his lips lightly grazing her ear. "It's OK. It's OK. They've gone now."

"Why? Why have they done this? For pity's sake, they must know that the island isn't defended!"

"I'm not so sure about that."

Abruptly, she drew away from him.

"Not sure? But it's common knowledge that all the British troops have been evacuated from Alderney, and that all the other islands in the bailiwicks were demilitarized ages ago."

"Common knowledge here, and in England, maybe. But there's a chance that the information hasn't even been relayed to the Germans. If it had, I doubt whether even they'd have been cowardly enough to launch an indiscriminate attack on an undefended target. Waste of good bombs, if nothing else.''

"But I don't understand. You mean the government hasn't even told the Germans that the islands are undefended?"

"They can't tell them, not through official sources. As soon as war was declared all diplomatic channels were cut. Only a representative from a neutral government could do it for them . . . like us, for instance. Joe Kennedy's the U.S. ambassador in London . . . whether they've asked him to relay a message to our embassy in Berlin is anyone's guess. From what's just happened I'd reckon they've left it a bit late in the day. Just like the British always do. No offense.''

For a moment they looked at each other. There was no anger in his eyes as she'd seen that day at the cove, when he'd rescued her from the sea. He went on gazing at her without speaking. One side of her face was smudged with dirt, and there were tear stains around her green eyes. Her hair had come undone from its ribbon and was falling all around her shoulders. He felt such a powerful urge to kiss her that he almost wished the German bombers would come back again, giving him an excuse to hold her. But he knew he mustn't give way to it; he couldn't. She was another man's wife and he had no right to. Instead he looked away to the scene beyond them, at the people rushing to pick up the dead bodies, the buildings on fire in the distance, the ground littered with wreckage and broken glass.

"Hey, come on. Let's get the hell out of here before they come back for another spot of target practice. Here, let me help you.''

Her stockings were laddered. One of her earrings was missing. A few yards away her bicycle lay twisted and charred. She ran her hands through her disheveled hair.

"How can I get back? I must find a telephone.''

He took her by the hand.

"You're in no fit state to go anywhere, little lady. I'll take you back to where I'm staying with my friends, and you can get cleaned up there. Then I'll ring your folks and tell them you're OK. I'll drive you home. No sweat.''

"I don't know how to thank you.'' She paused. "For a second time.''

He put his arm around her shoulders and they began to walk in the direction of Trinity Street, where he had parked his car, past shattered buildings and smoldering rubble, the wrecked houses on South Hill.

"There's no need. I'd do the same for anyone."

The news of the bombing attack at La Roque and the town harbor had already reached the house, even before Ross Klein's phone call. Julia and Blanche were waiting on the doorstep to meet them. Richard was inside the house with Frederica Tregeale.

"Thank God you're safe!" Blanche burst out, as soon as she set eyes on Evelyn. Blanche ran over to her and threw her arms around her as Ross Klein helped her from the car. Blanche turned to him. "And you. How can we ever thank you?"

He shrugged and smiled.

"No big deal."

"Please . . . you must come into the house. My mother wants to thank you herself, and not just for today. But for the last time you helped Evelyn."

He shook hands with Julia at the door and followed them inside.

"We found out about it a few minutes before you rang," Julia said, ushering him into the drawing room. "Some friends of Mother's were on their way from the village to St. Helier, when they saw the planes dive-bombing into the harbor. When they heard the crash, and then saw the flames, they realized what was happening and turned back. They were both in a terrible state—we had to give them double brandies. In fact they only just left a few minutes before you arrived."

"A car passed us back there on the road."

"Was there much damage done to the town?"

"There were several casualties, that's for sure. The planes just swooped out of nowhere, machine guns blazing. Anyone unlucky enough to be in their way wouldn't have stood a chance. I saw stores set on fire in Commercial Buildings, houses wrecked up on South Hill, and the Weighbridge is ankle-deep in broken glass. We were real lucky, I guess. I'd just spotted Evelyn when I saw them coming down on us, and I took hold of her and we made a dive for the nearest cover."

Frederica smiled her approval.

"Thank God neither of you was hurt!"

"Some folks down there weren't so lucky."

"Please stay and have a drink. It's the very least that we can offer you."

He smiled. "That's real kind of you, ma'am." His eyes rested on Evelyn for a moment, and unaccountably, she felt herself flush. "I'll take a straight bourbon with ice, if you've got it."

Julia rang for Etienne.

"This isn't the first time you've been to Jersey, is it? You were here a few months ago, when you saved Evelyn at St. Clouet's Bay."

"That's right. I'm staying with David and Caroline Sherman up at their place, just outside of St. Helier. They're real good friends of mine. Caroline went to high school with my sister, and after they'd both graduated and gotten married, they stayed in touch. When all the war talk started a while back, my sister and Caroline's folks back home started getting real edgy, and since I was going to be in London anyway, I decided it was the least I could do to make the trip here and try to persuade them both to come back with me to the U.S. Just as a precaution in case anything came of the rumors. Which it has." Ross smiled and sipped his bourbon. "Guess I was just wasting my time, though. Neither of them'll budge an inch."

"If that's the case then what are you doing back here on the island?" asked Richard from across the room in a chilly voice.

Evelyn looked at him in surprise. Ever since she'd got back with Ross she'd been waiting for him to thank Ross profusely, and to embrace her with happiness and relief that she was safely home again. So far he hadn't attempted to do either. While Ross Klein talked on with her grandmother, Julia, and Blanche, she could feel Richard's eyes watching her, and for some reason she felt strangely uncomfortable, a new sensation where Richard was concerned.

"Your friends, the Shermans," Blanche said now, "they bought the old Sorel house, didn't they?" She glanced at her mother. "Years ago, before they left the island, their eldest daughter was Mother's greatest friend. She knows the house well."

"Is that so?"

"Many years past," Frederica smiled, a little wistfully. She turned toward Richard. "This is Evelyn's husband, whose mother was the youngest of the Sorel sisters. He came back to Jersey a few months ago to look us up, and he still hasn't made the trip up to the old house to see where his mother's family lived for so many years. I told him that if he asked Mr. and Mrs. Sherman and explained who he was, I was sure they wouldn't mind showing him around.''

"It'd be their pleasure," Ross said, to Richard's stony faced profile. "They'd enjoy hearing about the old house's history. Kind of interesting to meet someone whose mother was born and brought up there."

"I'm sure it's been altered out of all recognition now," Richard answered, unsmiling. "And I wouldn't want to bother them with something so trivial."

There was a short silence.

"I'm having a small dinner party tomorrow night," Frederica said, breaking in. "And I'd be delighted if you and your friends the Shermans could come over. It might sound strange, having a dinner party after what's happened down in St. Helier today, but if my instincts are right and the Germans are getting ready to land on our doorsteps, we might as well make the most of what little freedom we have left."

"Why, thank you, Mrs. Tregeale, ma'am, I'd like that." He looked at Evelyn again and smiled, and she smiled back. "And I know David and Caroline'd love to accept." He stood up. "I'll go back right now and tell them, and Caroline'll call later to confirm. Even if they can't come, I sure will."

Blanche showed him to the door.

"We'll look forward to seeing you. Be careful on the way back."

"Sure thing." He looked back at Evelyn. "Take care of yourself, OK?"

"I'll come and see you out."

"Evelyn!" Richard got to his feet, steely-eyed. "I want to talk to you."

"In a minute, when I come back." She turned and went after Ross Klein.

"Will I see you again?"

"Sure you will—tomorrow night."

"I meant after that."

"Before I go back to the States?" He smiled as they strolled side by side toward the car. "Sure. I'll drop by to say goodbye."

"But if the Germans have occupied the islands by then won't it be difficult for you to get out?"

"I'm a U.S. citizen. They can't stop me from going anywhere while the States stay neutral, provided I have my passport and all my other papers in order. There's a risk on the boat trip back to the mainland, yes. But if I wait and see what's happening over the next few days—and my guess is the Krauts are planning to land—then they can see to it that the boat has a white flag or Red Cross sign so it won't be attacked from the air by their bombers." They reached the car and he took the car keys from his pocket. "No big deal. I'll be OK."

Their eyes met and held, and she felt the flush rising back to her cheeks.

"I expect you'll be glad to get away from here?"

"No way. What makes you say that, Evelyn?"

"You must miss America. And flying planes."

"Sure. But when I leave here I'll sure as hell miss you." Her face suddenly felt like fire. She couldn't speak. "And that reminds me . . . thanks again for that sketch of me you had sent over, it was just great. And you've got real talent, too. Never did get round to telling me you were an artist, did you?"

Inexplicably, she felt ridiculously shy, like a fourth-form schoolgirl on speech day. "I'm glad you liked it."

"One thing I couldn't figure out, though. We were only together a little while, yet you'd got every detail in my face. That was kind of flattering. To think that you'd remembered me as clear as that when we'd only just met."

"I wanted to give you a memento of being in Jersey—just a small token of thanks for what you did for me."

He leaned against the side of the car, and the late afternoon sunshine picked out little golden lights in his thick, straw-colored hair.

"I tried to call you that evening, just to ask if you were OK. But you weren't there."

Evelyn frowned.

"The same evening you brought me back from the bay? But I was here." She tried to think. "Who did you speak to?"

"Oh, some girl. I didn't ask who she was. I just asked if I could speak with you and she said you weren't there. So I left a message."

"I never got it!"

"When you sent the sketch I was just about to leave, and

there wasn't time to drive over before my boat sailed. So I wrote you a note instead. Did you get that?"

"No." She was frowning more deeply now. "What address did you put on it?"

"Miss Evelyn Tregeale, the Tregeale house, near St. Helier. Sorry, but I didn't know what this place was called, nor did Caroline or David. But I figured that there'd be only one Tregeale house so it couldn't get lost. Guess I was wrong about that." He laughed. "Are they always that inefficient with your mail?"

"I don't understand . . ."

"No big deal. Just that if you didn't get my note after you went to all the trouble of doing me that sketch, you must have thought that I was one hell of a bad-mannered guy."

"No, of course I didn't! I didn't expect an answer. I just can't understand why no one gave me your phone message and the note never turned up. It doesn't make sense."

"Not to fret over it, baby. Couple of wires crossed someplace. Maybe the girl who took the call just plain forgot about it. Maybe some thick head in your post office lost the note along the way. It happens. Sometimes things are more likely to go astray on a little island like this one than they are in a place as big as the United States." High above them, from one of the windows in the house, two pairs of eyes watched them. Neither noticed. "Well, I guess I'd best get back to Caroline and David." He smiled and got into the car. "See you here tomorrow night. Sweet dreams."

After the car had gone from sight she stood there watching the empty drive for some while. Then she turned and walked back into the house.

"What did he say to you, Evelyn? *What did he say to you?*"

"Richard, for God's sake! Whatever's the matter with you? He saved my life! I went back with him to the Shermans' house so that he could ring you to say I was all right, then he drove me home here. Why are you behaving like this? You never even thanked him!"

"These friends of his, these Shermans—were they at home when he took you there?"

"No, they were out, but—"

"I might have guessed it!" He came over to her and gripped her tightly by the arm.

"You're hurting me!"

"Answer me, damn you! What did he say to you when you were alone with him? What did he do?"

She tried to shake herself free, but he tightened his grip on her arm until she cried out in pain.

"I won't let go until you tell me."

"I don't remember . . . just things . . . we just talked about ordinary things . . . why he's here. That Caroline Sherman is his sister's friend . . . that he's a pilot in the U.S. Air Corps . . . just ordinary things . . ."

"What did you do with him? What happened when the Krauts bombed the harbor? Where did he take you when you ran for cover?"

"There was a cart about twenty feet from where we were standing . . . he pulled me underneath that and we stayed there through the whole attack. I was petrified. I really thought they were going to drop a bomb on us, or kill us with the shrapnel from the guns." She started to cry. "For Christ's sake, Richard . . . I thought we were going to die!"

"What did he do while the attack was going on? What did he talk about?"

"Richard—"

"I said, what did he talk about?"

"I can't remember! Please, stop it." She put a hand to her aching head. "I don't know what he said . . . just comforting things . . . things you'd say to someone who was as terrified as I was . . ."

"Did he put his arms around you?"

"Of course he put his arms around me. He'd have put them around anyone who was shaking with fear—wouldn't you?"

"And you let him?"

"If he hadn't been there, Richard, I don't think that I'd be standing here now. Maybe you'd prefer that? Maybe you'd rather I was one of those bodies that I saw, lying there covered with blood and broken glass, riddled with machine-gun bullets?" Her spiraling anger made her shout. "By the look on your face when we came back, I'm not sure you were even pleased that we'd got out in one piece at all!" She went over to the door to leave the room. "And shall I tell you something else? I felt ashamed of you downstairs. Yes, that's right. Ashamed. You didn't even have the good manners to thank him for what he did!"

"Thank him for putting his bloody arms around my wife?"

"Get out of my way, Richard! I don't even want to speak to you after the things you've just said! They're so ridiculous they're not even worth answering!" She tried to open the door but he rushed over to it and pushed the full weight of his arm against it to stop her.

"Oh, no. You'll leave when *I've* finished! What's the big hurry all of a sudden? What are you going to do now? Ring up your Yankee friend and see if he's got home safely?"

She looked up at him incredulously, realizing for the first time why he was behaving like this.

"You're jealous of him, aren't you?"

"That'll be the day. When I need to be jealous of a bloody Yank! What did you say he was? A pilot in the U.S. Air Corps? Pull the other one! If that's true what the bloody hell is he doing idling around here?"

"He injured the bones in one of his arms and in his wrist, several months ago, when his plane's engine failed in a routine exercise, and he had to crash-land. It's not knitting the way it should and because of that he's been grounded until it does. Satisfied? And he's here twice to try to persuade his friends to go back with him to the States for the duration of the war. Caroline Sherman is one of his sister's best friends."

"Oh, I see. You had a real heart-to-heart talk? I suppose he told you how beautiful he thinks you are?"

Angrily, she pulled away from him again.

"Richard, I've had enough of this!"

"Answer me, damn you! I want to know every word that bloody Yank said to you when you were alone, and I want to know now!"

"If I didn't know any better I'd say that you've had too much to drink!"

"Too much to drink? I'll save that privilege for your crazy aunt!" He grabbed her wrist. "And that bloody Yank that you so conveniently keep bumping into won't be the only one on this island with broken bones if you don't hurry up and tell me the truth!"

She turned on him.

"The truth? All right. I'll tell you the truth, Richard! I'll tell you exactly what we talked about! The Germans. And what we can expect them to do next, after dropping bombs on half of St. Helier harbor! Ross thinks they did it to find out if we have any defense system or not . . . now that they know we haven't even got a single antiaircraft gun to shoot back at them with, they'll probably invade the island within the week! We'll be occupied by enemy forces! And God knows for how long, or what'll happen to any of us when they do. But you don't seem to be concerned about that, do you? While everybody else is quaking in their shoes, all you can think about is whether your vanity's been wounded because I was saved from being machine-gunned by another man! You make me sick!"

She flung his hand away and ran out of the room and downstairs. For a few moments she hesitated in the middle of the hall. Then she went out and into the old tower.

All her half-started canvases were exactly where she'd left them, weeks ago. Her tubes of oil paint were gathering dust. She stood there looking at them all for a long while, trying to compose herself, to calm herself after the unpleasant scene with Richard. Then she propped one of the canvases up onto her easel, pulled on her white smock, and picked up her brush and palette, ready to paint. But, try as she might, she found it almost impossible to concentrate.

She loved him so much. Needed him. Wanted to be close to him. But, bulldozing over her feelings, angry, suspicious, he was gradually pushing her away.

Wearily she raised her brush toward the canvas.

"That fucking Yank!"

"Richard, for Christ's sake, keep your voice down!" A low, female voice spoke from somewhere in the shadows. "Do you want one of them to overhear you?"

"Them? They're all downstairs! They can't overhear." He clenched his fists till the knuckles showed white. "That bloody old woman, inviting the lot of them over here for dinner tonight. Just what I didn't want. I could wring her fucking neck!"

"It would've looked more odd if she hadn't invited them. Him, at least. After all, he's saved her precious granddaughter twice!"

"So everyone never gets tired of reminding me. Bloody Yank, coming over here, interfering. We never bargained for that, did we? And precious granddaughter my bloody foot! If she thought so much of her, why didn't she give her those bloody emeralds and some of the paintings as a wedding present, like you thought she would? Tight-fisted old bitch. She wouldn't give away the fillings in her teeth! She'd just better have left them to Evelyn in the will, that's all!" He turned round, angrily. "If you'd stayed and listened outside the door longer when she had Philip Le Haan here, we would have found out for sure!"

"It was too risky, I've already told you. Supposing someone had caught me? I've already told you everything I know, you know that. I've already done everything you've asked me to. And more besides. I'm sick to death of crawling around that filthy attic on my hands and knees, hardly able to see my hand in front of me because of the bad light. My eyes have been sore for weeks!"

He swore under his breath and lit a cigarette.

"Look. This was just as much your idea as mine, don't forget that. You found the record of the painting, and there's no evidence that anyone in the Tregeale family ever sold it again, so it's got to be somewhere in this house. That's just fucking logical!"

"Stop swearing at me! You'd never talk to her that way!"

"Fuck her and all the Tregeales! I don't give a bloody toss for the lot of them. All I want is what's coming to her from the old woman, and that bloody painting, one way or the other." He stubbed out his cigarette, still only half finished. "If we don't find it, then we do what I said in the beginning. And the Krauts occupying the island are going to make everything that much easier for us."

"How?"

"Because if Evelyn won't play ball, I can use Blanche for leverage . . . after what you've told me. It's perfect. And don't worry. When the Germans get here I won't waste a minute getting in with them." He laughed, harshly. "I'm sure they'd be more than interested to know the names of everyone on the island who's hiding a secret food store in certain secret places . . . and other things!"

"The last thing you want is to get known as being a collaborator!"

A hint of annoyance. "Do you think I'm that bloody stupid? The only way in this world to get what you want is not to let anybody else know that you want it."

Down in the courtyard, the Shermans' car drew up in front of the house.

* * *

It was cool outside in the growing dusk, and, pulling her simple silk shawl around her shoulders, Evelyn walked from the now-deserted dining room across the stones, her high heels making noises that echoed in the peaceful silence.

She went to the edge of the terrace, where a flight of wide stone steps led down onto the lawns below, and stood there, clutching the railing with cold, tense fingers, trying desperately to compose her thoughts.

Richard had scarcely spoken to her all evening; Ross Klein, seated opposite to her at dinner, had scarcely taken his eyes from her face. What was tearing at her was not only Richard's sudden, inexplicable hostility, but also her growing feelings for the American, which she had at first tried to deny, then fought to stifle.

Battling with her new unhappiness and guilt, she lifted the trailing hem of her black taffeta evening gown, and slowly went down the row of steps into the gardens. She walked, thought, and walked again, her feelings confused and unresolved. Absent-mindedly, she picked a flower and twirled it in her hand. It was beautiful in the silent garden, with the neat box hedges and flower beds, the ornate statues and sunken pond. She stood at the edge of the pond staring into the water, at the tall rushes that grew in profusion around its edges, at the lily pads floating majestically across the glittering surface. Then, just as she was about to turn away and go back toward the house, she heard a sound a little way behind her, and, suddenly, across the grass beside her, fell the shadow of a man.

"Hi, there!"

"Ross!"

"Aren't you cold out here?" He smiled, and she felt another stab of painful guilt because her heart had immediately begun to beat faster.

"No. No, I'm not cold." She had to do something. Distract herself. If she kept talking about trivial, unimportant things it would force her not to think deeper thoughts. "I was just about to go back inside, though." She smiled back at him. "It was rude of me to leave my grandmother's guests . . ."

"You want to walk awhile?"

Part of her, the part that belonged to duty, conscience, Richard, told her that she should say no, because, for her, a young married woman, that would be the right thing to say. But her lips could not speak that single word. Whether it was right or wrong, she wanted to stay out there, in the peace and coolness of the warm summer evening, she wanted to be alone with him because his very presence calmed and comforted her.

"Something bothering you?" They strolled on through the shrubs and trees, side by side. "If you want to talk about it, I'm listening."

"The Germans, I suppose." She wondered if that were really true. "Living under occupation. Everyone says it can only be days away, maybe even hours." She glanced up sideways at him. "It's fear of the unknown . . . not knowing what to expect. Wondering how long it will be for and if it might even go on forever . . ."

"No way. Sooner, later, we'll be in this goddamn war. Then we'll go over the whole goddamn Kraut nation like a bulldozer."

"You're very confident."

"That's how they train us. What we're brought up to believe. Nothing's ever impossible. There's always something you can do about everything. Because we believe in that, we do it. Thinking some guy can beat hell out of you and there's nothing you can do to stop him is the surest way I know to end up in a goddamn heap. Just tell yourself I'll do it! And then you do."

She found herself smiling.

"I love your optimism." They stopped walking. A wide stone bench sat back against the hedge, and she spread the material of her gown and sat down on it. Ross Klein sat down beside her.

"Don't tell me you're not an optimist, too?"

"I try to be. Sometimes it isn't easy."

"Is it just the thought of the Germans occupying the island that bothers you, or is there something else?"

How she longed to tell him how she felt. Impossible.

"Oh . . . I've often wondered, over the past few months, whether it was a mistake for me to come here." She looked down at her hands, folded in her lap. "Jersey hasn't been very lucky to me . . . if you believe in luck. Twice I've almost gotten killed. Then war's declared. They say that bad things always come in threes."

"The first two times weren't bad times for me, Evelyn."

Butterflies turned over in her stomach.

"You could have been drowned yourself that day at the bay, rescuing me! And killed by machine-gun fire from the bombers at St. Helier harbor! You don't call that good, do you?"

"Both times were good, because they brought me close to you."

"Ross . . ."

"I know what you're going to say. But you don't need to say it. I already know I'm way out of line because you're some other guy's wife and I shouldn't be here with you. But I have to leave this island in a couple of days, Evelyn, to go back to the States to fly planes, and I can't go before I've told you that even if we never meet again I'll never feel for any girl the way I feel about you . . ."

She could feel the hot flush rising inside her, taking her over. She could feel her whole body trembling and there was nothing she could do to stop it. She wanted to hold him and be held by him so much that it was almost a physical pain to not reach out and touch his hand. But she dared not.

"Ross, you don't know anything about me . . ."

"I know all I need to."

"Ross, we can't say these things to each other . . . we must go back in. If Richard knew I was out here with you . . ."

There was a sudden silence between them.

"Are you happy with him, Evelyn?"

For a fatal split second, she hesitated.

"Of course I am . . . I—I love him. We've only been married for a little while, just a few months."

"Then why did you hesitate when I asked you?"

With the last vestiges of inner strength, she got to her feet. "Ross, we must go in now. We can't stay here!"

Before he could say another word she had gathered up her trailing gown and run indoors.

20

Frederica Tregeale leaned forward on her stick in the huge leather winged chair and stared at the nervous group of assembled servants, then at the rest of them, one by one. Then she adjusted her reading glasses and held out the single sheet of paper in her hand.

"This document was hand-delivered to me this morning, with a note from the bailiff. According to what he says here, a German plane flew over the island a few hours ago and dropped three copies of this enemy proclamation stating that if we refused to surrender, the island would be heavily bombarded. As you can all imagine, he had no choice but to comply with the order. He goes on to say that we are required to show our agreement to the terms of surrender by raising a white flag from every building." She looked up again, briefly. "This is a translation of the communication the enemy addressed to the governor . . . I shall read out the relevant parts so that you'll all be fully aware of what we must do in these perilous circumstances, and what will happen if we refuse to comply with the Germans' wishes." She cleared her throat. " 'From the commander of the German Air Forces in Normandy. First of July, 1940. To the chief of the military and civil authorities. Firstly. I intend to neutralize military establishments in Jersey, by occupation. Secondly. As evidence that

248

the island will surrender without resistance, a large white cross is to be shown together with white flags.' That, I've just explained to you. 'Thirdly. If these signs of peaceful surrender are not observed, at seven A.M. on July second, heavy bombardment will take place. Fourthly. The signs of surrender must remain up to the time of the occupation by German troops. Fifthly. Representatives of the authorities must stay at the airport until the occupation. Sixthly. All radio traffic and other communications with authorities outside the island will be considered hostile actions and will be followed by bombardment. Seventhly. Every hostile action against my representatives will be followed by bombardment. Lastly. In the case of peaceful surrender, the lives, property, and liberty of peaceful inhabitants are solemnly guaranteed.'" She lay down the paper and looked up. "Etienne, Jean-Louis. Fetch the ladders from the old stable and Martha will find you a large sheet to hang from one of the parapets at the top of the house. Make sure it's secure. To the rest of you . . . just carry on your duties as usual, but no one is permitted to go far from the house, even during time off. Not until we know more about the situation. Julia. Go and telephone the bailiff's office and see if there's any more news." She made a sign of dismissal with her hand, and the servants filed out silently, one by one, faces pale, eyes downcast.

"Bloody hell! So the Krauts have got us over a barrel!" Richard took out his cigarettes and lit one. He sat down on the arm of the nearest chair. "Well, it might not turn out to be so bad as everyone thinks, provided we all keep our noses clean." He looked at Frederica. "But if I was you I'd find a safe place for all your jewelry and anything else that they might be tempted to salvage for the war cause, if you take my meaning. I've heard plenty of stories about certain Krauts with sticky fingers."

"All my jewelry is already in the safe."

He exhaled a cloud of cigarette smoke.

"I don't think you can afford to leave it there. It's too risky. After all, it's the first place they'd look. Where is it—behind one of the pictures?"

"Are you saying you think the Germans might loot us?"

"They won't give it as crude a name as that, but that's exactly what it'll be. They'll dress it all up in some fancy terms like gift to the Fatherland, or donation to the war cause of the

Third Reich, but in plain English it'll just be old-fashioned daylight robbery. Resist and they'll consider it a hostile action. Those emeralds that you wore that evening, the set that you told me had been in the family for—how long was it? That'd fetch the Kraut bastards a few Reichmarks on the black market!"

"Richard, please. Kindly moderate your language! I understand your feelings . . . we all share them. We're all in the same boat and likely to remain there for a long time to come; since the British government saw fit to leave the islands to get on with it and take care of themselves as best they could, none of us has any choice. But occupation or not, I've never tolerated bad language in my house and I don't intend to start lowering my standards now."

"My apologies," he said shortly, without sounding in the least sorry. "So what are you going to do about the things in the safe? Hadn't we better start searching for somewhere else to hide them? It's nearly four o'clock now. When the Krauts see the white flags and crosses, they'll swarm in here faster than bees in a hive. I don't trust them an inch!"

"Surely they won't interfere with the civilian population on the island?" said Julia, agitatedly. "Mother? If we comply with the terms of surrender, surely they'll leave us alone. You don't really think they're likely to start conducting house-to-house searches, looking for forbidden goods?"

"They'll ban all the radios for a start. Anyone caught with one'll be for the high jump straight away, no messing!"

"Julia. When Jean-Louis and Etienne have finished outside, get them to take this radio and the one in your father's old room out to the stables. If anyone comes here, we'll simply tell the truth. That they've not been in use for years and are dumped outside. If they want to confiscate them then let them do so. I never listen to them anyway."

"What about the paintings, and the porcelain?"

"What about them?"

"Most of them are worth a small fortune!" He stubbed out his cigarette. "Evelyn was telling me that that religious thing in her old bedroom is worth a mint. Haven't you heard the stories coming out of France about certain Nazi officers with a particular taste for priceless works of other people's art? They've practically denuded some of the Jewish aristocrats' private collections and shipped them back to Germany. Do you want to lose everything you've got? Pictures that have been in your family for hundreds of years? There's a war going on here, Frederica, and the Germans are winning it. When they walk into occupied territory they can take anything they damn well please, and find an excuse to justify it later. You won't be in any position to argue!''

"I already discussed the valuables with Julia weeks ago, and we agreed that it was better to leave everything as it is, except my jewelry. Think about it. If I'd ordered all the pictures to be taken down from the walls, and then the Germans came to the house, the white patches where they'd been hanging would stick out like sore thumbs! Use your common sense.''

"But the painting in Evelyn's old bedroom. She said it's a rare French master . . . You're not going to risk leaving that up there, are you?''

"I think Richard's right," Evelyn said. They exchanged a brief, unsmiling glance. Ever since the German bomb attack in St. Helier and his outburst over Ross Klein, they'd barely spoken to each other. He'd rebuffed, abruptly, all her gestures of affection. She couldn't remember the last time they'd made love.

"It's too large to be hidden anywhere they'd never think of looking," Julia said, turning to her mother. "There's the attics, but if they did search the house for any reason—and they can make up any reason they like, after all—an attic is bound to be the last place they'd look.''

Suddenly, Richard Mahone began to smile. He rubbed his chin, thoughtfully. "Got it!" They all looked at him. "None of the Krauts we're likely to get over here are going to be art experts, are they? So we'll be able to pull the wool over their eyes and get away with it. Take down the painting. Put it in Evelyn's tower. It badly needs cleaning, anyway. When the paint looks bright and new—and if anyone asks—she's painted it herself. She did it in London. A copy. From the original in some London gallery. They'll swallow it whole, won't they? Find something else to hang in its old place and nobody'll ever be the wiser. How's that.''

Frederica Tregeale looked at him as if he was mad.

"Don't be ridiculous, Richard. That painting was bought for an enormous sum of money, more than 160 years ago, by my late husband's great-grandfather when he was in Italy. It's an almost priceless work of art painted by a great master. Not even an idiot, much less the Germans, would believe that someone like Evelyn was capable of making a copy of it that would in any way bear a credible resemblance to the original. They only have to look at it to see that it's a genuine piece of art.''

He glanced across the room to where Evelyn sat, an unpleasant look in his eyes that he'd had when he looked at her ever since their quarrel over her and Ross Klein.

"Is that so? Well, I have news for you, Frederica. And you too, as well. You just don't realize what a brilliantly talented niece and granddaughter you've got." He smiled. "She forged a painting in London for her married lover that was so perfect, not even the president of Delacroix Art Syndicate could tell it from the real thing . . . that's why she had to pack her bags and come here in such a hurry." A deliberate pause while they all took in the shock. "Oh, dear . . . didn't she ever tell you?"

"Forgery!"

"It wasn't like that! I made a copy of a painting—"

"Intended to cheat and deceive!"

"That wasn't the way it was! I didn't know what Jack Neville was doing, I swear it. Not until it was too late. Because I loved him so much I believed the story he told me. I never dreamed of questioning the truth of it for a single moment, because I thought he loved me, too. When I found out why he really wanted me to copy it, and how he'd used me, all I wanted to do was curl up and die."

"You expect me to believe that?"

"I'm telling you the truth. If you don't want to believe it there isn't much I can do about it, is there?"

Her grandmother's cold, steely eyes bored into her. "I should have known that there was some other reason for your coming here. How short-sighted of me not to have guessed that there was much more to it than just an immoral relationship with a married man."

"That isn't fair! There was nothing immoral about my love for Jack Neville, nor about his for me!"

"He loved you so much that he was quite prepared to have you commit a criminal act on his behalf, not to mention collaboration in his schemes to sell the painting, and at the end of it all he happily abandoned you to your fate and went back to his wife. Quite some demonstration of love, indeed!''

"He wasn't the first man to put his own interests above his love for someone, and he won't be the last. Men seem to be conditioned that way!'' In her anger she failed to see the changed expression on her grandmother's face. "Yes, I made a bad mistake. I've never denied that. But I told Richard about it in confidence, I trusted him to keep it to himself, and he promised to. He had no right to humiliate me this way!''

"Have you been in trouble with the police over this forged painting? The truth, Evelyn.''

"No.'' She walked away, pacing about the room in agitation. It was part of the past, the part she most wanted to forget, and it was being dredged up and held up for everyone to see. The fury she felt against Richard for so flippantly betraying her trust made her almost hate him. "The president of the Delacroix Art Syndicate is a man called Robert De Braose . . . his daughter is Jack Neville's wife. He chose to keep the whole thing covered up, for reasons of his own. To protect the reputation of the syndicate, to stop people gossiping about his daughter's marriage. He didn't want anyone to know that Jack was in love with me.'' She stopped pacing the room and stared into space, unwillingly remembering. "He got me fired from my job and made sure that no one in London of any repute would ever employ me as an artist again. So now you know it all, don't you?''

There was a long silence while her grandmother went on looking at her critically with cold, disapproving eyes.

"I don't think so.''

"I don't know what you're talking about.''

"I'm talking about you and Richard. Things haven't been right between the two of you for several weeks now. Julia mentioned to me more than once lately that she's overheard the two of you, bickering. And I also understand that a few nights ago, Richard even went back and slept in his old room. I don't know what your quarrel was about, Evelyn. But I can tell you that for any marriage quarrels don't augur well.''

"Who told you that Richard spent a night in his old room? Julia?''

"Martha Le Bon.''

Evelyn was outraged.

"*Martha* told you? How dare she! My God, who the hell does she think she is?"

"A trusted, faithful employee of many years' standing. And a good woman. She couldn't help but notice because Richard asked Jeanne to put fresh sheets on the bed. Because she couldn't understand the reason why and was confused, she came to check with me."

"She has no right to go running to you with tales!"

"Don't twist the truth, Evelyn. Asking me to clarify something is not running to tell tales."

"She didn't have to say anything. If Richard wanted the bed made up she should have just seen to it and left it at that." They glared at each other. "She's never liked me. Not from the very first. I could see it, in her eyes. She thinks I'm an intruder and that I have no right to be here, just because I wasn't born on the island!"

"Nonsense. Martha has no interest in you one way or the other. Now, enough. The subject is closed."

"Enough? You're damn right it's enough!" She turned and ran out of the room and up the stairs, looking into every bedroom until she found him. Back toward her, peering through an old suitcase of clothes.

"You bastard!"

"What the hell!"

She slammed the door after her. "You dare treat me this way! Deliberately betraying my trust, humiliating me in front of Julia and Blanche, telling what I'd told you in confidence of my grandmother . . . my God, how could you do it, Richard? How could you stoop so low?"

"I thought you'd already told her everything."

"Liar! You knew damn well that I hadn't!" Her throat was tight with rage. "I told you what happened to me in London because I thought you were the one person in the world whom I could trust, the one person who'd listen and understand and then keep what I'd told you between the two of us. But you couldn't even do that, could you? You had to go and shoot your mouth off—to my grandmother, of all people! And right there in front of Julia, who hates my guts!"

He lost his temper.

"OK. So I told them. So what? You should have come clean with them a long time ago, when you first came here, instead of going around pretending that you were Miss Lilywhite-who'd-never-soil-her-pretty-little-fingers! It's no good trying to cover up your past just because you don't like the way it looks. You did what you did and there's no getting away from it. I said what had to be said to convince the old battleaxe that that was the best way to fool the Germans over the painting. Christ knows why I bothered! It's no skin off my arse if the Krauts take everything in the whole bloody house!"

"I'll tell you why you bothered. To get back at me. That's the real reason for all this, isn't it? The cold shoulder, picking quarrels, letting that hatchet-faced bitch Martha Le Bon know that you'd spent a night away from me in your old room, sulking, so that she could go running to my grandmother with the latest titbit! All of it, to punish me. Because when they bombed St. Helier and I was so scared I thought I was going to die, I let the man who saved my life put his arms around me for comfort!"

"That bloody Yank you're so sweet on!"

"Don't talk rubbish. He's saved my life, twice. Doesn't that mean anything at all to you?"

"Yes, it does mean something to me. Like too much of a coincidence to be true."

"What are you trying to say?"

"He's got his eye on you . . . oh, yes! I'm not stupid. It all adds up, doesn't it? He didn't have to come back to Jersey. That bloody Yankee wife of Sherman's already said that she wouldn't leave the island unless her husband went too, and he refuses to budge! Why did your darling Ross Klein bother to make another trip then, all the way from the bloody U.S.A.! It stands out a mile."

"Don't talk rot, Richard. I hardly know him. He came back again because after war was declared he thought the Shermans might listen to him and change their minds about leaving. As for me, he'd have done exactly the same for anyone, because that's the kind of man he is."

"He's the kind every bloody Yank is. Woman mad. Drape a skirt round a tree and they'd turn and stare at it!" He was beginning to shout. "And now he's conveniently been on hand to save you twice, you owe him a double favor, don't you?"

"I'm not going to listen to any more of this!"

He grabbed her by the arm and pulled her back again.

"You came here and started this, and by Christ I'm going to bloody well finish it! I'm warning you, Evelyn. If I catch you so much as within a yard of that bloody Yank, what the Krauts did that day to scare hell out of you will seem like something out of kindergarten—do you hear me?"

"Let go of me!"

"I'll let go when I'm good and ready!"

"You're hurting my arm!"

He took her roughly by the shoulders and swung her round to face him, then he grasped her by the hair and yanked her face toward his. Furiously, she struggled with him. "You bitch! I'll bet you didn't fight off Ross Klein when he put his arms round you! Did you? *Did you?*" He forced his lips on her, brutally. But as she felt her mouth crash onto his she bit his with such force that he gave a shout of pain and let her go. "You bloody little bitch!" Shock and anger brought tears to her eyes. They welled up and spilled over, running down her cheeks.

"Why are you doing this to me, Richard? Why have you changed?" Her voice broke in midsentence. "Why are you behaving this way?" More tears. "I thought you loved me . . ."

He stood there glowering at her, his face dark with anger, holding a handkerchief over his bleeding lip.

"Get out of here before I really give you something to snivel about!"

She stared at him almost without seeing him, trying to find the Richard Mahone she'd run to from the house that night, mistaking him for Jack Neville because they looked so uncannily alike; but only a stranger's eyes looked back at her.

21

Blanche pulled her cardigan closer around her shoulders and shifted her position on the chair. She rubbed her hands together, uncomfortable in the chill of the old tower, but she watched with complete fascination as Evelyn worked.

"If only I could paint like that. I'd give almost anything to have some special talent." She went on gazing at the half-finished picture, her chin propped on her hand. "Daddy used to take Gilbert and me to all the important art galleries in Paris. He had such a love of all beautiful things . . . he could see the finer points, the details that other people are blind to. I've known him to pick a flower and examine it for a long time, turning it one way and then the other . . . every flower and tree is a small miracle, he used to say. He appreciated everything. Things no one else ever takes time to look at, or even think about. And he loved music—I told you that before. He'd play a favorite piece of music and say that every time he listened to it, it was different. The same, but different." She got up and came closer to where Evelyn stood, smock tied around her waist, brush and palette in her hands. "He'd have loved you." She smiled, a little sadly. "If only he hadn't died when he did, everything would have turned out so differently." She went over to the window and looked out. "Oh, God, Evelyn . . . what's going to happen to us all? They're all out there, aren't they, somewhere? The Germans. Philip said that they've hung swastikas from all the public buildings, and that they've commandeered a lot of the big houses on the island for their quarters. Evelyn . . . you don't think they'll do that here, do you? You don't think they'll send any of us away to one of those labor camps? Not the ones I've heard about, in Germany . . . I just couldn't bear it. I know I couldn't. I'd rather be dead!"

Evelyn put down her palette and brush.

"Blanche, don't . . . don't. It's going to be all right. We'll pull through." She put her arms around her. "We just have to be strong. Not think about things that'll probably never happen. They don't have any reason at all to send anyone on the island away."

"But what about the things they've done to the people in the countries that they've invaded and annexed? What about them? I've heard about places like Dachau, and Sachsenhausen . . . Buchenwald . . . they throw anyone they want to into those places, they make up reasons if they don't have any. I've heard that the prisoners are flogged, and tortured, and sometimes starved to death . . . worse . . . Evelyn, do you really think all those stories are true?"

There was no point in lying to her, yet she shrank from escalating her alarm.

"Blanche, I'm sure everything will be all right. We just have to go on trusting, hoping that right will win and that one day we'll all be free again. We can't do any more than that."

Blanche nodded, slowly.

"Can I ask you something else? I'm not trying to pry, please don't think that. It's just that—well, it's about Richard . . ."

"I know what you're going to ask. And the answer is yes. We have separate bedrooms."

"But why? You were so much in love . . . you were so happy . . . it was after the Germans bombed the harbor that you started to drift apart . . . or is it just my imagination?"

Evelyn sat down.

"I don't know how to answer you, because I just don't know myself anymore. He just seemed to change, so subtly that I didn't notice it at first. Then we had our first real quarrel . . . that was really the turning point. He said so many cruel, hurtful things that I couldn't bring myself to feel the same way about him as I did at the beginning. It's as if the person he was then and the man he is now are two different people, and I don't know him anymore."

Blanche was silent for a moment.

"If you were really honest with yourself . . . did you fall in love with him for what he was, or just because he reminded you of Jack Neville?"

Evelyn hung her head.

"If I was really being honest? I suppose I was looking for a kind of substitute for Jack and Richard looks so very much like him. I missed Jack so much . . . I tried and tried, I fought, but I couldn't get him out of my system. I'd keep thinking about all the times past, times when we'd been together, and they were so real that I just couldn't believe that they were over, that I'd never see him again." She looked down at her hands. "When I first saw Richard, I transferred all that pent-up love and need onto him. I didn't look below the surface . . . now, only now, when it's too late, I can see that I've been a fool for the second time."

"Are things really that bad between you?"

Evelyn didn't answer. She got up and went back to her brushes, taking those she'd used yesterday from their pot, ready to be cleaned and dried.

"I've no more white spirit." She looked around her. "Do you think Jean-Louis has any in the garage?"

"Shall I go and see while you go on with your painting?"

"No, I'll go. I feel I need to get some air. Here . . ." She opened a wooden chest and took out a pile of sketchbooks. "You wanted to see these . . . start at the bottom and work up to the top. Every sketch I ever did!"

She wandered out into the courtyard and made her way toward the old stables, which had been converted into a huge double garage for the cars. There was no sign of Jean-Louis or Etienne, and for several minutes Evelyn poked around inside, moving old tins and empty gasoline cans, boxes of rusty tools, discarded bundles of old, oily rags. No white spirit. She went farther back to search, pulling out drawers and opening old cupboards festooned with cobwebs, still without any success. Then she spotted a battered old chest, stuck against the wall on the other side of the building, that seemed the only likely place left to look. She went over to it, opened the lid, and began to rummage inside. And then she saw it. Stuffed away at the bottom of the chest, half concealed by old newspapers and rags, was the jar of cold cream that had caused Blanche's disfiguring rash, the jar that she'd given Richard that morning to take back to La Riche. For a moment she held it in her hands, staring at it, trying to understand how it could have gotten here and, more important, who had deliberately hidden it. Then she heard footsteps on the gravel outside, and quickly hid it inside her cardigan. She turned round and came face to face with Jeanne.

"Oh . . . Evelyn . . ."

It had been a long time since they'd talked together as friends, a long time since Jeanne had even smiled at her. Like Richard, over the past months Jeanne had somehow seemed changed. Evelyn blamed Martha for that. Martha, who watched and spied; Martha, her grandmother's toady. But she was still Jeanne's mother and Jeanne was between two fires. On the one hand she liked Evelyn and wanted them to be friends, on the other she owed her loyalty to her mother. But Evelyn understood.

"Long time no see."

Jeanne smiled, a semblance of her old, genial self.

"Mother's been keeping me busy."

"Yes, I can imagine."

"Evelyn, I was looking for Jean-Louis . . . have you seen him?"

"No. I came looking for him too. I don't have any turpentine or white spirits left in the tower, and I must have some to clean my brushes. I thought he might know where I could find some. Ever since the bombing raid in St. Helier everyone's been afraid to go out in case the planes come back."

"That's why I was sent to get him." Her face looked strained. "Mother thought she saw a column of military traffic coming along the St. Helier road, a long way in the distance, too far to make out who they were. Mrs. de Corbiere thinks it might be the Germans. She wants all the servants to go into the house, in case it is them, and they come here."

"Oh, my God!"

"She tried to ring the Tostains, and then Mr. Le Haan, a few minutes ago to find out if they knew anything, but there's something wrong with the line . . ."

Evelyn was already running out into the sunlight.

"I must go and tell Blanche!"

• • •

They watched from the upstairs window, huddled together, as the dark shapes moved closer to them from the deserted St. Helier road. There were three cars, the last two that made up the convoy seemed to be crowded with men. Then, as the vehicles turned slowly into the drive and emerged from the barrier of the trees, Evelyn could see the bright sunshine glinting on an array of metal helmets. She gripped Blanche's hand beside her.

"It's them!" said Richard, not taking his eyes from the drive as they approached. "It's the bloody Krauts!"

Blanche moved closer to Evelyn.

"What do they want with us? Why have they come here?"

Her sister answered dryly before Evelyn could.

"There's only one way to find out."

All of them had seen pictures of the Germans. They knew the color of their uniforms; the peculiar shape of their helmets; the could recognize, without ever seeing one in real life, the hated symbol of Nazism, the swastika. But when the drawing-room door swung back and they were suddenly confronted with the sight of more than two dozen German soldiers, armed with rifles, every one of them felt the cold fingers of fear running up and down their spines. It was a shock.

Frederica Tregeale had seated herself in the huge winged chair, ready and waiting. Julia and Blanche stood behind, one on each side of her. Richard Mahone sat apart from them, on the arm of another chair. Evelyn stood by herself across the room, leaning nervously against the support of the wall. The palms of her hands felt hot and sticky. Her heart was beating fast. For a moment nobody moved and no one spoke. Then the ranks of the soldiers parted and a German officer, in full dress uniform and shining knee-high boots, came into the room.

"Madam, I am Korvetten-Kapitan Josef Deitmar, here on behalf of the new commandant of the island." An odd word here and there betrayed him, but otherwise his English was almost faultless, with little trace of an accent. "The commandant wishes to inform you that as from today, the first of July, the island of Jersey is under occupation government, and you are required to comply with all German orders that may be brought into force. My orders are that all large houses throughout the island are to be inspected, with the purpose of securing those deemed most suitable for our use." He turned and spoke in rapid German to the soldiers behind him, and half of them disappeared in several directions all over the house.

"This is an outrage!" Cold-eyed, Evelyn watched her grandmother face him with harnessed fury. "I shall complain at once to your superior officer!" She leaned forward on her stick. "Is this how the Germans intend to treat peaceful Jersey citizens? Marching into my home and telling me to my face that, at my age, I am to prepare myself to be thrown out of my own home?"

"Madam, I am only following orders . . . from my superior officer. I apologize on his behalf for any unavoidable inconvenience." His eyes darted about the room, looking at each of them in turn; then they rested for several moments on Evelyn. He inclined his head toward her and smiled. "Of course, our presence here to inspect the possible suitability of your house for our purposes does not in itself imply that you will be required to be rehoused elsewhere."

"Housed elsewhere? Am I to understand that both myself, at my advanced age, and my entire family and not inconsiderable number of domestic staff are to be booted out, lock, stock, and barrel, so that your superior officer can turn my home into a German army barracks?"

"Madam, all these factors will, I assure you, be taken fully into the commandant's personal consideration." At that moment one of the soldiers came back and said something in German in a low voice. "Will you please excuse me for a moment?"

The sound of their heavy boots on the polished floor sent a chill through the room. No one spoke. No one moved from his place. When he came back, all were still exactly in the same position, as if they were wooden dolls in a toy theater.

"You have a very fine house, madam. Many rooms. And considerable ground that surrounds it, yes? I admire also the many paintings you have. They have been in your possession for a long time?"

She exchanged a brief glance with Richard Mahone.

"All of them have been in my husband's family for several generations, yes. My husband is dead."

"I am sincerely sorry to learn that." Another glance toward Evelyn. "I would be obliged to have the full names of every member of your present family, if you please. And also the full names of your domestic servants. Also the date and place of birth for everyone in the house. This information is required by the commandant for his records, and will be collected tomorrow. On his behalf I thank you for your cooperation." He inclined his head again toward Evelyn and went out, the line of soldiers falling into a column behind him. As soon as the door had closed Evelyn sank into the nearest chair, Blanche sighed with relief from fright.

"Dear God . . . I've never been so afraid in all my life!"

"Be quiet, Blanche! Pull yourself together. Julia. Wait until they're all gone, then try the telephone again. I must get hold of Philip Le Haan."

"If you're thinking that he'll come up with some watertight legal reason why the Krauts can't take over your house if they feel like it, forget it. This is war, they're in the driving seat and we've got no choice but to knuckle under. Military necessity, that's what they call it, an unavoidable emergency measure. And there's not a bloody thing any of us can do about it."

"Where are you going, Richard?"

"Oh . . . just outside."

In the hall he peered from the window and watched them, standing in a group in the courtyard, Deitmar staring toward the stables where the cars were kept, then back to the old stone tower. He smiled to himself. He glanced quickly over his shoulder. Then he opened the front door and went on outside.

"Kapitan Deitmar?" He smiled and held out his hand. "I'm Richard Mahone. Mrs. Tregeale's granddaughter is my wife."

"Ah, I congratulate you. Your wife is extremely beautiful."

Richard shrugged.

"She's also a great admirer of the Germans. Of their enterprising spirit . . ."

"I am most flattered. Please give her my compliments." He looked around him. "Was there something in particular that you wanted to say to me?"

Richard fished in his pocket.

"I thought you might like to have this . . . a very detailed map of the island." He smiled again. "In the strictest confidence, I do happen to know that when news of your imminent arrival came, certain persons took it upon themselves to destroy every map of both Jersey and the other bailiwick— purely out of spite, I'm sure. I think you'll find everything you could possibly need on this one."

"Your cooperation will not go unappreciated," Dietmar

answered. He pointed toward the old tower. "My men have been unable to carry out an inspection of this part of the building. The door is locked. Is it used as some kind of store-room?"

"No. My wife uses it to paint in. At least, the topmost room—it has a good north light. If you want to look inside it won't take me a minute to fetch the key."

"Tomorrow will do." He stroked his chin, thoughtfully. "Your wife is an artist, you say? How interesting. I myself have always been fascinated by art. Which is why I so much admired the lady's collection of paintings. From my limited knowledge of such things, I would think that most of them are extremely valuable. And some of them very rare."

"Yes, I believe they are. Though I doubt if my wife's grandmother really appreciates them. All they mean to her is a decoration for a bare patch of wall and a burden on her insurance bill."

"You have a sense of humor, Mr. Mahone." He looked back at the tower. "I like that. You appear also a man of sound common sense. Someone who is intelligent enough to realize that no one can alter the inevitable."

"You mean the occupation of the island? I welcome it, personally. The English were never very good at running anything that bordered on the complicated. If you could have been here when the evacuation started, and seen the panic . . ."

"I can imagine. I trust that your fellow islanders will find us not the ogres made out by your British propangandists." He called several crisp orders in German, and the soldiers got into the cars. "I shall return tomorrow for the list of names, Mr. Mahone. Until then . . ."

"Just one more thing . . . do you really mean to take over this house for military purposes? I mean—where are we all to go if you do?"

Deitmar smiled as he climbed into the car beside his driver. "The commandant will only utilize those properties put forward on my recommendation. I think you can rest assured that that list will not include yours—on the understanding, shall we say, that in return for my deleting it from my list, you will be prepared to grant a few . . . small personal favors?" He tapped the folded map and slipped it into his uniform pocket. "Until tomorrow, Mr. Mahone."

Richard Mahone stood watching them as the convoy of cars

drove slowly away along the drive, then disappeared from sight onto the road beyond. Then he smiled to himself, turned back, and went into the house.

"Richard?"

The unexpected sight of Evelyn, waiting for him in the hall, startled him and made him jump.

"Do you have to stand there like a bloody ghost?"

"I want to talk to you."

"Oh? What about?"

"I'd rather tell you upstairs."

For a moment he hesitated, torn between irritation and curiosity. Then he led the way to the old bedroom he'd used before they were married. "All right. No one can hear us. So what do you want to say? If it's to ask me to move my things back into your bedroom, don't bother. I prefer it in here."

"Why were you talking to the Germans?"

"Because I wanted to know if we're likely to be kicked out of this house."

"And are we?"

"He didn't say. Is that all you wanted to ask me?"

"No, Richard, it isn't. What I want to ask you is what you really did with that jar of cold cream that burned Blanche's face. That morning when you left for St. Helier, the morning I went to St. Clouet's Bay . . . you promised to take it back to La Riche for me and complain to the manager, but after everything that happened that day, I forgot all about it."

He started to laugh.

"I don't believe this! We're overrun by the bloody Kraut army and half the bloody world's at war, and you want to know what I did with a jar of bloody women's face cream . . . how many months ago was it?"

Slowly, she took the jar that she'd found in the chest out of her cardigan pocket, and held it up.

"What's going on, Richard?"

"And what the hell is that supposed to mean? Where did you get that?"

"I found it, hidden in an old chest in the garage, while I was searching for some white spirit to clean my brushes, and it's the same jar that I gave to you that day."

"It can't be."

"Why are you lying to me, Richard?"

He lost his temper.

"OK. OK. So I didn't take it back. So I stuck it in the first place I could find where I never thought you'd look. Guilty. I didn't take it back because I wouldn't be seen dead standing at some bloody cosmetics counter, haggling over a bloody jar of cold cream. Satisfied? Now, if there aren't any more questions, Sherlock Holmes Tregeale, I've got things that I want to do." He pushed past her and went out.

For a while she stayed were she was, wondering what to do next. The Germans had worried and disquieted her; the feeling of being imprisoned and watched under some alien military rule, fear of what would happen to them and of what the future held, all crowded down upon her and she felt weak, helpless, impotent. She thought of Ross Klein and wondered where he was now.

He had promised to call by before he finally left the island, but she had neither seen nor heard from him since that last day. Had he already gone, she wondered, and not come back because he had forgotten her? Why, in spite of herself, did she find that he was somebody almost impossible to forget? For a moment she felt almost envious of him, a citizen of a neutral country who could leave the island whenever he pleased.

If only Richard had listened to her. If only they'd all gone while there was still time. But it was too late.

"So . . . you're saying that if the Germans insist on requisitioning the house, there's absolutely nothing that I can do to stop them?"

"More or less," answered Philip Le Haan. They were seated opposite each other at the library table. In the far corner, Richard Mahone was engrossed in a book. "They'll obviously insist that the requisitioning is totally necessary, that you'll be adquately compensated and satisfactorily rehoused . . . so you'll have no legitimate cause for complaint. You can always protest directly to the commandant, of course, but since the requisitioning is done on his orders, that would obviously be pointless. On the other hand, you can plead age, infirmity, the size of your family, and also your not inconsiderable obligations toward your domestic staff. More than three quarters of them know no other home than this, and have no other means of supporting themselves financially once removed from your service. Of course these are all small considerations when put alongside what the Germans consider an unfortunate necessity.

Soldiers do take up a lot of space, after all, and you have more rooms empty in the house than rooms being used. Still, let's not look on the black side of things—not yet, at least. If it comes to you, you can all stay in St. Helier with me, apart from the servants."

"But what about Martha and Jeanne? Martha's been my housekeeper for more than twenty years! Do they expect me to put her out on the street like a worn-out carpet?"

"Martha wasn't born on the island, was she?"

"What has that got to do with it?"

"At this point, with the occupation government only a few days old, almost nothing. Later on it might well take on a much greater significance."

"Why the hell should it?" said Richard Mahone from his place in the corner of the room.

Philip turned and glanced over his shoulder at him.

"Didn't you say that Deitmar was coming back to collect a list of everyone in the house, together with details of age and place of birth?"

"Yes. So what?"

"It's just a guess—and admittedly a long one—but I think the Germans want to find out exactly who among the population was born in Jersey and who wasn't. Why? Because they could well be thinking along the lines of having to deport non-native islanders elsewhere, if supplies of food and fuel get dangerously short."

"I'll fight tooth and nail to stop them sending away Martha!"

"I'm not saying it'll come to that. After all, Martha's lived on the island for more years, all told, than I have. Maybe they'll even deport me, since I spent fifteen years of my life in England. God forbid. But I'm convinced that if the war goes on for a long time—and it probably will—then getting rid of non-Jersey-born islanders will be a measure the Germans will have to think about."

Richard lay down his book, thoughtfully.

"Where does that leave Evelyn?"

"And you?" He glanced back at Frederica. "Of course, Evelyn and Richard both have one parent, at least, who was born in Jersey, so that would probably make them exempt. It's much more likely to be foreign workers and English settlers whom they'll get rid of first. Not people who have actual family ties. Contrary to what we've heard about them, I strongly believe that the Germans are anxious to preserve at least a veneer of public goodwill. They want to prove that all the propaganda about them is just that.''

"And the house? If they requisition it, what of my furniture and paintings, and my china and silver plate? They're all worth a small fortune . . . and irreplaceable, as you know full well. Are they to be taken away from me against my will, as well as the very roof over my head?''

"They can't take your personal property, Frederica. Compulsory requisitioning of a building or dwelling for a legitimate military purpose is one thing, outright theft is quite another.''

"Tell that one to the rich Jews who've had their entire art collections plundered in the last year, since the Krauts overran half of bloody Europe!'' said Richard Mahone from his corner. "Talk about daylight robbery . . . if that wasn't a threat of your money or your life, I don't know what is!''

"We can't believe every single story that we hear. We can only take the Germans as we find them.''

"A Kraut's a bloody Kraut in my book!''

The library doors opened, and Evelyn came in, unobtrusively.

"Well, Philip . . . since you've come all the way from St. Helier to advise me, you might as well stay to tea. When that German captain comes back, I want you here to back me up if he brings a requisition order. As my lawyer you can protest formally on my behalf. That'll carry more weight with the commandant.''

"Of course.'' He glanced toward Evelyn, smiling at the smudges of oil paint on her hands and smock. "I see you've been busy painting in your tower.''

"It helps me to pass the time. Though how much longer I can paint with oils is anyone's guess. The Tostains say that the stocks they had from London and Paris six months ago have almost run out. They've been kind enough to put by a special boxful for me, but after the bombing I've been too afraid to go back to St. Helier and collect it.''

"If I'd known that I could have brought the stuff over here myself. Though there's no danger now, provided you get back before curfew. That reminds me, Frederica . . . I think there's a strong chance they'll requisition one of your cars. They've passed an order requisitioning every vehicle under ten years old, which I know lets you out . . . but since you have two cars I hardly think they'll allow you to keep both of them."

"That'll be no hardship. Jean-Louis takes Martha to the market and us to church on Sundays in the '28. The other one is hardly ever used."

"Not since our wedding," said Evelyn to herself. She turned to follow them out, but Richard's voice called to her and she hesitated.

"You don't usually come in here. Are you that bored?"

"Evelyn . . . please." He put down the book. "I've been meaning to talk to you." He came to her and held her gently by the shoulders, the look in his eyes something of the old, caring Richard she'd known before. "Look. I'm sorry about the way I spoke to you yesterday . . . I shouldn't have done it. I know things haven't been the same between us for a long time now, but I want you to know that it's all my fault."

"Richard . . ."

"I've felt angry and resentful toward you, Evelyn, because now I know you were right and I was wrong about leaving the island before the Krauts came. We should have gotten out while we had the chance."

"You only did what you did because you thought it was right at the time, I know that. Richard, I don't *blame* you . . ."

"But I blame myself! I was bloody stupid not to see it. Curfews. Shortages. Being watched, spied on. And things'll only get worse, you wait and see. They'll be rationing. No petrol. People'll start turning against each other, informing on a neighbor who used to be a friend just because he's got a tin of ham or a half a dozen eggs that they haven't. War brings out the worst in human nature, believe me!"

"We don't have any choice but to stay."

He gave her a long, penetrating look before he answered. "There's just a chance that we might."

"What do you mean?"

"That Kraut captain who was here yesterday . . . Deitmar. I thought I'd heard that name somewhere before. Last night, lying in bed, I remembered. There's a Kraut general called Deitmar, on the East European front. They might be related somehow. I remembered that this Deitmar was involved in confiscating the art treasures from the homes of rich Jews the Nazis had deported to their work camps . . . only rumors, true. But as they say, no smoke without fire. From the interest that Kraut showed yesterday in the paintings in the house, the thought struck me that he was ready-eyeing one or two things, if you get my drift.''

''But he can't take anything from here! We're not Jews and they have no reason to confiscate anything. It would be illegal!''

''Since when have legal niceties stopped the Krauts from taking what they want? Evelyn, listen to me. If you and I box clever, and you do everything I say, I'm convinced that we can get ourselves off this bloody island.''

''How? There are German troops everywhere . . . even if we could get hold of a boat, all the beaches are being mined.''

''I'm not talking about escaping, that'd be crazy. I'm talking about being flown off, to a neutral country—Portugal or Ireland—by a German pilot. By courtesy of the Third Reich.''

''Have you gone out of your mind?''

''Far from it. I've thought of nothing else in the past twenty-four hours. All we have to do is give the Germans something that they can't possibly get hold of anywhere else . . .'' He turned away and picked up the book he had been studying when she came in. ''Take a look at this, Evelyn.'' He handed it to her. ''A priceless Italian Master said to have been Raphael's finest painting . . . stolen from the Orsini Palace in Italy in the middle of the eighteenth century, and never seen or heard of again. Where is it now? Can you even begin to imagine how much a painting like that would be worth today? It's completely unique. If it appeared in the saleroom, every major art collector in the world would be fighting to bid for it.'' He reached over her and turned the page. ''See this? This is the drawing of the Madonna made by Raphael himself, before he went on to do the painting . . . the only likeness in existence.'' Their eyes met and held across the open book. ''Evelyn . . . you know what I mean, don't you? Yes, I'm serious. I was never more serious in my whole life, because so much is at stake. I wouldn't even suggest it if I didn't think that you could do it.''

''Richard, this is madness.''

''It's our ticket out of this bloody Godforsaken hole, don't you understand that? Don't you think a man like Deitmar would give anything to get his hands on that painting . . . for nothing, if he knew that it existed? Look, listen to me, will you? I've thought it all out, every detail, every risk, every single thing that could possibly go wrong, and I know that it can work—because I trust you. All you have to do is to make a painting, using the Raphael drawing as your guide, and leave the rest to me."

"Even if I agreed, and if I could, I don't have enough oils left."

"You would if you stopped painting bloody cliffs and pictures of wild Jersey flowers! I'm sorry, I'm sorry. Look, this has got me all wound up . . ." He ran his hands through his thick, dark, wavy hair. "Will you just listen, Evelyn. Please. I've had a lot of time on my hands these past few weeks, and hardly anything to fill it in with . . . at least, anything worthwhile. So I came in here one afternoon and started looking around. I found a pile of old receipts and bills in one of the boxes inside that old bookcase over there . . . here, I'll show you. And they made fascinating reading." He found them and gave them to her. "They're the original bills of sale for all the paintings in this house . . . and look at the dates. They go back, some of them, to the beginning of the eighteenth century. But it was this one here that really struck me, because I'd already read about the Orsini Madonna in that book about the history of art." He pulled it from the pile and read it aloud. " 'Sold, on twenty-first April 1788, one painting in the style of the Italian School. A Madonna. To William Tregeale, Esquire.' Now, I know which one this is—it's that hideous, depressing thing that hangs in one of the empty bedrooms—but the Krauts aren't to know that. This is what gave me the idea. This bill of sale could easily fit the description of the stolen painting, couldn't it? Remember, it disappeared from the Orsini Palace around 1750, so it was lost for thirty-eight years before it was bought by William Tregeale in France."

"You really think Deitmar is likely to believe that?"

"Why not? I get to talking to him, tell him casually that I was going over these receipts for want of some other way to pass time, and I came across this. I tell him that I've searched the house high and low but I can't find this particular painting that the bill of sale seems to refer to. Get him curious. Get him intrigued. Let him believe that somewhere in this house there's an art treasure so rare and so unique that anyone who had it would own a fortune . . . and the finest painting that Raphael ever created. To an art fanatic like General Deitmar, to get his hands on something like that—a once-in-a-lifetime opportunity—there's nothing he wouldn't do for the person who could give it to him."

"How do you know that the Deitmar who was here yesterday is in any way related to the general? They could just share the same name."

"I'm convinced they're related. The elder Deitmar—who is either his uncle or his father—is a close friend of Hitler. He was one of the men instrumental in Hitler's rapid rise to power."

"I can't do it, Richard."

"You did it for bloody Jack Neville!"

"This time it's different! There's too much at risk, too much that could go wrong, and probably would. These men are ruthless, Richard, don't you understand that? Even if I agreed to do it, if they found out what we'd done, what they'd do doesn't even bear thinking about!"

"*If* they find out."

"Richard . . ."

"But they won't, because I've seen what you can do. You *can* do it, Evelyn! You *can*, you *can* . . ."

"Copy a genius like Raphael?"

"You copied Giorgione's Venus in London and fooled the head of the Delacroix Art Syndicate. Why not the Nazis? Do you think Deitmar could recognize a forgery when De Braose couldn't?"

For a moment she fell silent, her chin in her hands. Why didn't he leave her alone, why couldn't he leave her in peace? Was he really sorry for the way he'd treated her, or was he simply pretending to be so that she'd agree to what he wanted? She looked up at him, trying to see him as she'd first seen him, trying to resurrect the past and what they had lost somewhere between then and now. She wanted very much for him to love her, to fill the gaping void that Jack Neville had left inside.

"All right, I'll try. But if, when I've finished it—if I can scrape up enough paint—if I don't think it's good enough to fool Deitmar, then we forget the whole idea."

His eyes lit up in a way she'd almost forgotten.

"That's my girl." He sat down beside her and took hold of her hand. "Look. It can work. I know it. We've just got to be clever, and careful, that's all. The first thing we'll have to do is to get rid of that Madonna—the one in the empty bedroom that this bill of sale refers to. I'll go down to the cellars later and see if there's not a good place there where we can hide it. Just in case. No, wait. It'd be better to destroy it altogether. Then we can be sure that nobody will ever find it."

"But you can't do that!"

"It's too much of a risk to have it anywhere in the house. If Deitmar was the least bit suspicious, he might search the place from top to bottom—on another pretext, of course—looking for any picture that this bill of sale might refer to. We can't afford to take that kind of chance. For Christ's sake, Evelyn, I'm talking about our freedom. Don't you understand that?"

"What are you going to ask him for in exchange for giving up the painting?"

"Safe conduct off the island to neutral territory. For you and me."

"But how do you know you can trust him? What's to stop him from taking the painting and then doing what he likes with us? You'd have no guarantee that he'd ever keep his word."

"Wrong. I've already thought of that. We take the painting with us in the plane. When we've landed the pilot just takes it back again to Deitmar on the return journey."

"You really have thought of everything, haven't you?"

"Well, when will you start doing it? How long will it take you?"

"Longer than it took me to copy Giorgione's Venus."

"But why? This is a much smaller painting."

"It's half the size, yes. But you're forgetting that I don't have anything to copy from . . . I have to improvise the colors and the texture as I go along. That isn't easy, Richard. Not if you expect it to look anything like an original Raphael when it's finished. Then there's the problem of the colors themselves. In the sixteenth century artists used different pigments from those that were used later, and none of them are easy to duplicate."

"But when you worked for Pellini in London didn't you ever do work on any Raphael canvas?"

"Plenty of other fifteenth- and sixteenth-century Italian masters, yes, but none of his works. He was in a class of his own."

"But you know enough about his technique to imitate his style?"

"I'll do what I can, Richard. I can't promise any more than that."

He put his hand on her shoulder.

"One more thing that we'll have to be careful of . . . don't let Deitmar see any of the paintings in the tower. Hide them. Leave a few half-finished sketches about, make out that you're just an amateur, that you simply draw for a hobby. Whatever happens we just can't take the risk of inviting any suspicion. If he thought you were a professional . . . if he should talk to you and ask what you did in London, tell him you were a secretary, a shop assistant, anything like that. Even if he knew the truth, he'd never dream that you were capable of copying to such a fine degree that nobody but an expert would be able to tell the difference from the original . . . but we can't be too careful. Now, we'd best go in to the others, before Deitmar comes back for the list."

Evelyn frowned.

"Why do you think he wants it?"

"Ask Philip Le Haan. He reckons that if the occupation goes on for any length of time, supplies of everything are going to run so low that there won't be enough to go round. Don't forget that besides the civilian population, we have Christ knows how many thousands of Kraut soldiers to feed as well. Imports from England have been cut off. Only limited supples can be sent to us from France. Philip thinks that when the chips are down, anyone who can't claim to have been born on the island is likely to be deported. And what he says makes sense. Think about it. It was what he said that really decided me on this plan . . . because not only you and I are non-Jersey-born," he planted his final dart with care, "Blanche wasn't born on the island, either. Remember? She was born in Switzerland." A long, hollow silence while Evelyn's mind took in the unthinkable implication. Weak, tearful Blanche. Dependent. Unstable. To be sent away from everything that was safe and familiar to her would surely destroy what little self-control she had left. She swallowed.

"Believe me, Evelyn, we'd be the first ones to go."

"Go where?" she asked, already half knowing and dreading the inevitable answer.

"To one of the work camps in Poland or Germany."

Ross Klein slowed the car and shifted down to first gear as he caught sight of the road barrier up ahead. There was a group of German soldiers standing on each side of it, all armed with rifles and machine guns, and as he approached them one disengaged himself from the rest and stepped out in front of the car, holding up his arm.

"*Halt!*"

He turned off the engine and wound down his window.

"You will get out of the car, if you please."

He got out, looking around him. A temporary sentry shed had been erected on the far side of the barrier. From where he was standing he could see two German officers sitting at a small table, papers in front of them.

"What is all this?"

The German soldier merely pointed his rifle toward the table, and Ross walked over to it.

"You have driven this car from St. Helier?" asked one of the German officers, in tolerable English.

"From a couple of miles outside the town, yes."

"Do you have some business on this side of the island?"

"I'm paying a call on someone. Before I leave Jersey."

The German officer's eyebrows raised.

"Before you leave?"

"I'm an American citizen. On a temporary visit only."

"Your passport?"

"I don't have it with me."

"Do you have some other means of identification?"

"Not on me, no."

The two men had a short, rapid conversation in German, then the first one looked back at Ross.

"You cannot pass the barrier without identification. We regret that you must return and come back with your American passport."

"Look—"

"These are the orders of the commandant. You will please get into the car and turn back."

Angrily, Ross did as he was told, with ill grace. Halfway along the road back again, he suddenly realized that he was running short of gas and that because of the strict rationing in force even before the Germans came, it would be difficult, maybe even impossible, for David Sherman to get more. He felt guilty at using more than his fair share of it without thinking how they would manage after he was gone.

"It doesn't matter," Caroline said, when he'd finally gotten back to the house to collect his passport, "David doesn't use the car that much, not usually. And as far as I know, he has about a gallon left of his ration in a can in the garage. Use some of that."

"I could walk."

"It'd take you all day!"

He merely shrugged.

"Why don't you telephone instead?"

He hesitated, having already asked himself that question many times, over and over again.

"Because I want to see her again."

Blanche walked into her room and switched on the light, then stopped in the middle of the floor, abruptly. Someone had been here.

Her eyes traveled over the dressing table, then to the half-open drawers, a feeling of horror and panic rising in her. The top of the dressing table was completely clear, the drawers where she'd kept her spare supplies of lipstick and face powder were empty. She ran toward them, feverishly pulling out every one and throwing it hysterically onto the floor. She began to cry. She began to tear at her hair.

Then the door behind her opened and she swung round and came face to face with her sister, Julia.

"What have you done with them?" Her voice rose to a shout. "What have you done with all my things?" She went over to her and shook her. "Where are they? Tell me where they are, damn you!"

Julia pushed her away.

"If I didn't know better I'd say that you've been drinking!"

"Liar! I haven't touched a drop for months and you know it!"

"And how long will you keep that up, Blanche? How long can you keep a grip on reality this time, before you fold up like the weakling you are, and drink yourself senseless? I wonder!"

"You tell me where you've put my things or I'll choke it out of you!" Desperately, she looked around her. She pulled open the doors of her wardrobe and threw out everything inside. She opened drawers. The cupboard beside the door. Then she noticed that her suitcase, the suitcase in which she kept all her photographs and cuttings, had been pulled out from beneath the bed. She ran over to it and flung open the lid.

"It's empty! All my pictures are gone!" Her hands began to shake. She began to cry. *"My pictures of Daddy!"*

"Your pictures? *Your* pictures of Daddy?" Julia sneered, baiting her. "You think that he belonged to you, don't you? You think that you were the only important thing in his life?"

"I loved him as you never did, as you could never know how to! Because you're like Mother, aren't you, Julia? You're incapable of feeling real love. Or giving it. That was why Daddy loved me best, me and Gilbert."

"You, you . . . *always you!* You and Gilbert! He was my father too, but you took him away from me, and I'll never forgive you for that, for as long as I live! Nor will Mother. Before you were born he was close to us. He was part of us. Then you came along and everything changed." She pointed a shaking finger toward the empty case on the floor. "While you and Evelyn were out, I came in here and looked through every single picture in there, and do you know what I saw? Every photograph of Daddy was taken with you! Holding you. Kissing you. Sitting you on his knee!" She took something out of her pocket and held it up. "Do you see this one? This is the only one I kept. Take a look at it, Blanche. Take a good, long look. This is the only one I found of myself . . . of the four of us, all together. But look at it closely . . . do you see what I see? Something wrong, isn't there? Because we're not together at all. Here's Daddy, with his arms around you and Gilbert. And here's me, standing alone, like the stranger I was to him!" She tore it into little pieces and threw it in Blanche's face. "You took him away from me! He would have loved me if you'd never been born. He was my father before he was yours!" Spittle appeared at the corners of her mouth. "I've always hated you, even before Martha told me the truth . . . that you're not really my proper sister at all." A cruel smile touched her lips. "Yes, I thought that would shock you. All these years, Mother's kept Daddy's secret, out of a false sense of respect and loyalty. She even kept the truth from me. And I'd have never known it, but for Martha. She thought that I had the right to be told."

"What are you talking about?"

"She's always detested and despised you, because ever since you were born, you've taken the love and attention from Daddy that he should have given to me!"

"Liar!"

"I wonder what he'd think if he could see you now? A has-been. A miserable drunk. His precious little girl who never knew how to do anything except paint her pretty doll's face!"

"I don't know what you're talking about! What have you done with my pictures, you bitch? You give them back to me, you hear?" Blanche's strained voice had risen to a shout. "If you don't, I'll go straight downstairs and tell Mother!"

"Tell Mother? Mother's out, visiting the Le Fevres." Cruelly, she began to laugh. "You're all alone with me, little sister . . . just like all those other times, when we were children . . . do you remember? When I used to lock you up in one of the cupboards, and then sit there, listening to your screams?

"You want your pictures, do you? Well, you can't have them. I've got Martha to burn them all on the fire."

Blanche fled downstairs, tripping over her own feet in her desperate haste. She ran along the corridor, flinging open the door of every room. They were all empty. Then she heard noises in the depths of the silent house, from what seemed a long way away. Breathless, half crying, she ran down the steep steps into the kitchen and came face to face with Martha Le Bon.

"Give those to me! They're mine! All I have left of Daddy. You have no right!"

Julia had followed her downstairs. She stood there, a few feet away on the staircase, watching Martha throw the pile of photographs and cuttings one by one onto the kitchen fire.

"Stay where you are, Blanche."

"No! *No!*" She tried to lunge forward toward Martha, but her sister leaped forward and pinioned her by the arms. When she struggled to break free, Julia twisted one arm behind her back till the searing pain made her cry out, then pushed her toward the door.

"Burn them, Martha. Burn every one."

"I hate you!"

"Shut up, you worthless bitch, or I'll make you sorry that you ever saw the light of day!" Julia came toward her, brandishing her mother's walking stick. Then she hit Blanche so savagely across the face that she split the skin across the bridge of her nose and Blanche screamed out in agony.

"You hate *me?* You don't know the meaning of the word.

You can't even begin to imagine the hate I've had for you all these years, the hate I was forced to hide because Mother and Daddy wanted to protect you from the truth!" Her voice shook with uncharacteristic emotion. *"You bastard!"*

Sobbing, hair hanging in her eyes, her face blood-spattered, Blanche stared at her.

"Daddy . . . Mother?"

"Not *your* mother! Gilbert's. Mine. But not yours. Your mother was a cheap French whore Daddy met in Paris!"

Blanche swallowed. The whole room swam. Round and round. She opened her lips to speak through her appalling pain, but no words came out. There was a sudden terrible silence, broken only by the sound of Martha throwing the torn-up pictures relentlessly into the crackling fire.

"Mother was heartbroken. He wanted to leave her for his little French slut. She had no one to confide in except Martha, and she made Martha swear never to speak a word of the truth to anyone, least of all me and you. If Martha hadn't seen the way he favored you above me, his true daughter, she would never have told me what happened. But she thought that I had a right to know the truth. And I have.

"Mother loved Daddy very much, and he betrayed her. She begged him not to leave her, said that if he stayed she'd pretend that you were hers. That's why he took her away to Switzerland, where you were born." A triumphant pause. "But if you look at your birth certificate, you'll see that you're nothing more than a French whore's bastard. Nothing can change that."

"No!"

"It's true! They went abroad for more than a year, so nobody on the island would ever suspect. He planned it all, to protect you! And if your whore of a mother hadn't died having you, he would have left all of us to go to her!"

The tears of anguish and pain ran silently down Blanche's cheeks, and she looked at each of them in turn. She could see the hate in their eyes. She thought of her brother, Gilbert, laughing, teasing her, calling gaily to her as he threw the bright red ball at her across the beach, his childish voice echoing back across the lost years. *"You're so different from them, Blanche . . . you even look different. Almost as if you weren't related to them at all."*

"Why didn't Mother tell me the truth?"

"Because she was too ashamed. Because she'd promised Daddy that she never would. But now the Germans are here on the island, soon everybody is going to know."

"I don't understand."

"Before long, there won't be enough food for everyone on the island, anyone not Jersey-born will be deported. You're not Jersey-born, are you, Blanche? You're just the bastard of a long-dead French whore with a blank space on your French birth certificate where the name of the father should be. And that is exactly what I shall tell the Germans."

"No!"

"Do you know what they'll do to you, Blanche? Have you any idea what it will be like, a prisoner in a work camp with thousands of others? Where you can't wash, where you have barely enough food to keep you alive, where your body becomes filthy and covered with sores, and your hair is crawling with fleas and lice?"

"Stop it! For pity's sake, please!"

Julia came over to where she was and thrust her face close to hers.

"I hope they make you suffer before you die."

Wildly, she fought with Julia and pulled herself free. Then, screaming and sobbing, she fled up the kitchen steps and on upstairs to her room, where she threw herself on the floor and pummeled it hysterically with her fists. No Evelyn. No Richard. The house was empty. No one to hear her. No one to help her. She was alone. Alone.

There was a sudden creaking of floorboards outside her door, and she peered up, slowly, fearfully, through red, swollen eyes and a tangled curtain of hair.

A woman's feet were all she could see at first, until she raised her head and saw the rest of the body, and then the face.

"Miss Julia thought you might like to have this, Miss Blanche," said Jeanne Le Bon, holding out the bottle toward her. She smiled, looking down at the prostrate figure on the floor with light, malicious eyes, amused at the shock on her face. "Yes, I know the truth about you, too. Mother told me." She put the bottle down on the floor beside her. "Here . . . take it . . ."

22

As Evelyn heard the sound of the approaching car on the road behind her she stopped and stepped back onto the grass verge. But instead of passing her by it slowed down rapidly, and as it drew level with her came to a halt.

"Hi there!"

"Ross Klein!"

He switched off the engine and got out.

"I was on my way over to see you. Now I can give you a lift back."

"You were coming to see me?"

"I promised to, didn't I? I promised to call on you to say goodbye."

She tried to keep the smile alive on her lips, so that he wouldn't see her disappointment.

"Oh, I see . . . you're leaving the island. When do you go?"

"On Sunday morning."

For a moment they just looked at each other.

"What are you doing out here, anyway? Just taking a walk?"

"It was a fine day. A bit stuffy working in the tower. So I decided to bring my sketchbook and make a few pictures."

"Can I see?"

They sat down on the grass bank side by side, and she handed him the book.

"Very good. I'm impressed. You have a lot of talent." He went on turning over the pages, one by one.

"Thank you."

"I'm not being patronizing. I really mean that. Do you ever paint things, too?"

She looked down at her folded hands.

"Sometimes. Since the Germans came it's been almost impossible to get hold of fresh supplies of oil paints, mainly because ordinarily they're imported direct from London or Paris. It's hard to say if I'll be able to get any more at all."

"Maybe I can do something to help, if you let me have a list of what you want."

"I'd really appreciate that." She couldn't quite meet his eyes. The memory of sitting side by side with him, like this, on that long-ago evening in the garden at the Tregeale manor came back to her, and the words that had passed between them. She fought with herself. Against what she truly felt for him. Against a sense of disloyalty to Richard, despite everything. "But I've caused you quite enough trouble already."

"Oh? How come?"

"You know how. If it wasn't for you I wouldn't be here now."

"Big deal. I'm glad I've done something worthwhile in my life, leastways," he said, smiling, leaving her wondering if he was teasing her or not. She felt her face growing hot as he looked at her. For a moment there was silence between them.

"Before I go, Evelyn . . . there's something I've been wanting to say to you . . ." He leaned forward. "An apology, really. Looking back, I was real hard on you that day at the bay. My tactics were all wrong. I didn't mean to sound so mad at you."

"I deserved it."

"No way. It was my fault, not yours. I spend so much of my life flying airplanes that I'm no good at saying the right things to crying women."

"Is that what you'll do when you get back home again? If they pass you fit this time?"

"Sure, it's my job. It's what I was trained to do. And when we get into this goddamn war, I guess I'll do a lot more. Shoot down a few goddamn Kraut planes before they shoot me."

She looked at him sharply. She suddenly felt like crying. "Don't say that! Please, don't say it. Please don't talk about dying."

He tried to make his voice sound flippant, normal.

"We all go sometime, honey. For fighter pilots, it's just an occupational hazard."

"But America isn't part of this war."

"You said that before. But we will be, sooner or later, I told you why. I have a big hunch that Hitler's going to get real ambitious, pretty soon, and because even the Third Reich doesn't have enough soldiers to fight a war on every front, he's going to have to start looking for bigger allies . . . like the Japanese. There's no way Roosevelt could ignore something like that . . . the Pacific's right on our back doorstep."

A silence.

"Ross? Could I ask you for a favor before you go? Could I make another sketch of you, for myself this time . . . just as a keepsake?" She tried to keep the tone of her trembling voice light, so that he'd never notice the depth of her emotion. "I shall call it, 'The Man Who Saved My Life Twice.' There, what do you think of that?"

"Sounds great. Not sure if I really deserve it. But it's fine with me, if I can have a favor from you?" He reached out and touched her hair, and electricity passed between them. "A lock of this." He was no longer smiling now. "So that every time I look at it I'll be reminded of you."

"Ross . . ."

He stood up, unexpectedly, taking her by surprise. "How about doing that sketch right here and now? And I'll have that lock of firebrand hair. Then, when I get back home I'll be able to say . . . this lock of hair was given to me by a very famous artist." He smiled, and the moment of danger when he'd almost betrayed himself passed. "That's what you'll be one day . . . you know that? When this war's over . . ."

He'd dropped her at the end of the drive and she'd walked slowly along it back to the house, but when she reached it she hesitated before going inside. She looked up at the tower, then turned away and went up to her studio on the top floor. One of the wooden chests she'd brought with her from England stood back against the wall, and she opened the lid and rummaged inside it until she found what she was looking for.

Slowly, she began to turn over the pages one by one, until she came to the sketch she'd made of Jack Neville, so long ago. For a time she stared down at it, remembering, struck again, as she'd been before, at his likeness to Richard. Then she ripped the page from the book and crumpled it up in her hands.

"Where's Blanche?"

"Where do you think she is? Didn't you see from the outside when you came back that all her curtains are drawn? There was a single bottle of brandy left in the cupboard and she's taken it and locked herself in her room!"

"But the cupboard was locked!"

"She stole Martha's spare keys from the pantry. We found them by the empty cupboard on the floor." Julia seemed unusually agitated and ill at ease—or was it just Evelyn's imagination? "How could she do this? A few minutes ago we got a call from Peter Tostain. The Germans are coming round searching all the houses to see if anyone has any stores of foodstuffs or drink that have been prohibited. If they come here and see her in that state . . . we're not supposed to have any brandy . . ."

"They won't look upstairs. If they ask you'll just have to say that she's feeling ill. I'll go to her."

"She won't let you in. I've already tried."

As Evelyn started to go up the stairs she hesitated and looked back.

"Why did she do it? What upset her? I've never known her to just drink, not unless there was something wrong that pushed her over the edge . . . like all the other times."

"With Blanche, nobody can ever tell."

She caught sight of the single German car coming along the drive as she passed the upstairs landing window on her way to Blanche's room, and her heart missed a beat as she recognized the hated swastika symbol emblazoned on each side. The palms of her hands felt damp and sticky. She felt butterflies in her stomach, fresh fear at what Richard had compelled her to do, half against her will. All the risks, all the dangers that she'd tried to put away at the back of her mind came flooding back, like the tide, refusing to be still.

The car drew up at the front of the house. But to her surprise, only Deitmar got out of it. There was no driver. Not even a single German guard. Flattening herself against the wall, she wondered what he wanted, why he'd come here alone. As he suddenly glanced up toward where she was standing, she ducked out of sight and waited, heart beating fast, listening to the hateful sound of his heavy boots crunching against the gravel. Then he pounded heavily on the front door.

She didn't see who went to open it. She heard only his voice, then even that became fainter and finally disappeared, as whoever had let him in had taken him into one of the downstairs rooms.

As quickly as she could, Evelyn ran downstairs and out into the courtyard toward the tower. Then she dashed inside and up the narrow flight of steps to her studio above and began piling books rapidly onto the chest where her oil paints were hidden. She picked up some bundles of old rags that she used for wiping her palette and her hands, and put them on top of the books for good measure.

Sweating, she pulled on her smock and sat down in front of her easel, trying to calm herself. But her hand shook as she picked up a piece of charcoal and forced herself to draw. It was almost impossible to concentrate, her ears straining for the noise that would tell her he was leaving.

She waited for several minutes. Then several minutes more. But when, finally, she heard the sound of his boots on the gravel again as he emerged from the house, there was no sound of the car being started and driven away.

As the fear began to make the hairs on her neck stand on end, she listened, hardly daring to breathe, as the sound of his booted feet came across the courtyard to the door of the tower, then through it to the floor below. She waited, without making a sound, picturing him as he stood there in the middle of the bare stone floor, looking around him. Then his heavy footsteps began to climb the stairs.

When they stopped, she knew that he had reached the top and that he was standing there behind her, but she pretended that she was unaware of his presence.

"Good day," he said, in his near-perfect English. Slowly, she turned round, trying to look surprised.

"Captain Deitmar. I didn't realize you were here."

He smiled.

"Am I disturbing you?"

"Not at all." She forced herself to turn back to the paper on her easel. "Is there something that you wanted?"

"I'm interested in watching you at work." He came nearer to where she sat, and she felt herself recoil. "It is very difficult to create something beautiful in charcoal, which is so black and ugly, yet you have done so. I admire very much your gift for this."

"It's only a bowl of Jersey lilies," she said, trying to keep her hand steady. "Nothing special."

He walked around the little circular room, too close to the chest where she had hidden the oils. He hesitated, still looking around, then he came back and stood behind her chair. "I think there is something wrong here." She stared up quickly, almost dropping the piece of charcoal from her hand. "Someone who is as beautiful as you should be the subject, not the artist."

She tried to make herself smile.

"I have embarrassed you?" he asked. When she made no answer, he reached out and lightly touched the side of her face. "Tell me, are you happily married, you and your husband?"

"I . . . yes. Yes, of course."

"You hesitated before you answered me."

"Only because your question took me completely by surprise."

"Is that so?"

"It isn't a question that I would expect to be asked by a perfect stranger."

She could feel his eyes watching her, and she kept her own turned stubbornly on the easel in front of her.

"It is your choice if I remain a stranger."

She looked up then, for the first time feeling real fear. She had felt it, a faint ripple, that first day when they had come to the house and she'd felt the gaze of his hard eyes upon her then. So she had not been mistaken.

"I don't know what you mean."

"Then I must enlighten you . . . Evelyn. That is your name, is it not?" He took a chair from across the room and placed it close to hers, then sat down. He was so close to her that she could see the markings on his uniform, the German eagle, the swastika symbols sewn onto his sleeves. "It is unfortunate that our two countries are at war, but unavoidable. However, there is no reason why you and I should remain enemies." He touched her hair with his fingers. "After all, we have no quarrel, is that not so?"

"No," she heard herself say, reluctantly, barely above a whisper. "We have no quarrel."

"Good. I am most happy that you see it that way. Perhaps one evening I could send a car for you and you could come to my quarters in St. Helier . . . to do a sketch of me, if you would. I should like to send it to my uncle in Berlin. He, also, is a great lover and connoisseur of art; he would admire your drawing talent."

She remembered what Richard had said to her.

"Is he . . . in the army like yourself?"

"A general. You may have heard of his success on the Eastern Front."

"Yes . . . of course."

"I have a long way to go before I can ever hope to emulate him. I have always striven to. Since my father died many years ago, my uncle has taken his place. But his military successes will be hard for me to follow."

"I'm sure you'll do it."

She sat there, willing him to go, praying that someone would come looking for her so that she could escape from those hard, gleaming eyes, the thick, dry fingers that made her skin crawl each time they touched her. But no one came.

Finally she lay down the charcoal and got up.

"Please, you must excuse me. My aunt hasn't been well, lately, and I noticed that her bedroom curtains were drawn, I think I should go to her."

"As you wish." He stepped back to let her pass. "I shall send a car over for you . . . shall we say, tomorrow evening? I look forward to the pleasure of your company."

"I . . . I can't . . . the curfew . . ."

"Ah, the curfew. But you have no need to concern yourself on that point. In your case, it shall be waived."

"Isn't it a little unjust that everyone else on the island is compelled to be indoors by ten o'clock every night, and not me? If it was known, it would cause a great deal of resentment and bitterness. I should be accused of collaboration, and no doubt worse."

"Of course, you are thinking of your reputation. I understand that. Please let me assure you that everything will be . . . discreet." She tried to walk by him without touching him.

"Excuse me—I must go!" She ran on down the narrow little steps and back into the house. She ran down to the kitchen, looking for Jeanne, but there was no sign of her. She turned and went back upstairs, and shut herself in her room, trying to stop the sick feeling in the pit of her stomach, the shaking in her legs and hands.

Richard found her, huddled on the bed, the quilt thrown over her.

"Hey, what's this? You're not ill, are you? For Christ's sake, Evelyn, you've got to make a start on that bloody painting!"

She sat up, her red hair falling all around her shoulders, her green eyes huge in her pale face.

"That German officer! That Deitmar! He was here, today, less than an hour ago! I was working in the tower and he came up. He makes my skin crawl! And I know what he's after . . ." She burst into tears. "I didn't know what to do. I just had to sit there, pretending I didn't mind!" She told him about the car. "He said he wants me to do a drawing of him to send to his uncle in Berlin. Only a fool would believe that one!" She dashed away her tears on the back of her sleeve. "Well, he knows what he can do with his car! When it comes tomorrow evening, I shall be here. In bed. Stricken by some illness or other. I'll think of something."

She expected him to be horrified. To take her in his arms and hold her, to tell her that they were going to get away, that everything was going to be all right. But, to her astonishment, he just stood where he was, staring at her.

"Evelyn, you can't do that. He'll know it's just a trick. An excuse. He isn't stupid. You have to play along with him. Pretend you like him. For both our sakes. You know that . . . it's the only way."

"Do you know what you're asking me to do?"

"All I'm asking is that you be nice to him. You know as well as I do that we just can't afford to make him an enemy."

"I thought he already was!"

"Look, I know how you feel. I hate the thought of all this, too. But we don't have any choice." He came over to her and grasped her by the shoulders. "Evelyn, for God's sake, use your head!"

"I won't go!" She flung off the quilt and struggled to her feet. "I won't do it, Richard! Not for you or anyone!"

"Keep your bloody voice down! Do you want the whole house to hear? Listen to me. If you don't want to make Deitmar suspicious, you'd better start using that head of yours. I've planned this thing down to the last detail, Evelyn, and I'm sure as hell not going to let you foul it up—do you hear me? You've got Blanche's safety to think of as well as ours."

"Are you telling me that you don't give a damn if I'm pawed by a German officer, as long as you get what you want out of it? Is that what you're saying?"

"No! No, of course I'm not. You're my wife, for God's sake! Don't you think I have any feelings?"

"Richard, I don't know what to think anymore."

He came to her and held her against him.

"I know this isn't going to be easy, not for either one of us. But we can't afford to make any mistakes. Just trust me, Evelyn. Just trust me."

She slid her arms around him and lay her head against his chest. She desperately wanted to please him, to make things between them as they once were.

"I was so afraid. Afraid when he came near me. Afraid when he started walking around the room, those black, hard leather boots that they wear squeaking as he went." She swallowed. "Then he stopped, right in front of the chest where I'd hidden the oil paints. I was so scared he'd open it. He had no reason to, except out of curiosity, but I was so scared I could hardly breathe . . ."

He stroked her hair.

"It's all right . . . it's going to be all right." He paused. "Did you say Tostain had some more oils for you? The last of his old stock?"

"He has a box at the house, but I haven't been into St. Helier because of the petrol rationing. My grandmother and Julia are going to the Le Fevres' tonight, but I can't go because I have to work on the painting." She looked up at him. "If you went with them you could collect the box from Peter Tostain."

"We could be stopped and searched by the Germans. Just as a matter of routine. A box of oil paints isn't in itself suspicious, but we can't take any chances." He rubbed his chin, thoughtfully. "If I took a box, with say, some sugar or honey in it, a box with a false bottom, if I were stopped and searched I'd be covered. Yes, that's what I'll do. And put a few eggs in for good measure. Neither the Krauts nor the Tostains will think twice about it, except that I'm just being generous and neighborly. Will you have enough oils to do the whole painting with?"

"I think so."

There was the sound of a car drawing up outside, and Evelyn jumped.

"It's Philip Le Haan," Richard said, pulling aside the curtain to look. "I wonder what he wants."

"I brought these papers back for you to sign, Frederica. I'm sorry if I've called at an inconvenient time."

"No inconvenience." Frederica Tregeale made a sign to Julia, who brought her her spectacles. "We've been invited to supper with the Le Fevres' tonight. We have to leave early because of the curfew." She picked up her pen and dipped it in the inkwell. "That, and the petrol rationing, are making life more difficult for all of us, to say the least."

"We're all in the same boat."

"And the sea is certain to get even rougher before very long . . . all the signs are already there." She blotted her signature and pushed the papers back to him across the table. "Margaret Le Fevre told me on the telephone that people are having to bring their chickens into their houses at night, to keep them from being stolen. Imagine that. Fowls, indoors! And garden sheds are being broken into to steal other stores. Some people are blaming the foreign workers and the troops. But the greatest offenders are islanders themselves. Can you imagine the kind of pariah who'd stoop to stealing from his own neighbor?"

"In wartime it's dog eat dog."

"I need hardly be reminded of that."

"Jean-Louis has brought the car round, Mother," Julia said, from the doorway.

"I'm coming." She let him help her to her feet. "You should have telephoned first, Philip. Then we could have saved you the journey and your petrol. You could have brought the papers to the Le Fevres' tonight and I would have signed them there."

"I had another reason for coming over." He picked up the

documents and put them back in his case. "I wanted to see Blanche."

"Then you *have* had a wasted journey. She's gone upstairs and locked herself in her room. I doubt if any of us will see her before tomorrow."

"Is something wrong with her?"

"Oh, come, Philip. You know Blanche better than that. Although you've never been so indelicate as to speak about it outright, you've known for some time about her dependence on the bottle. When she gets a fit of depression on her, the first thing she reaches for is a glass of hard liquor."

"I think she should see a doctor. I've said that for a long time."

"Please, Philip. It's not a subject I wish to discuss. To begin with, Blanche has rejected everything I've tried to do to help her. Julia will bear me out. Nothing works, and nothing will ever work. You know as well as I do that she can't be cured unless she wants to help cure herself. And she shows no sign of that." She walked toward the door, leaning heavily on her stick. "Blanche is the cross I have to bear."

"Do you mind if I stay behind and try to talk to her?"

"Suit yourself. But she won't open her door to you or anyone else. Evelyn's already tried it."

He stood on the steps and watched them get into the car. He went on watching as Jean-Louis climbed into the driving seat and they moved off. He glanced up at Blanche's window, where the dark curtains were still drawn all the way across. Then Evelyn, her artist's smock tied over her clothes, came out of the house.

"You didn't want to go with them?"

She smiled.

"I'd rather stay here and paint. It helps me to escape, at least in thoughts."

"This isn't going to be easy for any of us."

She let her eyes follow his, up to the curtained window. "I tried to make her open her door and talk to me but there was no answer. Maybe . . . maybe if you came upstairs she'd talk to you."

They turned and went inside together.

"Can I get you something to drink? There isn't much left, I'm afraid. There was one bottle of French brandy, but Julia

said that Blanche opened the lock on the cupboard and took
it."

"I'm not thirsty."

It was cool and silent on the upstairs landing. Somewhere, a
large clock ticked, deeply, melodically. They walked along the
passageway together and stopped outside Blanche's room. The
door was open now, slightly ajar, and they exchanged puzzled
glances before Evelyn pushed it forward, then peered inside.

There was no sign of Blanche. Her dressing table was empty.
Her suitcase, the suitcase in which she had kept all her
photographs and treasures, lay empty on the floor. The bed had
been made, though Evelyn knew that nobody had been able to
get inside the room to make it, so it had been made by Blanche.
The brandy bottle, half empty, stood beside her glass and water
jug on the little table beside her bed.

They went outside, calling her name.

"She's up. She must have gotten dressed and gone downstairs."

"No. She hasn't been down since yesterday. I would have
seen her."

They walked on, side by side, along the passage. Then
Evelyn stopped abruptly, staring in disbelief toward the
bathroom door. Philip Le Haan had seen it too, and he
suddenly cried out Blanche's name, and broke into a run.

Water was pouring from beneath the door, dark and
glistening on the landing carpet. They could hear the sound of
it from inside, rushing from the taps.

"Blanche! Blanche! Open the door!" They both pounded on
it, shouted together, Philip shaking the handle, throwing
himself against it with all his strength. "It's no use! I'll have to
get something to break the lock!"

"For God's sake hurry!"

She heard him run back down the stairs while she went on
hitting it, impotently, screaming Blanche's name. But there
was no answer.

"It's me, Blanche. Evelyn. Please, I beg you . . . please
open the door!"

She heard him coming back, racing, breathless, the wood
axe from the kitchen in his hand. As she stood back, her heart
in her mouth and her whole body shaking, he swung it against
the door and there was a shattering, rending sound of

splintering wood. As it gave way and they both burst inside.
Evelyn froze with horror.

Blanche lay there in the overflowing bath, her face half
submerged, her dark hair floating round her, one wrist hanging
lifelessly over the side . . . and the water that filled the bath
and flooded over the top of it onto the floor was no longer
colorless, but dark red with blood.

He ran forward crying out her name, then turned off the taps
and lifted her limp body out and into his arms. He shouted to
Evelyn to run down to the telephone, and as her wooden limbs
began to move, he ran out ahead of her and into the nearest
room and lay Blanche down upon the bed. When she came
back he was ripping up the sheets to make bandages for her
wrists.

"Oh, my God, Philip . . . oh my God!"

"Did you get through to the doctor?"

"He's coming straight away. I told him what she'd done."

He went on ripping the sheet into bandages; then he wound
each length round and round her slashed wrists and tied it
tightly with all his strength. As gently as he could, he turned
her over and began to knead her shoulders with both hands.

*"Come on, Blanche . . . come back . . . come back,
please . . ."*

"She's still breathing."

"I know that . . . but she's lost so much blood!"

He turned her over, stroking her ashen face, cradling her wet
head in his arms. "Why, Blanche, why?" Tears began to run
down his face. His clothes were stained with blood. "Why did
you do it, Blanche? Why did you?"

Down on her knees beside the bed, Evelyn took hold of one
of her limp hands. And then, slowly, while they both held their
breath, she gradually opened her eyes.

She stared up past Philip toward Evelyn, fighting to mouth
each painful word, hampered by her ebbing strength.

"Had to . . . nothing left . . . Evelyn . . ."

"Blanche." Tears ran down her cheeks and into her mouth.
"They're coming . . . they're coming to take you into the
hospital . . ."

"Don't . . . cry . . . not for me. I've been happy . . .
long time ago . . ."

"Don't talk."

". . . when I was . . . young . . . someone loved me . . . I loved him, Evelyn . . ."

"Blanche, don't—"

". . . but . . . he was married . . . Julia told Mother . . . sent him away . . ." Evelyn and Philip looked at each other. "I was . . . beautiful, then . . . wasn't I, Philip?"

"Blanche, you still are."

"Daddy loved me . . ." She swallowed, then closed her eyes. "So glad . . . she isn't . . . my mother . . ."

"Blanche?"

Her breath began to come in quick and painful gasps. She squeezed Evelyn's hand in her own. "Don't trust Martha . . . Jeanne . . ."

There was a sudden, heavy silence, broken only by the faint ticking of the clock across the room. Then the screeching of a vehicle down below coming to a halt. Scrambling to her feet, Evelyn rushed over to the window.

"They're here!" She turned round to Philip. "I'll run down and let them in!"

Slowly, he let go Blanche's limp hand. He covered his face with his hand.

"It's too late."

"You were in love with her, weren't you?"

"How long have you known that?"

"I should have known it a long time ago, when I first saw you in the church that day . . . it was the way you looked at her . . ." She looked across at him with swollen, pain-filled eyes. "When you looked at her today, the way you cradled her in your arms, that was when I knew for sure." He turned away, a tear rolling down his cheek. "Philip, why didn't you ever tell her?"

There was a long, painful silence before he answered.

"I've loved her from the first moment I saw her, when she was sixteen. My God, I'd never seen anyone so beautiful! She took my breath away." He tried to smile. "She was walking toward me across the lawn, hand in hand with her father and her brother, Gilbert . . . she was laughing, smiling . . . happy. Her eyes were alive with the sheer joy of living . . ." He hesitated. "I was spellbound. Tongue-tied. A shy, gawky boy who was so insecure and unsure of himself that he didn't even have the courage to tell her how wonderful he thought she was.'' He fell silent again. ''She sparkled. Everywhere she went, heads turned.'' He lowered his eyes. ''She could have had any man she wanted, just by crooking her little finger. I never told her how I felt because I was afraid of being rejected.''

''Philip!''

''So I went away to finish studying in England. When I came back, I was stunned to find that she'd never even married. After her father died, she seemed to withdraw from everything, from everyone. I hardly ever saw her, from one month to the next. Slowly, she turned into another person, a woman that I scarcely even recognized . . . that white, mutilated body in that bath, that wasn't my Blanche, the Blanche that I first set eyes on that day, walking between Gilbert and her father . . . where did she go?''

Neither of them spoke again for several minutes.

''Jeanne telephoned Julia at the Le Fevres' . . . will you wait until they come home?''

''I'll stay with you if you want me to.''

''But you'd rather go back and be alone?''

''Will you be all right by yourself, Evelyn?''

''Jeanne's here. She'll be waiting for me downstairs.'' A pause, then a frown. ''I wonder why Blanche said what she did about Martha . . . then asked for Jeanne? It doesn't make sense . . .''

''I don't know.''

''Why did she do it? Was she drunk? Didn't she realize what she was doing?''

''I think she knew exactly what she was doing.'' They all stood there, still in their evening clothes, staring at her. Beside her, Jeanne squeezed her hand.

''And what exactly do you mean by that, Evelyn?''

''What did you say to her yesterday? What did you do to upset her so that she broke into the cupboard and took the last bottle of brandy? Don't try to tell me it was nothing, because I wouldn't believe you. I've been in this house long enough to know that Blanche only got drunk when she was pushed to it!''

''Blanche was unbalanced and you know it. She never needed a reason to do anything, least of all to drink herself stupid! Nothing about her was normal. Julia and Martha can testify to that. After her father died she withdrew into a world of her own, and nothing I tried to do could stop her. So I left her to herself. I gave up trying. I was ashamed. Yes, God help me . . . I admit that, too. Because I'd somehow failed." Emotion broke through the usual tight-lipped demeanor. "I promised her father that I'd always do my best for her, and I failed. But I did do all I could. I pleaded with her to see a doctor for her drinking and her depression, but she refused to see one."

"For a woman who's just learned that her daughter has killed herself you don't seem to be very upset."

"How dare you speak to Mother like that!"

"It's all right, Julia. I forgive her. I understand just how Evelyn feels. To discover anything so gruesome as a body in a bath full of blood is enough to unnerve and upset anyone. And Blanche was closer to her than she ever was to either of us." She nodded to Jeanne to leave the room. "Richard, I think you should take Evelyn upstairs to bed. And get Martha to bring her up a hot drink, to calm her down. She's had a very bad shock."

Evelyn pushed away his hand.

"Get Martha to bring me up a hot drink? As she used to for Blanche? What's going on in this house? And don't tell me nothing. One of the last things Blanche said was not to trust Martha." She turned to Richard. "Do you remember that night when I told you I'd been down to the kitchen to bring up Blanche's hot milk, and save Martha doing it? And how I said that I thought it smelled strange?" She looked back at Julia and her grandmother. "It's all beginning to add up. The smell of that milk in Blanche's cup was identical to the smell of the coffee in the flask that I was given to take with me to St. Clouet's Bay. After I'd drunk it I was out cold."

Julia's face turned pale.

"What the hell are you talking about?"

"What I talked about to Richard, which he dismissed as nonsense. Now I know better. Martha was putting something in Blanche's drinks to keep her knocked out. The same thing that she put in my flask of coffee that day. And by God I'm going to find out why?"

"This is madness!"

Evelyn ignored them and pushed away Richard's restraining hand. "No, Richard, I won't come upstairs with you . . .

because I haven't finished yet. I want this out and I want it out now."

Her grandmother sank into the nearest chair.

"These wild accusations are nothing but madness, out of shock and grief for what happened today . . ."

"No!"

"Whatever Blanche might have said before she died, Martha is an old and trusted servant of many years' standing, and completely loyal to this family. I ask you to remember that. For some reason, Blanche never seemed to like her, but then all her life Blanche had likes and dislikes that had no rational explanation. This business about Blanche's milk and your coffee is entirely a figment of your imagination. Evelyn, be rational. What possible reason would Martha—or anyone else—have to drug either of you? The very idea is completely ludicrous."

"I'll tell you the reason. Because after Blanche got drunk and blurted out the truth that you'd both tried to hide all these years—about Julia's husband—you were both afraid that when she'd had too much to drink again she might blurt out something else!"

"Blanche was an alcoholic and you know it!"

"She was a drunk because you made her life a misery, Julia! Ever since I set foot in this house I felt your resentment and hostility—to Blanche as well as to me. A hundred times I asked myself why. Why any normal woman wouldn't show a single spark of affection for her sister . . . or a normal mother for her daughter . . . and in my ignorance I thought that I knew the answer.

"Because Blanche was different. Because her father had loved her most. More than either of you. But I was wrong, wasn't I? None of those reasons was the real one. And I only realized the truth today, when she said something to me that took all her strength to say, something that fitted together with some other words she told me a long time ago, like missing pieces from a jigsaw." She paused. "She said that my father once told her, 'You're so different, Blanche. So different from Julia and Mother. Almost as if you weren't related to them at all.' The last thing she managed to say before she died was 'So glad . . . she isn't my mother . . .'" She paused again. A wild shot in the dark. "Blanche wasn't your daughter at all, was she?"

For a long, terrible moment there was silence. Then her grandmother turned away, moaning, her hands over her eyes, and leaned against the mantelpiece.

There was a photograph of Roland Tregeale there, in a large, ornate silver frame, and she stood staring at it for a long time. Then she lay her head against it, and sobbed.

"Mother!"

"I loved him . . . I loved him so. With all my heart and soul. I thought he was happy with me. But I was wrong . . . wrong. Because he betrayed me. Humiliated me. I gave him my trust and he went behind my back with another woman." She swallowed. "And I had to pretend, to playact to all our relatives and friends, while all the time I was crying inside!" The tears ran down her cheeks. "I was so naive. Blind. I never realized at first what he was doing. I really believed that all those business trips to Paris were nothing else but that. It was only when his French mistress became pregnant with his child that he told me the truth." Bitterly, she faced Evelyn. "Do you know what she was? A creature who earned her living by dancing half naked at the Folies-Bergère . . . And he wanted to be with her instead of me. He wanted to take Gilbert with him and start a new life with his whore and her bastard child! My son, to be brought up by that cheap little slut! And I was helpless. I cried. I begged. I pleaded with him not to leave me. I used to go to church in St. Helier every day and kneel there for hours on end, praying for a miracle that would bring him back to me . . . but the only reason he came back was that when she had his child it killed her." She paused and looked at each of them. "He made me agree to pass the child off as my own, because he refused to give her up. That's why we went to Switzerland, so that nobody on the island would ever find out the truth. And, because I loved him in spite of what he'd done to hurt me, I brought up that child." Slowly, she went back to her chair and sank into it, heavily. "I tried to treat her outwardly just as I did Gilbert and Julia. As God hears me, I tried. But in my heart I could never love her, because of what she was." Her eyes fell to the floor. "A constant reminder that my husband had betrayed me with another woman."

"Mother," Julia said, going to her side and kneeling beside her. "Don't. Please, don't . . . don't cry. He wasn't worth it!" Her cold eyes glared up at Evelyn, hate-filled. "Are you satisfied now? Does that answer all your questions? My God, it was a sorry day for us when Mother agreed to let you come into this house!''

Evelyn somehow found her voice.

"I'm sorry. Truly, I'm sorry. I can understand how you felt—"

"You understand?" mocked Julia, getting to her feet. "What the hell do you know about it? You don't know what it feels like to be betrayed by the man you love. On the contrary. From what I know of your life before you came here, you're more likely to have sympathy with my father's slut of a mistress than you are with any decent woman!"

"Julia! That's enough!"

"But Mother!"

Evelyn and Julia stared at each other.

"I feel pity for you. Pity, because whatever you do or wherever you go, you'll never be happy. You're sick and twisted inside with envy and hate. I saw that from the beginning and I tried to ignore it. You see ugliness in everything that's beautiful. You call a woman a slut just because she loves a man who happens to be married to somebody else. No woman in her right mind would choose to fall in love with a married man . . . and I speak from experience. Your father was an exception. Most men break your heart and then go crawling back, tail between their legs, to their families and their wives . . . and you're left all alone, helpless. With only your loneliness and your pain for company.'' A lump had come into her throat. "But that's something that you wouldn't know anything about, is it, Julia?" She turned and ran out into the passageway and into the hall. She threw back the bolts on the big front door and flung it open, then she ran out into the darkness and toward the tower.

The lamp that she used was standing beside the door and she knelt and lit it, then holding it up to light her way, ascended the steep, dangerous stone steps to her studio. There was another lamp there and she lit that, too. Then she pulled on her smock, took the canvas of the Orsini Madonna from its hiding place, and set it up on her easel.

Her hands shook as she dipped the tip of her brush into the paint on her palette, then held it above the painting. She closed her eyes. She took a deep breath. She got up and walked around the floor, trying to compose herself, trying to pull herself together. Pictures tortured her, pictures of Blanche, lying in the flooded bath, her dark hair floating in the bloodied water all around her like weeds floating in a pond. Blanche slumped across her bed as she'd first seen her, moaning, drunk, pathetic, a shell of what she'd once been. The crumpled, faded photograph she'd held up for her to see, of her as a child with her beloved brother, Gilbert, laughing as she'd clutched her father's hand . . .

Evelyn sat down again before the painting, her hand steadier, her brush poised. But as she tried to look in front of her at the image on the canvas, all the colors became blurred and ran into one another like a rainbow, distorted by her tears.

"Evelyn! For Chirst's sake what are you doing up here at this time of night?" said Richard from the top of the stairs, behind her. "It's bloody freezing in here. Come on. Put all that away and come into the house . . . come on, come to bed."

"No," she answered, without turning round. "I'm staying here. If I have to paint all night, and the next night and the night after that. I'll sit here until it's finished. Whatever it takes, whatever I have to do, I'll do it. Because I want to get away from here, from this house, before it destroys me as it destroyed Blanche."

She heard him cross the stone floor and come to stand behind her. Then she felt his hands resting on her arms.

"You're tired . . . you can't concentrate when you're tired . . . you mustn't make any mistakes."

"I won't make any."

He was silent for a moment.

"You're very clever, Evelyn. I never realize just how clever you really are until I look at something like this."

She went on painting, straining her eyes in the inadequate light. "Please, Richard. You're standing in my light. Go on back to the house and get some sleep. If you want to help me, just leave me alone. Besides, I can't work with anyone looking over my shoulder." Instantly, she thought of Ross Klein, doing just that as he'd watched her put the finishing touches to his sketch. A whole world away. No. She mustn't think of him. He was gone, out of her life now. He'd never come back. He'd go back to America and fly his planes, and meet some nice, ordinary, respectable girl and get married. Their paths had only been meant to cross fleetingly.

He went without speaking again. She heard his footsteps as they crossed back over the bare floor and then on downstairs, echoing eerily. Then the heavy tower door banged shut, and there was silence once more.

She had no watch, she had no conception anymore of time. Pushing herself, defying her drooping eyes and aching body, she went on working through the night. When the sky outside the window was still dark but streaked with faint flecks of gray dawn light, she lay down her brush and pulled herself up from the chair.

It took her several minutes to clear away all traces of her work. Then she put the canvas back in its hiding place and blew out the lamps.

Slowly, she went back down the steps and across the courtyard to the house. She bolted the front door behind her and went upstairs. But when she opened the door of their bedroom and went inside, she received the biggest shock of her life.

There, both naked, lay Richard and Jeanne Le Bon.

She was so stunned that for a moment she couldn't even speak. Then they saw her.

"You bitch!" she shouted wildly, running to the bed and dragging Jeanne out by the hair. "You no-good, underhanded little slut!" She slapped her across the face with all her strength. "And I trusted you. I liked you. I thought you were my friend!"

"Your friend?" Sneering, Jeanne pulled herself free and pushed Evelyn from her. She stood there, defiant in her nakedness. "I despised you from the first moment I saw you. You and your airs and graces, coming here from London with your expensive clothes, giving me your castoffs like Lady Bountiful and thinking you were doing me a favor!"

She looked from her to Richard.

"Why, Richard? Why have you done this to me? How long have you been going with her, sleeping with her behind my back?"

"He was my lover long before he ever set eyes on you!"

From the bed Richard laughed.

"Not quite true. I did have a glimpse . . . and I did very much like what I saw. Especially as it belonged to my cousin." Evelyn stared at him. "You see, Evelyn, it isn't really surprising that I look so much like him, because Jack Neville and I are cousins." She couldn't speak. She tried to move her body but it stayed rooted to the same spot. "When Julia went

to London looking for you and took Jeanne as her maid, she
left Jeanne alone in your old flat while she went off somewhere
or other trying to find where you'd disappeared to. I didn't
know that you were planning to leave, and when I knew you'd
broken up with Jack I came round to look you up and get
myself a piece of the leftovers." He smiled. "I always did
admire Jack's taste in women—except that bitch Laura De
Braose—and I reckoned after he'd turned yellow and ditched
you, you'd be grateful for a shoulder to cry on. But you'd
already gone. So I took up with Jeanne instead. If only Julia
had known what was going on right under that self-righteous
nose of hers! While she had early nights at the hotel, I took
Jeanne out on the town and we ended up in bed at my flat off
Piccadilly!" He rocked with laughter. "When we compared
notes, it seemed that it was well worth my while following you
to Jersey. After all, you're the old bitch's only granddaughter.
She ought to leave you most of what she's got. Trouble is, she
isn't going to. Jeanne stole her desk key and had a look at the
draft Philip Le Haan made out for her new will, and it seems
that she's going to leave the whole fucking lot to some medical
foundation. How's that for irony?"

"You *bastard!*"

"Red hair. Hot temper. That's what Jack said. About
redheads. He never could resist them. And he did say that you
were very good in bed."

Tears darted into her eyes. She dashed them away.

"You. Both of you. You're the lowest of the low!"

Jeanne's pale eyes gleamed maliciously. A stranger's eyes.

"You thought he was in love with you? He never was. You
never meant a thing to him."

Truth suddenly dawned.

"You're not Diana Sorel's son, are you? You were never
anything to do with the Sorels at all. It was Jeanne who told
you that my grandmother was so close to them, before they left
the island, and you knew that would be the perfect way to
worm yourself into the house without anyone being suspicious.
I can see it all, now. She told you everything you needed to
know!"

"Every man for himself, Evelyn. These are hard times we're
living in."

She fought with herself not to cry.

"It's a pity you didn't drown that day at the cove," Jeanne

said, bitterly. "If that bloody American hadn't come along you wouldn't be here now, complicating everything."

"Hold on, Jeanne, we need her to finish the painting—that's our oneway ticket off this fucking Godforsaken island!"

Evelyn looked at her.

"It was you, not Martha. You put the drug in my coffee. Knowing I'd fall asleep. Knowing that by the time I woke up the tide would have cut me off . . . but you were so clever. You even pretended that you'd fastened the strap on the picnic basket, and brought my attention to it being undone, so that even if I thought someone in the house had tampered with the things inside, I'd never suspect you." Everything began to fall into place, piece by piece. "The jar of cold cream . . . that was you, too . . . you went upstairs that night and put some kind of acid into the jar so that when I used it on my face, it would disfigure me . . . you didn't know Blanche went into my room after you'd left and borrowed it, because she had none herself." She let her disgusted eyes rest on Richard's face. "That's why you offered to take it back, so that I'd never find out. And then hid it in that old disused chest in the garage."

"That wasn't my idea. Or the drugged coffee at the cove." He got up from the bed and pulled on his trousers. "I don't fool around with crazy jealous women's ideas. That's not my style. And I told her so, when she used to come up to my room in the middle of the night, hungry for sex. Your crazy aunt almost caught us, once, when we started arguing a bit too loudly. Luckily for us, she'd had such a skinful that even if she did remember anything the next day, she'd think she'd dreamed the whole thing."

"You animal!" As she tried to strike him he grabbed her roughly by the arms, calling to Jeanne to help. Together, they forced her back against the wall, pinioning her by her arms until she screamed out with pain. Hair loose and hanging in her eyes, she glared at him defiantly.

"I'm never going to finish that painting, Richard! Do you hear that? Never." Against her will she began to cry. "When I think of what you've done to me . . . how for weeks, night after night I've slaved over that canvas in the bad light, going without food, rest, sleep . . . and all the time you've been in bed with this cheap little whore!"

As Jeanne shrieked out in protest, he pulled Evelyn toward him and thrust his face into hers.

"You will finish it, Evelyn. You bloody well will finish it. You think I've come this far to turn back now?" He shook her until her teeth chattered. "Don't bother to cry out. There's no one to help. Nobody to hear you. A bomb wouldn't wake the old bitch if it fell on her. And Julia wouldn't lift a finger to help you even if someone held a gun to her head."

"Take your hands off me!"

"I've got a special rapport with Deitmar, did you know that? I've been able to tell him a few interesting things about some of the people on this Godforsaken hole of an island—like who's trading in black-market goods, who's got hidden radio sets and other things they shouldn't have . . . listening to the BBC when the Krauts have got their backs turned. Plus Deitmar's uncle the general's got a well-known itchy finger for other people's treasures." He laughed, unpleasantly. "But shall I tell you the best thing of all that I'm sure he'd love to know? About that bloody Yank of yours who saved you from the dive bombers and pulled you out of the sea—U.S. Air Corps pilot, isn't he, didn't you say? Well, I'm sure Deitmar'd find that little titbit really interesting . . . the Yanks aren't in this bloody pain-in-the-arse war yet, but odds on they soon will be. Now, I wonder what an American pilot is doing, coming backward and forward to a little way-off place like Jersey? Enough to get the Krauts wondering about that, too . . ."

"You know damn well why he came here! To try to get his friends to go back with him before it was too late!"

"Maybe. But these Krauts are a bloody suspicious lot, wouldn't you say? They see treachery everywhere.

"It wouldn't take much for me to suggest to Deitmar that he might have been sent here for a very different purpose. After all, it's possible."

"They'd soon find out you were lying. And why."

"Possible. But it's amazing, I've heard, what things a man'll say when he's tortured."

Fear shot through her.

"You wouldn't stoop so low!"

"Wouldn't I?" He thrust his head under her chin and with the other one squeezed her throat so tightly that she thought he was going to choke her. "Don't push me, Evelyn . . . I've got too much to lose." He tightened his grip and for a moment his face receded, the whole room began to tilt and spin before her eyes. "When we go to Blanche's funeral tomorrow, you keep your eyes on the ground and your mouth shut!"

Slowly, he released the pressure of his hand. "I'm warning you . . . if you try to speak to that Yank—or anyone else— just one wrong move . . ." They went away and left her there, in a worn-out, crumpled heap in the middle of the floor, crying silently, her face covered with her hands.

Now she understood what being alone really meant.

23

She stared numbly from the window of the car as it drove slowly along the main street from Royal Square toward the Norman church, the same route that she'd driven along, so many months ago, to her wedding. The veil that fell from her black felt hat to her shoulders hid her face, and her dark-circled, swollen eyes, and when the car stopped and one by one they each got out and made their way into the churchyard, Evelyn stood back so that she could go in alone.

She paused by the lych gate and looked back into the street, at the small groups of people standing there, watching silently, her eyes beneath the camouflage of the veil searching every face, looking for his. But mercifully, he was not there. Soon he would be gone, never to come back. But she smiled to herself to think that, a few hours from now, he'd be safe somewhere far away, where danger couldn't reach him, and that thought oddly comforted her in her loneliness and misery.

A group of German soldiers, armed with rifles, had come to stand and stare at the cortege from their post across the square, and the sight of them, with their ugly, domed helmets and the hated swastika symbol emblazoned on their sleeves, made her blood run cold. Turning away, she went on into the church.

• • •

Josef Deitmar took the single sheet of yellowed faded parchment from Richard Mahone's hand and sat studying it for several minutes. Though he must have read and reread it several times over, he made no movement, but continued to stare down at it. Richard shifted his weight onto his other foot, and glanced at the huge round school clock hanging on the opposite wall, between the flags bearing the swastika.

"It's just as I told you," he said, unable to bear the silence any longer. "Now you can see for yourself. A painting, in oils, by an artist of the Italian School . . . I'm convinced it could be the lost Raphael Madonna." Deitmar nodded, very slowly, never taking his eyes from the sheet of parchment, but still he said nothing. "I looked up every written record there was in that library . . . there were letters and papers, receipts, bills of sale dating right back to the end of the seventeenth century . . . and from some of the letters I was able to find out that William Tregeale traveled extensively in Italy and France over a period of ten years near the end of the eighteenth century."

At last, Deitmar looked up.

"My uncle, I know, would be most interested to see the painting alluded to in this receipt." He looked at it again. "He has a particular interest in artists of the Italian School. Of course, to own an original work of art by such a painter as Raphael . . ."

"When my curiosity was aroused, I started to search through all the books . . . histories of art . . . and I found an illustration in one of the oldest volumes that showed a reproduction of the drawing Raphael did himself, before he started the painting. From the description on the receipt, the coincidences were too great for me not to think that there was every possibility of a connection."

"One thing I do not understand . . ." The cold, penetrating eyes rested on him. "Firstly, why the painting bought by William Tregeale is not to be found in Frau Tregeale's house, and secondly, why such a rare and coveted work of art should be offered for sale to an ordinary gentleman. These are things that—how would you say?—puzzle me."

"Who knows who stole it from the Orsini Palace, or why? Or where it was for more than thirty years before it was offered for sale to William Tregeale. Maybe whoever stole it got frightened, maybe they thought that if they were ever caught they'd never again see the light of day. Maybe a servant who worked in the Orsini Palace took it, not realizing its true value, and then when the theft became widely known, was too afraid to do anything but hide it away. After all, if the thieves had tried to sell a Raphael to a French or an Italian collector, it would have been put on view and its real identity soon discovered . . . think of the danger of that to a thief. William Tregeale was the ideal buyer. He was wealthy, he lived on a tiny island in the middle of the Channel, halfway between England and France. The true identity of the picture was scarcely likely to be discovered if it was taken there."

"Yes . . . yes, that is possible. Highly possible."

"As to why I haven't been able to find it . . . and Christ knows I've searched high and low . . . maybe some time ago one of the Tregeales found out that it really was the stolen Raphael from the Orsini Palace and hid it because he was afraid of the consequences."

"That could well be so . . . yet . . . ." He picked up a pencil and began to chew the end of it. "It seems too great a stroke of good fortune."

"I've said nothing about my theories to my wife's family, you understand."

"Of course."

"And it isn't easy to search thoroughly when they're all in the house. Today is the first time the house is completely empty, even of the domestic servants, because of the funeral . . . yet I can hardly absent myself from that and go back to look around . . . ."

"You've searched the attics of the house?"

"As well as I can. And the cellars. But so far I've found nothing."

"Could it be that that is because the painting was sold, and is no longer in the house? You don't seem to have considered that possibility."

"I have considered it. But I rejected it because of this bill of sale. You see, I found the original bills of sale for every other picture that is hanging in the house . . . every ornament, every item of furniture. I'm convinced that if this Madonna had been sold by the family at any time since it was purchased, this record of the original sale to William Tregeale would have been destroyed. After all, there was absolutely no reason for the family to keep it." He felt on firmer ground now with Deitmar.

He felt almost relaxed. He smiled and took out a packet of cigarettes, and held them out. "You know . . . there is one possibility that I never thought about until now, but it's a possibility nonetheless. The Orsini Madonna could have been hidden behind one of the other paintings in the house. If the family ever discovered that they'd bought a stolen painting. There was an outcry over the theft at the time—a huge reward, several million lira, a fortune in those times, was offered by the Orsinis—yet nobody ever came forward with any information. Then the trail, such as it was, went cold. It was never seen or heard of again. Consider it. A canvas, without its frame, is only a very flimsy thing. If it was lodged carefully behind another picture of roughly the same size, the deception would never be noticed."

Deitmar took one of the cigarettes and Richard lit it for him.

"That is a very intriguing theory. And highly possible. Hide it where nobody would ever think to look. Are there many paintings in the house of the approximate size of this Orsini?"

"A few. Mostly, they're large religious scenes." He dotted his ash into the wastepaper bin at the side of Deitmar's desk. "Not my taste at all. I like those big, buxom Rubens ladies, all breasts and legs bare."

Deitmar laughed.

"There is a club, in Berlin, one that my uncle told me about, where you would find exactly that kind of—ladies—everything to suit your personal tastes, however bizarre . . ."

"Berlin . . . I should be interested to visit Berlin."

"Perhaps that can be arranged at some time in the future. Now. I have kept you far too long . . . the service at the church . . ."

"Yes, of course. Poor Blanche. My wife was especially close to her. She's taken this all very hard. In fact, she refuses to come back to the Le Fevres' house where the family have arranged to have refreshments after the funeral. Because of the petrol shortage, it seemed wasteful for everyone to go back to the house straight after the service, and then those invited being obliged to make two separate journeys in their cars. Evelyn decided that she would walk back."

Deitmar leaned back in his swivel chair, thoughtfully.

"Your wife is going back home alone, you say?"

"Yes. I'm afraid she disapproves of people eating and drinking straight after they've buried somebody. I suppose it does seem rather callous, but then, life must go on. We must eat and drink to stay alive."

Deitmar got up from his chair and went over to the cupboard on the other side of the room and opened the door. He took out a bottle of whisky.

"A small token of esteem. With the compliments of the Third Reich."

While the rest of the family sat, heads bowed, in the front-row pews, with the servants and the rest of the mourners seated behind them, Evelyn remained where she was near the back of the church, a pale, solitary figure in black. She scarcely heard the words of the service. Scarcely mouthed the meaningless ritual of the printed prayers. To Blanche, the hypocrisy would have been obscene, and empty, and because she had loved her they were obscene and empty to her, too. Before the service was half over, she got up silently, without a word, and slipped unobtrusively from the church.

The square and the street alongside it were almost deserted. Shops were closed and shuttered. Some buildings that had been badly damaged by the shrapnel and bombs of June 28th were boarded up altogether. As she began to walk back the way they'd come, she looked up and saw the Nazi flag flying from the top of the town hall, and from the Crown Hotel in Royal Square. Lowering her eyes, hiding her grief for Blanche behind her veil, she ignored the groups of German soldiers that halted and stared after her as she hurried by.

It was a long walk back to the house, and after several minutes her feet, in their high heels, began to ache. But she quickened her step.

She stopped halfway along the drive and stared toward the house. It stood there, brooding and silent, eerie in its desertion. She began to walk on, more slowly, reluctant to reach it, her eyes on the windows of Blanche's room, with their curtains drawn.

She opened the front door and went inside, putting back her veil. Then she went upstairs and stood on the threshold of Blanche's room.

It was as if she had never existed. Gone were her creams and lipsticks and boxes of powder. Gone her beloved photographs and cuttings. Her bed had been stripped and remade with cold, white, starched sheets, hospitallike and clinical. Hesitantly, Evelyn went over to her wardrobe and opened it, and saw that someone had removed all her shoes and clothes.

A lump in her throat, she turned and ran out of the room. She ran downstairs, back through the dark, musty hall and into the fresh air outside. She looked toward the tower. The painting. It must be finished. Finished before it was too late.

She went up into the cold, half-empty studio and took the canvas from its hiding place. Then she set it on her easel.

She sat there gazing at it for a long while. She rolled up her sleeves. She got out her palette and her box of oil paints. But the mood, the inspiration to go on would not come. She was still sitting there when she heard the sound of an approaching car, pulling into the courtyard down below. So he had come back. Come back to bully and cajole. She tried to blot out the picture in her mind of how she'd seen them last night, him and Jeanne. She tried to think of Blanche, the Blanche she'd known from long ago, the Blanche whose letters she still treasured, whose face, young and beautiful and laughing, still looked up at her from the faded pages of her sketchbook.

She heard him close the heavy tower door below, she could hear his footsteps on the stairs.

"I've nearly finished it," she said, without looking at him. "It'll be finished by tomorrow night. Then I want you to take it away and never let me see or hear of it again!"

There was a long pause, and then a voice that was not Richard's answered.

"I am deeply impressed, Mrs. Mahone. Deeply impressed."

She spun around, her heart racing, and found herself face to face with Josef Deitmar.

She tried to speak but no words came. She tried to move but her body refused to obey her will. She just sat there, paralyzed by fear, as he walked slowly across the bare stone floor, the silence broken only by the hateful sound of his creaking, glossy boots.

He reached out and touched the canvas.

"The paint is still wet here . . ." She lowered her eyes. "But it is brilliant. Truly brilliant." He came closer and stood beside her. "Your husband is . . . an extremely resourceful man, Mrs. Mahone . . . Evelyn. I have always thought what a beautiful name Evelyn is." He went on staring at the canvas. "An English name . . . but, as I believe I said to you before, merely because my country is at war with yours we need not be personal enemies." She made her eyes rise to look at him. She felt that he was playing with her, a cat with a mouse that is cornered and knows it can never get away. He looked down at her now. "You do realize what this means, do you not? For your husband and yourself?"

"I have nothing to say."

"I assure you that I have a well-deserved reputation as a reasonable man . . . except to those who try to make a fool of me." She lowered her eyes again. "Tell me . . . was this . . . your husband's idea, to forge the lost Orsini Madonna?"

"I can't say anything about it."

"Were you . . . aware, Evelyn, of the price he asked were this painting to be delivered into my hands?"

"Yes."

"A German plane, to take him—and one other person—to the territory of a neutral country. Did you perhaps know that the 'other person' he wished to take was not to be you?"

"Yes, of course I knew that," she said, flatly, seeing no reason to deny it. This was the end. There was no escape. She was trapped, and there was no one to help her, nowhere to flee.

"This leaves me with one final question that I find myself intrigued to discover the answer to. If you were aware of this, that he intended to leave you behind, what possible inducement could he have made you to continue working on the painting?"

She got to her feet. Her legs were shaking and unsteady.

"I already told you that I have nothing to say. Now will you please go?"

"Go?"

"My aunt was buried today!" she cried out, struggling against the sudden flood of tears. "She's dead. She's dead and I loved her! I don't want to talk to you. I don't want to talk to anyone. I just want you to go away and leave me alone!"

He came over to where she was standing and stroked the side of her face, and she recoiled from him. But his hand shot out and grasped her tightly by the wrist.

"If I chose to, I could make life very difficult for you. For what you have done . . . here . . . attempting to deceive and defraud an officer of the Third Reich . . . your punishment could be something that even in your wildest nightmares you would never dream about. I advise you to think very carefully about the consequences should you displease me a second time." He pulled her toward him, and she tried to strain away from contact with his body. She twisted her face away from his.

"You forget that I'm a married woman!"

"That trifling circumstance is not a barrier to what I want from you. And what you will agree to give me."

"My husband would think otherwise."

"When he was planning to go away with someone else and leave you behind in Jersey? I think not. Besides which, that is not the impression that he gave me."

"What do you mean?"

"I mean that in return for his freedom, he was willing to give me not only the painting, but you."

"That isn't true!"

As he came toward her, she darted out of the way. He sprang at her, and she cried out in fear. But she ran across the room, grabbing everything in her path and throwing it at him, desperately. She grasped the canvas of the Orsini Madonna and tried to hit him with it. But it was no use. He lunged and caught her with one hand, and with the other hit her a stinging blow across the face. Then he took her by the hair and dragged her brutally toward him. Crying, screaming, trying to flail at him with her fists, she kicked and fought, but he was too strong for her. Throwing her down on her back on the icy floor, he sat astride her and hit her, again and again, until her arms fell down at her sides and her whole body went limp with surrender.

Sobbing, trying to pray, she closed her eyes to blot out the sight of his heaving, sweating face. Then she heard footsteps running furiously up the stairs, and a voice that she'd never thought to hear again yelled out in fury.

"You goddamn Kraut bastard," said Ross Klein. "Get your lousy hands off of her!"

"Ross!"

Deitmar swung around, stunned by surprise. Before he could get up Ross had dived at him and punched him so hard in the face that he went spinning away across the floor.

"OK, Kraut. You're real good at hitting defenseless women . . . now let's see what you can do with someone your own size."

As they fought Evelyn flattened herself against the wall,

heart hammering, half crying with fear, hands crammed into her mouth to stop the screaming. They rolled over and over. Kicking, punching. First one on top and then the other. But then Deitmar raised his booted foot and caught Ross a stinging blow in the mouth, knocking him away. In the split second that it took Ross to stagger back on his feet, Deitmar had pulled out his pistol.

A slow smile spread across his face. He raised his arm, pointing the barrel to take aim. As he leveled it exactly between Ross's eyes, Evelyn threw herself against him and the pistol went off with a loud and sickening bang, then went spinning from his hand and landed near Ross's feet. Without hesitating, he grabbed hold of it and shot Deitmar at point-blank range.

"Evelyn!" He threw down the pistol and pulled her into his arms, holding her as she sobbed against his neck. "Don't cry, baby. Hold on to me. I'm here. I'm here now."

"What are you doing here . . . for God's sake . . . you're supposed to be gone . . . if they find you . . ."

He stroked her hair. He squeezed her tightly against him.

"I didn't know about Blanche . . . we only heard this morning . . . I tried to ring you at the house, but you'd already left. I was all packed and ready to go . . . the Krauts had checked my U.S. papers and my passport . . . David drove me down to the boat an hour ago . . . but I couldn't do it, Evelyn. I couldn't bring myself to go without seeing you again. I wanted to tell you how sorry I was about Blanche." He looked down at her. "We went into the church, looking for you, but you weren't there. David only had enough gas left out of his weekly ration to drive me and my stuff down to the harbor and then drive back home again. So when I found out where you were, I walked here. Thank Christ I did." He gently moved away from her and knelt on the floor beside Deitmar's body. "We've got to be quick. In case anyone comes looking. Here, help me."

"What are you doing?"

"Taking off his clothes."

"I don't understand."

Ross looked up.

"There's only one way for you and me to get off this goddamn island, and that's just what I aim for us to do."

She knelt on the floor beside him as he began unbuttoning

Deitmar's clothes. "Ross, listen to me! You've got to get out of here! You can go. You can leave by boat. You're a citizen of a neutral country and the Germans can't stop you. I'm different. I've got no choice. Ross," she grabbed his sleeve to plead with him. "I won't let you do it. I don't want you to take any more risks for me!"

He dragged off Deitmar's uniform and then started to pull off his boots. "No can do, baby. You go with me or else I don't go at all. Hurry now."

Down in the courtyard Deitmar's car was parked outside the house, and Ross helped her inside. Then he got in and switched on the engine.

"What are you going to do?"

"Get us out of here." He put the car into gear and they moved away, gaining speed as they reached the end of the drive and turned out onto the St. Helier road. Her heart lurched into her mouth as they approached a German roadblock.

"Ross!"

"Just sit tight." As they slowed down at the approach to the barrier, the German sentry caught sight of his officer's uniform, and the swastikas painted on each side of the car, and waved them through with a salute. When they reached the other side he drove on in silence for several minutes until they came to a small clearing in the woods by the side of the road, and pulled into it.

He turned toward her.

"This isn't easy for me to say to you . . . and maybe I have no right . . . I told myself, over and over, that you were another guy's wife, that even though I could see things weren't good between you, it was none of my goddamn business to interfere—no, let me go on, because we haven't much time. Part of the reason I made up my mind to see you again was something I saw, a while back—something that made me tell myself I shouldn't have any scruples about doing what I wanted to do, because your husband didn't have any about what he was doing to you." He took hold of her hand and held it. "I saw him, with a pale, fair-haired girl in a car . . . they were parked way up near St. Aubin's Bay . . . I won't hurt you by going into any more details . . ."

"Jeanne Le Bon," Evelyn whispered, almost to herself. She looked up into his face. "I only found out a few days ago. I'd thought she was my friend . . ." She gave a small, bitter little laugh. "I've found out so many things, these past few days . . ."

"Evelyn, I've wanted to say this to you for so long . . . ever since that first time I saw you, when you were sitting there in that car with that rug round you, with seaweed stuck in your hair and those big, sad eyes looking at me from that white, wet little face . . . and when we met again, that day when they bombed the town harbor, I wanted them to come back so that I could keep on holding you . . ." He reached out and took her chin in his fingers, then leaned forward and kissed her lips. "I couldn't tell you then, but I can tell you now. I'd never leave without you, Evelyn. Because I love you."

For a moment they looked at each other. Then he leaned over and took her into his arms, and their lips met. Fire shot through her, taking away her breath, and she clung to him.

"Ross . . . I'm so afraid. Just hold me tight."

"It's OK, baby, I'm here. I'm right here." His lips grazed her eyelids, her forehead, her ears, her hair, then stole back to her soft, damp mouth. He wanted her more than he'd ever known it was possible to want anything, but as he felt her become limp in his arms, a sudden realization hit him. "Christ, baby!" He sat up, pulling her with him. "We can't go on with you dressed in that goddamn funeral garb! It's too risky." She stared at him, not understanding. "How could I be so goddamn stupid? Come on, we'll have to turn back and get something else for you to put on. It won't take long to drive back to the house, and I'll come in with you." He started up the engine again. "Just go back to your room and put on the brightest, flashiest dress you got!"

"But why?"

" 'Cause you gotta look like a Kraut's slick piece, that's why."

Ross drove the German car straight into the empty garage and closed the doors behind them. Then, hand in hand, they ran back across the courtyard and into the house. No one had gotten back from the funeral, and the huge hall clock ticked loudly in the eerie stillness, the dim, musty hall looking deserted and lonely in the late afternoon light that crept through the stained-glass window behind the door.

"Where is it?"

"This way!"

Together, they ran up the staircase, taking the stairs by twos and threes, then dashed along the landing to Evelyn's room. Feverishly, she flung open the door of her wardrobe, revealing a row of suits and dresses.

"That one," Ross said, without hesitation.

Helping her swiftly out of the black suit she'd worn for Blanche's funeral, Ross quickly fastened the tiny, awkward buttons that reached from the neck to the waist of the bright, flowered silk dress.

"OK. That's great. Let's go!"

"I'll need a hat."

"Get one then."

She tugged down half a dozen hat boxes from the top of her wardrobe, flung off the lids, then pulled out one with a wide straw brim and put it on. Then she pulled out a drawer in her dressing table and fished inside it for a pair of white crepe gloves.

"I'm ready, Ross!"

"You look just great, baby!" He grabbed her hand and they rushed out of the room, along the landing and halfway down the stairs.

"Well, well . . . what have we got here?" said Richard Mahone from the bottom of the staircase, hands on his hips. Behind him stood Jeanne and Martha Le Bon, both dressed in black. "Going somewhere, Yank?"

Slowly, still holding Evelyn tightly by the hand, Ross Klein came down the remainder of the stairs one by one. "Get out of my way, Mahone. We're leaving."

"You might be. But my wife stays here."

"I'd say that was up to her, wouldn't you?"

Richard looked at her.

"Trying to run out on me, are you, you no-good little bitch! I knew you had a thing for this bloody Yank right from the very beginning. Well, you're not going anywhere." He was standing right next to the telephone and he reached out and lifted the receiver. Evelyn could hear the dial tone from where she stood. "If you don't go back upstairs, Evelyn, I'll ring straight through to German headquarters and get Deitmar . . . and tell him that the two of you are going to try to get off the island." He laughed, unpleasantly. "Christ knows how you think you're going to manage it! Smuggle yourselves out in a fishing boat? Or were you just planning to take her to your pals the Shermans, to give her a good fuck before you swan off to the States? Unless she's let you have it already which wouldn't surprise me . . ."

In an instant, Ross had let go Evelyn's hand and was down the rest of the stairs and had hit Richard Mahone with such a stinging punch on the jaw that it sent him reeling like a cartwheel into the table behind, and the vase full of flowers that had been standing on it crashed over and shattered into pieces all over the floor. Jeanne and Martha Le Bon started screaming. Julia ran out from the drawing room into the hall.

"You yellow-gutted bastard, Mahone. I know what you've tried to do to this girl!" He stood over him, coldly furious. "You ever speak that way about Evelyn again, and I'll bust your ass!" He turned to walk away, toward Evelyn on the stairs. But in a split second his feet were kicked from under him and Richard Mahone charged him headfirst, knocking him to the floor, throwing himself on top of him. Ross threw him off. He flung himself back again. They punched each other, they grappled, they rolled over and over, crashing into furniture, sending the telephone and ornaments flying in all directions. Then Ross Klein hit him so hard that he cried out, jackknifed backward, and lay in a crumpled heap beside the stairs, blood oozing from his nose, his lips, a vicious cut above the eye. He lay there, exhausted, panting, knowing he was beaten. But as Evelyn looked down from her place on the stairs, she saw what he was looking at at the same time that he did, and shouted out to Ross. But it was too late. In the fighting, Deitmar's revolver had fallen out of Ross's pocket onto the floor, and Richard lunged at it.

Laughing, spitting blood from the tear on his lips, he pointed it straight at Ross Klein's head.

"He that laughs last—heard of that saying, eh, Yank?"

"*Richard, no!*"

She ran down the remainder of the stairs, her heart racing.

Her whole body froze, like a block of ice, as a loud, sickening shot rang out. A thick, choking sensation clutched at the muscles in her chest so that she could scarcely breathe. Terrified, shaking, she raised her eyes and looked. The revolver that Richard Mahone had been holding a moment before lay there, unused, on the floor beside him, while he groveled like an animal on the floor, pawing at the gaping wound in his arm.

There, in the doorway of the drawing room, stood Frederica
Tregeale, a cumbersome, outdated army pistol clutched in both
shaking hands. Slowly, she lowered it.

"You vermin!" Her voice was so deadly soft that Evelyn
could scarcely hear it. "You lied your way into my
home . . . you tried to make a fool out of me." There were
tears in her eyes. She took one hand from the pistol, reached
into the pocket of her costume, and took out a small book.
"You dropped this, behind the tallboy in your old room—or
did you hide it and then forget it?—one of the maids found it
when she was cleaning behind the furniture." She held it out to
him. "You recognize it, Richard? You should. It's your
detailed diary of everything, right from the moment you met
Jeanne in London. And all the things she taught you about the
Morels that you wrote down to memorize and learn off by heart.
Very clever." Slowly, she replaced it in her pocket. "You know
what this means I have to do?"

"It was her idea! And her bloody mother was in on it from
the start! Ask your lilywhite daughter, Julia. She and Martha
are bosom pals, isn't that right, Martha?" He went on and on,
not caring what he said anymore. Let them all be dragged
down with him. "She's had her hands more than soiled, I can
tell you. She and Martha used to smuggle up bottles of booze
to Blanche's room, so she could drink herself stupid whenever
she was depressed." The searing agony of the gunshot wound
made him vicious. "Loyal servant my fucking eye! She hated
Blanche's guts just like her sister did, because she was her
father's favorite!"

"Don't listen to him, Mother."

Dull-eyed, Frederica looked at her daughter, then at Martha
le Bon. "She told you, didn't she, Julia? Martha broke
her word to me and told you that Blanche was illegitimate.
All these years, while I thought it was just our secret, you
knew. You've known all the time . . . and I trusted you,
Martha . . ."

As if she was shell-shocked, Evelyn came down the stairs,
and Ross put his arm around her.

"Mrs. Tregeale . . ."

"There's no need for you to say anything." She glanced
down at the pistol in her hands. "This was my husband's old
army gun . . . and I kept it only because it was his . . .

silly sentimentality. I never thought that one day it would b
useful." A small, tight smile lit her pale lips, and as she looke
at Evelyn her bright blue eyes seemed almost soft. "I don'
know where he's taking you, but I do know that he's a goo
man and that you can trust him. Go with him, Evelyn."

When they came in sight of the airfield he slowed the ca
Then, giving a salute to the sentry, he drove it to a parkin
place in a line of other German vehicles and helped her out
"Act naturally. Smile. Laugh a little. Remember, you'r
supposed to be one of those loose-living dames that are happ
to collaborate with the Germans, and I'm your Kraut captai
lover who's brought you up here on a sightseeing tour to look a
our planes."

"Ross, supposing they come up to us and talk to you?" He
eyes darted nervously around. She tried to hold on to he
fluttering hat in the strong wind.

"No big deal. Didn't I tell you? My granddaddy was Swis
and between what he taught me and what I learned in hig
school, I can speak Kraut like a native."

She put her arm through his, and they walked on togethe
slowly, looking casually around them. Every now and then h
stopped and pointed at a plane, and she pretended to b
interested too. Nearer to the airfield they went, on towar
where Ross could see a German Dornier D. 17, and next to it
Messerschmitt 110.

"See that son-of-a-gun," he said, pointing to the Mes
serschmitt. "That's what the goddamn Krauts used to bli
Poland with in '39. Poor Polish sonofabitch didn't stand
chance: 348 miles per hour, two 820 kW Daimler Benz pisto
engines, two twenty-millimeter cannon and four MG 17 gur
in the nose firing forward, and one twin gun in the cockp
rear."

"What kind of planes do you fly?"

"P-36, P-38, P-40, Mustang. You name it, I fly it." H
smiled at her and squeezed her hand. "Now just keep o
talking and laughing, baby . . . we're almost there."

A Messerschmitt fighter stood about fifty yards in front c
them, and Evelyn could see two German soldiers and a man i
soiled overalls standing by the nose of the plane. As the
looked round and caught sight of her and Ross, they stoppe
talking and stood to attention. He walked forward, giving th

Heil Hitler salute, then stood with them for several minutes, speaking in rapid German, gesticulating toward Evelyn and then to the plane. Finally, as they began to walk away, he beckoned to her.

"Quickly," he whispered beneath his breath, "before those goddamn Krauts come back. I told them you were my girlfriend and I'd promised to let you sit in the cockpit of a Messerschmitt fighter."

"Ross!"

"Here, let me help you up!"

With his help she clambered into the cockpit with difficulty and he came in behind her. "OK. I'm going to strap you in. Sit tight." He winked at her. "I'll be back in two shakes." Before she could say a word he'd jumped down, and was walking casually away from the Messerschmitt across the airfield, in the direction of a huge pile of metal barrels. Then, momentarily, he disappeared. When he came into sight again, she saw him take his cigarette lighter from his pocket, flick it open and turn up the flame, then turn and toss it over his shoulder like a cricket ball. For a moment nothing happened; then the huge pile of barrels behind him spiraled into leaping flames, and he began to run toward the plane. A siren screamed, half deafening her. Panic, shouting, men running in all directions.

Her heart was in her mouth. Her whole body felt like jelly. When he swung himself into the cockpit in front of her, she felt dizzy from fright. He slammed down the cockpit cover. "That'll stall 'em a while. By the time they've doused that goddamn fire, it'll be too late for them to bother following on our tail. Now . . . when I start the engine and we take off, I want you to duck down real goddamn low, in case anything goes wrong and they start firing at us."

"Ross, the antiaircraft guns . . ."

"We can fool 'em. They don't suspect anything, so we've got the edge, the element of surprise. OK." But as he double-checked that the cockpit roof was clamped down, he suddenly caught sight of two German soldiers running toward them, waving rifles in their hands.

"Down, Evelyn!" He grasped the pistol that he'd taken from Deitmar and fired straight at them, and before they could recover from their surprise the plane's engines began to whir, deadening the noise of the wailing siren and the German guns. Looking out, he could see an armored car speeding toward them, and from the opposite side of the airfield, a dozen or more Germans brandishing rifles and machine guns.

"Here we go!"

Lying there, her heart racing, her stomach in her mouth, clinging to his thigh with both hands, Evelyn closed her eyes and prayed. Then the Messerschmitt shot forward and sped along the runway, and she felt it shudder, then lift itself at high speed into the air. As it climbed upward, the sound of the engine drowning out the impotent firing of the guns now far below them, she felt his hand come down and gently stroke her face.

"Hey! We done it, baby! We done it!" He started to laugh. "Full steam ahead to the south Irish coast, then dump this Kraut heap and on to the U.S. of A.!"

Trembling with excitement and relief, she dashed away the tears from her eyes and peered out, half disbelievingly, from the side of the cockpit to the ground far below them, at the fast-disappearing line of the Jersey coast.

For a split second, she thought of Blanche, and how happy she would be to know that, at last, both of them were free.

Biting back the lump in her throat, she lay her head against Ross's arm.

"I love you, baby. Don't look back."

ACKNOWLEDGMENTS

My special thanks are due to three different sources who very kindly gave me the benefit of their help with information which, in varying degrees, I have used in this book.

First, to BBC Radio Jersey, for supplying tapes concerned with many details about the German occupation. To Michael Ginns, Hon. Secretary of the Channel Islands Occupation Society, for answering several questions I would not have found the answers to so rapidly elsewhere. And last, but by no means least, to Frank W. Gadbois, of the United States Air Force Base Library, Mildenhall, for going to so much trouble on my behalf.

The Author,
April 1986

New York Times bestsellers— *Berkley Books at their best!*

___ 0-425-10005-7 **THE EIGHTH COMMANDMENT** $4.95
by Lawrence Sanders
Sex, corruption, scandal...A priceless Greek coin is stolen and another priceless Sanders suspense is born!

___ 0-425-09884-2 **STONE 588** $4.50
by Gerald A. Browne
A valuable gemstone drives men and women to obsession and murder. "Dazzling!" —New York *Daily News*

___ 0-425-10237-8 **"AND SO IT GOES"** $4.50
by Linda Ellerbee
"Funny, honest stuff that's all too revealing about how T.V. works." —*People*

___ 0-515-08973-7 **BESS W. TRUMAN** $4.50
by Margaret Truman
A triumphant and intimate portrayal of the remarkable First Lady—as only her daughter could tell it.

___ 0-425-10179-7 **DREAMS ARE NOT ENOUGH** $4.50
by Jacqueline Briskin
From the bestselling author of TOO MUCH TOO SOON comes the sizzling tale of Alyssia Del Mar, the sultry star of the silver screen who lives in a world where passion is power, and money buys everything.

___ 0-441-69400-4 **Q CLEARANCE** $4.50
by Peter Benchley
A novel of intrigue in the White House from "the man who brought chills to millions of summer vacations with *Jaws* and *The Deep!*" —*Time*

Please send the titles I've checked above. Mail orders to:

BERKLEY PUBLISHING GROUP
390 Murray Hill Pkwy., Dept. B
East Rutherford, NJ 07073

	POSTAGE & HANDLING: $1.00 for one book, $.25 for each additional. Do not exceed $3.50.
NAME_____	BOOK TOTAL $_____
ADDRESS_____	SHIPPING & HANDLING $_____
CITY_____	APPLICABLE SALES TAX $_____ (CA, NJ, NY, PA)
STATE_____ZIP_____	TOTAL AMOUNT DUE $_____
Please allow 6 weeks for delivery. Prices are subject to change without notice.	PAYABLE IN US FUNDS. (No cash orders accepted.)